PRAISE FOR

"A glittering small-town romance, delightfully angsty and heartfelt, packed with sizzling tension, heat, and sweet, swoon-worthy moments. Wilde's voice is fresh, authentic, and wonderfully charming."
—Peyton Corinne, author of TikTok sensation *Unsteady*

"Achingly tender and deliciously sexy, *Only in Your Dreams* is everything readers are looking for in a brother's best friend romance! Wilde's writing is brimming with palpable tension and deeply relatable characters, and my heart was completely enthralled by every moment."

—Jillian Meadows, author of *Give Me Butterflies*

ALSO BY ELLIE K. WILDE

OAKWOOD BAY Series
Only in Your Dreams

SUNSET LANDING Series
The Sixty/Forty Rule
The No-Judgment Zone

Only Between Us

A NOVEL

ELLIE K. WILDE

ATRIA PAPERBACK

New York   Amsterdam/Antwerp   London
Toronto   Sydney/Melbourne   New Delhi

ATRIA
PAPERBACK

An Imprint of Simon & Schuster, LLC
1230 Avenue of the Americas
New York, NY 10020

First Atria Paperback edition July 2025

ATRIA PAPERBACK and colophon are trademarks of Simon & Schuster, LLC

Simon & Schuster strongly believes in freedom of expression and stands against
censorship in all its forms. For more information, visit BooksBelong.com.

For information about special discounts for bulk purchases,
please contact Simon & Schuster Special Sales at 1-866-506-1949 or
business@simonandschuster.com.

The Simon & Schuster Speakers Bureau can bring authors to your live event.
For more information or to book an event, contact the Simon & Schuster Speakers
Bureau at 1-866-248-3049 or visit our website at www.simonspeakers.com.

Interior design by Lexy East

Manufactured in the United States of America

1   3   5   7   9   10   8   6   4   2

Library of Congress Control Number: 2024951312

ISBN 978-1-6680-9383-2
ISBN 978-1-6680-9384-9 (ebook)

To anyone sitting on a dream,
this is your sign to go for it.

Only Between Us

Chapter 1

Brooks

"I ever tell you how much I hate you?"

With a sinister-as-hell smile curling the corners of his mouth, Parker drops the five-pound plate he'd been in the process of adding to my squat.

He picks up a ten and feeds it onto the bar instead. Adds one more to the other end while I stand here like a chump, unable to do a thing about it because the bar's already loaded with another too-many-fucking-pounds across my shoulders.

"Despise." I grind my teeth as he assumes his position behind me, arms outstretched to spot me. "Have I ever told you how much I despise you?"

"Multiple times a day." My best friend seems to pride himself on it. He smirks real hard at my reflection in the wall of mirrors in front of us. "Squat the damn bar, Brooks. We've got to be out on the field for drills in thirty."

From an alternate universe somewhere out there, a very different Brooks Attwood shakes his head at my sweaty form in abject disgust.

Look at you. You call yourself a big-shot NFL starting wide receiver?

I do not, in fact, call myself that. Nor has anyone else since a miserable spring day, two years ago.

Alternate Brooks, who's currently nine years into his pro football career, could squat this bar no problem. He'd scored three touchdowns in the second half of his last Super Bowl game to bring his team as close as they'd come to a championship in over two decades.

Unlike me, that Brooks didn't leave that game limp and unconscious on a stretcher, six minutes and eleven seconds after his last touchdown. He didn't spend months recovering from a crippling concussion, thinking he'd never make it out of a dark room again let alone survive another tackle from men twice his width. And he didn't retire from the league while at the very top of his game.

The lucky bastard's probably sitting pretty on some beach during his off season. Maybe with a wife and a kid on the way.

He's certainly not here.

In the gym at the University of Oakwood Bay, deserted but for me and Parker as the school year winds down.

"Two more reps and then thirty seconds of rest." In the mirror, I find Parker frowning at my form. He taps my left thigh as I lower into a squat, and I adjust the bend in my knee.

I lucked out, having two physical therapists-slash-trainers for best friends. Parker and our friend Summer have been whipping my body into athletic submission since January, when I quit my only season as wide receiver coach for the UOB Huskies football team to focus on an unlikely comeback to the NFL. They've been helping me build enough endurance to sprint the length of a football field as fast as I did when I played, without vomiting violently on the sideline. Reminding my feet what it's like to twinkle-toe through a course of intricately laid orange cones without wiping out and breaking my neck. And building enough strength not to crumble under the weight of the godforsaken bar currently perched on my back.

It's a long shot, no doubt about it. A player pushing thirty, attempting to come back to the league as a free agent, after a bad concussion and two-year retirement? It's unheard of.

Laughable, depending on which sports pundit you ask. Since the day my agent leaked the news that I've been working on a comeback, you'd be hard-pressed to find a media outlet that hasn't run at least one segment a day about it. Either talking up my audacity or mocking my delusion. And all of them chalking it up to my being yet another athlete who can't bear to let the game go. To see the end of his glory days.

I'll take those assumptions any day, if it means they never catch wind of the humiliating truth: that my obsession with this comeback is fueled by neither audacity nor delusion, but by the cold sweats waking me up in the middle of the night. The tossing and turning until I give up on sleep and drag my ass out of the house for a long, exhausting run, bringing along my poor German shepherd simply for the sake of his company.

I squat the final two reps, sweat absolutely pouring down my temples, and rack the bar. Parker hands me the towel I'd slung on the black workout bench in front of us.

"Your knee keeps turning inward on the descent. Does it feel tight?"

I run the towel over my face. "It's been locking up on and off since yesterday's drills."

Parker swears under his breath. "You're supposed to tell me these things. How do you expect me to help when you're out here pretending everything's fine?"

"Everything *is* fine. That knee just squatted my body weight on a bar."

Parker's eyes close. He sucks in a long breath as though willing away all his problems in life. Which, I suspect, mainly consist of me at the moment.

He points at the workout bench. "Sit down."

"The knee's fine. Let's keep going."

"Sit the fuck down, Brooks."

I sigh like he's *my* biggest problem and drop onto the bench, leg extended. Parker crouches and gets to work digging his thumbs into the muscles around the joint. I think making it hurt on purpose, just to prove a point.

The doors at the opposite end of the facility bounce open, smashing into the walls, and we look around to find Summer striding into the otherwise empty space. She's been in the adjoining athletic rehabilitation center with a client all morning, and I wonder whether the session went to shit, considering the look of murder on her face.

"Look who I found trolling the rehab center." She widens her eyes at us. And then I spot Josh, the agent who's been in charge of my career since my rookie season, following several feet behind.

"Heard that," Josh tells her.

"Meant you to." Summer runs a frustrated hand through her shoulder-length brown hair.

I don't blame her. Josh is an ass on his best day.

But he's an ass that got me nearly everything I'd dreamed of as a kid hoping to one day go pro. Drafted second overall by the Los Angeles Rebels, during my junior year here at UOB. A lucrative six-year contract extension that bought two homes for me and one for my parents. Multiple cars I really didn't need, outrageous holidays my ex-girlfriend enthusiastically bragged about on social media.

He and his five-percent cut had jumped at the opportunity when I'd called about this comeback.

Josh rounds Summer to set a laptop on my workout bench, looking ridiculously out of place in his crisp pinstripe dress shirt and slacks. His hair is neatly pushed back in a way that would take my unruly waves a good forty-five minutes of styling to accomplish. Not that I'd ever waste a second attempting it.

He does a double take when he sees Parker working on my knee. "What happened?"

Summer, too, looks concerned by the sight. She assesses the movement of Parker's fingers around the joint. Seems to sigh inwardly when she connects the dots.

"Nothing happened. Just resting before the next set." I stand despite Parker's obvious disapproval, and the now outward sigh from Summer. But these two are my ride-or-dies. They know how easy it is to set off Josh at the mere mention of a papercut on my multimillion-dollar hands, let alone a tight knee. So they keep their mouths shut as I line up at the squat rack. Simultaneously, they move to either side of the bar and remove fifty pounds off the ends.

"Cool-down set," Parker explains when Josh raises an eyebrow.

Satisfied that my body is still in working order, Josh decides to ruin my day in a different way. "Bad news, Brooksy."

I almost falter mid-squat. "Not something I want to hear, man. Is this about your call with the Rebels? How'd it go?"

Josh had arranged a call this morning with Jackson Ford, head coach for the Rebels, to discuss the prospect of my return. Because it's not enough to rejoin the league. I've set my sights back on my old team. Two years later, they're still among the top four teams. And the last time I wore their royal purple jersey also happens to be the last time I truly felt alive. Three feet in the air, catching a football a heartbeat before I was on the receiving end of what I'd then decided was a career-ending tackle.

The Rebels are where I need to be.

"You wanna know how it went?"

Squat.

Josh flips open the laptop he'd placed on the bench.

Squat.

The screen comes to life. It takes me a second to make sense of the picture in front of me. It's dark and a little blurred . . .

And then my eyes adjust. It's me. Me and . . .

"What the—" My knees buckle. Behind me, Parker darts to grab the bar, helping to get it back on the rack.

Who is that woman?

I've got her backed up against an alley wall I recognize as one next to Beehive, a Hollywood nightclub frequently attended by Rebels players. The photo's close up, but grainy in a way that tells me whoever took it captured it from afar. I've got my mouth planted on this woman's neck, and her fingers seem to be fumbling with my belt buckle.

"What the fuck is that?"

"That," Josh jabs his finger at the screen, "is the reason you're not getting signed to the Rebels. They gave me this. A file full of photos just like it."

My body goes cold. "Since when is a consensual make-out in a back alley an unsignable offense?" I sound outraged. But I remember full well what else happened in that back alley.

And it was far more than a make-out.

Josh hits a button on his laptop. It's another photo. The same alley outside of Beehive, but my clothes are different. My shirt's all the way open this time and . . . that's definitely a different woman.

Josh clicks again, and another photo floods the screen. Same alley. Different woman.

Humiliation trickles through every inch of my body. At my side, Summer whispers a very sad, "Oh, Brooks."

I've done my best to forget the six months I spent aimlessly wandering LA after my retirement. Not just because I'd been brokenhearted over losing my dream career at twenty-seven. But because the day I'd announced my retirement—already the worst day of my life—was also the day I caught Naomi, my then-girlfriend of eight years, cheating with my own teammate.

She'd taken my barely beating heart and turned it into a lifeless husk. The months that followed were a blur of Hollywood nightclubs, nameless women I'd never see again. Too much liquor and brain-numbing hangovers. Living on instant gratification. Anything and everything I could do to forget that I'd just had the soul ripped out of me, losing my dream career and college sweetheart in a single day.

I was a walking disaster of a human. Treated my body like shit until my poor mom finally broke down in a fit of tears over the phone one night. It crushed me so bad, I got my ass into therapy the very next morning.

"It's an unsignable offense," Josh continues, "because the Rebels are a family-owned business. Passed down through generations of the Dupont family, who very much value their reputation as a squeaky-clean organization. And according to this slideshow, you seem to have fucked your way through the state of California the last time you lived there."

"I haven't done that in a long time." My voice comes out paper-thin. I'm fixated on the photo on screen, the way I look . . . barely *there*. Barely alive.

"Since you moved to Oakwood to coach," Josh specifies. "I know. You cleaned up your act, did something with your day that didn't involve drinking and fucking. But as far as they're concerned, you got your act together *after* leaving the Hollywood scene. They're convinced that bringing you back will set you off. That you'll humiliate the organization with more of this very public indecency the moment you set foot in that town again."

I shake my head, rejecting the thought that the Rebels might not want me back because of the stupid things I'd done in a drunk and depressed fog. "This is bullshit. You see that, right? I haven't been that guy in years. I've . . . I've been productive and responsible—"

Josh hits that damn key on his laptop and the next photo puts me way back on my heels. It's set at Oakley's, the only bar here in Oakwood. It's a grainy photo again, taken from across the room, but it's clearly me. Sitting in a chair with a petite blonde in my lap.

Josh raises his eyebrows. "You had an affair with your best friend's girlfriend just a few months ago—"

I cough out a breath. Beside me, Parker mutters "Oh, Jesus" and runs his fingers through his hair. Summer chokes on a startled laugh. Probably because the woman on screen is our friend Melody, who also happens to be Parker's twin sister and our friend Zac's now-fiancée.

"That wasn't real." The satisfaction of finally being able to explain something forces a laugh out of me. "I was her fake boyfriend. We pretended to date each other so Parker wouldn't know she was really hooking up with his childhood best friend. If anything, *she* was the one having an affair, seeing as she had two boyfriends on the go. One real, one fake."

"What the fuck are you talking about?" Josh demands.

"It wasn't real. That one-time lap-sitting was as far as it ever got with us, and Zac—her real boyfriend—was in on it. It was fake. I was her fake boyfriend."

"Fake boyfriend?" Josh blinks. "That's the stupidest thing I've ever heard."

"*Thank* you." Parker shakes his head at the photo of me and his sister sitting together. Summer huffs a laugh. "Absolutely stupid."

"Point is, all you have to do is explain that to the Rebels, and this'll be squared away."

"And the other women?" Josh flies through the back-alley photos again. "Were you fake-dating them, too?"

"That's . . . No. It's exactly what it looks like. But I wasn't in my right mind then." I white-knuckle the racked squat bar, willing away the nausea that rumbles through me with every picture that flashes on his screen.

"That's enough." Parker moves to my side. His body is tense like he expects to have to jump into a brawl at any moment. "He gets the point, Josh. Knock that shit off."

Summer snaps shut Josh's laptop, removing the photos from my sight. The tension in my chest eases almost instantly. They've spent the past few months tirelessly working to get me into playing shape, but I've never been more grateful for the both of them.

"All right." Josh sighs. It's as close to an apology as I've ever heard from him. "Look, Brooksy, you know there's no one more invested in your comeback than me."

Summer snorts. Parker rolls his eyes.

"Fine. Tweedledee and Tweedledum over here aside." Josh waves a dismissive hand at them.

"Don't." Summer flings an arm out in front of Parker without even looking his way—probably sensing, by virtue of their twenty-six years of friendship, that he was about a moment away from throttling my agent. He's always been an *act first, think later* kind of guy.

Parker's body immediately deflates.

Josh watches it unfold with amusement, and I think I might throttle him myself. "Is that what you've come here to tell me, Josh? That the only team I want to play for won't have me? That there's no chance of my signing with them?"

Josh turns his attention back to me. "That is what I'm saying. Before our call today, I would've given you a ninety percent chance of receiving an invite to their training camp in a couple months' time."

"And now? What chance do I have?"

"Unless you find a way to convince the Rebels owners that you're no longer the kind of person who meets with random women in back alleys—*yes*, I know it was consensual, Brooks." He stuffs his hands into the pockets of his slacks, shakes his head at the beginnings of my protest. "It doesn't matter to them how ready and willing these people were. Unless you can somehow prove you've settled down, that you've turned over a new leaf? You can kiss your chances of signing with them goodbye."

I sag against the cool metal squat bar. "And how do you expect me to do that?"

"Any chance you've got a wife or long-term girlfriend you've been hiding from me?" Josh shrugs when I shake my head, in a move I'd almost call helpless. "Then I'm sorry, Brooks. It's time to consider other teams. And do yourself a favor and keep it in your pants."

He collects his laptop and spares Summer and Parker a glance before turning on his heel and making for the gym doors.

"And if I don't want to consider other teams?" I call after him.

He doesn't answer. Josh shoots me a genuinely sad smile over his shoulder.

And that's how I know how serious he is. How absolutely shit out of luck I am.

Chapter 2

Siena

"Slow down. For the love of God, act natural."

I hiss the words at Shyla's back, hurrying to catch up as she hustles down the UOB football field at a clip that announces that we're somewhere we're very much not supposed to be.

I'm certainly no stranger to being in places I shouldn't—trespassing, breaking and entering, outrunning beach security when they catch me skinny-dipping in the bay in the middle of the night.

But this particular scenario—interloping on a busy college football stadium in broad daylight among dozens of people—requires a different kind of finesse.

The kind of cool and calm Shyla clearly doesn't possess. Her bright blond hair flutters behind her as she hurries across the busy football field toward the black, white, and maroon husky painted at the fifty-yard line.

"Act natural?" Shy throws over her shoulder with a laugh. "What's natural about two women and a toddler loitering around a football field? I can't believe I let you drag me into this."

"You can't? You'd think after eighteen years of friendship, you'd be used to all the dragging. And there's no one I'd rather share this moment with than my two besties." We come to a stop in the very middle of the field, and I nuzzle the blond, curly-haired two-year-old hiked over Shy's hip, whispering, "Don't tell your mom, but I can't wait to corrupt you the second you turn sixteen."

Shy laughs as Rosalie clumsily grabs for my face. "Can't you at least wait until she's twenty-one?"

"Says the woman who got us our first fake IDs at sixteen."

"*You* got us those fake IDs."

"Oh, right. That was definitely me." I tweak one of Rosie's tiny pigtails. "My dad was so pissed when he found those. Stomped around the house for days."

I take in the field around us. We're surrounded by several tall, deliciously built men tossing footballs. Some of them hopping around sets of orange cones laid out. A couple running laps at the far end of the field. And, strangely, a towering, dark-haired man with the tightest bubble butt I've ever seen, chatting up some girl with a massive German shepherd on a leash.

The sight makes me breathe easier. If Shy, Rosie, and I aren't supposed to be here, that dog certainly isn't. It'll be the perfect scapegoat in case of emergency.

Your Honor, I call the happy, oversized dog to the witness stand.

The man tosses us a glance over his shoulder. I can't make him out too well from here. But by the way he lingers on us, I think he knows we shouldn't be here.

For some reason, that only makes me laugh.

"So, now that we made it, what do you want to do?" Shy asks, drawing back my attention.

"Honestly, Shy? I didn't think that far ahead." I hook my thumbs around the straps of my white overalls and turn on the spot, eyeing the stands towering behind both sidelines. "I kind of wanted to make it down here just to say I did."

I find what I'm looking for in the top left corner of the far stands.

Two seats that look like all the others around. But those seats were home to some of the best nights of my life. The very best memories with Dad during the college football season.

Mom would join us sometimes, as would Shy and her parents, but football was our thing. Mine and Dad's. It started mere months after Dad caught me breaking into their home and raiding the kitchen in the middle of the night. After Mom and Dad took me in at thirteen, like I'd been theirs all along.

"Oh, Cee." Shy loops an arm around my waist and tugs me into her side when my breath hitches. I shut my eyes and employ every ounce of self-control not to tear up. "He really would have gotten a kick out of seeing you down here."

I manage a pinched smile. "Yeah. He would have."

Which is why Shy, Rosie, and I spent the last twenty minutes playing covert ninjas inside the stadium, trying to make it here without ending up in the slammer.

This time last year, on the first anniversary of his death, I'd settled for spending a couple extra hours at Ship Happens, the bait and tackle shop I inherited when Dad died. Spent the rest of the night listening to Mom, and Carla and Evan—Shy's mother and father—tell stories about him over a cribbage board.

This year, though, it's like my dad was calling me here. All the way to Oakwood, the next town over from Baycrest where I grew up, both before and after the new life he gave me.

And it wasn't about coming here to sit in our old season seats. For whatever reason, I felt like Dad wanted me *here*.

Down on this field. Standing right in the middle, where I am now.

My gaze affixes on a football being thrown nearby. It arcs perfectly between a guy in an official-looking UOB T-shirt and the aforementioned bubble-butt owner, who shuffles to make the catch with the kind of grace, agility, and glutes I shamelessly admire.

"Daddy," Rosie coos.

"That's not Daddy, Ro. Daddy is away, remember?" *Misses her dad*, Shy mouths at me when I shoot her a curious look. My heart pinches. There's a lot of that going around.

Shy turns her attention over my shoulder, in the direction of the guy I'd just been ogling. "He's cute. You want Rosie to wing-woman you an introduction?"

I *think* we're looking in the same guy. It's slightly confusing, considering *cute* is the last thing I'd label him. Even from here, I can tell he's something else entirely. He's got two full tattoo sleeves, for crying out loud.

"Hell no. He looks like one of them."

"Oh, yes. The big bad athletes you refuse to go near after Tom. Shame." She tilts her head, perhaps just now noticing his killer ass. Not sure what took her so long. "Here, let me take a picture of you on the field. Your mom will love this."

Shy's right. Mom had always been more tolerant of the batshit habits I brought into their home—the sneaking out at all hours of the night, cutting out of class, slowly corrupting good-girl Shy when we became friends after my parents took me in. Found them entertaining, even.

I hand Shy my phone and shake out my shoulders and the heavy weight of grief off my chest. Gussy up my hair for the picture, straighten the straps of my overalls.

Ignore the sudden commotion on the field behind me.

"Hey—*hey*—watch your head, lady—"

Shy's eyes go wide, tracing a trajectory in the sky behind me. She drops my phone and shields Rosie with her body just as something painfully solid smashes into me, knocks the wind out of me. Sends me careening forward. Flailing my arms to break my fall, keep from smashing my face on the field beneath me.

I land on the ground with a shocked yelp. Face down, overalled ass up. And the wrecking ball that just did its best to obliterate me lands behind me.

Or rather, he landed draped *over* me, in a melee of muscled arms wrapped around my waist to catch me. Break my fall as though the damage hadn't already been done. A thud of thick, solid thighs hits the backs of mine, and the juncture of bent-over hips slaps into my ass in a way I'd very much appreciate if I hadn't just nearly swallowed a mouthful of grass.

All things considered—and by all things, I mean the stinging pain in my elbows and knees—this isn't so bad.

Mr. Wrecking Ball may need to brush up on his knight in shining armor skills, but he smells like a delicious mix of heady pine and clean man-sweat. His body certainly feels like the impressive product of the aforementioned man-sweat, all hard and strong behind me.

Really, this isn't so bad at all.

His arms clench around me, lifting me with perfect ease to allow me to plant my hands underneath me. He dips his head, peering over my shoulder—trying to make eye contact I'm frankly unready to return given the way he's still cuddling me doggy-style on this well-attended football field.

"You all right?"

I clear my throat. "I definitely didn't expect to get trampled close to death today, but there are much worse ways to die."

Flash.

Our heads snap up.

Shy peers over my phone with as close to a shit-eating grin as I've ever seen on her. "Now, this is one hell of a picture."

Mr. Wrecking Ball peels himself off me and scrambles to his feet. Sitting back on my heels, I'm struck by the length of this man's shadow. He's a giant.

"I am so sorry." He steps around me as I brush the grass off my overalls.

What do you know? Mr. Wrecking Ball happens to be the grace, agility, and glutes I watched catch that football a minute ago.

Up close, I see he's much more than a backside and athleticism. He's high, sharp cheekbones and a perfect jawline. A full mouth. Wavy dark hair, a little floppy on top, and an intriguing scar slashing across his left cheekbone. Full tattoo sleeves along both arms. He's deep, earnest brown eyes that belong around your mother's dinner table at Thanksgiving, as he regales the family with wholesome stories of cat rescues and road-side cleanups.

Then the corner of his mouth stretches in a smile and . . . no. I was wrong. This isn't a nice boy you simply bring home to Mom. This is a man who charms the pants off your parents, opens the car door for you after dinner, and drives you to a dark corner of a nearby parking lot to fuck you lights-out in the back seat, because he couldn't wait 'til you got home.

Also, he looks incredibly familiar.

"I hope you're okay." He holds out a hand to help me up with an impressively fretful furrow to his brow. Once I'm on my feet he reaches for me again, eyeing my grass-stained front. As though he means to brush me down but then thinks better of touching a strange woman in the breast area.

What a shame.

"Totally fine." I wipe off my overalls. "Can't say the same for my knees tomorrow, but who hasn't woken up a little banged up after a doggy-style tryst on the ground?"

The man chuckles almost uncertainly. Like he wants to laugh but can't decide whether it's particularly gentlemanly to laugh at a joke like that. His gaze drifts to Shy, as though seeking her permission.

Where the hell have I seen him before? The face, that build . . . I'm positive that I know him.

He seems to relax when Shy offers her own laugh and hands me my phone. "Here, I assume the photo shoot's over."

"Daddy." Rosie throws out her arms toward the man.

"Not Daddy." Shy kisses the top of Rosie's head and shoots Mr. Wrecking Ball an apologetic look.

"She's very sweet." He waves at Rosie. Then he zeroes in on my phone, and there's definitely no trace left of that amusement. "Hey . . . I know this is probably a weird thing to ask, but is there any chance you can delete that picture?"

I swipe at my phone, bringing up the photo in question. There I am on all fours, pink in the face, hair disheveled, with this beautiful man plastered on top of me. And we look *good* together.

I turn the screen around, letting him have a look. "Are you sure you don't want me to send you a copy instead? This is definitely *plaster above your bed* material."

He peers at the screen one long moment, and I certainly don't miss the twitch at his jaw as he stares at us all tangled up. Nor the way his eyes find me beyond my phone, taking me in like it's the first time he's seeing me properly.

He clears his throat, gaze cutting to Shy before settling back on me. "It's not really a good time for me to be seen having a public . . . What was it? 'Doggy-style tryst on the ground'?"

"Oh, now I'm intrigued. You're saying there's usually a good time for it?"

His lips twitch. "You'd be doing me a favor. If you deleted the picture."

My thumb moves over my screen. "There. All gone."

"Thanks." He pushes the hair off his forehead a little uncertainly and holds my gaze, doing his very best to hypnotize me with the deep brown of his eyes and that hint of a smile. It might have worked, had I not been too busy trying to place him.

Shy hikes Rosie up her hip. "Cee, maybe we should . . ."

She indicates the opening under the stands we'd snuck out from. Because we're not supposed to be here, and we're definitely not supposed to be drawing attention to ourselves.

"Right. Well, it was nice to meet you. Sort of." I hook an arm around Shy and start leading us back to the exit, but the man catches up quickly.

"What brings you out here, anyway? The school only gives special permission if you're working with one of their trainers." Shy and I double our steps. Mr. Wrecking Ball tucks his hands into the pockets of his black athletic shorts. He's keeping pace with us, and without looking I can tell he keeps shooting sidelong glances my way. "By the awkward silence, I'll assume this isn't exactly sanctioned?"

"Of course it is." I don't slow down in the slightest. "We're upstanding citizens, me and Shy. Rosie especially. And I resent the accusation."

"She's an alum," Shy adds. "Helping out the Huskies with . . . you know. Their social media. Hence the photo shoot you ruined."

"Exactly." I suck in my cheeks to keep from laughing, patting Shy's arm as we move around a set of orange pylons on the field. "We'll get 'em next time, when the mean man isn't here to run me over."

"The Huskies' social media, huh?"

The edge in his voice tells me he didn't buy that for a second. Also, that he's willing to make us pay for it.

Mr. Wrecking Ball cuts us off, coming to a stop in front of us, forcing us still. He shoots a quick grin at Shy. Or rather, at the overload of cuteness in her arms.

He isn't wearing UOB-issued clothing, so maybe he doesn't work here. His friend is, though. The guy with the light brown hair and curious frown making his way over to us now.

Shit.

I'm going to get a two-year-old imprisoned. Her mother will kill me.

Mr. Wrecking Ball settles an amused gaze on me. "I'll tell you what. You need a good shot of the field for the Huskies? I know where to get you one."

Chapter 3

Brooks

This isn't one of my smartest moves.

Sure, I managed to get that unintentionally hot photo of us deleted before it leaked online, stoking the fire of my apparent slutty reputation.

But bringing this woman to a private, deserted corner of the Huskies stadium, high above the field and away from onlookers, probably doesn't give me the chaste, family-oriented allure Josh says I should be going for. Especially since her friend with the cute kid declined the excursion.

Couldn't help it, though.

Something about that quick mouth got to me down there. The way she knew I wasn't buying the bullshit about working for the Huskies but was willing to go down in flames with it anyway. And now we're up here. For the sole purpose of seeing how deep she's willing to dig her heels on this.

I lead her through the small coaches' booth lined with tables and swivel chairs. The lights flicker on automatically as we move toward the floor-to-ceiling windows overlooking the field.

"This place is usually buzzing on a game day." She follows me a few steps behind. "You'd have a small army of assistant coaches up here, watching the game and feeding intel to the rest of the team through headsets. If the Huskies need a good picture of the field, this is the place to get one."

She shoots me a cutting glance. Knows perfectly well that I know they were bluffing down there. Refuses to back down. "You seem to know your way around the place pretty well. Do you work here?"

"Not anymore. A couple of friends of mine work down in the athletic rehab center. They've been helping me train during the off-season."

I don't elaborate, but it piques her interest anyway. She studies me with those blue-gray eyes the same way she had down on the field. Like she's on the verge of inviting me over for a private *doggy-style tryst* but also like she's trying to place me. That look you give when you know you're supposed to know someone, but you can't quite figure it out.

"Here, give me your phone. Let's get you those pictures, huh? Are you supposed to be in them?"

Another searing look in my direction. She's still unwilling to admit defeat as she hands me her phone.

The woman positions herself by the windows, and I'm struck again by how stunning she is. And I mean *struck*, like a truck hitting me head-on, then reversing just to get me again. Down there on the field, she'd damn near turned me into a bumbling mess just by looking at me.

The long dark hair, almost black and so fucking shiny. And those eyes. Bright and lively. This woman is always on the hunt for laughs, I can feel it.

She's tall, and so lusciously curvy. Hips you want to sink your fingers into, leave a couple prints for her to wake up to in the morning so she remembers who those curves belong to.

She's got the kind of body and face you just don't share.

"Question for you."

"Hm?" Fuck. I've been staring at her way longer than is chaste or family-oriented, and she's definitely noticed.

"Am I . . ." She shrugs casually. Toys with the necklace she's wearing. A silver chain with an anchor charm dotted with sparkling blue-gray stones, just like her eyes. ". . . about to get murdered, maybe?"

My eyebrows shoot up. "Come again?"

She gestures around us. "Well, it's just that I'm suddenly realizing that I've come all the way up here with a stranger. Who's now holding my phone. Also, aside from telling my friend we were going to find a good spot for a picture, no one knows exactly *where* I am with said stranger. And while this is kind of par for the course for me, the whole getting-myself-into-difficult-to-get-out-of-pickles thing, this one in particular feels like it'll end with my untimely demise."

She delivers the entire diatribe in one long, breathless flow, and I let out a single burst of laughter when she finishes. I'd love to know what kind of pickles she gets herself into. I bet they're good.

"So . . . will it?" she continues—casually, like she hasn't just asked me whether I'm about to do away with her. "Am I about to get murdered?"

"Am I?" I counter.

"Are you what?"

"Am I about to get murdered? Because if that logic stands, then I'm also up here with a stranger, without anyone knowing. So . . . am I about to get murdered?"

I've amused her. The corners of her mouth lift just slightly, eyes twinkle as she assesses me. Just a small taste of what's got to be a real killer of a smile.

That look is a tease.

Addictive.

It's equivalent to a pat on the head, and now I want the whole goddamn gold medal around my neck.

It's an urge I haven't felt in years.

"Statistically . . ." She blinks up at me slowly from under those long, dark lashes. Little flirt. "About ninety percent of all homicides are perpetrated by men. So, if anyone was likely to be chopped up and served as a meat-loaf treat to the coaches here on game day, it would be me."

"Pretty sure whoever pulled those stats hadn't met you. How many poor fuckers have you brought to their knees with that little look of yours?"

Her mouth curves just another millimeter. "Which look?"

I jerk my chin at her. "That one. That ghost of a grin and the twinkle thing you're doing with your eyes. You want me to wonder if you're flirting with me. Want me to dial it up, work a little harder to impress you, while you decide if I'm worth your time."

I know I'm real close to getting a proper smile now, because her teeth sink into that plush bottom lip. "Is it working? The look?"

"You want it to?"

She tips her head. "Undecided."

I release a tortured breath, because, yeah—the look works. "For fuck's sake, put me out of my misery and tell me your name."

"It's Siena."

"Siena." I take my time letting it roll off my tongue, tasting it, weighing it. It suits her, as far as names can suit a person. "After the color or the city?"

"They spelled it like the city but probably meant the color." She shrugs. "I couldn't know for sure."

I'm still holding her phone, and her eyes lock with mine as it passes from my hand to hers. Her gaze flickers to my mouth, back up again.

"Brooks. My name, in case you're curious. It's Brooks."

She hums, inching back to get a proper look at me. Assessing whether the name matches the guy, maybe.

And then I see it. That spark of recognition. Siena looks from me to the football field behind her. Back to me.

"Brooks . . . Attwood."

I lift and drop a shoulder. "Brooks."

Her eyes go wide. "You're Brooks Attwood."

"Brooks." I nod. "It's nice to meet you, Siena."

"But—but you're *Brooks Attwood*. My dad grew up a Rebels fan. And his dad before him. And me, since I was thirteen. I knew you looked familiar—you know when you don't expect to run into some-one, so it takes a while to click?"

"Your dad and grandpa are Rebels fans, and you didn't hop on the wagon until you were thirteen?"

"He didn't become my dad until I was thirteen. God, this is . . . Today of all days." She looks around in utter awe. "I wish he could see this. Brooks Attwood. Your comeback is all over the news."

"Comeback attempt. The rest remains to be seen."

She waves away my words, like there's no doubt in her mind this comeback is happening. "Hey, listen, will you take a picture with me? My mom will get such a kick out of this. Please?"

Please. Like I wasn't already running through a list of excuses to get near her again. "Here, my arms are longer."

Siena hands me her phone and slides under the arm I hold out for her. I snap some photos, only half paying attention. She smells like . . . what is that? I turn my chin, momentarily burying my face in her hair, trying to pin down her scent.

Salt water? Sunshine?

Does the sun have a scent?

She scrolls through the pictures when I hand her back her phone. "Your eyes are closed in half of these." She chuckles before tucking it into the pocket at the front of her overalls. "Well, as nice as this was, shall we head back down?"

I put an arm out, blocking her path as she heads for the door.

"Hold up. Aren't you supposed to be posting pictures for the Huskies?"

She tenses against my arm. Definitely avoids my eye. "As soon as we get out of here. I don't want to hold you up."

"I've got time. Unless you're ready to admit you were actually trespassing down there?"

I beam when she gives me a sharp look, pulls out her phone, and taps away at it.

"There. Pictures posted." She gives me a saccharine smile as she waves the screen, flashing a glimpse of photos of the field on a social media feed. "Satisfied?"

"Incredibly."

"Fantastic." Siena tugs at the door of the coaches' booth. Then again. And again when it doesn't budge. She turns an inquisitive look on me, moving aside when I reach for the door myself.

Definitely locked. From the outside.

Siena tsks. "I'm getting *chopped into meat loaf* vibes again, Brooks Attwood."

"I didn't plan this, I swear." I slide down the wall by the door, sitting on the ground and pulling out my phone. "Let me message someone to get us out of here."

"Oh. I can just—"

"It shouldn't take long. My friend Summer was with a client in the gym, but she should be wrapping up soon."

After a moment's hesitation, Siena sits on the floor beside me. I peek at her from the corner of my eye. Find her doing the same with me.

We soften into simultaneous chuckles. I can't remember the last time I hung out with a woman I wasn't related to, fake dating, or best friends with.

It's . . . nice.

I hadn't intended on staying single after things ended with my ex. In fact, the prospect of dating was just about the only bright spot once I stopped self-destructing. I figured losing football might get me closer to what I wanted: a partnership like my parents'. A little hellion like my sister's son, Leo.

And I'd be able to find the right person this time. Someone who wanted me and not, it turned out, the allure of my ex-career. Who wouldn't throw away an eight-year relationship and find another pro athlete to sink her claws into, after my own career in professional sports went bust.

Instead, I traded liquor and back-alley hookups for second-guesses and paranoia, and every woman who looked at me twice became heartbreak and betrayal just waiting to happen.

When the dating thing never went anywhere, the idea of a comeback to my old team became an obsession. At least I could have football. I could be back with the coaches and teammates I'd loved playing with. One out of two isn't bad, as far as life goes.

Except now, the Rebels won't touch me.

Sighing, I rest my head against the wall behind me and pick at the sole of my sneaker.

"Midnight skinny-dips."

"Pardon me?"

"Midnight skinny-dips." Siena's almond-shaped eyes look at me like they're trying to pierce into my brain, my soul. Trying to figure out this silence. "Whenever I sigh that hard, I strip down and hop in the bay in the middle of the night. Doesn't always work, I'll admit. But nine out of ten times, it gets me out of whatever funk I'm in. Give it a shot. Report back." She gives me an expectant look, and when I don't say anything, she adds, "Or not. What's your thing? When you're sighing that hard?"

What does it say about me that I come up with nothing?

Sleep, run, work out, drills, run, sleep. It's how my days have looked since I decided on this comeback four months ago.

Even before, what did I have? A coaching job I hated. Happy

friends moving on to bigger and better things. A too-big, secluded house just outside of town. My family across the country.

I rub my arm, feeling the suffocating weight of . . . nothingness.

Peter. I have Pete.

"I have a dog." I feel like an inadequate idiot the moment I say so. She's trespassing into a stadium, skinny-dipping in the middle of the night. Probably the kind of woman who goes skydiving on a random Tuesday morning. And here I am telling her about my dog.

He's a really good boy, though.

"Show me." When I stare at her uncomprehendingly, Siena nods at the phone sitting in my lap. "Show off your dog, Brooks Attwood. I want to see."

"Yeah?"

She nods her encouragement. Probably just humoring me, but it doesn't feel like it. She's smiling from her eyes.

I tap my phone to life, and Pete stares back at us from the lock screen, lying belly up in the grass at home. "His name is Peter. He's a hundred-and-five-pound German shepherd who thinks he's a lap dog. He was down there earlier."

She grins at a video of me and Pete wrestling over a mini football. "That was your dog on the field? He's cute."

"Funny, most people describe him as terrifying as fuck."

"Who, this guy? A harmless pup if I've ever seen one." Siena pries the phone out of my hand but pauses with her thumb over the screen. "Which way do I scroll for more Peter? We should build up to the dick pics."

With a laugh, I lean over and scroll through my phone. It's all Pete. Napping, panting for treats, destroying stuffed toys. "No dick pics in either direction."

Siena clicks her tongue. "Shame."

I sit back, just watching Siena scroll through my camera roll. Strangely, every bit of the weight I'd felt just a minute ago has lifted.

"Brooks, he's adorable."

From my pocket, I pull out a round lollipop and twist off the purple wrapping before reaching for another and offering it to Siena. "He's a good boy. I adopted him from a rescue when I moved back to Oakwood."

"You carry candy in your pockets?" Siena accepts the lollipop and sticks it in her mouth.

"In case of emergency. I grew up in my mom's bakery, so the sugar addiction started early. Never know when the craving will strike."

"Or when you'll be in the mood to lure a woman in a locked room."

I finger the stick coming out of my mouth. "Really not doing much to talk you out of the murder thing, am I?"

"I'm as convinced as ever. How many times have you run this play, Brooks Attwood?"

"The stuck-in-a-coaches'-booth-with-a-pretty-girl play? You're my one and only."

"Perfect answer." Siena holds my gaze. I haven't flirted in . . . Fuck, when had I last flirted? I swear, it's that smiling thing her eyes do, bringing it out of me. The old me. The one who laughs and plays, with no guard searching for a motive. "So, are you allowed to tell me how your comeback is going? Full disclosure, I *will* turn on you if you tell me you're signing with any team but the Rebels, because . . ." Siena pulls out her phone when it starts *dinging* in her front pocket. Her face falls. "Oh, shit."

"What is it?"

"Those pictures. The ones I posted online." Siena turns her screen around so I can see. She swipes through a carousel of pictures of the field she'd posted to her social media account, until she lands on one of . . . us.

We're standing by the window; she's tucked under my arm with her hand splayed over my chest. My head is turned toward her, looking down in some kind of awe—like she's the first woman I've ever laid eyes on.

Shit, I really need to get out more.

"I haven't had pictures go viral in, like, a year," Siena muses, tipping her head at the phone.

My stomach plummets. *Viral?*

Stuffing my lollipop into my cheek, I reach for her phone. In the ten minutes since she posted it, it's well into the five-digit likes, and there are hundreds of comments below it.

Now, that's one hell of an UPGRADE! Go Cece!

It's a long stream of messages along the same lines—little fires and something about revenge being best served with a side of *football daddy?*

What the fuck is a football daddy?

"What's this about an upgrade?" My ringtone cuts off whatever she was about to say. I dig my phone out to find Josh's contact lighting up the screen. "Shit, it's my agent. He's probably pissed about the picture."

"Oh, it's definitely about the picture." Siena turns her phone around. It's an article on the *All-Stars* website. An online tabloid.

The online tabloid.

COMEBACK KID BROOKS ATTWOOD COZIES UP WITH CECE PIPPEN, JUST MONTHS AFTER HER BREAKUP WITH NFL STAR THOMAS IVERS

Chapter 4

Brooks

"You're fucking brilliant, you know that?"

Wind rushes over Josh's voice, like he's driving with the windows down, and for a second I think I hear him wrong. "I gotta tell you: I thought this fake girlfriend thing was peak stupidity. But you really know what you're doing, don't you? Fucking *brilliant*. It's already all over the internet—it just came up on ESPN radio, for fuck's sake. The Rebels ownership team forwarded me an article, asking how long you've been dating."

"I . . . Hang on a minute—"

"No idea how you managed to snag someone this quick, let alone some beloved, internet-famous girl, but you really knocked it out of the park." I've never heard Josh this pumped up. "You'll have to really sell this, Brooksy. Get her to post pictures of you both on social media—hell, get Pete in those pictures. People love dogs, they'll eat it up. Bring her to that Huskies alumni game you're hosting next week. If we can convince the Rebels you're in a loving, stable relationship, you'll be on that training camp invite list in no time. I guarantee it."

My stomach sinks, heart pumps furiously. *Beloved? Internet famous?*

"Hang on, Josh. This isn't what you think—I never said I was going to do the dating thing."

"What the hell are you talking about?"

"I'm saying this is a misunderstanding. I don't even know this girl. There's no way I'm dating her." I wince, turning to Siena, who looks deeply amused by the entire thing. "No offense."

She widens her eyes, plucking the lollipop out of her mouth. "Your loss."

"Brooks, let me be very clear about your situation, in case you didn't quite get me before." All traces of energy have been sucked out of Josh's voice. "I don't care if it's real or fake, if you just met her or have known her since you were both snot-nosed kids in diapers. This isn't going to be yet another photo of you and a woman looking cozy, only for her never to be seen again. Not when that's the one thing keeping you from a contract with the Rebels. Am I getting this wrong, Brooks? Do you *not* want to sign with the Rebels? Should I focus my efforts elsewhere?"

"No," I say quickly. "That's where I want to play."

"Then I don't care if you have to get on your knees and beg her to date you. I don't care if you have to pay her a damn salary. You stick with this girl until that contract is signed and sealed. You get me?"

Siena is texting away beside me, oblivious to the mad scheme she's being weaved into over the course of this phone call.

"These girls are all about chasing clout," Josh continues. "You're all over the news. You can talk her into it."

These girls?

I hate his words, the tone of his voice. I especially hate that all of it is pointed at the woman beside me. Except . . .

JUST MONTHS AFTER HER BREAKUP WITH NFL STAR THOMAS IVERS

Thomas fucking Ivers. Star quarterback for the Ravens, the second team out in Los Angeles. He's the face of the NFL, at the very top of the pay scale. I know the guy, have met him countless times at events around LA.

Suddenly, this is all too familiar.

After announcing my retirement, I'd escaped home to find Naomi swapping spit with an ex-teammate, right in our driveway. Her bags were packed by the front door, and she'd apparently been anxiously waiting to dump me while I was out ending my career.

It all came together then. Where she'd been while I was in bed for months, scared and recovering from my concussion. Why she'd fought so hard against my decision to retire.

When she and I had gotten together here at UOB, I was already being hailed as the NFL's top prospect in my future draft class. She dropped out of college to move with me across the country when I got drafted by the Rebels. Encouraged me to take every single sponsorship deal that came my way; to buy the biggest house I could afford, a garage full of nice cars I didn't need. To attend every glitzy gala I was invited to, always with her on my arm.

Naomi had managed to build her own adoring social media fanbase surrounding her lifestyle as an NFL girlfriend by the time I scored my first touchdown in the league. I had a bona fide second career as her personal photographer, and a third making cameos in the photos and videos she'd post online.

There was always somewhere to go, some fancy party to attend. She lived off the team's celebrity connections. Loved the attention from fans.

At the peak of my career—and right around the time I got injured—she'd been getting papped on the way to the goddamn grocery store. I thought nothing of it all until she dumped me, and it became clear just how replaceable I was. Turns out, it didn't matter whose arm she was on as long as it was attached to a pro athlete.

There's dead air in my ear. I've been so caught up in a panicked spiral that it takes me a few seconds to realize Josh has already hung up the call.

I shoot a glance at Siena, who's still typing away at her phone. She looks entertained as hell by the entire thing, and I can't figure it out. Whether she caught on to who I was from the jump, down on the field. Whether she was playing me, posted that particular picture on purpose, knowing the attention it would get her.

These girls are all about chasing clout.

My phone chimes, announcing a text from Josh, who seems to have sensed my downward spiral from wherever the hell he is.

JOSH: Rebels ownership wants to arrange a phone call tomorrow. They're loving this. Don't fuck it up.

Shit. He's right, isn't he? If the Rebels changed their tune this fast . . .

This is my way in with the team. Dating Cece Pippen. Beloved, clout-chasing ex-girlfriend of the face of the NFL.

I clear my throat, tossing my phone to the side. "Cece—"

"Siena," she corrects with a grimace at her phone. She's texting someone named Shyla—her friend with the cute kid? "My ex called me Cece. Sadly, it stuck."

"Right. Well, those articles. The reason people seem to care we're getting cozy? Why would that be?"

She shrugs. "You're all over the news."

"And you? Why are your pictures going viral?"

She rests her head on the wall at our backs, the stick from her lollipop protruding from her mouth. "Well, part of that probably has to do with who my ex is."

"And the other part?"

Siena shakes her head, a wry smile playing at her mouth. "There was a video that went viral, just a few months before our breakup. I was sitting behind the benches during one of his games. A fan for the other team somehow managed to set a bevy of doves loose on the field while they were lining up at the seven-yard line, about to score a game-winning touchdown. I guess it was supposed to be funny because their team was playing the Ravens. And then—"

"That was you? The girl in the clip?" I turn to get a proper look at her. "That video was on every sports reel for weeks."

"Slow news weeks."

They weren't slow news weeks. It was simply that the video taken from the stands was just that good. I remember it vividly. Doves hobbling around the field, stadium staff scrambling to catch them, both benches clearing to help.

And then, out of nowhere, the birds simultaneously take flight. They make a beeline toward the stands and land one by one around a woman sitting in the crowd, casually munching on popcorn. She visibly freezes, you think she's about to run off screaming, and instead she . . . just starts sharing her popcorn with the birds. Like some Disney princess kind of shit, before they all fly off into the sky.

"ESPN named you—"

"Cece Pippen and the Seven Yards." Siena gives a rueful shake of her head. "Insane. My social account blew up overnight. I couldn't shake the attention as long as Tom and I were together—people would do this bird chirping sound at me whenever they saw me. They still do, sometimes." She demonstrates, attempting a whistle that comes out as more of a wet exhale than anything else. She shrugs, laughing to herself. "I could never whistle worth shit."

Tom. Her very famous, very talented athlete of an ex.

I try to fight the bad taste in my mouth, but I know it's a losing battle. I feel it in my stiffening muscles, in the inches I add to the space between us.

These girls are all about chasing clout.

Is there a neon sign above my head? *Gullible man found here. Come get him while he's hot.*

What *had* she been doing on the field? Am I really supposed to believe that I ended up locked in a room with Thomas Ivers's ex-girlfriend by complete coincidence?

I think back to how thrilled she'd been when she supposedly figured out who I was. How quickly she asked for that picture together. And now, we're all over the internet.

How the *fuck* did I manage to attract another Naomi into my life?

"Did you know who I was, down there?" I ask quietly.

Despite mounting evidence of my own naïveté, I hate myself the second the question leaves my mouth. But I've been through this before. Naomi and her insatiable desire for that WAG title. No matter how many athletes she had to fuck to keep it.

Siena glances up from her phone and plucks the lollipop from her mouth. "What?"

"On the field." Have I ever sounded so cold in my life? I didn't know I was capable. "Did you know who I was? Did you get me up here alone on purpose?"

The smile fades slowly off her face. "*You* brought me up here."

"You weren't supposed to be down there at all. Then you ask for a picture with me and turn around and post it."

"*You* challenged me to post those pictures." Her brows pull together. "Just so you're aware, it sounds like you're accusing me of either jersey chasing or stalking."

"Why not both?"

She scoffs, eyes widening in disbelief. She sweeps the room, as though she expects to find someone with which to exchange a stunned *are you hearing this shit?*

"Did you do this on purpose? You figured out I was training here, found a way onto the field—"

"Wow. You are so full of yourself, it's almost impressive." Siena gets to her feet, brushing the back of her overalls and dumping her half-done lollipop into the trash.

I stand and do the same with my candy. "It's all a little convenient. You're telling me I just happened to get locked in a room with Thomas Ivers's internet-famous ex?"

Her eyes pierce mine. Not in that cute way, either. In a way like she wishes her stare was made of actual daggers, stabbing me in the face. "Besides the fact that I don't fuck around with athletes—"

"Unless they're on a roster, right? And the face of the league."

Her mouth twists furiously. "Well, that disqualifies you, doesn't it? Seeing as you're neither."

Siena's words hang between us, a low blow kicking me right in the sternum, filling my veins with the kind of hostility I haven't felt in years. Not since my ex calmly explained that she'd been fucking my teammate for months before she left me for him.

I catch a flash of regret on Siena's face before she smooths it right out. She unzips her purse with such force, I'm shocked the zipper doesn't fly off its track.

I force a breath into my body. "We need to talk."

"I think we've done more than enough of that. What we need to do is get the hell out of here. Never see each other again."

"Sadly, that'll have to wait." I rub my face roughly. "We're stuck together until I get a contract with the Rebels."

Siena freezes, hands still on her bag. "Excuse me?"

Going off on her right before asking to date her probably wasn't my smartest move. "Turns out the internet loves us together. So do the Rebels, who, until a few minutes ago, refused to touch me based on my apparent inability to settle down in life. One look at that picture of us together, and they're hot on me again."

"And why am I supposed to care?"

I have no desire to get into the story of Naomi, so I give her the half-truth. "I went on a bender after my injury, partying and . . . trying to cope with my retirement in all the wrong ways. It poses a bit of a problem for the Rebels."

Understanding seems to dawn. "Because they're known for signing strait-laced, family-friendly players."

"Meaning they've shut down any talk of my coming back, unless I can prove that I've changed. That I keep my . . ." Why did I gesture at my dick like that? "Point is, it's supposed to look like I've settled down since then, and this picture of us makes it seem like I've settled down with you." I throw out my arms. "Congrats, Cece Pippen. You just bagged yourself a fake boyfriend."

Siena bursts into laughter. "You're kidding, right?"

"My agent seems to think this is the only way out of this mess. You'd be my ticket back to the Rebels, and I'd be your ticket to some more of that internet infamy. Brand deals, whatever. Based on those articles, it's already working."

She digests my words. "*Fake dating?* Who does that?"

"I do. I once fake-dated my best friend's girlfriend for a while and . . ." I trail off when her eyes grow in alarm. "Forget it. It'll be temporary. Surface-level. We won't even need to see or speak to each other outside of public appearances where we'll have pictures of us taken with my dog."

"Let me see if I understand this clearly. You want me to pretend to be your girlfriend for however long it takes you to sign with the Rebels."

"That's the gist of it."

Her brows pinch together. "You want me to make appearances with you where we'll presumably be photographed together, so that the Rebels management team thinks you've settled down."

I think she might really be considering this. "Exactly."

She combs her fingers through her hair, thinking hard. "And once you sign, you'll move away. We'll pretend to . . . what? Break up because of the long distance?"

I jab my finger in her direction. "Perfect."

She hums, nods along with me. "And what I'll get out of it are cuddles with your German shepherd and more internet fame as an NFL girlfriend?"

"See? It's win-win."

Siena snorts, and the pensive look melts right off her face. "I'm going to have to pass. As tempting as it is."

"You won't do it?"

"Of course I won't do it!"

"Why not?"

"Oh, I don't know," she says sarcastically, pacing to the windows. "Maybe because—contrary to your glowing opinion of me—I don't care about being internet famous. Besides, you're a total stranger." She turns on her heel and makes for the locked door of the coaches' booth. "A scheming stranger, who probably lured me up here knowing we'd get stuck together, just to convince me to pretend-date him and his dog."

Siena whips a credit card out of her wallet and moves for the door. She fiddles for a few moments until an unmistakable *click* breaks the silence.

What the fuck? "How'd you know how to do that?"

Calmly, she replaces her credit card and wallet into her purse. "I've been jimmying locks since I was a kid."

A number of questions bounce around my head. I settle on "And why didn't you do that to begin with?"

"You didn't seem especially concerned that we were stuck. And I'll admit I was . . . intrigued. Now, though?" When she finally looks at me again, it's with something akin to disgust. She indicates me with a flippant flick of her hand. "No, thanks."

Siena grips the door handle just as it swings open on its own. For the second time today, I throw my arms around her, catching her around the waist before she face-plants into the ground.

"What the hell is going on in here?" We look up to find Summer, still dressed in her UOB faculty gear. Her hair swishes as she looks between us. "I got your SOS. I thought you said the door was locked from the outside?"

Siena smooths her hair, wafting some of that sun-kissed, ocean scent to where I stand behind her. "It was."

Summer eyes Siena with interest. "Hey, you're the girl from the picture. It's all over ESPN down in the gym."

Fucking. Awesome.

Definitely no way out of this, then.

"That would indeed be me." Siena clutches her purse. "Well, I'm out. Thanks for the attempted save . . ."

"Summer."

"Thanks for the attempted save, Summer. And . . ." Siena's gaze cuts to me. "Good luck with everything. I'd say I'm going to miss you, but honestly? It turns out you're kind of a conceited prick."

She heads down the hall without another word. Not even a glance back. Something sharp kind of carves up my insides at the sight of her walking away.

In my peripheral vision I see Summer lift an eyebrow. "*Conceited prick?*"

When I don't do anything but stare at Siena's retreating figure, stomach sinking to my feet, Summer clears her throat.

"Hey, Cece," she calls down the hall. Siena looks back over her shoulder. "I don't know what happened in there, but for the record? This is a guy who sobs at dog shelter commercials. Seriously, all it takes is the opening bars of that Sarah McLachlan song and it's game over."

I nudge Summer and give her a searing look.

"What?" she whispers. "I'm helping you out."

"By making me out to be a sensitive sap?"

"You *are* a sensitive sap. Embrace it."

Siena watches our hushed exchange. "Thing is, Summer? I like to think I don't need four legs and a tail to have someone's respect."

Damn.

She turns on her heel, leaving me in the dust feeling about two inches tall, and every bit the asshole I was in there.

Chapter 5

Siena

WhatIsAFootballDaddy01: Did you know there are exactly 174 Cece Pippens on this app? Took me a while to realize you'd be on here as Siena, given the whole nickname-from-your-ex thing, but I sorted through every single Cece trying to find you. It was kind of like being on hold with the bank. Scared to hang up just in case you're next in line, you know?

WhatIsAFootballDaddy02: Apparently this thing only lets me send you one unanswered message before it blocks me? Had to make another account just now. Anyway, you can ignore all that. This is what I get for sliding into someone's DMs at 3:15 in the morning.

WhatIsAFootballDaddy03: This is Brooks, by the way. Please message me back.

I snort, dropping my phone on the checkout counter at Ship Happens, the one and only bait and tackle shop on Baycrest's boardwalk. I can admit to having been initially charmed by the messages, and the fact that the man created three accounts solely for the sake of rambling into the void of my inbox. Just as I'd been charmed by Brooks Attwood before our short acquaintance went to hell.

But all it takes to cleanse me of that is remembering how he levelled those accusations. How humiliated I'd felt. How grieving Dad that day was bad enough without being looked at like I was Satan's personal envoy, come to ruin this man's life.

How much of a hypocrite he'd been.

Accusing me of scheming to earn all the supposed perks of dating a professional athlete, when he'd asked to fake-date me for the sake of his own financial gain.

The balls on that guy.

It was a busy day on the boardwalk today, the first week of consistently warm May weather. Tourists were out in droves, all coming to the blip on a map that is Baycrest because, somehow, our small town managed to monopolize the entirety of the short waterfront of Oakwood Bay. Meanwhile, the bay's namesake, Oakwood, is nested in mature pine trees with no view of the water to speak of, until you drive to its outskirts.

The busy days are the good ones.

They fly by in a blur of hobby fishermen not unlike my dad. Except, where these fishermen visit Ship Happens to stock up on gear before hopping on their boats at the marina down the way, this shop was Dad's life's passion. He and Mom built it from the ground up years before I joined their family, and it was always part of my plan to take it over. It just happened a lot sooner than I ever thought it would. Mom's arthritis became such a challenge that she retired, then Dad passed, and suddenly the shop was mine.

I have no particular affinity for the worms and minnows that make the shop a must-visit prior to fishing excursions. Nor for fishing in general.

But I love how much Dad loved this place. I loved the weekends and summers I worked here with my new parents, loved that I was giving back to them, earning my place in their family when they'd gone through hell to keep me in it. Every corner of the shop is proof that Dad existed. From the colorful lures on clear fishing lines I'd talked him into hanging from the rafters, to the football-shaped bob-bers on a spinning display on the checkout counter.

Those bobbers have been there for ages. Can't remember the last time I sold one.

But Dad had gotten such a kick out of them when he'd stocked them. Two of his favorite things combined into one.

"Hey, Aidan?" I call into the shop. "Can you make sure to check the—"

"Already on it."

It's a testament to Aidan's unyielding patience that he doesn't even look halfway annoyed as he doubles back down aisle three, where I hear him fiddling with the large refrigeration unit holding our latest shipment of live bait. It's been on the fritz for the past week, flickering on and off at random times. Never long enough to risk our stock of worms and minnows, but just enough to fray my nerves, con-sidering those little containers house our biggest draw for customers.

Aidan and I grew up on the same street, have been friends since I moved in with the Robertses. He's just a couple of years younger than me and my thirty-one years, helping me around the shop between the surf events he travels the country to compete in. He's tall, with skin that really soaks up the sun—a Surfer Ken if I've ever laid eyes on the type.

In the months since my breakup, we've also become the kind of friends who meet for late-night movies and naked tussles.

He's Ship Happens's only other employee—if I can even call him that, with his minimal hours and all the traveling he does—because fishing is a seasonal business in this part of the country. The majority of our summer earnings need to cover an entire twelve months of commercial rent, maintenance, and my paychecks, in addition to the significant cut I funnel to Mom for the mammoth second mortgage on her house.

It's the least I can do, seeing as I was the reason she got it.

Aidan reappears at the front of the shop. "Unit looks good, Cee. Up and running as usual. Are you all good here?"

"Yup, I'm almost done. Thanks for your help today."

My phone lights up with another string of messages like those I've been getting for the past week.

Comments from the masses on my supposed relationship with a beloved past and future NFL star. Brands reaching out with partnership and advertising offers. It appears that my stock has skyrocketed with Brooks's star power behind me—they're offering over double the kind of fee they did at the peak of my Cece Pippen and the Seven Yards days.

Not that I'd ever taken them up on it.

"How many articles today?" Aidan grins when I only raise my brows. "Articles shipping you and your supposed boyfriend. I still can't go out for a drink in town without reaping the rewards for knowing you, which I thank you for."

I snort. "You mean the women who keep kissing your ass in the hopes of one day crossing paths with him?"

"They're rabid." He shakes his head.

"Uh-huh," I say with a smirk. "And you're telling me you haven't indulged a single one of them?"

"You're the one dodging me this week. What am I supposed to do?" It's true that I haven't been in the mood for our evening visits lately. Aidan's phone begins to ping enthusiastically, lighting up with texts that he scrolls through with mild interest. "When you do wrap up here?"

Our code for *want to come over and bang tonight?*

And . . . nothing.

I feel nothing, just like every other time he's asked this week. No twinge below the waist. Not even the desire to shrug and say, *Why the hell not? Beats sitting at home bored and alone.*

My libido has just . . . disappeared. Into thin air. I haven't so much as looked at *myself* naked all week.

"Cee?" Aidan prompts when I've been quiet too long. He tucks his phone into the back pocket of his shorts. "You doing anything tonight?"

"It's cribbage night at my mom's." I'm grateful for the built-in excuse to dodge him again, even though there's no reason for the nerves. He's taken all my *no*'s in stride, no questions asked.

"Oh, that's right." He straightens off the counter, shoots me a parting grin. "Then I'll see you—"

A shrill beeping breaks the silence, from the very back of aisle three—a mean, urgent sound I've never heard before, but I know instantly.

Those goddamn worms and minnows are about to ruin my night. And my tomorrow.

My several tomorrows.

~~~~~

The cribbage game is well underway by the time I make it to my parents' house, and I take the opportunity to stop at the mirror by the front door to smooth my wind-swept hair.

Because my car broke down.

Broke down.

As though I hadn't just spent the past three hours arguing with a refrigeration company. Trying to offer fixes for the busted unit like I knew anything about refrigeration to begin with, before being plainly told that it was twenty years old, far beyond repair, and that its replacement would cost me $10,000.

Which isn't ideal, considering money is tight—*always* tight for a seasonal business—but I could have cut my own pay for a few weeks, paid rent on my apartment from my savings, and it would have been fine.

But that rusty old bitch of a car died on the way over, and though

I'll have to wait until morning to know what the damage will be to my wallet, I can't help but wonder what kind of energy I've been putting out into the world.

You'd think I had enough for one week.

To have the anniversary of Dad's death, and my face plastered on every sports and D-list celebrity website, after suffering the indignity of being called a gold digger by my supposed boyfriend. The articles online aren't all bad, but the nasty ones make me glad for my thick skin.

I close my eyes, effectively blocking out the sight of the nest on top of my head from the windy bike ride over to Mom's. Gulp down a long breath to cut off the acute panic rising up my throat.

Gulp another when it doesn't work.

And a third, and fourth, until I'm nothing but calm control, smiling back at myself in this mirror.

"Who's winning?" I call as I stroll into the small living room with the same worn-in floral couches my parents have had since I moved in.

Maybe I didn't need those deep breaths.

The familiar sight of those beat-up floral cushions lifts my mood in an instant. This whole house does. Has since the second time I set foot here, invited for dinner by Mom and Dad just twenty-four hours after they caught me breaking into this very home at thirteen. Starving, too skinny to be healthy. Holes in the soles of my shoes.

By then, I'd been sneaking into neighboring houses for food for three months straight. After my birth parents woke up one day, decided they'd had enough of me. And vanished before I'd even rolled out of my cot in the basement.

This tiny house is the first place I was ever truly happy. The first house where I felt cared for, loved. All because Dad found me waist-deep in their fridge one night and took pity on my skinny ass instead of calling the cops.

Mom is huddled around the coffee table with Carla and Evan.

Mom on the sofa because her arthritic joints don't do well on the ground, and the other two sitting cross-legged on the carpeted floor.

"There you are, angel!" Mom offers me her cheek when I give her a peck and then smacks one of her own on my forehead. "Everything all right at the shop?"

"All good, just took a bit longer with the inventory tonight," I say, ignoring the pang of guilt over the lie.

Better that than to worry Mom or force Evan and Carla to spring to action, solving a problem that's mine. They've made it their business to keep Mom company since Dad passed—coming around for dinner a couple of times a week, inviting her to travel with them. I couldn't love them more for it.

Wouldn't know how to begin repaying them for that level of kindness.

Certainly not by adding my own messes to their plate, especially when they've got their own businesses to worry about—they own the marina just down the boardwalk from Ship Happens, and charter out their own sailboat during the summer months.

And Mom . . . well, she and Dad have done more than enough for me. The least I can do is take care of the shop, like I have for years.

And years, and years.

"Well, you're doing a fabulous job with it, angel," Mom says happily. "Dad was right to leave the shop in your capable hands. You're doing him so proud."

And years, and years, and *years*.

"Was it the inventory, or was she sneaking around with her new pretty-boy lover?" Carla shoots me a smirk overtop of her playing cards.

"*Ha-ha.*" It's been a running joke all week, since that stupid picture from the Huskies stadium went viral, regardless of how many times I assured them that the media had it brutally wrong.

That there was not, nor would there ever be, anything going on between me and Brooks Attwood.

I move around the room, offering Carla and Evan hugs before plopping down next to Mom. "I thought Shy and Rosie were coming tonight."

"There was a last-minute playdate with a new neighbor's kid." Carla surveys the cards in her hand before her gaze bounces between Mom's and Evan's, as though she's got the X-ray vision required to see through them.

"Oh yeah? She didn't mention. I'm glad she's getting out, though." I tuck my legs underneath me. Since her husband, Max, was deployed six months ago, Shy's been a walking ball of stress, missing him and caring for Rosie. Shy and I aren't a required presence on cribbage night anyway, seeing as they play on a three-person board. It's just an excuse to get together, drink too much wine, and tease our parents for reaching the golden age of cribbage in the first place.

"You can say that again," Evan mutters as various cards hit the wooden coffee table. "I keep telling her we'll watch Rosie so she can have more of a life, but she's worried about Rosie missing a parent enough as it is."

I think of that afternoon on the Huskies field, the way Rosie called out for her daddy when she laid eyes on my *new pretty-boy lover*. My heart clenches for her and my best friend.

"You're preaching to the choir, Evs, and we've just established that Shy isn't here." Carla leans over under the guise of patting his arm, head straining around her husband's handful of cards. She's really hamming it up, like she wants to be caught.

"For shit's sake, love." Evan catches on to his wife's antics, whips his hand away from her prying, cheater gaze. He gives her a slow, exasperated shake of his head while a reluctant smile pushes through his stern expression. Mom and I laugh quietly on the couch.

I've watched Shy's parents together for nearly twenty years, but they still give me the same butterflies I felt when I met them as a kid. There's something so charming about their dynamic. The way she goes out of her way to tease him, annoy him. His feigned irritation, the way he can never stay stern with her longer than a few seconds before hearts start pouring from his eyes.

He can't even manage a *for shit's sake* without tacking on an endearment.

Not that I'm especially itching to date given the recency of my breakup with Tom, but that's the dynamic I long for. Playful and affectionate.

"Siena . . . you didn't ride your motorcycle here, did you?" Mom's hand smooths over the top of my head, drawing my attention. She's staring at the messy bun I'd thrown my hair in—my signature look when helmet hair can't be helped.

I should have known better. Mom *hates* that motorcycle, the graduation present I bought myself with accumulated earnings from working at Ship Happens since I was fourteen.

"It was all right. Just a five-minute ride." I lean over the coffee table to pick a piece of cheddar off the cheese board they've been nibbling at. "I considered walking, but . . . exercise." I make a retching sound, exaggerating in the hopes that Mom will forget to scold me.

"Exercise." Carla wrinkles her nose and shudders in palpable disgust. A woman after my own heart. "Hey, remember the day we all went out looking for the girls when school called to tell us they cut out of gym class?"

I groan and bury my face in my hands. "Carla."

"Oh, no. Don't you dare act ashamed of yourself now," Mom says with a laugh, fortuitously swept up in the story.

Carla shakes her head. "I still remember that little shit-eating grin you gave us when we found you back at the marina, trying to get our sailboat off the dock."

Evan grunts. "Out of your damn mind, girl."

I resurface from behind my hands and lift them in surrender. "It was Shy's idea—"

"No, it wasn't," they all say together.

I drop my hands to reach for Mom's glass of pinot grigio. "Fine. Just admit you'd all have been bored without me. I really know how to give you your money's worth."

"Made my hair turn gray sooner than it should've in life," Evan grumbles.

I snort into the wineglass. "You were bald when we met, Ev."

"It fell out in preparation. Knew exactly what we were in for, even before we did." He picks up the discarded playing cards sitting on the table and shuffles them into the deck. "You were trouble if I ever saw it."

Mom and Carla chuckle. Evan even musters a look that might pass for affection.

But I sink back into the couch. Take a long sip of wine to cover the way the short-lived pride on my face falters.

You'd better hope you're worth all that trouble.

None of them hear the dark echo of the words that have haunted me since I first heard them, almost exactly one year after I'd been taken in by the Robertses, who'd go on to sacrifice so much just to keep me with them. I'd have ended up in the system without their help.

My phone vibrates in my lap, signaling a handful of fresh notifications and a welcome distraction. More brands reaching out with ad offers, and . . .

Shit.

A text from Marty Wilson. My landlord. The man who owns the only apartment building in Baycrest.

MARTY: FYI, rent for the building goes up by 10% in thirty days.

What? My stomach plummets.

FYI? *FYI?*

That isn't an FYI. On top of the fridge and the car, that's the final nail on the coffin of my destitution. Apparently, bad things really do come in threes; I am so screwed.

Mom nudges me, staring at the way I hold the stem of her wineglass in a death grip. "Are you okay, angel?"

Okay? The backs of my knees are sweating profusely, probably staining this ancient sofa. I can't afford a ten percent hike in rent.

"Totally fine." I force a grin. "Just zoned out for a minute."

I take a quick sip of wine. Sweet, blessed Carla distracts her by playing a card.

MARTY: Happy to come up with an alternative arrangement if that doesn't work for you.

MARTY: Stop by my place when you get home.

Goddamn it, Marty.

Make that my *creepy* landlord. He's asked me out consistently since the day I moved into the building five years ago. Didn't seem to care that I'd been with Tom for two of those years.

Or maybe he did.

Since Tom and I broke up last year, Marty's gone from asking me out for drinks to blatantly inviting me over for *alternative arrangements.*

SIENA: No arrangement needed. Have you found someone to fix the lock on my front door?

No reply, of course. I've only been asking him for weeks. The strength of my grip on the wineglass doubles. I imagine it's Marty—my fingers wrapped around his sleazy, money-hungry neck.

What are my options here?

I could move back in with Mom, but no part of me wants to burden her during her peaceful retirement. I could try to find somewhere to live in Oakwood. But rent is far higher in Oakwood, given they have the demand from college students.

Fuck. Fuck, *fuck.*

My phone vibrates again, and I tap it to life, dreading yet another text from Marty. It's not, though.

It's my stupid social account. Nothing new from any of the **WhatIsAFootballDaddy** accounts, but there's an ad offer from a swimwear company that's apparently discovered that I spend my days working on the boardwalk. And . . .

They're offering me enough money to cover a couple months' worth of increased rent. Just to post one single, measly picture of myself in their swimsuit? It's absurd.

All this, just because people are convinced I'm dating . . .

Oh God. This is it, isn't it?

This is my way out of this mess. This is how I afford the new fridge at the shop and still get to pay myself. How I can get my car repaired, bank some cash to afford the higher rent.

I wouldn't have to ask anyone for a penny. I'd earn it all myself.

This idea has *disaster* written all over it. I can't stand the guy, and he thinks even less of me.

Still, I tap open my thread with **WhatIsAFootballDaddy01** and stare down at the message that's gone unanswered all week.

Chapter 6

Brooks

I choke on a sip of water so hard, Parker has to thump me on the back.

"You told them we're really dating?" I cough into my fist. A few gym-goers nearby turn toward the racket I'm making, pausing with interest when they recognize me.

When Josh only gives me an odd look—probably because my words weren't actually discernable over all the coughing—Parker translates: "He's asking you to confirm that you've really told the Rebels ownership team that he's dating an internet-famous ex-NFL WAG that he's only met once and hasn't heard from since."

"Oh," Josh says, leaning casually against the squat rack I'd been working at, like he hasn't ruined my day in the five seconds since he showed up. "Yeah, that's correct. You're officially dating Cece Pippen, as far as they're concerned. For the long haul, etcetera, etcetera."

I swear, every time this guy talks to me, it's something new. He's my personal grim reaper. Backing me into sticky corners.

Maybe I . . . fuck.

What are the odds I can find someone in this town who could pass for Siena Pippen? Convince *her* to fake-date me for a few months . . .

"How long is long-term?" I ask Josh, downing another sip of water to soothe my aching throat. "How long have we been together?"

"You met shortly after her relationship with Ivers ended. You've been together nine months, though you kept it quiet until now. It's serious. You're talking about a future together. Moving in together, getting married, the whole *shebang*. Your parents love her, she's become best friends with your sister. Your dog likes her better than you. You'll have kids one day, probably."

I stare. He's just laid out an entire future ahead of me.

Except I haven't heard from this woman in days.

"Would your sister consider dyeing her hair?" I ask Parker.

"What?"

"Melody. Would she ever agree to dye her hair dark? Just for a few months, so she can pass as Siena. She can go back to blond the second this nightmare is over. She'd fake-date me again, right?"

I pull out my phone to message her, because this is it. My only option. Fake-dating my best friend's sister and pretending she's Siena. The Rebels won't know any better.

Parker's hand comes down to cover my screen. "That's not gonna work."

"Why not? I mean, she kind of owes me—I did it for her last year."

"It's not gonna work, man. This woman has her own cult following in the football world—there's no way someone won't realize she got a whole new face."

"He's right, Brooksy." Josh tucks his phone in his pocket. "I don't care how you do it. As long as you get this Cece to make doe eyes at you—"

"It's *Siena*. Her ex called her Cece."

He lifts his eyebrows. "Let me let you in on a little secret, Brooks: *I don't care what her name is.* Cece, Siena, Amethyst, Charlene—as long as she attends this alumni game of yours over the weekend and pretends to be madly in love with you, I'm good."

And I'm . . . not good. They're right—I couldn't parade around a fake Siena. Every year, the UOB Huskies put on an alumni game stacked with players who'd gone on to play in the NFL, past or present. Seeing as I'm the big draw and the face of the event this year, there'll be no flying under the radar for me, or whoever I manage to convince to respond to the name Siena Pippen.

People will see through it in a heartbeat.

Josh straightens off the squat rack, shoots Parker a look like he's personally holding my friend responsible for helping me figure this out, and walks off toward the exit.

I direct an unrestrained groan at the ceiling. I am so. Fucked.

"You know, I've always liked the name Amethyst. There's something so whimsical about it. She definitely lives in a yurt somewhere. Frolics through fields to pass the time . . ."

"What the hell is a yurt?" I mutter to the ceiling. So completely and fully *fucked*.

"Brooks?" Parker nudges me.

I catch sight of a head of dark, shiny hair in the wall of mirrors ahead of me. Turn on my heel, barely daring to let myself believe she's really there—

She is.

Siena with her hair tied up, sitting on a workout bench behind us. No overalls today, just a simple white polo shirt and navy skirt that hits just above the mid-point of her curvy thighs. She has her legs stretched out and crossed casually at the ankles, and looks grim as she stares back at us.

How does she keep sneaking into this facility, anyway?

And how does she get her hair so shiny? It really is luscious—

Clout chaser. NFL girlfriend. Beloved, social-media famous Cece Pippen and the Seven Yards.

Naomi 2.0.

I'm uninterested. Can't be thwarted by her ability to lift me out of a funk within two seconds of meeting me. I will not succumb to that single, sweet freckle whispering at me from the top of her cheekbone.

Come on, baby. Could someone so pretty ever sting you that bad?

Yes, she could.

"That guy's a total prick, by the way." Siena nods toward the exit, presumably meaning Josh. "I can see why you get along."

Behind me, I hear the distinct sound of Parker's chuckle. Siena fights her own laugh, and I'm glad everyone is so entertained at my expense. Meanwhile, I'm still standing here dumbstruck. "How much of that did you hear?"

"All of it. Frankly, I was hoping he'd get around to telling us how many kids we're about to have. I'm dying to know."

"Please tell me that means we're doing this."

Siena blows out a long breath, then shoots Parker a tight smile before settling her attention back on me. "Yeah, Football Daddy. We're doing this."

Chapter 7

Siena

We've been sitting in awkward silence for the past few minutes, just staring at the field. Losing his friend's company—a buffer, fleeting as it had been—has left us to examine the cold hard facts of our short acquaintance:

I think he's an arrogant jerk.

He thinks I'm a gold-digging jersey chaser.

But if we've got any hope of convincing anyone we've been secretly dating for nine months, we're going to have to figure out how to get past all that. Or at least learn to fake it.

"What changed your mind about dating me?" The wind catches in my ponytail, and he watches the dark strands billow off my shoulder.

"*Fake*-dating you." I smooth back the wisps of hair fluttering around my face. "You caught me red-handed, Attwood. I'm in it for the money, just like you predicted."

"Of fucking course." He sighs sharply, staring out at the field. "How much do you want?"

God, he's so fucking insufferable.

"I'm not asking *you* for money. I'm asking to be seen with you looking happily in love. It turns out dating you fetches a pretty penny on the social media market."

Brooks rubs his face. "Yeah. I'm well aware."

The words send a rush of anger through me. "Do I really have to point out that, once you get signed to the Rebels, you'll get far more money out of fake-dating *me* than I'll ever see out of you? What are you looking at, Attwood? Twenty million a year? Thirty?"

"It's not about money for me. It's about playing with the team I grew up with. It's also closer to my hometown."

"And you'll be moving closer to your hometown with your multimillion-dollar bank account, to play on a multimillion-dollar contract. You'll forgive me for needing a bit of money to keep myself afloat."

I pin him with a look, daring him to counter the argument. Fortunately, he doesn't. He looks . . . appropriately humbled.

Good.

Brooks wipes his palms up and down the front of his shorts. "What do you need the money for?"

"Pretty clothes and shiny shoes." No way am I getting all touchy-feely with this guy. "Look, this is less than ideal. We're clearly incompatible. And as much as I'd like to do us both a favor and vanish from your life, we need each other. I don't know about you, but I really—*really*—need this to work."

If it doesn't, I'll be homeless and carless. And we'll cut the shop's seasonal earnings in half without that refrigeration system. Already, I've had to halve this week's stock of bait without anywhere to store it.

"So we ride each other's coattails until I get signed," Brooks says. "Break up once I move away."

"Perfect."

He sucks in a long breath, looking anywhere but at me. "I'm hosting the annual alumni game here this weekend. It's probably a good place to start."

I bob my head. "And we make sure to give the crowd something to talk about. Something worth posting online."

"Doubt we'll have to work too hard at it."

Brooks tips his head to the left of the field, where a guy seems to have stopped mid-drill to check his phone. I've seen this move before though, when I dated my ex. He's filming.

And here we are, sitting with two whole empty seats between us. The same thought seems to occur to Brooks. He stands, drops into the seat next to mine. He's so big and long-legged that he barely fits in the tiny chair. His knee juts out, brushing my thigh, and I hastily cross my legs, cutting off the contact.

"Wow," Brooks deadpans. "The picture of true love."

"I didn't expect to have to start *now*. I thought I'd have more time to mentally prepare." I uncross my legs. Hesitate before pushing my knee back against his. "There. Happy?"

Brooks stares down at our connecting knees. It might be a trick of the afternoon sun, but he almost looks amused. "Hate to break it to you, Pippen, but this"—he gestures between us with a finger—"started nine months ago."

I attempt to keep my glare to a minimum. "What do you expect me to do? Let you bend me over in one of your naughty back alleys?"

Shit. Didn't mean to let that slip. Once it became clear I wouldn't be falling asleep easily last night, I caved and fired up an internet search on the man at my side. Doing it felt dirty after a while, though. I quit the second I caught sight of that first back-alley picture.

"You know about that," he says grimly.

"Not until yesterday. I figured if I was going to do this, I should probably know what kind of guy I was getting in bed with. Or, you know, into a back alley with."

He gives me a single, curt nod. "So, that's a *no* to the naughty back alleys, then. Noted."

The joke catches me so off guard I have to turn my chuckle into a cough. "Cute."

He shoots me a wink. "So they say."

What the hell was that?

"Attwood," I say, a sarcastic warning in my voice. "Don't you know you're not supposed to flirt with your stalker?"

"Not according to the stuff Summer reads." He chuckles to himself, then jerks his chin toward the field. "There are about three phones pointed at us right now, Pippen. I'm gonna need you to look like you can stand me, at the very fucking least."

Right.

"Four phones." I sweep the field below us. What the hell did I just get myself into? "We should probably come up with some parameters, then. Ground rules for this dating thing, so we're on the same page."

"Probably a good idea." Brooks sinks in his seat, then does a double take when he notices me looking at him expectantly. "What?"

"What do you mean, *what?* You're the one who's done this before. How am I supposed to know how to fake-date someone?"

"Ever *dated* someone before? The point is to make it as close to the real thing as possible, if you want a shot at convincing anyone." He glances pointedly at our knees. "Though if this sad display of affection is any indication, we're about to have a relationship-ending blowout."

"Would you like me to mount you, here and now? I thought we were going for wholesome."

"We're going for madly in love."

I pull out a pad of paper I'd brought with me from the shop and poise a pen near the top. "I'm not used to it, all right? Tom didn't do PDA."

"How is that possible?" He stares at me, looking strangely disturbed.

"How's what possible?"

"Nothing." He runs a hand over his face. "Ship Happens? What is that?"

I stare at the logo on my notepad. An anchor bisecting the words *Ship Happens*. "It's my family's bait shop. My dad had a great sense of humor."

"Had?"

I feel Brooks's gaze on me and kick myself mentally for bringing up Dad. He'd been such a fan of Brooks's, both with the Huskies and the Rebels. How unfortunate that he's turned out to be so disappointing.

I fiddle with the anchor charm on my necklace, a gift from my dad for my twenty-second birthday. It's nothing special at all—he'd bought it from a sidewalk vendor on the boardwalk. But every little thing feels like a big deal, a prized possession, when you make it thirteen years without a single birthday celebrated.

"Rule number one: no personal questions. This fake relationship stays as surface level as it gets."

"If we're trying to convince anyone that we're on the brink of marriage, or whatever bullshit story Josh fed the Rebels, shouldn't we know everything there is to know about each other?"

"Feel free to make up my life story. You didn't have trouble doing it last time. We'll keep our lives as separate as we can. You don't meet my family and friends, and I don't meet yours. If you can keep things discreet, you're welcome to smuggle anyone you want into a back alley and vice versa—"

"No."

"Pardon me?"

"You heard me." Brooks sits forward, pressing his elbows onto his knees. "Fake or not, my girl doesn't fuck other people."

There's an edge in his tone that tells me this is a sensitive subject for him, but I don't press for details, per rule number one, and he doesn't offer anything more.

"You might rethink that when you hear the next rule: No intimacy whatsoever. We keep all physical touch to . . . I don't know. Holding hands. Hugs. In public only. Not that we'd have the opportunity to do that in private, because rule number three is that we're not seeing each other anywhere our picture can't be taken."

"Fine. As long as you don't go looking for it elsewhere." Brooks lifts a single eyebrow. "That a problem for you? Holding off for a couple months?"

My gaze floats over the field below us. I'm not sure what's happened to the guy who used to get it on in public dark corners, but me? Cutting myself off for the next few months is rough enough. Doing it while pretend-dating Brooks?

When he forgets to metaphorically double-check that I haven't made off with his wallet, I can't deny that the man is hot as hell. Everything from the dark hair he keeps having to push off his forehead to the scar on his cheekbone. The tattoos and huge hands.

He has *I dare you to make bad decisions with me* written all over him. And I've always been a sucker for bad decisions.

"Fuck. Okay." I give up on the pen and paper, stuffing them back into my bag. "I need to break the news to Aidan."

Not that I've had any desire to hook up with him, but I'm bound to bounce back from this libido slump eventually.

Brooks tips his head to glare at the sky, silently berating it for some unknown offense against him. I was right—this is definitely a touchy subject. "Aidan?"

"He's a friend," I explain. "He helps me around the shop sometimes and . . . we hang out, if you know what I mean."

"End it." It comes out like an order. He clears his throat, maybe trying to soften his tone when I raise my brows. "For the sake of the . . ."

"Fake relationship?"

"Whatever. Just end it. Would it help if you fired him, too?"

I roll my eyes. "I'm not firing him—he barely even works there. I'll end it with him tonight."

Brooks cuts his gaze away, blowing out a breath that sounds suspiciously like *fucking Aidan*.

We sit in awkward silence a while, Brooks eyeing the field, me trying to make out the intricately inked lines on his arms out of the corner of my eye.

"So, is that it? We get started here, this weekend?" I get to my feet when he nods. "Then I need to get back to the shop."

Brooks and I exchange numbers, and after an awkward beat in which we spot a group of guys shooting us covert looks, we figure it's probably the right move to leave the stadium together.

We walk with several feet between us. He clears his throat when I head for the parking lot with only a nod in his direction. When I double back, it's for an awkward-as-hell one-armed hug he scoffs at.

There's no way in hell we're convincing anyone we're in love.

Chapter 8

Siena

The stadium parking lot is absolute mayhem.

It's packed with pedestrians decked out in maroon-and-white Huskies gear, waiting at various food trucks and booths, and even though I haven't been to one of these alumni games since Dad passed away, the chaos feels familiar. Almost soothing.

There's a long line to enter the stadium at the nearest gate, but I follow Brooks's instructions and veer off to the players' entrance at the side of the building. Somehow, it's even louder here. I follow the floor-shuddering music and deafening cheers to the season-ticket-holder signing event, stopping just short of going inside.

I shoot Brooks a text that I made it, and he appears through the doors almost right away, carrying a brown paper shopping bag.

Both times I've met him, he's been covered in a sheen of well-earned sweat and dressed in a variation of a gym shorts and T-shirt combination that most definitely does him and his absurd physique justice. Today, he's cleaner and more covered up than I've ever seen him, wearing dark-wash jeans, stylishly beat-up sneakers, and a maroon number eleven Huskies jersey.

I can't decide which version suits him most.

Then Brooks turns around to set the paper bag on a nearby table. *Dear God.*

Forget the gym clothes. Those jeans do his football-player ass serious justice.

"Pippen."

I snap out of my ass-induced trance to find him looking far too pleased with himself. "I think you sat on some gum."

He snorts, doesn't buy it for a second. "Did you make it here okay?"

"Really, no witty reply? You're letting me get away with staring at your ass like that?" I clasp my hands together, sighing dreamily up to the heavens beyond the raftered ceiling. "It happened. I broke him."

Brooks's gaze cuts to something behind me. He frowns. "What the hell is that?"

"What?" I wheel around, looking for what he means.

"And *now* we're even."

I glance over my shoulder to find him staring blatantly at my ass. A burst of laughter escapes me before I can stop it.

With a hint of amusement, Brooks jerks his chin at me. "We need to talk about this look."

"Really? Do I have helmet hair?"

I had to ride my bike here after being officially told that my car engine is beyond repair. The upside is that, without a car to fix, I can set more money aside for the uptick in rent. I've already cashed in on a couple of brand deals in the days since Brooks and I made it fake-official. Enough to pay for the new refrigeration system at the shop.

"Helmet hair?" Brooks eyes me, pushing a loose wave off his forehead. "You rode a bike from Baycrest to Oakwood?"

"My car is out of commission. And, to be fair, my apartment building is practically on the edge of town." I take in my sneakers, strategically ripped white jeans, and top dotted with flowers. "You know what? I stand by this outfit. It's cute."

"Not sure I'd use the word *cute*."

Dick.

And then Brooks's gaze drops in the region of my hips, and the deadpan look flickers before he wrangles it firmly back in place.

Oh. "Uh-oh, Attwood. Did you forget you're supposed to hate me?" I point to my face. "Gold-digging hussy, remember?"

Brooks gestures between us. "Lovey-dovey fake couple, remember?" He reaches into the shopping bag he brought and produces a maroon jersey with his last name stretched across the back. "Put this on and let's get this night over with."

I take it from him, examining it between my hands. "And so, the jersey chaser becomes the jersey receiver. Interesting turn of events."

Brooks shakes his head, delightfully exasperated. "Just put it on and let's go."

I raise my hands in surrender, then slip the jersey over my clothes before moving for the doors.

"Wait."

Brooks reaches for my throat. For a panicked split second, I think, *This is it, my smart mouth is finally getting me killed.*

But then his fingers find my anchor necklace, the clasp in the chain having slid to the front, and he carefully feeds it in place behind my neck. He doesn't meet my eye. Just stands there, brows furrowed in concentration as he fixes my necklace.

Warmth erupts deep in my stomach, radiating outward, tingling in my fingertips.

Fifty thousand eyelashes.

The man has fifty thousand of them. Dark, and sweeping his skin as he fiddles with the anchor around my neck, setting it carefully in place over his jersey.

"My dad got it for me," I say for some reason. A *thank-you*, maybe, for so sweetly and unintentionally caring for my most prized possession.

He nods like he understands but doesn't dwell on the moment. Brooks moves for the metal doors. He rolls back his shoulders, stretches his neck from side to side, getting ready for our show. Then he holds out a hand, fingers open and waiting for mine.

"You with me, Pippen?"

I think it's one million eyelashes. "Yeah. I'm with you."

The second our fingers lace, he throws open the door and ushers me into pandemonium.

~~~~~

"You'll be signing right over here."

A volunteer leads us through the masses of lined-up season-ticket holders and tables manned by large men I recognize as past Huskies and recent or current NFL players. They're signing autographs, flanked by people I assume are their partners and children.

Even with all this star power, Brooks and I draw most of the attention as we move through the maroon-colored space. Plenty of stares and phones point in our direction. And mixed in with the cheers, I hear whistling bird chirps definitely directed at me.

It's perfect.

Exactly according to plan. The more photos of us there are out there, the higher my stock online, and the more likely they'll make their way to the Rebels for Brooks's benefit.

"You okay?" My breath hitches when Brooks's hand touches the small of my back. He speaks quietly into my ear. "I know it's a lot."

"I can handle it." I choose not to remind him that I'd previously trailed my ex as the masses fawned over him.

I was a common fixture at his games in our first year together, when Tom played just a couple of hours away from Baycrest. Then he'd demanded that trade to the Ravens in LA and moved all the way across the country while I stayed behind to take over the shop.

After that . . . I'd become living proof that *out of sight, out of mind* was pretty much right.

Brooks slides an arm around my waist as we pass the legions of screaming fans. He's surprisingly at ease for our first time out as a pretend couple.

But then, he's done this fake thing before. Knows exactly how to play it up, doesn't he?

We approach an empty table in front of a moon-sized poster of a younger Brooks grinning behind his helmet on the Huskies field. This college-aged version of him looks so sweet. Not unlike the way he'd laughed with me in that coaches' booth, before it all went to shit.

Brooks flinches when he catches sight of the picture. "Not ideal."

Again, my body tenses. A visceral reaction to that low, smooth voice delivered with his mouth at my ear.

"What's not ideal?"

"You think I enjoy sitting in front of my face?" He shoots me a look. "Don't."

I raise an innocent brow. "Don't what?"

"I know there's a face-sitting joke simmering in that head. Don't say it."

"Oh, come on. It's a good one!"

He shakes his head, exasperated, but there's definitely a twitch at his mouth. "It's a family event, Pippen."

The volunteer seats us behind the table where Brooks will be signing. She leans in between our seats so we can hear her above the cheers. "You're on the hook here for the next hour and a half. Then you'll head to the locker room to prep for the game, Brooks. And Cece will head out into the stands."

"It's Siena," Brooks and I correct in unison.

Our gazes clash, mine more than a little surprised he remembers my disdain for the nickname my ex saddled me with. Let alone that he'd bother to correct someone over it. He'd done the same thing with his agent at the gym earlier this week. Brooks ducks his chin to focus on a spot on the maroon tablecloth.

Fascinating.

In a bizarre Jekyll and Hyde kind of way.

The man acts like he can't decide whether to hand me a parachute before pitching me off a cliff.

~~~~~

Jekyll and Hyde is right.

The next hour is an uncomfortable glimpse of the Brooks Attwood I'd met before our fauxmance hit the internet. He manages sincere smiles. Dives right into easy small talk. Seems to personally know every local among the fans, recalling the most obscure details of their lives.

It's irritating.

A whiplash-inducing experience, seeing as he's served me only snark and disdain since that picture went viral. Other than fixing my necklace, which I'm not convinced I didn't imagine.

"Here we go." Brooks eyes the next fans in line, and his face transforms into another wide grin. "Moment of truth. You ready to really sell this, Pippen?"

Nerves pang in my chest. "What? Why?"

He's been good about introducing me to fans throughout the event—seeing as it's the whole point of my attendance. But other than the quick introduction and polite small talk, I've been able to slip right into the familiar role of *athlete's silent and doting girlfriend.*

A group of women about Mom's age approach our table. They don't even bother pretending to ask for his autograph, seemingly here just to fawn over Brooks. Dating Tom, I got used to the inappropriate flirting and touching from fans. Strangely, that's not what this is. They're all staring at Brooks like he's their personal pride and joy.

Brooks meets a silver-haired woman halfway over the table and plants a quick kiss on her cheek. The interaction feels so second nature I wonder whether she's his mother, but then, he'd mentioned a few days ago that his family lives across the country.

"Hey, Callie." He beams at her. "I see you convinced Amber to let you renew those season tickets."

"Just in time for you to jump ship from the coaching team." She attempts a stern look, but the adoration is plain in her eyes. "We saw on TV you've got *four* teams knocking on your door now."

Brooks gives a small nod. "I've been very lucky. Never thought anyone would be interested after I took so much time away."

"Oh, we just knew they'd all be dying to snap you up," another woman says, as the others nod enthusiastically.

Oh my God. Brooks Attwood has made proud aunties out of the women of this town. They're just short of pinching his cheeks and tucking him into a safe, warm bed. They continue peppering Brooks with praise, and he entertains them all with charming, humble words.

"Are you getting enough to eat, love? You're looking thinner in the face," Callie says.

One of the others turns to her. "It's called *getting ripped*, Cal."

"What does that mean, *getting ripped*?"

"It's to do with exercise."

Callie turns back to Brooks, completely perplexed. "I can drop off some food if you'd like? A few things you can keep in your freezer. For after all the ripping."

Beside me, Brooks gives a soft laugh. "Only if you bring over that chorizo lasagna, Cal. Best I've ever had—just don't tell my mom."

"Of course!" Callie reaches over the table to press a hand to Brooks's cheek. "Such a sweetheart."

Okay, screw him, but this really is kind of adorable.

I dig my teeth into my lip. Brooks glances over, gaze flickering to my mouth, noting the way I'm working hard to stifle a smile. "Have you met Siena?"

No less than ten aunties swing their gazes my way.

My stomach pangs. Make that ten overprotective aunties, all staring me down with varying degrees of skepticism.

"Ah, yes. We heard about this." Callie gives me an up and down. "How did you meet?"

Shit.

I'm sweating now. Everywhere. My eyelids are sweating.

My *fingernails* are sweating.

Is that possible?

I'd joked that we should just make up the details of our life together on the spot. But in the reality where I'm now being grilled by Brooks's personal fan club, surrounded by cheering fans, I'm realizing how stupid a plan that was.

It isn't a fucking plan at all.

"We met in Baycrest," Brooks says when I panic for a beat too long. "I took my sister and nephew out to the boardwalk when they visited last year, and Siena's family owns a bait shop there. We literally bumped into each other, and I pestered her until she agreed to go out with me. I couldn't stop thinking about her."

Damn. That rolled off his tongue so easily—was so plausible a story he's almost got me convinced.

One of the women pouts at him. "Why is it we're only hearing about this now, Brooks?"

"No one's more shocked than us that we managed to keep it under wraps for so long. It was all my doing, if I'm honest." He shoots me a sweet smile. "I wanted to be selfish with her. Keep her to myself for as long as I could."

Across the table, there's *aww*ing and pouting and clutching at hearts.

Brooks holds my gaze for a beat longer than appropriate, really selling it, and . . . I should have spent more time preparing for this, if the misguided stutter of my lungs is any indication.

How is he so damn good at this?

Frankly, I'd assumed Brooks would be the one to sink this ship, seeing as I do have experience with acting the loving girlfriend to a famous boyfriend. But that had been *real*.

There'd been nothing to fake.

And here's Brooks, carrying the team. Faking affection with ease.

"Well, we hope you're treating our boy right, Siena." Callie's eyes have softened on me after Brooks's glowing words. "He has the biggest heart."

"He . . . does. Yes."

Good grief, woman.

I scramble for something more to say—something *useful* to say. Under the table, Brooks squeezes my knee. A *get your shit together* if I've ever felt one.

To my relief, one of the volunteers ushers the group away. They go with parting waves at Brooks, and dubious looks in my direction.

Brooks leans in close, and my breath actually fucking hitches when he sweeps the hair off my shoulder to bring his mouth to my ear.

"You're really choosing this moment to go quiet on me, Pippen?"

It's the eyelashes. All twenty million of them, throwing me off my game.

"In my defense, I haven't done this before."

"What, had a normal human conversation with nice people?"

I hit him with a glare. "Faked a relationship. How'd you come up with all that on the spot?"

"I didn't. I'm serious about getting signed, and I'm not leaving any of this to *on the spot* inspiration. You've shown how well that works." Brooks drapes an arm over the back of my chair, gaze skating over my face with increasing fascination. "I know I'm supposed to be pissed about it, but I can't tell you how much I'm enjoying this plot twist.

Siena *Always Got Something to Say* Pippen. A deer in the headlights right when it counts."

"I think the true plot twist here is that Brooks Attwood is capable of enjoying something at all."

"Just *Brooks*, Pippen. We're supposed to be dating." He leans in, licking the corner of his mouth as he tries to hold back a laugh. "Fuck, you're so bad at this. It's awesome."

"I'm not bad at it. I can do this." I'm saying it mostly to myself. A self-wake-up call, because I refuse to be the lame duck in this operation.

Brooks's smirk turns into a bright smile as the next fan approaches. "Prove it, Pip."

Chapter 9

Siena

I sit with the other partners and families in the row directly behind the sideline.

The game isn't being played too hard, considering it's for charity and half the players invited back are retired and a bit out of shape. But the atmosphere is just as electric as you'd expect it to be with past fan favorites on the field. A team of miniature kid cheerleaders stands on the sideline, egging on the crowd with a series of clumsy dance moves.

My eyes track number eleven on the field, the way they have all game. Brooks looks so good down there, like a damn snack of a man in his padding. And it goes beyond the biteable ass. He looks *technically* good down there. I can't tell the difference between the players currently on an NFL roster and the man coming out of a two-season retirement.

A whistle calls the end of a play on the field, and Brooks tosses the football to a ref. Lola, the woman beside me who I believe is married to one of the cornerbacks, leans over.

"Your man always was great on the play fake. Bane of Jeremy's existence, whenever they played against each other."

Brooks, good at faking something? No shit.

"Oh, he is so sweet."

I follow Lola's gaze to find Brooks now with his helmet off on sideline. He's standing with his hands planted on his hips, grinning widely at the junior cheerleaders. They wave their tiny pompoms as they shuffle and shimmy in a dance, whipping their chins from side to side and sending their braids swinging around their heads.

I think that's all he's doing, admiring the little squad. Bopping his head in time with their clumsy movements. And then . . .

Oh, come on.

Six-foot-four, heavily tattooed Brooks Attwood juts out his arms, punches the air, and swishes his hips in time with the girls.

He's *dancing*, mirroring the little cheerleaders and laughing to himself. Either he's forgotten he has an audience of peers and fans who are all looking over, roaring with laughter, or he doesn't have a single speck of shame over the whole thing.

And why would he?

Even from up here, I hear the girls' excited laughs over their new dance partner. They start to move with even more enthusiasm, like they're testing whether Brooks really means business. Apparently he does, because he meets their every shuffle, hop, and kick.

He looks totally ridiculous and . . . astoundingly attractive.

And it's doing strange things to me. Odd tinglings in my stomach force an uncool giggle from my mouth.

There's a resounding round of applause and cheers when the routine comes to an end. I scan the crowd around us. Nearly every woman has their phone out, either pointing at the cheerleaders or typing at their screens. In the seat next to mine, Lola uploads what's clearly a video of Brooks's dance moves online.

I'm getting this all twisted up.

Of course he did it for the crowd pleasing. He's the face of the event, isn't he? And he needs the Rebels to see him in a fresh light.

Massive, tatted football player dancing with junior cheerleaders. It has *viral* written all over it.

Brooks moves along the line of tiny cheerleaders, high-fiving them all before finding me staring in the stands. He winks.

Winks.

I roll my eyes, mouthing, "Show-off."

His lips lift in a cocky smile, and he jerks a thumb at the end zone. "Watch this."

Another whistle goes off and he heads for the line of scrimmage. I don't know what there is for me to watch; they're all the way at the twenty-yard line, nearly at the opposite end of the field after a shitty kickoff return.

The play gets called, ball is snapped, and Brooks tears down the field, keeping an eye on his quarterback as he goes. God, I forgot how *fast* he is.

He's got four defenders on him by the time he catches the pass. The stands fall silent in anticipation, watching Brooks outrun every single one until there's a clear path to the end zone from the fifty-yard line. When he scores, the stands erupt. With the football in his hand, Brooks points into the stands, right at me, and the cheers get louder.

Lola leans into my side. "So cute! He's showing off for you."

No, Lola. He's showing off for the hundreds of phones currently pointing at him.

"Oh—look!"

I follow Lola's gaze to the jumbotron behind the end zone, where my unimpressed face stares back at me. Everyone else is on their feet after Brooks's heroic display.

I'm sitting comfy in my chair. Arms and legs crossed tight, without a fuck to give in the world.

Lola gives me an odd look. "Are you two okay?"

And now it looks like I despise my boyfriend, the town darling.

Quickly, I fix my attention on Brooks, who's nearing the benches with his helmet off. I give my best interpretation of an awed girlfriend of nine months. The way he shakes his head at me plainly says *Come on, Pippen. Is that all you got?*

Dick.

There's a smattering of bird whistling mixed in with the cheering now. That, along with his challenging look, gets me to my feet. Gets me crooking my finger at Brooks in a *get over here* motion.

The crowd is so loud, my ears will be ringing for days.

After a beat of surprise, Brooks closes the distance at a jog, reaching the barrier between my seat and the field. His brows shoot up in surprise when I throw out my arms.

"What are we doing?" Brooks says through a wide smile.

"I don't know." I cup his face between both hands, faking a smile just as big. "Just go with it."

He wraps an arm around my waist and hauls me off my feet and over to his side of the barrier, keeping me tight against his padded chest.

With a hand on each side of his face blocking the view, we should be able to pull this off. Fake a kiss. No one will know any better.

"You go left," I whisper.

Brooks's eyes widen in understanding. I lean in, then veer to the side at the last second. Meaning to place a kiss at the corner of his mouth. Except that it's not the corner of his mouth at all, because we move in the same direction.

Brooks's mouth presses against mine, and I can't hear my own shocked gasp over the insane screaming around us. I can't hear his grunt, either, but I do feel it in the kiss, in the way his body tenses against mine.

The crowd must be as stunned as we are, because every single person in this stadium goes silent.

In the back of my mind, I know that's impossible. That what's probably happening is that my own hearing has gone out at the feel of Brooks's lips.

I'm frozen.

He's hesitating. Then probably realizes how bad it looks, hesitating into a kiss with his supposed girlfriend of nine months. The future mother of his children.

So . . . he *kisses* me.

He sucks on my lip before tilting his head to go in for more. I'm only holding up my end of the bargain when I lick into his mouth. Brooks grunts again, body going pliant. He pulls back, nips my lip, then kisses me deeper, selling the act for the thousands of people watching. And that's exactly why I wrap my legs around his hips. Pull us closer together, cup his face the way I would if this were real. Breath hitching when he rests a hand under my ass to support my weight and sighing when he threads his other fingers through my hair.

We stand there, enduring this kiss.

This terrible kiss.

This kiss with his soft, plump, totally *fucking* kissable lips, oh my fucking *God* it's so good—

What the hell am I doing?

I wrench away and the screaming around us rushes back in. I do my best to ignore the noise. I wish I could equally ignore the smug look on Brooks's face, but I don't have any luck with that given it's only a handful of inches from mine.

"What the hell was that?" I hiss. "We said no kissing."

Brooks brushes my cheek with his thumb. "Smile, Pippen. People are watching."

I thread my fingers through his hair. There. We're just a couple having a moment. And Brooks Attwood is definitely *not* a dead man walking.

"*You did that on purpose.*"

"*Me?*" His eyes are hard, but he presses his forehead to mine with a sweet smile. "You said go left, so I went left. You're the one who swerved the wrong way."

I stroke the soft hair at the back of his head. "I told you to go *right*. You totally kissed me on purpose!"

"Un-fucking-believable. I never took you for delusional." His shoulders shake with an incredulous laugh that could pass for flirtatious. "Don't pin this on me. You broke your own rule."

I cup his cheek, feeling his stubble underneath my skin. "Well, I hope you enjoyed it, seeing as it was your last."

Brooks presses kisses along my jaw, all the way to my ear. "My last kiss ever? You might have a monopoly on the next couple months of my life, sweetheart, but the second this is over—"

I give him my best *I'm madly in love with my boyfriend* dreamy doe eyes. "I'm going straight back to Aidan."

"Don't *fucking* say his name," he growls, tucking me in closer so that my breasts press against the hard padding across his chest. He stamps a hard kiss on my mouth.

My satisfied smile grows, and I don't even need to fake it. "Oh, I'm sorry. Does that bother your caveman brain? The idea that I've had other men before I had you?"

"You haven't had me."

"Much to your disappointment."

"Mine? You just climbed me in front of forty thousand people."

"As if you don't like the attention. You get off on this, don't you? The adoring fans, the sound of your own name being screamed in your presence."

"The only time I care about hearing my name screamed in my presence is with a pair of thighs wrapped around my head." Brooks digs his fingers into my ass where he holds me, just roughly enough that I'd enjoy the hell out of it if we weren't quietly arguing in front of thousands of people. A traitorous whimper leaves my mouth, and he lifts an eyebrow. "Like it rough, Pippen?"

My heart fucking stutters.

It's the low tone of his voice, the stupid, sexy smirk. His hands on my ass. The way he looks at me like he knows the answer is *yes*. If I'm honest, it's the cheers around us, too. The fact that we're pulling this off. Together. Convincing everyone.

It feels too damn good.

"Put me down," I demand through my smile. Before I do something stupid, right here in front of all these people.

Brooks leans closer and sweetly grazes the tips of our noses. His gaze drops to my mouth. "Ask me nicely."

"Aw, baby," I let my voice go breathy, sugary, and bat my lashes at him, "would you pretty please get your hands off my ass and stop eye-fucking me in the middle of this stadium? It's making me nauseous."

Apparently, it's possible for the look in his eyes to go dirtier. "Say that again without looking like you're dying for me to fuck you with more than just my eyes."

I choke on my breath.

With a smirk, Brooks sets me on my feet back behind the fence, doing a much better job at ignoring the forty thousand pairs of eyes on us. He smooths the hair off my face in a move that elicits more than a couple of nearby *awws*.

I fist my hands at my sides, resisting the urge to punch him in the dick.

Brooks backs away toward the field, throwing me another stupid wink. "Enjoy the rest of the game, baby."

Chapter 10

Brooks

PARKER: Should I send out search and rescue?

BROOKS: What for?

PARKER: I'm at the gym before you for once. Which is saying something, seeing as they pay me to be here.

PARKER: Is Pete okay?

BROOKS: Pete's fine. Sound asleep on the couch according to the doggy cam.

PARKER: So that's a no to alerting the authorities?

The world's smallest white dog emerges from the low-rise apartment building I'm parked in front of. It's a cute little guy, a fraction of the size of Pete.

To my surprise, the small white dog is followed out of the door by Siena. She's wearing the same pair of overalls she had on the day I met her, with her dark hair floating freely in the breeze, holding a red helmet.

I'm not typically in the business of showing up at people's homes unannounced, nor staring at them from my car like a creep. But I plan on making my presence known eventually, and this woman has dangled the enigma of her life in front of me enough times that I can't help but take a couple of minutes just to see.

To try to understand what the fuck Siena Pippen has done to me, in the days since I met her.

She kissed me yesterday, and it took everything I had to keep the shock off my face. To keep up the act. Remember the boundaries, instead of pulling her back in for another, longer one.

That kiss is all I've been able to think about since.

And it pisses me off.

I don't know her. I don't trust her. And I should know better than to be distracted by stunning girls with joy-filled blue-gray eyes, laying one on me just for show.

Fake. Clout. NFL girlfriend. Beloved, social-media-famous Cece Pippen and the Seven Yards.

Naomi 2.0.

Siena leads the little dog to a patch of grass at the edge of the parking lot, letting it do its business before returning up the front steps toward an elderly woman who hovers with a walking cane. She hands the woman the leash before dropping to her knees and kissing the little dog, enthusiastically petting its belly when it flips over to offer it to her.

Something hums in my chest. My body goes warm—actually tingles. And it's fucking infuriating.

So she likes dogs. So she wasn't fake-fawning over Pete up in the coaches' booth.

Big fucking deal. Everyone likes dogs, and Pete is the best boy there is.

Upright again, Siena waves the elderly woman and her little pup into the building and heads for the parking lot.

I lower my window. "Pippen, over here."

Siena does a double take when she spots me, clearly struck dumb by my appearance, and I can't help the twinge of satisfaction. It's nice to be doing the startling for once.

"Whose—" I start as she approaches, but Siena holds up a hand to stop me.

"No, no. I need time to enjoy the fact that after all that talk about me being a stalker, *you're* the one showing up at my place uninvited." She chuckles to herself when all I do is glower. "How'd you find me, Stalkwood?"

"You said you live in an apartment building. This is the only one in town." She opens her mouth, no doubt to humiliate me for tracking her down. I quickly interrupt. "Whose dog was that?"

She peers over her shoulder. "Mrs. Robbins has a hard time with the stairs. I let her dog out every morning, but she still insists on walking with us to the front door so that I don't have to take Spike all the way back up to her apartment. Her dog walker doesn't come until lunch and her son can't come by to help until after work."

"That little thing's name is Spike?"

"Don't underestimate Spike. I once watched him douse a neighbor's pant leg in urine while looking him straight in the eye, just because the guy denied him a French fry."

My chest pinches at the thought of her running this puppy routine for her neighbor every morning before work.

And I'm pissed off at myself all over again.

"Get in. I'm taking you to work."

A beat passes in silence. "Why?"

I stare pointedly at the red helmet. It's a bit heavy-duty for a bicycle, but to each their own. "You said your car's in the shop."

What else was I supposed to do with that information? Let her fend for herself?

Siena hugs the helmet to her chest. "Actually, it's in a vehicular graveyard. But I still have my bike."

She jabs a thumb over her shoulder. I look for the bicycle in question, the one she said she rode all the way to the Huskies stadium last night. But the only thing behind her is a cherry-red motorcycle, in the same shade as her helmet.

My entire body goes cold. It's not a bicycle. She rode a goddamn *motorcycle* from Baycrest to Oakwood?

I suck in a long breath, forcing away the sudden tension in my shoulders. It doesn't matter.

Who cares if this woman seems to have a death wish? Between following me, a stranger, to an unnamed location the day we met, and riding a fucking *motorcycle* of all things, I have serious doubts about her desire for self-preservation.

But that's not my problem.

"And you call that a responsible riding outfit?" I demand, apparently making it my problem.

Siena takes in the overalls she's wearing, and the protective leathers she's not. "It's fine, it's just a five-minute ride to the boardwalk. I've been riding my bike for years."

"When does your new car come in?"

"I'm pretending to date you for money, Attwood. What part of that says that I have a new car on the way?"

Fuck. I figured this morning's detour from Oakwood to Baycrest would only happen once or twice, until she got her car fixed. It's shaving precious time off my morning training session—time I can't afford to lose, assuming I'll land an invite to the Rebels' training camp in a couple of months.

I rub my face with my hands. What the hell is she thinking, riding that thing?

Not that I care . . .

"New rule: no motorcycles for the length of this sham relationship." I hesitate. "Do whatever you want when we break up."

Theoretically, how hard would it be to destroy a motorcycle beyond repair, without raising suspicion?

"Brooks, no. You can't make up unreasonable rules. How do you expect me to get around?"

"This is Baycrest. Everything is within walking distance." I gesture at my steering wheel. "Besides, I'm here, aren't I? You're on my way to training."

Training which I'm already late for. May as well take an extra few minutes after I drop her off to come back and run that bike over with my car.

"Baycrest is on the way to training?" Siena says slowly.

I check the parking lot perimeter for security cameras. "Yeah."

"The training you do at UOB? Which is in Oakwood. Where you live." She breaks into a teasing smile when I only stare. "You worried about little ol' me, Brooks Attwood?"

I force my jaw to unclench. "I'm worried about my fake girlfriend ending up as roadkill on the side of the street, just as we got this thing going. Get in the car, Pippen."

She's laughing to herself as she rounds the car and tosses her helmet in the back seat. "Careful. Someone might get the impression you don't hate your completely repulsive fake girlfriend as much you let on."

"You're not completely repulsive."

"*Really*?" Siena fans herself. "You have such a natural way of making a girl feel special."

My focus snags on her wide smile. My stomach dips. Adrenaline hits my bloodstream, same as it did the first time she ever smiled at me.

I resent it. Despise it. Should know better.

But goddamn, she's beautiful.

How long, exactly, does it take to desensitize to the delicate shape of a woman's nose? To stop counting the pale flecks of blue in her eyes?

Shaking myself mentally, I pull the car onto the road. In the years I've lived in Oakwood Bay, both for college and in the time since my injury, I've spent little time in Baycrest. The town itself isn't especially different from Oakwood, with its colorful storefronts, cobblestoned main road, and vintage streetlamps. But while Oakwood is nestled in greenery and pine trees, with no waterfront to speak of, Baycrest sits on the bay itself.

We wind down a curved road at the end of her street, and the view opens up to the water. At least it's a quick drive down to the boardwalk. I'll be at the gym, where I belong, within a half hour.

"Attwood." I glance over to find Siena's eyes still shining with laughter. "Are we going to sit here ignoring the fact that every single cupholder in this car, front and back, has a coffee cup in it? Rough night last night?"

"They're for you. I don't know how you like to caffeinate."

With another laugh, she peers at the cupholders between us and the ones in the back seat. "And, what? You bought out an entire Starbucks to figure it out?"

"Of course not. That's ridiculous." I pull in behind a row of parked cars on the side of the street and check the cup closest to me.

"Then what—"

"You know there's no Starbucks around here. They're from the diner in Oakwood. Do you like vanilla? I think this is a latte." Her deadpan stare is fixed on me. No-go on the vanilla. I pick up another cup, checking the black marker scrawled across the side. "Coffee with cream and sugar? Or there's one with oat milk in it, whatever that is. Parker swears by it for his lactose intolerance—can you have dairy?"

She stares. I can see the gears turning in her head before a bratty little smirk pulls at her mouth. "Actually, I prefer tea."

"Which kind?" I reach into the back for the cardboard tray of teas sitting on the floor behind her seat.

The smirk flickers but she recovers quick. "Just kidding. I'm an iced-coffee-even-in-the-winter kind of girl."

That smirk dies right out when I pull a tray of iced coffees from behind my own seat. "Which kind?"

She stares at me double fisting trays of caffeine. "You seriously went out and bought one of everything because you weren't sure how I like my caffeine?"

When she puts it like that . . . well, it sounds mildly obsessive, which is not at all what I had in mind when I did this. I was shooting for . . .

Fuck, I don't know.

Siena stares down at the humiliating array of beverages before finally helping herself to the original vanilla latte. "Well, you've done it—I have no idea what to say to this." She pauses with her mouth on the lip of her cup. "They're not poisoned, are they?"

"No." I cough when my voice comes out grainy. "Not poisoned."

I watch her take a sip of her drink as she stares out of the window, and it stills the nonsensical nerves thrumming in my veins. Then she glances at me.

"Thank you." She shoots me a tentative smile. Same way she did yesterday, when I gave in to the inexplicable urge to untangle her necklace.

Something hot bursts in my stomach. Same as it did then.

"Yeah" is what I muster up. I hold her gaze and it feels significant. The way it felt to sit next to her in that coaches' booth, before our selfie went viral. And then she kissed me and . . .

Serious question for one Brooks Attwood: What the fuck is wrong with you?

I shouldn't care about her coffee preference. Shouldn't have brought her coffee at all, let alone a carful of it. I stash the idiotic trays of teas and iced coffees where they came from and get us back on the road.

"Consider this a thank-you for that nice little kiss from yesterday." I suck in my cheeks, holding back a laugh as she freezes mid-sip. "You know, I've been thinking about it all night."

"I don't need to know about your nighttime activities. That's between you and your hand."

"Well, me and my hand finally figured out how that kiss came to be."

She shoots me a glare. "You mean how I told you to go right, and you can't listen to simple instructions?"

"I mean how you definitely told me to go left, how you *know* you told me to go left, and then you decided to move the same way."

Her eyes narrow in thought. "That was a lot of words without saying anything."

"You wanted to kiss me," I say simply. "And instead of putting on your big-girl panties and admitting it, you tried to put the blame on me."

"I believe the saying is big-girl *pants*. Leave my panties out of your nonsense."

I lift my eyebrows. "But then we wouldn't be talking about your panties."

Her mouth twitches and she takes a long sip of her coffee, wincing as the hot liquid hits her tongue.

We turn onto a dead-end street lined with parked cars, with a glimpse of the boardwalk and the bay beyond it framed by peach-painted brick storefronts. Somehow the boardwalk is already packed with young families with overactive kids, older couples out for a walk along the water.

I pull into a vacant spot and climb out of the car. Siena throws open her door and hops out onto the pavement just as I reach for the door handle.

She freezes, staring at my outstretched hand. "Oh. You don't have to do that. There's no one around to see."

She's looking at me like I've got a screw loose, and this might be worse than the coffees.

"Right. Yeah."

She reaches for her helmet in the back seat. After another awkward beat, Siena gives me a parting nod and heads right for the boardwalk without another word.

"So, I'll see you back here tonight?" My voice bounces off the buildings on either side of us.

"What for?" she calls without stopping.

"I'm your ride home, Pippen."

She waves away the statement, turns the corner, and walks out of sight.

I stare after her. Wondering what the hell I think I'm doing and tugging at the drawstrings on my sweater just to occupy my hands.

Chapter 11

Siena

"Thanks for your help today."

Aidan follows me out of Ship Happens, hovering at my side as I set the alarm and lock the glass door. We finally got the new refrigeration system up and running at the shop, bringing our population of worms and minnows back up to a solid *too many for my personal liking*.

Maybe I had to bat my lashes at a guy to earn the money to do it, but it's for the good of the shop. That's what counts.

The Baycrest boardwalk is quieter now that it's dinnertime, though there's a solid line coming out of Molly's Chowder Cove, wrapping around the building and into the parking lot like it does every night from May to October.

Across the row of colorful shops is the water, endlessly open straight ahead and lined with a high cliffside topped with pine trees to the left. A few boats dot the bay, including the stunning sailboat owned by Evan and Carla. I haven't set foot on it in two years, but just the sight of it is enough to force a surge of nostalgia and longing up my throat. Some of my best memories with Dad took place on that ship.

"You don't have to thank me for helping you, Cee. We've been friends forever." Aidan's words pull me out of it, and I smooth out the hair in my ponytail, brushing off the memories and slapping on a smile. He shoots me a grin and leads the way down the weathered boardwalk. We pass the line of people waiting at Molly's, headed for the parking lot. There's a shortcut just right of the lot that'll shave a couple of minutes off my walk home.

"So, what's the deal with your bike?" He jerks his chin at the helmet tucked under my arm. "How come you didn't ride it to work?"

"Long story. You really don't want to . . . know."

Up ahead, against the driver's side door of a black SUV leans Brooks. Arms crossed, legs crossed at the ankles. And an unmistakably irritated tick to his jaw as he watches Aidan and me stroll into the parking lot.

He looks *pissed*.

It's the same look he gave my bike this morning before requesting I stop riding it for the duration of our sham. Like he wished for nothing more than to see it swallowed into a chasm in the earth.

But there's something else there, too. A tightness in his eyes as they flick from me to Aidan.

"Att—Brooks," I quickly amend, clocking the restaurant line-up and the handful of faces turned blatantly in our direction. "What are you doing here?"

At my words, his gaze rips away from Aidan. Brooks strides over, takes the back of my neck, pulls me in, and—

For the second time in as many days, I gasp against his lips. But there's no hesitation on his end as he kisses me this time. He tightens his grip possessively on the back of my neck and absolutely *destroys* me with his mouth. He parts my lips with his, strokes our tongues together, brings our bodies so close it takes nothing to dig my nails into his hips. He seems to like that. I hear his groan as he kisses me, feel the slight shudder in his body.

What the hell are we doing?

I pull away. Despite my shock, there's nothing like the sheer satisfaction of having felt that kind of want from Mr. I'm Fake Dating My Stalker. His jaw pulses. Eyes are on fire.

"Well, well." I smirk. "Still claiming I was the one who kissed you yesterday?"

His eyes close in sheer exasperation. "Please, just shut up."

Brooks crushes our lips together. Kisses me deeper, harder this time, and I don't know what the hell I think I'm doing, kissing him back like this. Moaning. Tipping my head, curling my fingertips into his sides just to feel his body react again.

And I hate it.

I hate how much I don't hate kissing him.

Brooks breaks it off, panting, *glaring*, and I press my lips together to keep from laughing at how clearly he despises himself for what he's just done.

"You're a good kisser," he accuses, prying the helmet from my hand.

"I know." I make my smile as obnoxious as humanly possible. "I can give you pointers if you're open to improvement."

"You were *moaning*. I don't need improvement."

"Two words: turbo tongue. Ease up a little, honey."

His stare is hard, and I am *shuddering* with unspent laughter. "I messaged you to see when you wrapped up at the shop. You didn't answer."

"How long have you been waiting?" He smells piney and freshly showered, and over his shoulder I can see his gym bag in the passenger seat. He probably came here straight from training.

He lifts an eyebrow. "The internet told me you close at five."

"You've been waiting for me since five?"

"Didn't I just say that?"

"Brooks, it's seven o'clock."

"I can tell time, Pippen. I'm not just a pretty face."

I blink up at him, unsure if he's being deliberately obtuse. Or maybe he simply doesn't care that he just sat in his car for two hours waiting on his fake girlfriend to finish doing inventory after the shop closed.

What the hell's gotten into this guy?

Brooks's gaze drifts over my shoulder. I follow it to find an audience: people lining up for dinner, and Aidan, who shoots me a wide-eyed look that says *holy shit, Cee.*

I trust Aidan, seeing as we were friends long before we started and stopped hooking up. But aside from Shy, I figured it was best to keep up the pretense of this relationship with Brooks. Less chance of forgetting who does and doesn't know and accidentally slipping.

I did have to tell him the media had the timeline of our relationship wrong, though. As far as he knows, Brooks and I met that day on the Huskies field, and he persisted until I agreed to go out with him.

"Oh," I say quickly. "Brooks, this is Aidan."

"Figured," he mutters, just loud enough for me to hear.

"And Aidan, this is—"

"I know," Aidan cuts in.

Brooks tucks me into his side and turns an unimpressed look on Aidan. "I've got her from here."

"Yeah, all right. I'll see you tomorrow, Cee." Aidan doesn't even spare me a look. He's still stuck on Brooks. Awed, like the massive football fan he is. He's been peppering me with questions since I told him we were together. "It was great to meet you, man."

Was it?

Maybe you needed to be pressed into his side to feel the arctic chill radiating from Brooks. So much for the charming guy at yesterday's signing event.

I wait until Aidan is out of earshot before splitting away from Brooks. "What's with you today?"

"What do you mean?"

With a hand on the small of my back, Brooks guides me to the passenger side of his car, clearing the seat of his gym bag and tossing my helmet into his back seat. He waits until I'm comfortably settled before making his way behind the wheel.

"The coffees, chauffeuring me around? You looked at Aidan like you were hoping the sky caves in on his head. You *kissed* me."

"The guy looks at you like he's seen you naked." He slices me with a look when I open my mouth. "Don't fucking say it, Pip. Or so help him God."

Oh my God. He's *jealous*.

I don't even know what to make of that.

There's an open pack of gummy worms in one of the cupholders between us, and I help myself to one. This guy and his sugar cravings. "Aidan is completely harmless. We've been friends since we were kids."

Brooks rolls to a stop at a sign. "Did you end it with him?"

"We haven't been together since you and I met."

He's silent for a beat. "Since we made the rule about not seeing other people."

"No. I mean, we haven't been together since you and I got stuck in the coaches' booth. We met and Aidan just didn't . . . appeal." I don't know why I cared enough to admit that, but the moment I see the flash of surprise in his eyes, I know I've done the right thing.

Even more so when Brooks holds my gaze and says, "Thank you. For doing that."

I nod, unsure of why I can't look away from him. "I said I would."

His smile comes and goes fast. "Yeah, well. Sometimes it's easier said than done."

"What, monogamy?" I stare at his profile. He doesn't reply, instead going for another gummy worm as the engine roars. "He's a huge football fan. Trust me, those looks said *fanboy*, not *fuckboy*."

The corner of Brooks's mouth ticks up. "You mean I should've offered to sign his ass?"

"He would've shamelessly agreed, then showed it off to whoever would look. The guy owes you one. He's been getting laid just by association."

"Does he always stay back late with you?"

"Only when I need the help with inventory. Everything else I handle myself."

"And you really run the shop by yourself?"

I fiddle with the zipper on my purse. "Ship Happens was my dad's baby—I don't trust anyone else to do right by him. Anyway, hiring people isn't in the cards. It's a seasonal business and we don't have the cash flow."

"Is that why you agreed to date me? To hire more people?"

I stall with a length of gummy worm, ultimately deciding I'm still not in the mood to share with him. "If you must know, I agreed to date you because of all the crazy rumors online about your huge, monster-sized—"

"Deflection dick jokes? Really?"

"—heart," I finish with a smile. "And I wanted to get a feel for it myself."

He chuckles, shaking his head as he pulls into the parking lot of my apartment building. By the time I've hopped out, I find Brooks awkwardly hovering by the hood, a little pink in the cheeks.

I think he'd been trying to open the door for me again.

He shoves his hands into his pockets. "I'll see you tomorrow?"

"I'm good." I lift my helmet from his back seat. "You don't have to drive me."

"So you keep saying." With an irritated tick at his jaw—which I'm starting to hope he reserves just for me—he jerks his chin at the car. "I'm keeping the helmet as collateral. Put it back where you found it and I'll see you tomorrow, Pip."

Chapter 12

Brooks

"Fucking crushed it."

With hands propped on his hips and unmistakable pride on his face, Parker watches me approach from the collection of orange markers I've been weaving through for the past twenty minutes.

I did crush it. My footwork feels so close to what it was when I last played. I'm appropriately winded, sweating no more than I should. I don't feel the churn of vomit in my stomach. I'm in the best shape I've been in years, certainly after the damage I did over the course of that six-month bender.

Parker tosses me my water and we sit on the long bench on the Huskies field. "Your time is only down by one-point-three seconds from where you were when you played. It's impressive."

I nod, swiping the sweat off my forehead with the back of my arm. "Thanks, man."

We eye a couple of guys tossing a football a few yards away. I recognize one of them as a tight end I used to coach on the Huskies. He wasn't drafted this year, so he's probably putting in the time to up his chances for next year. The other guy is middle-aged, with thinning gray hair. Probably his trainer.

My skin starts to itch. Knee bounces. Because I don't have a *next year*. This unlikely comeback is a one-time chance, and if the league—the Rebels—decide I'm not fit to return this season, I'll be written off faster than my ass can move through those orange markers. No one will bother with me a year from now.

And what then?

I go back to a job that made me ache with envy and loss? I keep living here, just me and Pete on the outskirts of town?

Am I supposed to learn to exist with this empty pit inside me?

A few yards down the sideline, the older man who'd been training the Huskies player jogs up to the stands where a redhead I presume is his wife waits for him. They chat for a moment before she slyly reaches around and pinches his ass.

Something in my chest pulls hard, leaving behind an ache so bad I stutter around my sip of water.

Envy. I'm so painfully jealous of this couple, copping a feel of each other, that I rub at my chest as though to scrub away the feeling. It's the playfulness that gets me. The way they've probably been together for decades and still flirt like a pair of shameless teenagers.

I hate that I've become that guy. I hate that I can't look at a woman without trying to pinpoint the way she'll inevitably fuck me over. Being one half of an aging, dirty couple has never felt less attainable.

Which is why this comeback has to work. At least then I'll have my career again.

I rub my face with my hands. "You think you can do an extra training session this weekend?"

Parker looks up from his phone. "What part of me telling you you're nailing your drills says you need an extra session?"

"I need to be at my old stats, not near them."

"You also need rest. You need to look after your body before it flips you the finger mid-game one day and shuts down after everything you've put it through." Parker leans his elbows on his knees. "I know how much it means to you to play again. But you need to be smart about it."

"Is that a no on the extra session?"

Parker's head dips, and he stares at the field under his feet. "If I say no, will you just go rogue at your gym at home?"

"Probably."

"You're an idiot." He shakes his head. "I'll meet you here on Saturday if you skip your morning run."

"Done." There's no way I'm skipping my morning run, but he doesn't need to know that.

"You're full of shit and I'm not stupid. I know you're not skipping your run."

Parker looks to our left, where Summer strides across the field from the entrance to the training facilities. Pieces of hair have unraveled from the two French braids she always wears for her sunrise surf session, and they flutter back with the force of her annoyed pace. When she's within range, she tosses me my phone.

"Your dickhead agent has been blowing up your phone for the past half hour."

My phone must be connected to one such call, because even over the activity on the field we hear Josh's distinct voice through speakerphone. "I heard that."

"Meant you to," she calls at the phone before turning to Parker. "Donut break?"

Parker nods once. "Donut break."

I lay my palm over my phone's microphone. "Save me one?"

Muffled under my hand, I vaguely hear Josh's protests of *nutrition* and *diet*. It only makes me laugh because half my diet comprises of candy that I offset in the gym.

"We'll save you ten," Parker calls over his shoulder as they walk off toward the inner facility. Just loud enough to set Josh off on another dickish tirade.

~~~

"I thought you said this was working."

Josh's voice is muffled on the other end of the phone, like he actually had the gall to cover the mic and conduct a side conversation with whoever he's with.

And then I hear the words *grande* and *cappuccino* and I fume. "I'm shaving one percent off your cut for every second you ignore me the moment I sign a goddamn contract—"

"I'm here, I'm here," he yelps into the phone. "What were you saying?"

I take the edge of the bench below me in a tight grip. "I thought you said this dating thing was working. A week ago, you were telling me the Rebels wanted to meet, and now . . . what? They lose interest all over again? There are pictures of me kissing my pretend girlfriend all over the internet, for fuck's sake. You're telling me it was all for nothing?"

"It wasn't all for nothing. The kissing thing is phenomenal. So was the bit with the kid cheerleaders. That video's up to nine hundred thousand views."

I'm so startled, I pull the phone from my ear. That wasn't a goddamn *bit*. The kid cheerleaders were cute.

"Then why haven't I been invited to their training camp?"

His heavy sigh assaults my eardrum. "I need you to swear you'll take this in stride, all right? When I tell you, there'll be no going off the rails. You'll stay focused on your training."

"Spit it out, Josh."

"The door is still open to you, but as of this morning, Doug

McDaniels is an unrestricted free agent and I'm hearing the Rebels are interested in having him back, too."

The pit in my stomach is painful, visceral at the mention of his name.

Doug McDaniels. Also a former wide receiver for the Rebels, who got traded shortly after I announced my retirement. Our stories with the Rebels are eerily similar. Including the fact that we've both dated Naomi Ward.

Except his dating of Naomi Ward happened to overlap with our eight-year relationship.

"I can feel your frustration—"

"I'm not frustrated," I bark. I clear my throat, willing myself to calm the fuck down. "Why would I be frustrated? He's got a fraction of the receiving yards from my last season."

"Which was two seasons ago. McDaniels is an active player—it's a less risky investment."

Fuck.

It wasn't bad enough to find out on the day of my retirement that my teammate had been screwing my girlfriend. Not enough that Naomi up and left me for him, or that they're still happily together, as far as I know.

Now this guy is what's standing in the way of my signing with the only team I'm interested in?

"What the hell's going on, Josh? Do I have a shot with the Rebels or not?"

"You definitely have a shot. It'll just take a bit more to finesse them than we initially thought."

"More than faking a relationship?"

"We need to make you desirable. The Tigers are interested. They've invited you to join them for an off-season scrimmage and their annual charity gala. To see whether you're back in playing shape. How you mesh with the team."

The Tigers? They're the top team in their division here on the East Coast. A stand-up organization from everything I've heard, and I'd be lucky as hell to return to the league with them.

But they're not the Rebels.

"We've gotta play the game a little. Nail this scrimmage with the Tigers. Bring Cece with you—"

"Her name is Siena."

"Whatever. Bring her, let her charm them. The second the Rebels catch wind that you're being wined and dined by the Tigers, they'll come crawling. They won't want you playing there."

I put the call on speakerphone and pull up my text thread with Siena. We haven't made an official appearance since the alumni game, so it's only a couple weeks' worth of the same type of texts every evening at around six thirty.

SIENA: Limo service requested, please advise ETA and provide the most expensive bubbly in the ice bucket.

BROOKS: I'm here.

SIENA: With champagne?

BROOKS: Get your ass over here, Pippen.

Even though she's relented on the rides to and from work, I've caught her trying to sneak her helmet out of my back seat on more than one occasion. I've never been particularly domineering as a boyfriend—of the real or fake variety—but I promised her that if she's ever riding that bike again, it'll be because I'm six feet under.

Which only prompted her to advise me to sleep with one eye open.

BROOKS: Can you get away from work next weekend for a scrimmage and gala in the city? It'll be a weekend thing.

My knee bounces as I stare down at my phone, waiting on her reply.

Since the day I became her reluctant chauffeur, I've felt trapped in a dizzying cycle with Siena Pippen. I know better than to trust her or become invested in anything more than the sham we've been thrust into.

But then there are the fleeting moments where I forget to be that guy. The overthinker, the one trying to sniff out a motive.

In those moments where I simply let myself be, I find myself irritatingly intrigued by the nuggets she lets slip about her life. I become irrationally driven insane over things that shouldn't raise my heart rate.

And yet, they do.

Several things about Siena Pippen have come to drive me insane, in fact.

I don't understand how her hair is so shiny. I don't get how her scent lingers. It *lingers*. In the air in my car. In my clothes. I take a whiff of anything and I'm served that bright, sunshine scent. I can't get rid of it, no matter how many times I put my clothes through a wash cycle.

Every day since starting my second career as her personal driver, she's greeted me with a freshly made, still-warm breakfast sandwich. Eggs, cheese, and bacon bits that belong nowhere near the diet of an athlete deep in training who reserves the bulk of his caloric intake for candy. But I eat that goddamn sandwich every morning, because it's her way of repaying me for the lattes and the rides. And it ticks me off that she wouldn't simply let me drive her around without feeling the need to repay the favor in the first place.

Plus, she admitted to cutting off Fuck Toy Aidan the day she and I met. Before we'd even agreed not to sleep with other people.

What the fuck was that about?

She could barely stand to look at me then. Meanwhile, Naomi slept with my teammate during a committed relationship. That confession and the fact that she handed it to me so readily, like she knew I needed it, makes it hard to slot the two women in the same category.

Except Siena is, quite literally, dating you for money.

I don't get it. Don't get her. Don't get why I even give a shit.

I'm vaguely aware of Josh prattling on, but I'm fixated on the screen as three gray dots flicker at the bottom.

SIENA: Let me consult with my manager.

BROOKS: So, yourself?

SIENA: Smart AND pretty. You're one hell of a catch, Attwood.

BROOKS: Aren't you a lucky girl.

BROOKS: Is that a yes?

SIENA: Separate rooms?

BROOKS: Separate floors.

SIENA: Deal.

I stare at my phone, waiting to see if she'll add anything else. Feeling that familiar prickle of irritation when she doesn't.

"*Brooksy,*" Josh shouts, startling my gaze off my screen. I swipe away from our messages as though I've just been caught doing something I shouldn't. "Am I talking to myself?"

"Yes," I admit. "Text me the details. I'll do whatever it takes."

Chapter 13

Brooks

"Door's unlocked."

Siena's voice is clear in the hallway outside her apartment, which is quiet except for the bizarre scene I just walked past—a man with his door propped wide open, vacuuming his place dressed in nothing but a pair of briefs.

"You keep your door unlocked for anyone to walk in?" I call when I'm inside, door firmly shut behind me.

Siena pops her head into the hallway. "The latch on the lock has been stuck for months. Haven't had the chance to look at it, and my landlord doesn't seem to care."

"Would that be the charming man cleaning in his underwear two doors down?"

"Oh, he's wearing underwear today? Good for him." *What the fuck?* My heart rate skyrockets the way it does around her. "Come in. I'm running behind."

We're making the three-hour drive to the city for the Tigers' minicamp and gala. The scrimmage today is straightforward enough. They'll put me through my paces. Make sure I'm fit to return after two seasons off.

It's tomorrow's gala that's the problem.

Specifically, it's the single hotel room the Tigers are putting us up in, and the apparent lack of spare rooms given the hotel is booked out for the party. I've called them to check.

Multiple times.

And I've been too much of a coward to inform Siena, in case sharing a room turns her off enough to back out of the entire trip. Like it or not, I need to be seen with her.

I join Siena in her kitchen. Her apartment is modest—I can take it all in from the spot where I'm standing. The open kitchen and living room, the short hall down to what I assume is a bedroom. I can hear a washing machine going off inside the bathroom. Somehow, though, the place feels oddly expansive.

Like the roomy inside of a Mary Poppins bag.

The kitchen cabinets are painted a blue that's somehow both bright and dark, the living room curtains thrown open to an outdoor patio covered in greenery. It's bright, lights on everywhere, and it feels alive in here. Hits of color all over the place, every shade you could imagine, and it somehow all works together.

Siena hovers next to me, watching me take in her space. My gaze flicks over her body, the silky blue robe she's wearing, and she shamelessly does the same with me. Taking in my athletic shorts and T-shirt, the socks on my feet. Eyes lingering on my tattoos.

Add it to the list of things about her that drive me insane. I hate how much I like it when she looks at me. It's shameless, with a greedy edge. Makes me feel wanted in a way I haven't felt in a long time.

I like looking at her, too.

"Is that what you're wearing to the scrimmage?"

Siena shimmies in her robe. "I figure if you turn into a lame duck out there, I can flash the other players to distract them."

"You flash, I score?"

As if seeing Siena Pippen naked wouldn't straight up turn me into football roadkill.

"That's what I call teamwork, baby." She heads for her bedroom. "I got caught up getting things done for work and then had to post a few pictures online wearing a dress for a brand deal. Take a seat, I'll be ready in a minute."

"Are you getting enough brand deals, then? To cover whatever you need the money for."

She turns, tips her head to the side. She's surprised I care enough to ask, and frankly, so am I.

"You mean you haven't been stalking my account, **WhatIsAFoot ballDaddy01**?"

"Not since I made that account to find you."

Her lips press together. Probably remembering the unhinged DMs I threw at her in the days after we met.

"In a totally unfortunate turn of events, all the bigger offers are from swimsuit companies, seeing as they've figured out I work on the bay. I've been turning those down."

"You don't strike me as someone who'd be shy in a swimsuit."

"You'd be right. But I figured the Rebels wouldn't like seeing your fake girlfriend's ass all over social media."

No, but nothing could get me to fire up that app faster.

"I've been sticking to cute clothes or makeup I'd buy for myself, that kind of thing," she continues. "It's not much, but it adds up if I do enough of them. And I figure it's on the safe side for the Rebels."

My chest floods with warmth, the same way it does every morning I watch her let her elderly neighbor's dog out. "How much money have you turned down?"

"Oh—it's insane. I told them all *no* and one company upped their offer to ten grand per post, for a three-post deal. I thought they were making fun of me for a minute." She laughs, heading for her bedroom. "Be right back. Have a cookie while you wait."

She motions to the open box of fudge cookies she'd been snacking on before I showed up, and there's no way I'm helping myself to one of those. I was raised on the best baked goods from my mom's bakery.

Instead, I clench the edge of her kitchen counter, my throat burning with something hot and thick.

She's turning down five-figure offers for my benefit.

Without being asked to.

Without even knowing this was something I'd struggled with before, or what it would mean to me if she did it. After she admitted she can't afford a new car. When she's resorted to fake-dating me for money in the first place.

Top that with the revelation about her ex-fuck-buddy, and Siena's showing me more loyalty than Naomi ever did.

My head is a mess of guilt. Confusion. I wonder if I'm getting ahead of myself, being so naively hopeful that a woman would choose me over her own personal gain. Putting Siena on a pedestal where she doesn't belong.

"So are you nervous for today?" Siena calls from her room.

I scrub my face with my hands. "I'm a four-time all-star and I've played in three Super Bowls. I'm not supposed to get nervous over an off-season scrimmage."

"And I've been riding my bike for years. Still get nervous taking her out some days."

I sort through her kitchen drawers until I find a knife and make my way back to her front door to get a look at this lock. It only takes a couple seconds of fiddling with my makeshift screwdriver to fix the sticking latch; you'd think the least that idiot Aidan could have done within their *arrangement* was fix the damn thing for her. Made sure she had a door that locked when she went out. While she slept.

Something claps down on what sounds like a wooden surface in her bedroom. "Well? Are you nervous, Brooks Attwood?"

I wander into the living room, taking a breath as I browse the wall of photos hanging behind her couch. "Yeah, I guess I am. It's the moment of truth in a way—I haven't played at this level in years."

"You think you can keep up?"

"I think if I can't keep up today, there isn't a chance in hell the Rebels will take me. If they hear the Tigers had me out there practicing and lost interest immediately after . . . Doesn't get any more clear as to why."

"So that's a *yes* on flashing my tits if things go south, then."

I huff a laugh, still scanning her wall of photos. Siena on a sailboat, with awesome views of the bay and the pine trees along the shore. Beaches and waterfalls, temples and pyramids I know don't exist anywhere near Baycrest. She's in all these pictures posing with Shyla, the blond friend I recognize from the day we met.

Except there's something off about the way the other woman is standing with Siena.

"Okay, I'm decent," Siena announces, entering the room. "You ready to kick off the performance of your lifetime?"

I pick a frame off the wall to get a better look at it. "Is this . . . You glued your friend's face on all these pictures."

Siena pops her head over my shoulder to have a look, assaulting me with that sunshine scent, but even that's not enough to distract me. Close up, it's obvious and crudely done: a clear cutout of Shyla's face pasted onto the original photo, over a disproportionately large male body.

"Oh, that." She grins wide, staring at the gallery wall with pride. "This is the product of a wine-drunk night after my breakup with Tom. Shy came over to help purge the place of him, but it felt like such a shame getting rid of all this. We ended up taking Polaroid shots of her, cutting out her face, and sticking them over his."

"That is . . ." I snort, eyeing the wall of photos. My grin grows an inch with every new picture, because this is truly some of the funniest shit I've ever seen.

"Slightly unhinged?"

"*Slightly*?" I laugh, jabbing a finger at her wall. "She's piggybacking you down a mountain in this picture—that woman is barely half your size. How bad was this breakup?"

"It was fine. But these trips were once in a lifetime, you know? I wanted to keep the memories, minus him."

She pries the frame from my hands and tosses it down on the couch.

"Woah, woah—this is how you treat a work of art?" I carefully place the photo on its hook, taking a step back to admire it. "This has to be one of the best things I've ever . . ." I trail off, catching a flash of tangerine in my peripheral vision. ". . . seen."

What was that about a work of art?

Siena's hair had been pinned back when I first came in, but it's loose now, sprinkled around her shoulders in thick, bedhead waves. Sex hair if I've ever seen it, and I glance around the apartment for any signs of a walking dead man named Aidan.

But it's just us. Siena standing there in a mind-numbing, curve-hugging dress underneath a denim jacket, and these strappy sandals with enough of a heel to bring her eyes, her mouth, tantalizingly close to mine. She does a little shimmy, curves bouncing as she does—drying out my throat, fucking *killing* me. Because I might be allowed to look, but I sure can't touch.

Not unless we're in public, putting on an act.

"What do you think? Is it giving *long-term girlfriend of an NFL star*? The dress is Tigers orange, too."

It's giving *I want to forget about this scrimmage and rip that off you with my teeth.*

"Pretty sure you won't need to resort to flashing. You look . . ."

"Hot as hell?"

I bark out a laugh. There's a smile in her eyes that tells me she's kidding. But also, she's not. Her confidence has been palpable since the second we met.

And that's as hot as she is.

"Yeah. God help me, you are." I take a breath and nod at the front door. "You with me, Pip?"

At her door, I lift her keys off a hook. Siena raises an eyebrow, watching me lock up behind us. "You're really good at this fake boy-friend thing, huh?"

Chapter 14

Brooks

For a scrimmage held a whole three months before the first kickoff of the season, these guys play without mercy.

I don't know whether they've been specifically instructed to really test me, or if this is how they always attack practices. But it's not hard to understand why this Tigers team has had back-to-back conference final showings. Why the end of this past season truly felt like an upset when they packed it in without a championship win.

They play fucking *hard*.

The whistle blows between plays and I take the precious opportunity to strip off my helmet and pat the sweat off my face with the hem of this black practice jersey.

I scan the lower rows of seats behind the benches for the stunner in tangerine orange among the other partners. I've done my best to keep my focus on the game, but more than once, I've found my attention drifting to the stands during breaks in play.

Siena is enthusiastically chatting with a woman beside her—quarterback Shawn Hartley's wife, if I remember right. She's slotted into their group almost seamlessly since we arrived, settling into her fake role a lot better than she did at the alumni game.

"You holding it together, old man?" The helmet on Shawn Hartley's head doesn't conceal his smirk. The quarterback fingers a football someone tosses him. "Old bones not what they used to be, huh? Never thought I'd see the day where Brooks Attwood alligator-arms a pass."

Fuck, I missed this. Nothing beats the shit-talking comradery of an NFL locker room.

"Maybe put a little more juice behind your next throw and I wouldn't have been in the line of fire. And are we gonna pretend I wasn't still in diapers while you were out having your first legal drink?"

Hartley breathes a laugh.

I zero in on Siena again. She's watching me back this time.

"Nice ass," she mouths.

I shake my head, trying to pull off the disapproving thing, but I'm suppressing a laugh.

Jay Adams, another receiver, lets out a long, low whistle. "Are you persona non grata around LA these days, Attwood?"

"Why would I be?"

"You've got Thomas Ivers's girl eye-fucking you from the stands, that's why."

I track his gaze back to Siena, who's now laughing obliviously with the woman at her side. In fact, several of these jackasses are openly staring at her.

"She hasn't been his girl in months, dickbag."

There's a smattering of *ooh*s around me. "Touchy subject?"

This teasing shit is par for the course among teammates. In the Rebels locker room, I'd be quietly laughing in a corner. Listening to those idiots try to get a rise out of each other or letting it roll off my back if they were salivating over Naomi.

It's nothing new. Doesn't bother me in the slightest.

Siena isn't a touchy subject at all. This relationship is a hoax, and any eye-fucking from the stands was probably done for the sake of onlookers.

They can tease all they want. I'm laser-focused on my game.

"Wouldn't mind getting a little touchy with that one myself—"

I grab a fistful of jersey on the nearest guy and yank him around so that he faces the field. Do the same to the other idiots around me.

"Eyes on the goddamn football. *That one*'s mine."

There's not a single guy around me not bursting into laughter. Adams claps me on the shoulder pad, proud as fuck for getting me to snap.

Jackasses, all of them.

"What the hell are you all standing around for?" Over on the sideline, Lamar Wentworth, the Tigers' head coach, gestures with his clipboard. "Are we paying you to gossip over tea and crumpets or play some football?"

I pull on my helmet as we position ourselves around the line of scrimmage, me on the far side of the field. I can't help another look at the stands. It's as if my brain can't go more than a few seconds without checking on Siena. Wondering what she's doing, whether she's giving her new friends that bright smile, or if she's tracking me on the field. The same way I can't help tracking her.

Focus. Let her play her part out there, while you play yours over here.

As soon as the ball hits Hartley's hands, the players unfreeze. Some crash together at the line of scrimmage while others take off down the field, me included, trying to stay open for a pass.

According to the play called, the pass isn't mine. I make a run for the end zone anyway, luring defenders with me and away from Hartley's real target at the other end of the field. But Adams gets caught between opposing players, so I slam on the brakes, killing my forward momentum so fast my defenders make it yards away by the time they realize I didn't go with them.

They converge on me the second I catch Hartley's pass, but I'm faster. I manage to split them, but just barely. One of them is a scrappy fucker. He knocks me off-balance just as I pass him, and I scramble to catch my footing.

Pain erupts in my left leg in response, but fuck if I don't keep tearing down this field anyway, not stopping until I cross into the end zone.

Fuck yeah.

A couple receivers meet me in the end zone, smacking me on the back. Just as the adrenaline starts to fade, someone hollers "He's still got it, baby," at the top of their voice.

Somehow, I manage a laugh.

Coach calls us in. The boys on the field head for the benches and the stacks of water bottles on the sideline. I follow them slowly, sucking long breaths through my nose. Grinding my teeth.

I don't need to work to catch Siena's eye as I move for the bench, because she's already looking. She's shaking her head with something like awe. By the time I make it to the sideline, though, the wonder has faded off her face. She takes the stairs, meeting me at the railing.

"What's wrong?"

We're far enough away from the other women that she doesn't need to whisper, but she does anyway, her expression laced with concern. I don't know how she figured out something's out of place from that far away. But her gaze moves over me, trying to pinpoint the problem.

I rip the helmet off my head. Grip the back of her neck and bring her close like I'm kissing her cheek. Instead, my lips meet her ear. "I fucked up my knee."

Chapter 15

Siena

My body chills, all the way down to my marrow.

I fucked up my knee.

Five devastating words for an athlete. Brooks keeps his face smooth, the picture of calm when he pulls back, but I see it right there in his eyes: devastation alongside frustration.

"How bad?"

I brace my hands on the fence between us, white-knuckling the metal, feeling so incredibly sad for him. Maybe we're not the best of friends, but Brooks is just a guy trying to do what he loves most in life.

I admire that—respect it. Not all of us have that option.

He's worked for this every day for months from what I hear. He wants this so badly he entered into a fake relationship with me, just to hedge his bets. And now this.

Brooks pries my hands from the fence, lacing our fingers. His hands are big and warm, rough and calloused around mine. He's the one who's hurt, upset, yet he caresses his thumb over my skin as though trying to erase my concern.

"People are watching, Pip." Brooks glances to the side, where players shoot the shit on the sideline and women do the same in the stands.

He flashes me a smile.

Right. He's acting the part.

Like we did at our last show, I lean in, trying to make this look like a breezy conversation. Playfully tipping my head to the side. To anyone on the outside, I'm just a girl flirting with her hot-as-hell boyfriend, who—despite the secret injury—just pulled off an incredible touchdown.

"I went one way, and my knee went the other. Don't think it's much more than a sprain, but I won't know for sure until Parker or Summer looks at it."

"You don't want the team doctors to have a look now?"

Brooks raises our intertwined hands and brushes the hair off my cheek. His fingers graze my skin and my heartbeat thumps in response.

It's fake. Fake, fake, fake.

"They can't know," Brooks tells me. "I can't come off as this fragile."

"But won't they know something's wrong when you don't go back out there?" I ask gently. My stomach sinks when the corner of his mouth flicks up in a tight smile. "You're not seriously planning to keep playing on an injured knee."

The happy mask must slip right off my face, because Brooks reaches for my waist and pulls me close. There's a railing between us from the hips down, so our bodies don't quite meet. But I'm close enough to breathe him in when he wraps his arms around me.

Brooks's brows are pulled together. He seems as baffled by my concern as I am. There's nothing fake about it. "I'll be all right, Pip." With a glance at our audience, he lays his forehead on mine. My lungs seize. "An injury right now would kill my chances. The news would make its way around the league in a second. I have to play through it."

My arms go up around his neck. "Brooks, no. This is the moment we planned for—I'll flash them, and we'll hightail it out of here. They won't know what hit them."

My sheer relief at the sight of him genuinely laughing catches me by surprise. And I'm just taking liberties now, leaning into the *fake* of it all and the prying eyes around us, when my fingers slide through the thick, short strands of hair at the back of his head.

His lips part with an exhale.

There's still that damn fence in the way, but when he tugs me closer, this time my breasts press into his pad-covered chest. My thighs push into the barrier, metal cooling my heated skin.

"It'll be fine. I'll be fine." Brooks's gaze falls to my mouth. "Hopefully . . . hopefully it can get fixed when we get home."

One of the hands on my back slips lower, fingers tightening over the upper swell of my ass, and I arch into him, flattening into the hard padding covering his upper body.

For the sake of the prying eyes.

"So, listen," Brooks says slowly. "I called the hotel to make sure we could have separate rooms this weekend, but it doesn't look like that's in the cards. They're hosting the gala, and it's completely booked up."

I pull back a fraction to look him in the eye. "And you're just telling me this now?"

"I didn't want you backing out." His fingers curve, digging into my ass. "I'm sorry."

"Really?" I eye the tiny uptick to the corner of his mouth, fighting off my own smirk. "Because you don't look sorry at all, Brooks Attwood."

His grin grows just as the sharp, prolonged sound of a whistle cuts through our bubble.

"Can we cut it out with the free porn and get back to the fucking field?"

We turn toward the sound, to the players tossing water bottles onto the turf. Some of them openly stare at our scene, others stare from out of the corner of their eye, and all of them are laughing at our guilty looks. The red-faced Tigers coach rolls his eyes.

Brooks chuckles. "I think we convinced them."

Given the accelerated pace of my heart, I think we might have convinced *me*.

He splits away but I catch the front of his jersey before he can get too far. "Brooks, are you sure about this?"

He untangles my fingers from his jersey before kissing the center of my palm. "I'll be all right."

Brooks dons his helmet as he goes. He's moving a fraction slower than usual, but he's as sure-footed as ever. His hands are clenching and unclenching at his sides, but there's no limp in sight.

Still, I can't help thinking he's being blind to the big picture. That maybe he can get through this scrimmage, but it'll be at the expense of an easier recovery from what's currently a simple injury.

He's an overconfident athlete if I ever met one, and I've met plenty. They all think they're infallible, can push their bodies to their limit and bounce right back the next morning to do it all over again.

From what I've seen, it always has a way of catching up to them.

~~~~~

Brooks drops our bags onto the carpeted floor of our hotel room and releases a desperate groan of relief when he sags onto the mattress of the solitary king-sized bed.

Through sheer force of will, he managed to pull through the rest of the scrimmage and an entire team dinner with the Tigers without a hint of discomfort. But he seems to be paying for it now, and I don't know how we're supposed to make it a whole other day tomorrow without letting on about it. Brooks kicks off his shoes and grips below his knee with both hands, attempting to rub at it without aggravating the injury. I can't make out his full expression with his chin tucked down, but there's a curve in his dark brows that makes me uneasy.

"What did your friends say about it?" He'd called his physical therapist friends as I took over driving for him after dinner, barely giving them one-word answers. He hasn't said much since.

"They don't think it's a sprain, seeing as the swelling isn't bad. Said it sounds like the muscles just locked up." He stares at his knee despite what sounds to me like a positive prognosis. There's no mistaking the way his shoulders, usually squared with confidence, deflate. "I couldn't even make it through a single game without falling apart."

The defeat in his voice has my heart sinking. I scramble for the right words. "It's just your first game. There was always going to be an adjustment period, wasn't there? This is . . . minor. Doesn't mean anything for your prospects."

"Doesn't it?" Brooks meets my eye at last, and I almost wish he hadn't. With his brows curved and the tight, almost lost expression in his brown eyes, he looks devastated. Like he's already written himself off. It's so unlike the man I know, who radiates self-assuredness like he's got endless reserves of the stuff inside him. Even on the sideline, he seemed confident in his ability to keep playing. Had he been faking that, too? "One game, Pip. A low-impact *scrimmage*, of all things. I couldn't keep up."

"But you did keep up. You played through it, stubborn man that you are. Played through it *well*." I prop myself on the dresser opposite the bed, watching his fingers move over his leg muscles. My arms wrap around my middle, hugging myself the way I'm suddenly tempted to hold him. He looks so brokenhearted. "If you're really worried, then let's call it and go home. Skip the gala tomorrow so you can get checked out."

"We can't miss that party. We're seated at a table with Shawn Hartley and a handful of the coaching staff, and I need this weekend to go well if I'm going to make the Rebels think there's a chance I'll sign with another top team. Might not be able to twirl you around the dance floor, though." The joke is barely half-hearted, delivered without a fraction of his usual ease, and I officially hate this. "I really need this to work, Pip."

"This comeback?" I hesitate, knowing this is in clear violation of rule number one, keeping us surface level, but I've already come this far. "Why are you so set on playing again? On going back to the Rebels?"

He's the one who hesitates now. This is unchartered territory for us. We've found somewhat of a groove with the ribbing and small talk, the way I annoy him and love every second of it. But we don't do *this*.

"I was happy when I played there. Was happy with that team." Brooks speaks slowly, like he's testing the waters. "It's been a rough couple of years."

"Rough because of injuries?"

"Not injuries. Life's been . . . I don't know." He gives up on his leg, instead rubbing his brow. It's a frustrated move but also reeking of deep exhaustion. "Blank. No thrill, no joy. Nothing's ever come close to filling the void, and I can't . . . I can't keep living like that, Pip."

I ache at that. Both for the heaviness in his voice and the fact that I get it. I spend about sixty hours a week at the shop without thrill nor joy.

"Surely there are other things . . ." I think to the day we met. His dejected sigh in that coaches' booth, and the flash of panic in his eyes when I'd asked for his version of my pick-me-up skinny-dips. The way he'd scrambled to find an answer before landing on his sweet dog.

Brooks's mouth tips in a lackluster smile. "I signed up for a fake relationship with a woman who can't stand me. I played on a bad knee. That's how bad I need this."

Guilt pounds at the wall I erected between us the moment he first threw those accusations at me. I assumed this comeback was in pursuit of money or born from an athlete's typical inability to let the sport go. Knowing he's been struggling like this . . . I'd love to pin this concern on the fact that I need to keep riding him and his NFL prospects to the bank for the sake of my finances. Which I do.

But damn my stupid heart, I'm worried about *him*.

"You're sure you don't want to see a doctor?" Brooks shakes his head, and, with a sigh, I lift off the dresser. "Out of the way, Attwood. My mom is arthritic. I learned a few tricks that might help."

I avoid his eyes as I kneel at his feet and take up his previous efforts. My fingers start below the knee, sliding upward and gently working muscles that are definitely tight. I'm close enough to hear a breath gust out of him, to sense his disbelief over the fact that I'm helping him. By kneeling at his feet, no less.

While he sits on a bed. But I'm not thinking about that pesky detail.

"Tom used to play injured all the time. I hated it, but it's part of the deal whether you're making a comeback or you've been playing for years." I keep my focus on his leg as I work, perfectly content not knowing how he's looking at me, and grapple for something to help lighten . . . him. This fake relationship is shaky at best, couldn't even qualify as friendship. But he doesn't deserve to feel like this. "At the risk of inflating your ego, you were amazing out there, Attwood. Injury and all."

Brooks gives a quiet chuckle. A hint of life. "My ego thanks you."

"Plus, if I'm going to get all dolled up for this gala—and this is me we're talking about, so you know it'll be good—I'm going to require a minimum of one dance to show off my outfit. So let's get this knee in working order, shall we?"

A beat of silence follows, but I still don't muster the courage to look him in the eye. "Yes, ma'am."

There's a slight laugh in those two words, shrinking the pit he put in my stomach. And then he fills it completely, seals it shut when he releases a sigh, thick with relief, as my thumb digs into his thigh.

I chance a look at him. Brooks leans back on his hands, head thrown back, eyes closed, a furrow in his brow. He inhales deeply and his T-shirt strains against every hard bit of his chest.

"That hurts so fucking good, Siena." *Jesus.*

The tentative air around us shifts, spikes with sudden, unbearable humidity. My lungs struggle to draw breath as a flush rises up my neck. I watch his chest lift and fall, almost in pace with my fingers. His massive hands are spread out over the white comforter, digging into the down.

I've never been more aware of a bed in my life.

"Is this how you act on the treatment table for your friends?" I force my eyes back to his knee, my entire body tense. All of it. Shoulders tight, toes curling, pussy clenching. "Because I'd urge you to consider reeling it in."

"You checking me out, Pippen?" I feel his eyes on me again. Hear the definite humor in his voice.

Don't look at him. Focus on putting air into your lungs. "Is this doing anything to help?"

"You're the one nursing me to health. You tell me."

"That doesn't sound like a thank-you."

I forget all about breathing when Brooks reaches for me, lifts my chin with a finger so that I'm finally forced to look him in the eye. He's perfectly calm, amused. Not at all the bundle of overactive hormones I've become.

"Thank you for helping me." His mouth tilts in a genuine half-grin, which does absolutely nothing to calm the fresh ache between my thighs. "Does this mean I can get some rest tonight? Fall asleep without worrying you'll off me just to ride that bike again?"

"I wouldn't get too comfortable." I run my thumb deep into a groove in the muscles of his calf. Brooks releases a soft breath that makes my thighs clench together. "Feel good there?"

He nods with his eyes on me. "Yeah."

I do it again, unable to help myself, and bite my lip when his jaw slacks. *Don't think about the bed. Pretend it's not there.*

"Fuck. Look at you blush." Brooks's eyes move over my face. "Is this rubdown for me or for you, Pippen?"

"Please. What could I possibly be getting out of this?"

"You're right." Brooks sits up straight. His shadow falls over my body. "Knee feels a bit better."

I know this is my cue to let go. Know he's said it for the sole purpose of proving his own point. But I can't stop touching him. His soft sighs are addictive. The way he looms over me, too. "So you'll twirl me around the dance floor, then?"

"If you play your cards right," he says without breaking eye contact. "I need you to stop touching me now. Really."

"Why?"

He tips his head in a way that says *are you really asking me that?*

I let my gaze fall down his body to find his cock straining against his shorts. Fuck, it's . . .

"Siena." Brooks's voice turns low, gravelly, that calm façade crumbling fast. "I need you to get up. Right fucking now."

I stare up at him, at the very clear threat in his eyes, before doing what he says. I get to my feet on shaky legs and find my spot leaning against the dresser. Try and fail to think of something to say to break this unbearable tension, until Brooks's phone starts ringing on the bed behind him.

"It's my mom. Probably wants to know how it went today." Brooks gets to his feet. He tests his knee, adjusting the front of his shorts before moving for the door to take the call. "I'll, uh . . . I'll sleep on the floor tonight."

I don't dare move until the door closes behind him.

Chapter 16

Brooks

Siena walks into the room just as I'm tossing a couple of pillows on the floor.

She's bare-faced, wearing a faded, oversized T-shirt that skims the tops of her thighs. She looks comfortable. Disarmed, at least in appearance. It looks good on her.

"I thought we'd have separate rooms and didn't pack bottoms," she says in apology.

As though I weren't snapping a multitude of mental pictures of those legs. One day, when I'm wrinkled and my body truly gives up on me after everything I've put it through, I'll stay warm remembering those legs and the fact that I once got someone as stunning as Siena Pippen to pretend-date me.

"It's not like I'm wearing much more." I gesture down my front, at the boxer briefs I have on, and nothing else. Because, fuck it. If I'm taking the carpet tonight, I may as well be comfortable. "I'm sleeping on the floor, anyway."

Siena pulls back the bed covers on one side of the bed. "Brooks, do you really take me for the kind of person who'd let an injured man sleep on the floor?"

No, but I really wish you were.

"All right." I sigh. I'd never been more relieved to see my mom's name across my phone than I'd been earlier. I don't know whether Siena feels it, too, but this room is running on depleted levels of oxygen.

Feeling her up on that sideline had been an indulgence.

Letting her touch me, kneel at my feet, just minutes before sharing a bed?

It was a mistake.

I climb onto the mattress with the stack of floor pillows. Siena flips off the light and . . . it's so much worse like this. I can't make her out as my eyes adjust, but my every other sense feels amplified. I hear her soft breath from the other side of the bed, feel the heat from her body nearby. That sunshine scent is drenching me. My skin feels pulled taut by awareness.

I straighten out my bum leg as much as I can in the space between us, trying to loosen it up some more. Trying to keep my earlier panic at bay and replaying Siena's soft encouragement when it comes close to gripping me by the throat.

You were amazing out there, Attwood. Injury and all.

I kept up with active players, despite the injury. Even Thomas fucking Ivers gets injured. And this one is fixable—minimal, compared to the concussion I survived years ago. Parker and Summer will murder me for playing on it, but it's not like I had a choice. Sitting out the rest of that scrimmage would have killed my already shaky career prospects, and making this comeback is how I get to feel better. Feel happy again.

And then there's Siena. I'd be lying if I said she wasn't part of what got me back on that field. She's used to running with elite athletes, and fuck, I really wanted to impress her.

I should know better.

After the way Naomi ripped me apart, I promised myself I'd

avoid this. That I'd never get involved with anyone who made me feel like I was only worth the trouble with a football in my hand.

I extend my leg farther, flexing my foot to try to get a good stretch in my calf, but end up grazing Siena in the process. "Shit, sorry. I'm not being a creep."

"Does your knee hurt? I can move if you need more room."

That, there.

That's the difference between them, isn't it? The look of deep concern on that sideline when I told Siena about the injury, and again when she massaged the muscles. She didn't have to do that.

She's been turning down an easy $30,000 she probably really needs, for the sake of my career. Didn't have to do that, either.

It's become impossible to slot her in the same category as the woman who called me a coward for retiring out of fear of my own brain damage.

A wave of shame washes over me, remembering the way Siena's beautiful smile faded in the coaches' booth after the things I said to her. I don't think I could have been more wrong about her if I'd tried.

"Siena . . ." I stare up at the sliver of light on the ceiling from a small split in the window curtains, trying to pick the right words while leaving out the gory details. "I've had an issue in the past. With people being with me for the wrong reasons."

Siena watches me in silence. In an effort to say as little on the matter as possible, I've ended up saying nothing at all. *Fuck it.* "My ex cheated with a teammate while I recovered from the concussion and then left me for him when I retired."

It spills out of me fast and breathlessly, but the words are followed by a surprising rush of relief. Like shedding an armor I never wanted to wear in the first place.

Siena's head lifts off the pillow. "Who?"

"Doug McDaniels. I caught them together." Her mouth pops open. She's a Rebels fan. Would have watched us play together for years. "It fucked me up, but I stopped loving her the second I figured out who she really was. She's nothing to me, but it still—"

My voice dies at the ache in my throat and burn in my eyes. I clamp my jaw, because God knows this woman has dealt with enough of my baggage already. I take a few seconds to fight the burn and point at my chest as a substitute for the rest of the sentence.

It still kills me that I wasn't enough.

Siena's legs slide under the covers, toes brush my calf. Just a whisper of a touch, but it's all I need to pull myself together. "That's why you turned on me after you heard about my ex."

"I shouldn't have said those things to you. I'm a walking cliché of trust issues, and you were an easy target."

"Tom and I met through our moms."

"You don't have to explain."

"I know. I want to." I swear, it could be pitch black, and the blue in her eyes would still shimmer. "Tom's parents retired in Baycrest. Our moms became friends and introduced us while he visited for the holidays. I didn't go looking for him—he's the one who asked me out, and I was the one to end it after two years together. The day I snuck into the Huskies stadium was the anniversary of my dad's passing. It was his favorite place in the world—well, second-favorite place, after Ship Happens. I wasn't trying to track you down."

Shame and guilt twist inside me.

"I'm so sorry. For all of it, Pip." I clear my throat when it comes out gravelly. "Accusing you of tracking me down for attention. For making an already bad day worse. And for what it's worth—which I imagine is very little—I don't think that about you anymore."

She offers me a small smile. "As for the reason I agreed to fake-date you . . . My rent went up. Things stopped working at the shop. My car broke down. All in the same day." She pauses, staring back at me. "The day we met, it felt like my dad was calling me to that stadium. I think maybe he knew things were about to go wrong, and he wanted to put me in a position to handle it. I think you were meant to crash into me on that field."

"You believe in that? Things being meant to be?"

"You don't?"

"I don't think so. I've lived through too many shitty things I can't explain."

An injury that almost killed me. Witnessing my ex's affair on what had already been the worst day of my life. If I'd been made to feel that one-two punch by a higher force on purpose, it's a cruelty I wouldn't want explained.

"I believe in it. My whole life has felt like a *right place, right time.*" She waits for me to argue, but what can I say to that? If it's something she needs to believe, who am I to talk her out of it? "You know, my dad would go nuts if he could see this. He loved you on the Rebels. And the Huskies. And look at me now, snuggling up in bed with Brooks Attwood."

Something about that hits just the right way. I like the idea of her dad liking me.

But that's weird, and I shove the thought away.

"Tell me this isn't how you've been snuggled in the past. There's a whole two feet between us." She laughs, and the sound is so pretty, just like the rest of her. "That wasn't rhetorical, Pippen. People need to know."

"Who are people?"

I lift up on an elbow and glare down at her. "Me. I'm people. Do I or do I not have to right a colossal wrong?"

She's curled up on her side now, laughing so hard at my outrage that the mattress shudders with her. It's never been quite this light between us. The practical guy in me knows how perfect this is. That we're far more likely to keep pulling off the act if we like each other as people.

The delusional part of me? He feels how *perfect* this is. Maybe she's here for practical reasons, but I haven't had pillow talk with a woman in years—hell, I haven't slept next to a woman in years.

I ache for this—always have. The sleepy conversations until the crack of dawn, the secret sharing. I'd say my ex robbed me of that, but it wasn't like this with us. The only words we ever exchanged in this position were sleepy goodnights.

And here's Siena, a woman I barely know, giving me that soft comfort. And it feels so . . . effortless.

"Rest easy, Brooks Attwood. I have indeed been properly snuggled."

"I might hate that answer more." I flop onto my back. "I think I'll start a Thomas Ivers troll account. Make fun of his completion percentage and taunt him with pictures of you in nothing but that T-shirt."

She winces. "Please don't do that. This is his shirt."

I sit up like I've just been sucker punched in the gut. I don't know where I get off being so goddamn possessive of this woman, but she's gotta be fucking kidding me.

I rub my face with both hands. "What are you wearing underneath it?"

"Why? You're gonna to rip it off my body, Attwood?"

Her amusement dies the second I look over and she sees exactly how fucking close I am to ripping it off her body. If she so much as gave me a hint that she wanted me to touch her . . .

We may be playing pretend, but there's nothing fake about the way my body wants her.

Siena inhales a slow breath. I know she was rattled earlier, rubbing my leg, but she looks like she's hurting now, watching me hover over her. Sitting so close we're almost touching.

"We said no fucking," she whispers, swallowing hard. Definitely rattled. I love it.

"That was your rule, Pip. Not mine." I tug at the sleeve of her shirt.

"Is this fun for you? Winding me up?"

"Yeah, it is. I have a feeling you don't let many people see you squirm. It's doing wonders for my ego."

That hits a nerve. Her eyes flare with something a little ruthless, and I know in an instant she's going to make me pay for this.

"You know, that was a really good question."

"What was?"

Siena releases a soft sigh, just short of a whimper. "What *am* I wearing under this shirt?"

She flips onto her back, shoves the comforter down to her waist, and my body clenches, lungs failing in anticipation of whatever torture I know she's about to inflict. Her fingers smooth over her body, her stomach, reach under the covers.

"Panties." She snaps the elastic band. The comforter ripples as her hands move inward.

It's a real whimper this time as she runs a hand between her thighs. Heat rushes down my body, straight to my dick.

Fucking Jesus.

"Brooks," she breathes. Her hand moves under the covers, eyelids dropping as she rubs her pussy. "Feels so good."

Oh, fuck me.

With another soft whimper, Siena abandons her efforts and yanks her T-shirt so that it sits taut over her body, outlining the fullness of her tits, every curve along her torso. Her nipples fight the cotton of her shirt.

Holding my gaze, she smooths a hand over a breast, thumb lingering over her nipple. My harsh breath cuts through the silent room.

"Definitely no bra."

"Fuck." I run a hand along my jaw.

"You wanna feel, Brooks?"

I groan. "Yeah."

She throws back the covers some more, and for a blessed split second I think it's in real invitation. But she zeroes in on the shape of my aching dick, and the corners of her mouth lift. She tucks us back under the comforter.

"Too bad. I'm exhausted—long day, and all that." Siena flicks a hand, motioning toward the other end of the bed. "Over on your side, Attwood. Try to get some rest, won't you?"

Siena flips over, giving me her back. Nuzzles her pillow. Yawns.

She fucking *yawns*.

Meanwhile, I lower myself down onto the mattress, body over-heating. I clench my fists to stop myself from giving my cock a des-perate tug.

Siena Pippen is dangerous. A special kind of drug.

The kind that has me in an emotional spiral one minute, hard and needy the next.

She's got me on the edge of my seat, just waiting to see where she takes me.

"Brooks?"

She's watching me over her shoulder. My heart pumps like it foolishly expects her to say *just kidding*, crawl over this mattress, and beg me to fuck her.

But then she gives me a soft smile. The one that makes my body hum whenever she lets me have it. "I really appreciate the apology. Means a lot."

With that, she settles back onto her pillow. I do the same, shoot-ing glances at her every so often, even after her breathing slows and I know she's drifted to sleep.

There's a knot in my chest and I have no idea how to unravel it.

Chapter 17

Siena

This is complete, unadulterated hell.

I had the time of my life teasing Brooks last night. Truly, there was nothing more satisfying than seeing that smug look wiped clean off his face as he watched me play with myself.

Except for the cold hard fact that I fell asleep aching. Woke up aching.

Spent the entire day aching at Brooks's side while being entertained by the Tigers owners back at the stadium, who aren't playing hard to get whatsoever in their desire to have him on the team. Great for him. Except that I've been unable to give myself a shred of relief, not even in the shower because Brooks was on the other side of the door.

Now, I'm sitting in front of the mirror in a fluffy white robe. Putting the finishing touches on my hair for the gala while Brooks takes his turn in the shower.

Naked in the shower.

This entire room feels several degrees too hot. Too tense. There's no way I can make it all night, let alone sleep next to him again, without letting off a little steam.

I just need a few minutes to myself.

Brooks's phone buzzes aggressively from the nightstand just as the shower turns off. It's the fifth call in a row from his agent, Josh.

"Hey, Brooks?" I can hear the rustling of fabric as he gets dressed. "Your agent is blowing up your phone."

Brooks emerges from the bathroom with his hair in wet curls, dripping over his face. His shirt is in a fist as he hikes up a pair of sweats. It takes every single ounce of my barely existent propriety not to look for a bulge.

Really, I deserve a medal.

"Thanks," he says, distractedly taking the phone. "I'll take it in the hall. We need to go down in the next twenty minutes."

Thank God.

The moment he's outside I hurry to my bag and dig all the way to the bottom for a pink, U-shaped vibrator. I'm the horny girl who travels with a sex toy, just in case.

Sue me.

In bed, I loosen the tie of my robe. Close my eyes. And because this is just a fantasy, I let myself pretend it's Brooks running his fingers over my chest, my breasts, lifting goose bumps along my skin. Imagine it's him skimming his hands along my waist. Smirking at the moan he gets out of me. I picture him pushing his fingers inside me the way my vibrator slides in, stroking my clit the way the toy sits on it now.

I lift my phone off the nightstand and fire up the right app, sorting through the controls to find just the right vibration.

"Fuck," I mumble into the room, throwing back my head.

I think of his mouth on mine. His mouth on every part of me, teeth grazing my nipples, tongue licking down my stomach. I imagine him digging his fingers into my thighs to keep them wide open for him as he kisses around my pussy before finally giving me what I need.

I think of how it would be to fuck him for the first time.

Wonder if it'd be so quick and so dirty our clothes would stay haphazardly on, his jeans pushed down to his knees, mine hanging around an ankle as he fucks me against the hotel room door. Or whether we'd let the anticipation eat away at us, really take our time. Licking and nipping each other all over before finally giving in.

My toes curl as my back arches off the mattress.

He'd feel so good fucking me. He'd taste so good in my mouth.

He'd make the hottest sounds.

"Oh fuck. Oh, *fuck*—"

There's a knock at the door just as my orgasm starts to crest.

"Pip? It's me, open up. I didn't bring a key."

My head snaps off the pillow.

"Siena, you there?"

I sob, feeling my body come down from the edge, left hanging and needing. This feels so much worse than it did a minute ago. Jabbing at my phone, I kill the vibrator. Scramble off the bed. Close my bathrobe as I wrench open the door.

"Hey." I'm panting. Fucking *panting*. I pivot back into the room the second he's inside, hoping my skin hurries up and cools down before he asks what I've been doing. "I'm almost ready, just need to put on my dress."

After grabbing it off a hanger in the closet, I hurry into the bathroom and nudge the door shut.

I hate myself.

In the mirror, I'm blatantly flushed and looking feral. Exactly how you'd image a woman on the brink of a badly needed orgasm, only to have it snatched away.

Brooks is moving on the other side of the door, the sound of hangers clinking together as he presumably gets dressed. "How long do you think you'll need to finish getting ready?"

"Um." I eye my dress, willing my voice to lose its tremble. "Just a quick second."

I'm so jittery it takes more than a second to make sense of the dress, which side of the shiny purple fabric goes up and which goes down. Where to stick my arms in with these crisscrossed laces on the back.

Calm the hell down, you sex-starved nympho.

I take a breath. "I'm done. Can I come back into the room?"

"Yeah, I'm decent."

Clutching the front of my dress to keep it from sliding down, I open the door. Brooks looks up from the tube of lipstick he picked up from the dresser, a shade that gives off the effect of love bites from a mind-numbing make-out session.

Decent?

He looks incredible in a tux, crisp white shirt, no bow tie. I go weak for this man in a T-shirt, tattoo sleeves visible. But a dressed-up Brooks Attwood could get me to rob a bank just to curry favor with him.

I shake my head in fake disgust. "Look at you. Take some pride in your appearance, for God's sake."

Brooks gives a husky laugh I feel right between the thighs. He gives me the same once-over. "I never thought anything could top those overalls."

I rear back. "My overalls? Seriously?"

Either he ignores me or doesn't hear me. His gaze rakes upward, off my body, and onto my face. It zigzags like he's looking for something specific. Or maybe he can't decide where to land. "You really are beautiful."

Oh.

My stomach swoops violently. At the words; at his rapt, shameless attention. There's something so soft in the way he looks at me now. It's the same way he did last night, whispering his apology in the dark.

"Thank you." I reach for his collar. Pretend to straighten it just as an excuse to touch him.

We're on more solid footing today and . . . I like it.

"Mind tying me up?" I smirk when he lifts an eyebrow, and spin around, giving him my back. "The dress. I need a hand doing it up."

Brooks sweeps the hair off my back and over my shoulder, gliding his fingers over my skin along the way. In the mirror above the dresser, I watch his gaze fall down my back. The dress is low, cutting just above my hips, with laces meant to crisscross all the way up. He ignores them and traces a finger along the upper length of my spine, mesmerized by the line of delicate star tattoos I got the day I turned eighteen.

"Attwood?"

"Yeah." The single word comes out grainy, like it's been dragged over gravel on the way out of his mouth.

"If you can't handle a little bondage—"

Brooks's eyes find mine in the mirror. In two smooth movements, he wraps the end of a lace around each hand and tugs so hard it yanks me back, forces the air from my lungs in a gasp.

"Don't test me, little Pippen."

Fuck.

I'm winded. From the dress, the way he looks so predatory now, gazing at my reflection in the mirror as he does up the dress with swift, harsh jerks of his hands.

"I think we can both agree there's nothing little about me. If you want someone to toss around, you might want to look elsewhere."

"Yeah?" I seem to have amused him. In a beat, I'm spun around, shoved back into the dresser as he steps into my space. His hand closes loosely around my neck, forcing up my chin so that I can look at him.

Yes. Please.

I grip the edge of the dresser behind me and various bottles and tubes topple over as the piece of furniture shudders.

"You look plenty small to me, Siena." Brooks's fingers tense around my throat before sliding around the side to possessively hold the back of my neck, sweeping his thumb along my jaw. "Plenty easy to throw around. Do whatever the fuck I want with."

Yes. Yes yes yes.

Brooks's thumb drags over my lower lip. He hums with approval when my mouth parts reflexively, then dips his finger inside.

"Suck."

My sound is halfway between a whimper and moan. I won't survive the night.

I close my lips around his thumb and do what he says. Swirl my tongue around his fingertip, hollow my cheeks, graze my teeth along his skin. Keep my eyes on his impassive expression, searching for any little hint that I'm doing this right.

The way he likes it.

But he gives me nothing. Just stares back, utterly calm. Amused more than anything.

And then Brooks plucks his fingers from my mouth so fast the wet sound fills the room. He reaches around me, presses something cold against my chest, and waits until I have a hand on it before releasing me. It's a shiny, rose gold tube.

"Fix your lipstick." I huff a breath. Turn around, lift the tube to my puffy lips with trembling fingers, dabbing on more lipstick. He stands behind me, watching my reflection work in the mirror.

"A little warning might've been nice," I say quietly.

"What for?"

"You're out there getting fawned over by women my mom's age. Dancing with kids. If only they could see their good little boy behind closed doors."

"Siena, I used to fuck in back alleys. What part of that says *good boy* to you?" He raises an eyebrow. "You call this a dress, by the way?"

"Are you going to order me into a different one? Can't stand the thought of other men looking at your pretend girlfriend?"

"No point. I could take you out in a paper bag and still have fuckers tripping over themselves to get at you." He takes me in, head to toe, and shakes his head. "Asking you to cover up would be like shoving a championship ring under the mattress. You better believe I'm showing that off front and center, spotlights and all."

"Consider me impressed, Attwood. That's a very mature perspective—"

"Obviously the ring stays in a glass cabinet, under lock and key. This is strictly a *look don't touch, under threat of immediate strangulation* kind of thing."

"And *there's* the ego I know and love."

The act of dragging his gaze off my body looks like it takes a whole lot of effort. Brooks offers me his arm. "Come on, Pippen. Let's get this over with."

It's not until the steel elevator doors slide shut that I remember the little pink vibrator, still tucked inside me.

Chapter 18

Siena

I haven't had this much trouble escaping to the bathroom since high school, when my history teacher finally realized that when I asked for the hall pass it was less about relieving myself, and more about making out with Dan Trenton in the back of his beat-up Impala during second period.

The hotel ballroom is packed with a few hundred people I don't know. Brooks and I have constantly been pulled in different directions by members of the Tigers organization—the entire night has been a perfectly executed rotation of players, coaches, and alumni selling Brooks on the team. It's made it impossible to slip away.

Brooks leans back onto the bar as Shawn and Bonnie Hartley—the Tigers quarterback and his wife, who are currently charged with our entertainment—order a beer and cocktail each.

He and I have been sipping on water. Brooks because he lays off the booze during training. Me because I'm sharing a bed with the most gorgeous man I've ever laid eyes on, and I need all my inhibitions firmly in place.

Which is a fucking chore right now, considering I've currently got a vibrator sitting snugly inside me. It's not running, but still pushing against my clit in the most tantalizing way.

The shit I get myself into sometimes. I swear.

"Thanks," I tell Brooks as he slides a fresh water toward me on the bar. He shifts his weight and I quietly add, "How's the knee?"

Brooks gives a half nod, half shrug in response. Beyond him, I notice a blond woman in a shimmering silver dress eyeing us curiously before lifting her champagne glass off the bar and heading for the dining tables. *Shit.*

"Hey, who is that?" I ask Brooks. I'd been whispering, but there's something funny in the way she was staring at us.

Brooks looks just as the woman glances over her shoulder. He pulls a face, giving her his back. "Lyndsay Brown. Her husband was with the Rebels in the earlier years of my career. She and my ex are friendly."

My stomach sinks. "Do you think she could've heard—"

"How're things at home?" Brooks interrupts, grinning as Bonnie Hartley turns back to us, putting away the phone she'd been typing at.

Bonnie gives a small laugh. "Mya's giving the nanny hell. Keeps bartering for more bedtime stories."

I fiddle with a bar napkin. "How many kids do you have?"

Feigning interest in my fake boyfriend's potential colleagues is part of the deal, but I genuinely enjoyed hanging out with Bonnie and the other women today. It felt like a day out with girl friends, watching our guys play in ass-hugging pants. In that way, I miss the comradery of a pro-sports family.

Not that I'd ever admit that to Brooks, when it feels like we're moving past the whole *Siena Pippen is a gold-digging hanger-on* thing.

Bonnie flicks through her phone and hands it to me. "We have one girl. Mya is nine."

"She's adorable." I tilt the phone to show Brooks a photo of the girl with hair so blond, it borders on white. "You remind me of me and my mom. A brunette and a blond."

Bonnie takes back her phone, smiling down at the picture. "We adopted her when she was five. Can't go anywhere without getting at least a few comments from strangers, though. I do worry it'll get to her one day."

I feel a fresh wave of appreciation for the woman in front of me. Mom and I used to get that all the time. "Trust me, it won't matter in the long run. She'll love you more than she'll care about inappropriate strangers. Blood relation is totally overrated."

"It sounds like you're speaking from experience."

I smile at Bonnie. "I was fostered at thirteen."

Brooks looks over. "You're a foster kid?"

"Yeah, I am." I've never been ashamed of this part of my life; how could I be, when it was the best thing to happen to me? "My birth parents up and left one day. No explanation."

"And you ended up in the system?"

"Not exactly. I hid out in our old house for a few months after they left and broke into homes around town to steal food. My parents— the ones who eventually took me in—caught me raiding their fridge in the middle of the night. I remember thinking I'd be in juvie by sunrise. But they ended up giving me a whole new life."

I smile to myself, remembering the way Dad and I stood in the dark kitchen with our hands up. Mine in surrender, waiting for him to call the police. His because he didn't want to scare me.

Scare me. As though he hadn't just caught me breaking into his house.

Brooks stares at my anchor necklace, the way it shimmers under the overhead lights. "You didn't have any other family to stay with?"

I take a long sip of my sparkling water. "There was an aunt on my mom's side. I didn't want to live with her."

And my parents were made to pay for that decision in the cruelest way. Over and over, starting just a year after they took me in.

"You didn't know this about her?" Shawn and Bonnie exchange a look.

Shit.

Brooks glances at me. Because I'm his girlfriend of nine months, and he should definitely know this about me.

"Of course he knows," I say quickly, stroking the hair off his face. "It's . . . the old concussion. It creeps up on us sometimes. He even called me by another woman's name the other day. I swear, I came within an inch of chopping off his balls, thinking he'd been messing around on me."

The arm he'd had draped along the edge of the bar drops, and Brooks squeezes my hip in warning. I try not to laugh.

"Of course. Head injuries are part of the deal in our world." Bonnie nods in understanding. "Most of our husbands are the same way."

"Shawn calls you by another woman's name, too?" I inject just the right amount of hope into my voice.

"God no, that's fucking *awful*—" Shawn catches himself and winces at Brooks. "No offense, man."

"None taken," Brooks says flatly. He gives my hip another squeeze.

The bartender slides Shawn's and Bonnie's drinks across the bar, causing enough of a distraction for Brooks to lean close. I tense the moment his lips graze my ear, feeling the touch all the way down my spine.

"You're gonna get it later for that little stunt." This is officially unbearable. My pussy clenches around the vibrator, begging for relief.

I pull out my phone, hoping to distract myself from the dormant sex toy lodged inside me. "Don't go dangling these empty threats. It's not nice."

"Who says they're empty?" Brooks reaches lower, takes a shameless handful of my ass. "Bet you'd look so fucking pretty bent over my lap."

My breath hitches. I'm so startled, so turned on, I end up fumbling my phone on the glossy ballroom floor. Looking all too pleased with himself, Brooks picks it up.

Does a double take at it.

"Shit, did the screen crack?" I peer over his shoulder. And my stomach plummets.

The screen's fine. Crystal clear and spotless, and open on the goddamn vibrator app.

"That's . . ."

A slow smirk stretches Brooks's mouth. "Is this what had you so flustered upstairs?"

"Me, flustered? Must have me confused with someone else."

I reach for the phone. Brooks jerks it away. His eyes skate over me, my flaming hot cheeks, and the teasing grin fades off his face.

"Siena." I've never heard my name sound so filthy in my life. He glances around us, at Shawn and Bonnie nearby, huddled over her own phone. "You still wearing this thing?"

My heartbeat stutters. "Am I wearing a sex toy at a black-tie function? Of course not."

He tips my head back with a finger at my chin, forcing me to look at him.

"Don't lie to me. Is there a toy in your pussy right now?"

My entire body throbs.

"I'll take that silence as a yes. Suddenly, this night's looking up."

Brooks releases my face and his gaze drops to my traitorous phone, still open on the app. I go to grab it again. Stupid, considering he has an athlete's reflexes. He catches my wrist, twists me around so that my back hits his front.

Fuck. "What are you going to do?"

Out of the corner of my eye, I see Bonnie tuck her phone back into her clutch. Shawn shoots me a grin.

"That shit you pulled last night in bed?" Brooks presses a kiss to my temple. "Consider this settling the score."

His thumb flashes over my phone. I gasp, absolutely *shove* my teeth into my lip to stifle a cry when the toy comes alive inside me, just as Shawn and Bonnie make their way over.

Brooks's mouth is at my ear. "Play the part, sweetheart."

"Sorry about that," Bonnie says. "I think we're going to try to slip away. Enjoy a good night's sleep with the sitter staying at the house tonight."

Yes. Please. Go away.

I grit my teeth, forcing my breath steady, but there's no winning this battle. The vibrator shudders inside me, strokes my clit, and I clench everywhere.

Fuck, that feels so good.

In my peripheral vision, I see Brooks fighting a laugh as he tucks my phone into his pocket. "Oh, that's too bad. We were having such a great time getting to know you. Why don't you have another drink with us?"

Asshole.

"We'll take you up on that another time. And maybe we can both knock that championship off our bucket lists this season," Shawn tells him. "You didn't miss a beat yesterday."

"Thanks, man. It's been an honor to be here." Brooks wraps a strong arm around my waist to secure me against him. "We've both enjoyed it. Such a pleasure."

Bonnie seems just as intent on torturing me as Brooks, because she turns her smile on me. "I'm sure it helps that the team only plays a quick three-hour drive from Oakwood."

"Y-yes. It's . . ." I swallow a whimper. My nails dig into my palms. "Fantastic."

Brooks peers down at me, strokes a thumb where he holds me at the waist. It's so good and so, *so* bad, intensifying the heat already radiating from my pussy as the toy pulses inside me. "Definitely a selling point, isn't it, sweetheart? It'll be good to keep you close. Right where I need you."

"Well, we're glad you both decided to join us tonight. Brooks, let's stay in touch, all right?"

Thank fuck.

The moment we're alone again—aside from the other few hundred people in the ballroom—I gasp a breath. "*Fuck*, Brooks. Please."

"Please what?"

Brooks turns me around to face him, cups the back of my neck, strokes his thumb along my jaw, the same way he'd done upstairs. I'd been clenching before, wound up and trying to keep myself from crumbling. But now that it's just us in this dimly lit ballroom, with the music loud enough to smother my panting, I'm shuddering.

I'm grateful.

I need this.

Now. Right now. Don't care who's watching.

"Brooks," I sigh.

"Never heard my name sound so good." With his thumb, Brooks lifts my chin, forces my gaze onto him. We're standing close enough together that I can hear the satisfied rumble in his chest as he takes me in. "You like this, don't you? Pussy throbbing right here, surrounded by people."

What does it say about me that I do like it? I like our secrets. I like the way his fingers curl into my waist, biting into my skin.

"Answer me." His voice is soft, but it's a command.

I whimper. "I like it."

"Fucking knew it. Pretty little Siena, with her winning smile and charming wit. Perfect pretend girlfriend. Perfect media darling. Fooling everyone but me." He licks the corner of his mouth, holding my gaze. "I knew you were a bad fucking girl from the second I met you. The kind who'd let me make that sweet pussy come in front of four hundred strangers. Aren't you?"

Brooks gazes back, utterly calm. The only things giving him away are his short, tight breaths and the hard length of his cock I can feel snaking down his pant leg. I push into him. Brooks releases a ragged breath.

God. He's so turned on.

This is back-alley Brooks, and I'm so damn happy to meet him.

"Do it," I whisper. "Make me come."

With his eyes on me, Brooks strips off his tux jacket and tosses it onto the back of a nearby chair. He takes my hand and leads us past the younger, burly players, to an unoccupied patch of the dance floor.

He pulls me right against his body. His perfect fucking body, hard and hot under my fingers. His arms wind around me, holding me in a way that makes me feel just as small as he claimed upstairs.

From the outside, we look like any other couple on this dance floor, holding each other and swaying to the music. In our own loved-up world, bodies pressed together.

But my pussy clenches around the vibrator, thighs slip together. I'm slick and wet, and dying for relief. His hand moves from my waist, grazes the exposed skin at my lower back before slipping a bit lower. He grunts at the feel of his hand on my ass. With the coverage from Brooks's body, I let my face crumble.

My fingers dig into his arms, nails scraping along his buttery shirt.

This is too much. Not enough.

The toy is still perfectly in place, tucked inside my pussy, hitting all the right spots. But I've never felt more empty. I'm craving a deeper stretch, a different kind of full. The tight press of his cock, pushing inside me. My back arching off a bed only to be shoved back down by his body, hands trapped over my head as he fucks me hard into the mattress.

God, I want to *taste* him. I want him throwing back his head. Groaning into the room, this time as he fucks his cock into my throat.

"Let's get out of here," I pant. "I want to touch you."

"But you set very clear rules, sweetheart. No touching, remember?" Brooks pouts. He's mocking me, the little shit. "You found me a perfect loophole, though, didn't you? We don't touch, but I still get to feel you squirm. Still get to know what you look like with your pussy aching, like the needy fucking girl you are."

"Maybe I changed my mind. Maybe I'll let you fuck me."

"A few minutes ago, I'd have fucked you, no question. But I'm not so sure anymore."

Brooks spins me so that I face out onto the dance floor. Tuxes and sparkly dresses blur around us under the pale glow of the overhead lights. I whimper, body trembling, sagging into him. His cock teases me, digs into my ass, and goddamn him he punches his hips.

"Maybe I want you up at all hours thinking about me, and everything I'd do to you. Maybe I want you racing to my house in the middle of the night. Pounding on my door with a soaking-wet cunt, begging to be fucked." He grazes my neck with his mouth. "So, no, baby. We're not fucking tonight. Instead, you're going to be the dirty girl I know you are, and you're going to come for me right here. In the middle of this party."

My phone flashes in my face, triggering the face ID.

I bite down on a cry as the pulsing inside me intensifies, stroking in my pussy, over my clit. My fingers dig into Brooks's arms, and his hips begin to move. Unmistakably grinding his cock into my ass.

Such tiny movements that you likely couldn't tell, unless you were actually feeling the steady rub of cock on your ass. But the idea that he's enough of a freak to do this in public makes me wild.

Makes me want him more.

I wish he was inside me. I wish he'd bend me over and fuck me right here—

Brooks groans softly in my ear, kisses my neck.

"I'm going to come. Brooks, you're going to make me come—"

He cups my cheek and turns my chin over my shoulder to see his pupils blown wide, the tick in his jaw. "I know. Those sweet little gasps can only mean one thing."

"Brooks. *Brooks*." His name is an urgent warning on my lips. I grasp onto the arm he has wrapped around my waist and hold on for dear fucking life.

He keeps his eyes on me, watching my face with hungry focus as a hot rush blasts through me, takes over. Forces a cry to rise up my throat—

Brooks crushes his mouth to mine at the very last second, swallowing my cries, clutching me to him as I fight to retain control of my body, keep it from shuddering. I let him hold me close as I come with his tongue sliding over mine.

The kiss is quick, just as long as it needs to be to keep me quiet. Another flash of my phone and the toy stills inside me. I slump against his body. Brooks strokes my hair, tucks me under his chin. "They really know how to throw a good party here, huh?"

I try to laugh but all that comes out of me is a weak moan. Everything around me is a blur as Brooks sits me down at our empty table and pours me a fresh glass of water. He crouches at my feet, hand on my knee as he watches me drink. "Talk to me, Pip. You okay?"

I nod, sucking in a breath. "That was . . ." *The single hottest thing that's ever happened to me.* I manage a smile, and it thaws the caution in his eyes. "I really needed that."

"Saying this seems pointless seeing as you're always the prettiest person in the room. But orgasms really suit you." He stands, drops a kiss to my forehead. "Sit tight. I need to take care of something."

He weaves through the crowd, head ducked to avoid getting pulled into conversation.

Brooks Attwood is about to go jerk off somewhere in this ballroom. And there's no fucking way I'm missing it.

I lurch to my feet, hurry to catch up as he turns down an empty hall leading to the washrooms. He's so sexy from behind. His dress shirt stretches over his muscular shoulders; his ass a dream in those pants.

We fall into step as we come in line with an open door. He peers

down in surprise a split second before I shove him with everything I
have, forcing him through the door and closing us in.

The overhead lights flicker on. It's an empty coat check closet,
small enough that we're no more than a few feet apart.

Brooks's back hits the far wall with the force of my shove. He
gives me a calculating look. "Pippen, what am I doing in a coat closet?"

My gaze drops to the front of his pants. "Are you going to take
care of that?"

He tilts his head. "Are you saying you want to help?"

"I'm saying it's only fair I get to watch."

I reach under my dress, finally pulling the toy from my pussy. But
before I can drop it into my clutch, Brooks snatches my wrist, lifts my
hand. And takes the wet end of the vibrator into his mouth.

Holy. Shit.

My pussy throbs, begging for release like I didn't violently come
just minutes ago. He sucks on the pink toy with his eyes glued to me,
then returns possession of my arm.

"You taste good." It sounds like an accusation.

I've never felt so damn feral. "Take your fucking cock out, Brooks."

He doesn't even flinch. Brooks makes quick work of the buttons
on his shirt until it hangs open over his sculpted torso. He yanks open
the cuffs in two deft movements before reaching for his belt.

My heartbeat is in my ears. Brooks pulls out his cock and my eyes
fall shut. Perfect, just like the rest of him.

"I was really hoping it was small."

He gives a husky laugh that twists around a moan and my eyes
snap open. Brooks strokes his cock in long, slow motions, gaze fixed
on me. Darting over my body, my face, my breasts peeking over the
top of my dress, my hips.

His attention is rapt enough to make anyone self-conscious,
but it's the last thing I feel. The power in it is intoxicating—the way
Brooks presses his weight into the wall behind him as though his

strong legs can't carry him. The desperate gasps and deep groans as he strokes himself, the way his unblinking gaze is fixed on me.

"You like this, Pip? Seeing how hard you make me?"

I nod fast, panting like he's touching me. Pussy gripping nothing this time. "You're really fucking hot."

He groans deep at that, hand moving faster over his cock. The tip beads with pre-cum I want to suck off him, tasting him the way he tasted me. His body is rigid as he works himself, abs flexed, shoulders bunched under his shirt. With a final thrust into his fist and a soft groan, Brooks throws back his head, hits the wall behind him. Paints over his fist and I wish I was touching him, feeling his stomach tense under my fingers.

I release a breath, dazed as I watch him come down. He's . . . fuck, he's a work of art, isn't he? I've never laid eyes on a more gorgeous man.

Brooks's eyes open, finding me as he works to slow his breath. Loud, happy voices echo in the hall on the other side of the closet door.

"Didn't quite think through this location, did you?" he mutters, lifting his soaked fingers. "What am I supposed to do with this?"

Biting down on a smirk, I pull him together. Tug up his pants, buckle his belt. Button his shirt. "Since you can't do it one-handed."

"And your mess?" He indicates his hand.

"Mine?"

"You made me hard. Made me lose my fucking mind to the point of jacking off in a coat closet at a black-tie event. So yeah, Pip. It's your mess. What're *you* gonna do with it?"

Brooks doesn't say anything more—just lifts a single eyebrow—but my heart thumps in my ears anyway. He's a fucking freak.

I love it.

"Ask nicely," I whisper.

"Pippen." Brooks licks the corner of his mouth, working a smirk off his face. He takes the back of my neck with his other hand. "Be a good girl and clean up your mess."

I don't know what's become of me, become of him.

Become of this night.

Not long ago, we were throwing jabs on a sideline. And now—

I bring his hand to my mouth and clean off his fingers one after the other until there's nothing left. He watches with his lips parted.

"You taste good," I tell him when I finish.

Brooks shakes his head, tucks his shirt into his pants. And when he catches up with me at the door, he takes my hand firmly in his before leading me back into the masses.

Chapter 19

Brooks

Siena unravels her hair from the messy knot on top of her head, letting it tumble over her shoulders. She shakes it out, massages her temples, and slides into her side of the bed. Completely calm in the wake of what happened down there. In fact, she's been completely calm from the moment we left that closet. Upbeat and warm to anyone who pulled us over for conversation. I've known she can handle emotionless sex—that moron she works with is an unfortunate living, breathing reminder of that.

But I expected . . . something.

Coy stares. Rosy cheeks. Anything but the master class in nonchalance lying in that king-sized bed. I turn back to my open suitcase, studying the stack of T-shirts I brought for the weekend. I'm debating putting one on to sleep this time, because fuck knows this thing flew right off the rails down at the party. Maybe we should reel it in a little bit.

I throw another glance over my shoulder. She's texting away, so unbothered. Not a damn care in the world and still wearing Thomas fucking Ivers's shirt to sleep. I eye her overnight bag, sitting open next to mine.

Fuck it. I lift my entire stack of T-shirts and stuff it into her bag.

"Attwood." Siena doesn't even look up from her phone. "What's going on in that pretty head of yours?"

I straighten and flutter my eyelashes. "You think I'm pretty?"

"*You* think you're pretty. Let's not pretend you don't normally spend all night whispering sweet nothings to yourself in the mirror. I'm sorry to keep you from it two nights in a row."

My face turns grave. "It's so hard. Thank you for acknowledging it."

Her eyes sparkle as she withholds a laugh. "I think this is a good time to renew our commitment to the rules."

"Which ones?"

"The no-touching one. Considering you were just making bitter eyes at your suitcase, we were right to agree to it in the first place."

"Except there was no touching down there. And I recall our first kiss being your doing."

"Conversation over." She buries her face behind her screen.

I can't help grinning on my way to the bathroom to get ready for bed. Finally ruffled her perfect feathers. Shiny feathers.

Shiny like her hair.

After a minute, Siena's giggle filters through the open door. I stiffen, toothbrush in hand. Who's she giggling with, and why isn't it me?

Jesus Christ, will you please calm the fuck down?

I roll back my shoulders. Trying to shove away the memory of her soft body near-limp in my arms, so sweetly satisfied. The way she looked at me with all the trust in the world.

But that look lingers, imprinted in my mind.

It lingers because, after she let slip about her upbringing, the way she was left to fend for herself at such a young age, that trust feels like a gift.

I picture a thirteen-year-old Siena, with her shiny hair and twin—kling eyes, forced to break into her neighbors' homes just to have something to eat. My heart fucking clenches.

It's so different from the pampered way I was raised. Two loving parents, a close relationship with my sister. Nice house, plenty of gifts at Christmas. They invested so much in my early football career, and I'd never have been able to reach the pro level without them.

Yet, there Siena is, giggling in bed. Still so full of life.

She's . . . unexpected.

I finish brushing my teeth at warp speed and hover by the bathroom door, watching her text away with about a thousand questions on my tongue.

"Can I ask you a personal question?"

Siena looks over, and there's nothing like the satisfaction of having her gaze rake up and down my body. I opted against the T-shirt, and she's rewarding me for it with that filth in her eyes.

"You expect me to say no to you looking like that?" She shakes her head and puts away her phone. "Ask away, Brooks Attwood."

"What were you like as a kid?"

She barks a shocked laugh. "Diving right in, huh?"

"I can't help it. You are . . . infuriatingly interesting."

She tips her head. "I can't decide if that's a compliment or not."

"It is. Even after that first day, I wanted to know everything about you. It pissed me off. I didn't want to wonder."

Siena's expression is one of pure amusement. She stares pointedly at the other end of the mattress. "Will you at least get in bed? Make this feel like less of a strip tease gone terribly wrong?"

"Why?" I crawl slowly over to her on the mattress, really playing it up with a growl. "You want more of this, Pippen?"

Laughing, she palms my face and shoves me away. "I gave you the gift of a lifetime down there. Count your blessings."

Counted them, need more of them.

I slide under the covers and turn to face her. She kills the light and settles in the same way. "Tell me what it was like growing up."

She hums. "Before my second life? I was an accident they ended up keeping. My birth parents liked to party with friends who weren't burdened by childcare. Our house was . . . always full of people I didn't know. I think I was offered my first joint at eight, and that was the tame stuff." Siena picks at a spot on the sheets between us. "I started to feed myself at seven years old, when my parents were too hungover one day to get out of bed. They saw me get the hang of it and decided I could take it from there. And they got more and more comfortable leaving me to it, until I guess they decided they didn't need to be around at all."

"At thirteen?" I knew the story wasn't going to be pretty, but I didn't imagine it hurting so bad, either. All my kids happen to be imaginary, a dream for the future, but I could never fathom doing that to them. "Did you ever look for them after they left?"

She shakes her head but doesn't look me in the eye. I don't push it, though, and there's a beat of silence as we listen to a door slam in the hallway.

"It's not like they were exceptional parents, even before they took off," Siena continues once it's quiet again. "And I had a home where I felt loved for the first time. My new parents helped me go to college. I took over the family business."

"Ship Happens. It's a great name."

"And it was my dad's pride and joy. I'd work there on weekends and every day in the summer growing up. Except the one day a week when he'd close up shop so that we could borrow a sailboat from our friends at the marina and go fishing on the bay."

Siena shifts, and the space between our bodies closes further. I can feel the heat rolling off her. Can't look away from her. I'm near-hypnotized by the sound of her voice. The fact that she's even telling me any of this.

Every damn thing out of this woman's mouth has me dying for more.

"Funny, I can't picture you fishing. Sitting still and quiet for a whole afternoon? Forget it."

She grins wide at that. "You'd be right—I *hate* fishing."

"But you work at a bait shop?"

"Like I said: Dad's pride and joy. He left it to me when he died. And my mom's arthritis makes it impossible for her to work, so . . . it's all mine."

I hesitate. "How did he . . ."

Her smile turns pinched. "He had issues with his kidneys."

I fist my pillow, wishing I could hold her and knowing she'd never let me. "Two years. That's still so recent." Siena nods, looking like she'd rather talk about anything else, so I say, "Tell me about your joy, then."

She blinks, caught off guard by the question. Stares back silently a while, and then, "Who said anything about me?"

I prop up on my elbow. "What kind of question is that?" She doesn't say anything. Just stares back at me, and it might be the effect of the low lighting but she looks almost . . . nervous. Like I've backed her onto a landmine, and she's calculating the safe way off. "Come on, what's your joy, Siena Pippen? Other than making me crazy and supergluing your best friend's face where it doesn't belong."

The tension trickles off her face until she's suppressing a tired smile. "If Dad's joy was fishing, mine was being behind the wheel of a boat. The wind, the way you sort of feel weightless, cutting through water. No straight lines or hard roads. There's something so freeing about it, you know? Especially with the way things are—*were*." She's stumbling over words, and I don't know whether it was a real slipup or the product of fatigue, but it's so unlike her it makes me uneasy. "Coming out of the situation with my birth parents, where it felt like my life was so . . . small. Limited."

Keeping those pictures in her living room makes sense now.

Memories of the places she probably never thought she'd see. Once-in-a-lifetime trips, she'd called them.

And now I'm fixated on the wild idea that maybe I could make those *once-in-a-lifetimes* fifty-in-a-lifetimes. Make her world feel so big she'd need a trail of breadcrumbs to find her way home.

Siena gives a full-body yawn, arms tensing under the covers. She pulls her anchor necklace from under that T-shirt—Thomas fucking Ivers's T-shirt—and fingers the charm. "Any more pressing questions?"

Yes, exactly how pissed off would you be if I caused irreparable damage to that shirt in the morning?

"Go to sleep, Pip. I'll take first watch." I know I'm taking advantage of her fatigue, but I smooth the hair off her cheek, lift the covers over her shoulder. Spin her anchor necklace around so that the clasp sits in the back. Her eyes close, face goes soft, and something twinges inside me. "What if you had it the wrong way, yesterday? What if everything went to hell for you with the shop and the rent so that you'd agree to date me?"

Siena gives a sleepy chuckle. "Fake-date you. I don't date athletes anymore."

My head lifts, hoping I heard her wrong. Siena pushes into her pillow as she finally drifts off.

I lie staring up at the ceiling long after she's asleep.

Wondering what in the hell I did to deserve wanting a woman who struck down any chance I have with her, the very second I realized I wanted one.

Chapter 20

Siena

Eager hands dart out the moment my cheese platter hits the coffee table. Predictably, they aim right for the sharp cheddar in a battle of flicking wrists and prodding fingers. Meanwhile, I take the liberty of sampling the soft, stinky one I can't remember the name of, but that looked intriguing enough at the market.

Cribbage night wouldn't be cribbage night without sharp cheddar, but I like to throw in a wild card here and there. Help Mom, Carla, Evan, and Shy broaden their horizons a bit. Even in the cheese department.

"Excuse me, I'm trying to feed a child here," Shy shout-whispers. She swats her mother's hand, trying to get at the cheese first.

Carla swats her back. "Rosie is dead asleep. In a completely different room."

I toss a cushion on the hardwood and settle into my seat, leaning my cheek against Mom's leg who sits on the faded floral sofa with Shy. Evan and Carla have claimed their usual spots on the ground.

The room goes quiet and every ounce of focus falls to the cribbage board on the coffee table. When my phone chimes, interrupting the silence, the cribbage and cheddar fiends glare over their cards.

I flick my fingers at the coffee table. "Don't give me that. I came bearing snacks."

BRATTWOOD: We have a problem.

I barely have a moment to soak in my instant dread when a screenshot follows. Since Brooks's injury on the Tigers' field, I've been on edge waiting for the other shoe to drop. For him to tell me the knee is worse than we initially thought. That he's been forced to give up on this dream of a comeback. It'd be unfortunate for me and my social media earnings, but knowing how badly Brooks needs this . . .

I recognize the picture he's sent me at once. It's the same one Josh has been thrilled about mere days ago, a photo posted to the Tigers' social account of Brooks and I laughing, dressed to the nines at the gala. Except, unlike the last time I saw it, there's a comment on the post from . . .

Lyndsay Brown. The woman who'd given us an odd look at the gala. I'd completely forgotten about her, given the . . . dancing that followed. *So happy to see you back, Brooks! Hope your knee feels better after the scrimmage!*

"Oh my God." My stomach has sunk so low, it's sitting on the floor with me. The comment seems innocuous enough, and yet I've been in these circles long enough to know how wrong—how utterly *malicious* it is for someone on the inside to publicly comment on a player's health like this.

All because I couldn't keep my stupid mouth shut.

Mom gives me a questioning look, but I shake my head at her, forcing a smile as I scramble to call Brooks. He sends my call to voicemail, and the guilt inside me turns punishing, clogging up my throat until he follows up with a text.

BRATTWOOD: Sorry, Josh is talking my ear off on the phone.

SIENA: Brooks, I am so sorry. I don't know what to say.

BRATTWOOD: Sorry for what? You didn't make her comment on anything.

SIENA: Except she heard it from me. How bad is it?

BRATTWOOD: Bad. He's been on the phone all day trying to counter it, but the goddamn rumor mill has taken off. The Rebels are concerned, and the Tigers don't know what to believe. I don't know how to fix this.

I picture Brooks at home, wearing the same defeat he'd worn after the scrimmage. It lights a furious, vengeful flame inside me, drowning out my guilt. I don't know what game she's playing or what she gets out of it, but this woman had to have known what she was doing with that comment. She's officially messed with my team, and I've never been one to endure my grievances in silence.

SIENA: We try to fix it the same way this all started. I'll come around to your practices, shoot some content with your knee looking better than ever. It's the least I can do.

SIENA: Your knee's still doing better, right?

BRATTWOOD: It's not at a hundred percent, but we're getting close. You'd really do that?

SIENA: On two very important conditions: One, you wear those ass-hugging shorts of yours to make it worth my while. And two, I myself won't ever be required to participate in physical activity. That's all you, honey.

BRATTWOOD: You got something against physical activity?

SIENA: If it doesn't end in a screaming orgasm, I don't want it.

So much for the boundaries.

Brooks had been oddly sentimental after we'd left that coat closet. But in the days since we've been home, we've settled into a groove where all rules are perfectly adhered to, and any teasing stays entirely verbal. No orgasms to be had.

Unless you count the ones in the privacy of my own apartment, where Brooks only makes an appearance through vivid memories of that coat closet.

SIENA: Ignore that. When can we start?

BRATTWOOD: I'm coaching the Huskies Tots and Touchdowns camp at the stadium this weekend. Maybe you can trespass your way in to join.

SIENA: Easy. Security's really lax there. Is that the camp with mini humans stumbling around for a football?

BRATTWOOD: Yeah, they run it once a year. Haven't missed it since I played at UOB.

BRATTWOOD: This plan has lowered Josh's voice by a solid two decibels. My eardrums thank you.

I gasp a laugh, relieved that he's managing to crack jokes through the mess I've made.

SIENA: Speaking of thank-yous, I found something interesting in my overnight bag when I unpacked it tonight.

BRATTWOOD: More interesting than the sex toys you travel with? Because I found those pretty damn interesting.

BRATTWOOD: Also, you would be one of those people who doesn't unpack for days after they get home from a trip.

SIENA: I am who I am. Can you explain how a whole stack of men's T-shirts that I don't own found their way into my bag?

Specifically, they were a whole stack of men's T-shirts that smelled pleasantly like Brooks's piney scent.

BRATTWOOD: The idea is that you'd wear one of them to sleep.

BRATTWOOD: And that either you shred the one you stole from your ex, or sink it to the bottom of the bay. Either works for me.

My chin jerks back noticeably enough for Shy to shoot me in inquisitive look. I suspected the T-shirt donation had been made in jealousy, but I never expected Brooks to readily cop to it.

The jealousy is unnecessary, anyway. My wearing that shirt had nothing to do with nostalgia, and everything to do with the fact that I hadn't done laundry in a while, and Tom's shirt was the last sad and crumpled option in my drawer.

Brooks putting his shirts in my bag, though? It's a ballsy move.

And I am thoroughly charmed.

"Oh, I know that look well." Carla eyes me over the top of her cards. "It's the look Evan gives me about a split second before he jumps my bones."

"Mom," Shy groans.

Evan gives his wife an exasperated look that reminds me all too much of the way Brooks shakes his head whenever I say something out of pocket.

Mom giggles, falling against the back of the sofa. "Leave the girl alone, she's in love."

Other than Shy, I hadn't had the heart to tell any of them that Brooks and I are faking it. Explaining it to Mom would require telling her I'd been struggling at the shop, and I couldn't stand to disappoint her after everything she and Dad have done for me. All it took to get her excited about the supposed relationship was assuring her that the media had it wrong. That I hadn't been hiding the relationship from her for nine months. That we'd met that day at the stadium and hit it off.

"In love with a fine piece of—"

"*Carla!*" we all shout-whisper, trying not to wake Rosie.

Carla cackles dramatically, proud to have gotten a rise out of us. She shuffles the deck of cards and starts dealing. "Tell us about Brooks, honey. Is he treating you well?"

Shy smirks. "Yeah, Cee. Tell them about his amazing dance chops."

That little bitch. I knew I'd regret telling her about that.

"Brooks is . . ." *Jerking off in a coat closet for me to watch, then asking me to lick him clean.* "Sweet. He fixed my front door the other day."

Evan looks up from his hand. "What was wrong with your door?"

"I couldn't get it to lock for a couple of months."

"For shit's sake, Siena." He sighs heavily, like I'm the cause of every headache he's ever had. "Don't tell me you've been sleeping in that place with an unlocked door for months. Why didn't you call me?"

"It's fine. I didn't want to be a nuisance." Evan's bearded face turns ruddy at my words, and I hurry to talk him down, throwing up my hands. "It's fixed now! Brooks took care of it."

Evan grunts, still steaming in disapproval. "And if someone had come in while you were sleeping?"

A grin breaks over my face. "Ev, I've been sleeping with a steak knife next to my bed since I was nine, just in case. I don't need saving."

You could hear a fucking pin drop.

I never knew who Patricia and Tyler Pippen had invited over on a given night, and I was wary enough to make sure I had the means to protect myself. There were only so many times someone could stumble into my makeshift room in the basement, supposedly looking for the bathroom, before things went south.

I guess not everyone can laugh at my history the way I do, but it's much preferable to the alternative—wallowing over things I can't change. They'd eat me alive if I gave them the room to.

Mom runs her fingers soothingly through my hair, though I have a feeling it's more for her sake than mine. To this day, she has a hard time hearing about the way I grew up before I joined her family.

"Guys, I'm kidding. I've never once slept with a knife. We can all take a breath and get back to this riveting cribbage match."

They don't believe me, but return their intense focus on the game as Brooks's name flashes at the top of my screen.

BRATTWOOD: I was kidding.

BRATTWOOD: Sort of.

I read through our messages. The previous two from Brooks that went unanswered, after I'd asked about the shirts he'd snuck into my bag. My silence was clearly making him sweat.

BRATTWOOD: You don't have to wear my shirt to bed.

BRATTWOOD: But you still need to shred his.

BRATTWOOD: Kidding. Again.

BRATTWOOD: Kind of.

I laugh at my screen. It's the same kind of digital word vomit he did in my DMs in the days after we met. It's as charming now as it had been then.

SIENA: I tossed his shirt this morning.

And I fully intended to wear one of Brooks's tonight. Without washing them. Because, frankly, they smell divine.

BRATTWOOD: Yeah?

I never planned on confessing that, seeing as I'm still wrestling with exactly what it means. Seeing as we're supposed to be playing pretend for the masses and not wearing each other's clothes in private.

But at that simple *yeah?*, I picture Brooks's hulking figure hunched over his phone. Captivated the same way he'd been in that bed as he listened to me talk. Undivided in his attention and looking inexplicably grateful for every word I gave him.

The memory makes my heart pinch.

I file that in the same drawer as my confession, to await examination at a later date.

Chapter 21

Siena

"My daddy says you're dating the bird lady."

I choke on my breath in the first row of the stands at the Huskies stadium, where I've been live-posting content as Brooks coaches a group of under-sevens through a series of practice drills that they execute with all the grace of baby giraffes.

Every so often, a kid will break away from the activity on the field to chat him up excitedly, including the three-foot-nothing boy now grilling Brooks on his apparent status as a bird-lady boyfriend.

"Oh my God, I'm so sorry. He's seen your video from the Ravens game," a man a few seats down the row tells me, cheeks flushed. "We're still working on manners."

"I'm still working on mine, too." I wave off his apology. "Manners are overrated."

On the sideline, the cute kid continues his interrogation. "It's true? You're dating Cece Pippen and the Seven Yards?"

"It's true, my man." Brooks crouches at eye level with the kid. "But she doesn't like that nickname. Her name is Siena. Can you call her that?"

"But why? Everyone calls her Cece."

"They do." Brooks nods patiently. "But we should let people decide what they want to be called, right? Everyone should feel good about their name."

The audacity.

Who the hell authorized this man to be so utterly charming?

He's been tense in the couple of days since the online speculation about his health started, but Brooks has been nothing but soft and patient with these kids today, determined to show them a good time despite the threat to his career. I haven't been the only one to admire it, either. The parents surrounding me have had their phones out all day, documenting as Brooks demonstrated drills and simple plays, some of them posting their videos online. Perfect for us, as we try to call off the dogs sniffing around for an injury.

A little girl appears at Brooks's side. "Coach, does Cece play football, too?"

"We call her Siena," the boy tells her, glancing at Brooks for his approval.

"That's right, we do. But Siena doesn't play football. It's just me."

Another girl appears. "Girls should play football. Should we teach her?"

Brooks finds me watching in the stands. I shake my head.

"Oh, I think we absolutely should teach her." Brooks rises, beaming as every little face surrounding him turns pleading eyes in my direction.

That little jerk. I lift a leg, indicating my heels. "We have a problem."

"Come on, Miss Siena!"

"Let Coach teach you how to throw!"

"Come on!"

Brooks's lips have disappeared entirely into his mouth as he bites down on a laugh. There's more of them now. A whole swarm of kids surrounding their coach. All calling me onto the field like the children of the corn, ushering me to my demise.

Or, at the very least, to my humiliation.

Brooks looks so utterly pleased with himself as I get to my feet. He comes to lift me over the barrier the same way he did at our first appearance here as a fake couple: arms around my waist, eyes squarely on me.

Except this feels nothing like that time.

This time, his smile is genuine. And my urge to dick-punch him has mellowed to a simmer.

"Sorry to mess up the outfit," he says once I'm on the grass and unstrapping my heels. I toss them off to the side. "I have some spare socks in my bag if you want them."

"I'm good." I wiggle my toes. I'll never complain about being barefoot in the summer. "Full disclosure, me throwing a football would end in an unintentional grounding call, every single time."

"There's no such thing as an unintentional grounding call."

"Exactly. That's how bad I am. They haven't needed it until me."

One of the boys hands Brooks a football. "Thanks, buddy."

Then, because these little hellions really want to kill my mojo, the kid turns and hollers for the entire field to come watch their coach show me how to throw a football. In the stands, I see a few parents pull out their phones and point them at us.

"Oh God," I mutter under my breath. "How mad will Josh be if a video of your girlfriend embarrassing herself on a football field makes the rounds online?"

"Can I tell you a secret, Pip? I can't throw a football worth sh—crap. Can't throw one worth crap. Hey, don't look at me like that—I didn't get paid to throw." He laughs, raises his hands defensively when my jaw drops. "Josh won't care about a video of you blowing a pass. Me, though? There's a good chance I end up the laughingstock of the internet."

"Please don't say that. I can only handle one internet crisis at a time." I contemplate him. "Hold on—you're telling me there's a decent chance I'd be better than you at throwing?"

"I wouldn't say *decent*."

"Dick." I shove him in the shoulder, but the damn wall of bricks doesn't move an inch.

Brooks tuts. "Language, Pip."

We have a full-on audience now—boys and girls watching us avidly, drills on the field long abandoned.

"Show her how you do it, Coach!"

"Yeah! Show us how far you can throw it."

Brooks stares down at the ball in his hands. "I assume that flashing diversion tactic of yours won't fly here."

"You assume correctly," I mutter through a smile. "We're effing screwed."

"We could fake our own deaths?"

I make a wishy-washy sound. "Tried that once. It's harder than you think."

A little girl approaches bravely, pointing at the ball in his hands. "You use the laces to help you throw."

"That's right, Brie. *Exactly* what I was just about to do." Brooks pokes my side when I fail to kill a laugh. He positions his fingertips along the white laces on the football, then turns to the crowd now surrounding us. "On second thought, who wants to demonstrate a pass?"

Several little hands fly into the air, some bouncing up and down as their owners hop on the balls of their feet.

"*Oh*, he's a quick thinker, folks. Consider me impressed."

"I'm more than just a pretty face, Pip." Brooks scans the group with all the patience of a seasoned schoolteacher before pointing to a tiny guy at the very back, doing his best to make himself visible above the taller kids around him. "What do you think, Jax? You want to show Siena how it's done?"

I try to stifle a laugh, which just comes out as a snort. Brooks reaches back and pinches my ass. The snort turns into a gasp as Jax works his way through the crowd with enviable confidence.

"In front of the kids, Brooks? What will they think?"

"That ours is truly a love to aspire to."

"Coat closet encounters aside?"

"I aspire to a thousand more coat closet encounters, so no."

"Bet you do, you horn dog."

Jax makes it to the front and accepts the football Brooks hands him.

"Are you going to catch my pass?" the little guy asks. His awe and excitement are so infectious I'm smiling, too.

"You better believe I am. Don't you dare go easy on me." Brooks waits until Jax lines up at the sideline, then gives me a pointed look. "Now, pay close attention, Siena. God knows you need the lesson."

The smattering of laughter from the kids weaves with my own.

Jax throws the ball in a perfectly executed spiral, but the real beauty is the show Brooks puts on. He launches himself through the air in an exaggerated dive to make the easy catch; crashes to the ground and widens his eyes comically big as he juggles the ball, only to let it fall a foot from where he lies.

"*Fumble!*"

With that, they all race toward him. Brooks's hands fly up to shield himself from their clumsy feet as they fight for the loose ball.

He's so sweet.

Once they take off down the field, Brooks reappears at my side. "And that's what I call a perfectly executed *divert and distract*."

"Evil genius." I stare at his profile, the scar across his cheekbone. "You're really good with kids. You dancing with those junior cheerleaders was real?"

Brooks digs into his pocket for two lollipops. He offers me one before sticking the other in his mouth. "Of course it was real. They're some of my favorite humans."

"Kids or cheerleaders?" I tease.

He pretends to think. "Were you ever a cheerleader?"

"God, no. That pyramid wouldn't stand a chance. Have you seen my hips?"

We're standing so close together, side by side, staring out at the field, that when he reaches for his lollipop, his arm grazes mine. "They're burned into my mind, Pip. All I ever think about."

A whistle goes off nearby. One of the camp volunteers calls for attention as she shuffles the kids between the sets of drills laid out on the field.

"So, you want to be a literal football daddy one day? Driving your own little team to practice in a minivan."

"F—*heck* no. The kids aren't setting foot on a football field unless there's confetti raining down on us and the Lombardi in my hands. I couldn't stomach watching them take a tackle. Getting hurt."

"Says the guy who played on a knee injury."

"Not my smartest move in hindsight." Brooks holds my gaze seven seconds past friendly, and a whole five past appropriate for a children's camp. "It's what happens when I want to impress a pretty girl. I start doing stupid things."

A warm summer breeze ruffles strands of thick waves on top of his head and causes the surface of my skin to tingle. Or maybe that's simply the combined effect of his words and the way he looks at me like I'm his favorite toy.

I don't think he's playing it up for the legions of parents behind us, who can't hear a single word of this.

Goddamn it, Brooks. This wasn't the deal.

"You were trying to impress the Tigers," I remind him.

"And you. Did it work?"

I almost melt into a puddle of overactive hormones then and there. Forward and confident is my catnip.

I eat it up. Would let him wine and dine me, work to impress me before eating *him* up, under better circumstances.

That breeze has done a number on his hair, throwing it forward over his forehead to skim his dark brows. He pushes it back carelessly. And he still hasn't looked away.

What's your angle here, Attwood? Are you trying to fuck me or wife me?

Does it even matter?

Fucking could get messy.

Dating would be . . . a hard limit. Because this particular man is angling to move across the country in a matter of months. Nothing douses the fire in my panties faster than the idea of a cross-country long-distance relationship, wrapped in an endless training and travel schedule.

Tried it. Got my heart broken.

I've never been one to repeat past mistakes. The way I grew up, I had to learn my lessons fast.

I fix my gaze on a boy hopping through an obstacle course of cones ahead of us. "Shouldn't you be coaching? You're depriving the children, Attwood. Not very *football daddy* of you."

"Tell you what: you explain why you don't date athletes, and I'll go out there and coach."

Ding ding ding. There it is.

I'd have preferred a naked proposition.

"Attwood." I shoot him a sharp look. "Why are you asking me that? We recommitted to the rules."

"Siena." The little shit shoots me a panty-melting smirk. "Answer the question. Do it for the children."

Fucking. Catnip.

And my pussy has sniffed it out, the greedy little bitch. He teased her good the night of the gala, and she's begging for more.

Come on, just rub up on him a bit. Give us a little taste.

"Tell me." Brooks steps right into my space, pulling the lollipop from his mouth. The breeze picks up again, feeding me that intoxicating scent of his. The one that lulls me to sleep, wafting off his T-shirts. "What does it take to win you over, little Pippen?"

His gaze rakes over every inch of me, like he expects to find the answer written on my skin. My heart thunders in my ears.

This is the answer. All of this. The sheer confidence, the vague smirk. That piney scent.

I'm a slut for his scent.

No use denying.

"I have to take this call."

One single corner of his mouth ticks up. "Your phone's not ringing."

"It's on silent."

"Then how do you know—"

The universe hands me all my well-earned karma when a loud chime erupts from the back pocket of my jeans.

"Told you." I wave my phone at him. It's Carla calling.

"Lucky break, Pip."

I press the phone to my ear. "Would you keep it down? I'm on a call."

Brooks shakes his head as he backs away onto the field. "Conversation's not over."

"Seriously, keep it down," I call back, before hustling down the sideline. "Carla—remind me to kiss you the next time I see you. You have no idea what you just saved me from."

"You're very welcome, but I think I'm about to do you one better. How would you like to run a charter for us in a couple weeks?"

My heart almost launches itself out of my chest. I yank the lollipop out of my mouth. "Seriously?"

I haven't set foot on the *Lilly Grace*, their sixty-five-foot sailboat, since Dad passed away. Carla and Evan let tourists charter it in the summer months, taking turns between captaining the ship and running their marina.

I've never run a charter by myself, but Carla had helped me get my certification a couple of years ago, once I confessed I'd been interested in the idea. Not that I ever ended up using it.

"I'm perfectly serious. We're hoping to take a few days off to celebrate our anniversary in the city, and it's the only day we can't find anyone to cover for us. Come by during your break tomorrow, let me give you a refresher."

"Carla." I spin, smiling stupidly at the field. I find Brooks with his arms spread wide, half-heartedly blocking a kid trying to round him with a football. He's grinning around the stick from his lollipop, and the sight is just too sweet. "Swear to me you aren't joking."

Carla laughs. "Not in the slightest. You in?"

"I'm so in. *Beyond* in. You just kicked up that little peck to a whole wet slobber of a kiss."

Chapter 22

Brooks

Through the windshield of my parked car, I watch Siena make her way to the boardwalk. She's wearing a skirt and polo combination that really does her legs, her waist, her fucking ankles justice.

She's so pretty from head to toe, and I sit behind the wheel, just staring after her on her way to Ship Happens like I do every morning. More than once, I've been tempted to walk her right to the shop itself. But seeing as she always leaps out of my car before I can even get the door open for her, I have to assume she'd laugh me right back into my seat.

She's self-sufficient. No doubt it's a by-product of having to raise herself until she turned thirteen, and I like that about her. Admire the hell out of it. But can't a man open her goddamn door once in a while?

Or, maybe they can. Maybe she lets them, if they're the right kind of guy.

Siena disappears around the corner to the boardwalk, and I groan into the silent car, bouncing my forehead on the steering wheel over and over.

I don't date athletes anymore.

I'd believed her that night in bed. Her words were such a blanket statement that my innate competitiveness got me past it. I figured I could dig up what that idiot Ivers did to her. Correct course on her opinion of athletes. Command myself never to bash in his face the next time I see him on a field, for his yet-to-be-uncovered offense against Siena.

But the more I analyze it, the more I think . . .

She told me her breakup with Ivers hadn't been a bad one. She still slept in his shirts, for fuck's sake, until I packed mine into her suitcase. This couldn't be about him.

Maybe it was her way of turning me down without hurting my feelings. Which she's perfectly entitled to do, but . . . Shit.

Between the online gossip and the injury, it's been hard to keep the faith that this comeback will work out. That I'm good enough to return, that teams—*my* team—want me to return. Only two things have managed to keep me grounded in the weeks since, and I can't even tell if one of them likes me back.

Pete, thankfully, lets me cuddle him without protest.

A sound chimes inside the car, and I find two phones tucked into the cupholders between our seats. They're identical, but when I tap the one lighting up with texts, its background is a bright picture of the bay with a sailboat in the distance.

Well, well. If I didn't know any better, I'd think this was fate acting in my favor.

I kill the engine and make my way along the boardwalk, scanning the row of bright storefronts until I find a square of navy blue bricks with the words *Ship Happens* painted on the large window.

The glass door chimes on my way into the small shop. Aside from the navy shiplap wall framing the checkout desk and the colorful lures dangling from the ceiling, it's exactly how I'd imagine the inside of a bait and tackle shop. Tall metal shelves flanking a handful of aisles, scuffed-up white linoleum. More bluish fluorescent lighting than natural light.

If I didn't find Siena busy behind the counter, I'd think I was in the wrong place.

She's told me just how much her late father loved this shop, how important it was to him. But seeing someone as vibrant as Siena in a drab place like this puts a pit in my stomach.

She belongs out there. Under the sun, in the water. On a mountaintop, doing that little shimmy she does when she shows off an outfit.

"Hey," she says when she spots me hovering by the door. "Everything okay?"

"Everything's fine. You forgot your phone in the car." I drop our phones on the counter and let my fascinated gaze wander again. "The infamous Ship Happens. Where all the magic happens."

Siena chuckles, tucks her chin to her chest as she refocuses on her laptop. "Not sure there's much magic left here."

It's a surprising slipup, seeing as I've never seen her do anything less than glow when she talks about this place. Or maybe it's when she talks about it in the context of her father.

"Excuse me." A man with a baseball cap low on his face pops out from behind me. "Where can I find your live bait?"

"At the end of aisle three, and to your right." Siena offers him a smile before turning back to me. "Stick around any longer and I might put you to work."

I can't tell whether she's gently dismissing me or giving me an opening to leave, but I ignore both.

"So put me to work, Pip."

I lean my elbows on the counter, leaving barely a foot of space between us. It takes no effort to fiddle with the anchor around her neck, straighten the chain. Siena stares at me while I do. She might cap this thing between us at flirtation, but she always blesses me with a glimpse of something sweet when I fix that necklace.

I can't tell whether she likes me—at least, not the way I like her—but she definitely likes it when I do that.

A woman approaches the counter, clearing her throat. "Where can I find the live bait?"

Siena darts upright, shooting me a look of warning like she hadn't been giving me doe eyes a second ago. "At the end of aisle three, and to your right."

The moment the woman is on her way, Siena heaves a sigh and stares at her laptop. My Siena—the one I know outside this shop—is all playful quips, laughter at my expense, and flawless smiles.

She's different in here, though.

"Busy day already?"

She nods. "Business is up since we started fake-dating. Have you heard back from Josh?"

"He says it's a wait-and-see game now, whether teams buy everything you've been posting." Siena's made it to a couple of training sessions since the kids' camp, posting a few videos of Parker putting me through the ringer. "If all else fails, maybe the ass-hugging shorts you requested will sufficiently distract them."

"I hope so. Keep me posted, okay?" No flirting, no teasing, no nothing. Siena's gaze drifts over my shoulder as the sound of quiet laughter approaches the counter.

"No, no, that's definitely her," a hushed male voice says. "Think her name is Cece."

"Imagine fucking all these players and still working the till, selling worms and fishing rods," another guy says with a laugh. Unlike his buddy, he doesn't seem worried about the way his voice carries. "The hot ones are always the worst on their knees, I swear."

I'm so shocked by what I'm hearing that it takes me a moment to react. Siena looks so bored by the whole thing I almost question hearing it.

Still, I straighten up off the counter.

Then she lifts her eyebrows, and it stops me right in my tracks. Suddenly she's there. Siena Pippen with that flare in those blue-gray eyes. The telltale sign that she's about to slice through your ego with a machete and enjoy the hell out of it.

"Do you feel that?" she asks me at full volume. "I *think* it's small-dick energy. But I've never been around one of those before now, so I can't be sure."

"Hey now, don't be mad." A future corpse in shorts and an open linen shirt sidles up to the counter, either unfazed or unaware that he's on the verge of death. "I don't have millions in the bank, but I can still show you a good time, baby girl. Teach you exactly how to suck good—"

"You watch your fucking mouth when you're talking to her."

My presence seems to finally penetrate his thick fucking skull. He pales like the little bitch he is and backs away from the counter, bumping right into his friend.

"Ah, fuck."

"That's the correct reaction." I take a step toward him, because it's about damn time he has his pathetic little neck snapped, but Siena's hand closes around my shirt.

"Don't worry, baby. I've got this." I don't know which part hits me hardest. The offhand *baby* or the utter, terrifying calm in her voice. Siena holds out her hand toward the man and crooks her fingers until he offers her the Styrofoam container he'd been holding. "Will that be all?"

He coughs. "Yeah. Just the bait. Thanks."

With a sickly sweet smile, she rounds the counter, pries open the lid on the container. And flips it over the guy's head. Damp dirt and worms rain over his hair, his face, his gaping mouth.

Goddamn.

Siena tosses him the empty container, which he fumbles, then calmly takes her place behind the counter like nothing happened. "Get the fuck out of my shop."

They start hustling to the door but hit the brakes when I get in their way.

"You're forgetting your manners." I tip my head in Siena's direction. "Apologize."

"She covered me in fucking worms, man—"

"I'll cover you in worse in a second." I jerk my chin at the check-out counter. "Apologize."

They mutter their apologies to a deadpan Siena and scurry out of the shop before my next breath. Leaving me simultaneously raging, ready to punch through a wall, and insanely turned on by the way she handled them like the trash they are.

My badass girl can hold her own, and it's the hottest thing. But Siena is already typing at her laptop, so unbothered I'm once again questioning whether I imagined the whole scene.

Too unbothered.

"What the fuck, Pip? Has this happened before?"

"They're not the first, won't be the last. I've been dealing with creeps like that since I was a kid. You should meet my landlord."

"*Your landlord?* Is he inappropriate?"

"He's fine. It's under control." Unfazed, she reaches for a broom in the corner behind the counter. "The *spreading my legs for millions* thing is a new angle, obviously. For every person who likes us together, there's another two coming in here swinging their micro dicks with something to say."

"Jesus." I rub my face and cut her off before she makes it around the counter, taking the broom from her. "Let me do that."

"I've got it."

"I didn't say you didn't. I said I wanted to do it for you." I get busy sweeping the earthy fallout into its original container. "You sure you're all right, Pip? None of that was okay."

"I'm sure. They caught me on a good day." Siena pauses her typing long enough to shoot me a smile. "Though I appreciated the backup."

"Not that you needed me," I mutter, sweeping up the last of the damp dirt streaking over the linoleum.

"If you'd laid a hand on them it would have been the nail in the coffin for your chances with the Rebels. And men with egos like that? They don't make a peep about being knocked down a peg by a woman."

I'm on the verge of telling her exactly how many flimsy shits I give about my chances with the Rebels when it comes to people talking to her that way. But the shop door chimes open ahead of a man with shaggy gray hair, and he's not three feet into the shop before calling, "Do you have any live bait?"

"For fuck's sake with the live bait," I mutter. I replace the lid on the filled Styrofoam container and hand it to him. "Here you go."

"Oh. Thanks." The man's gaze bounces between me and Siena before he inches farther into the shop. "I'm going to . . . look at a few more things."

"Take your time." Siena's smile falls the second the customer is out of sight. It's not hard to miss that she looked more alive lighting up those assholes than she does right now. Than she has at any point since I've walked into this shop.

It's like this place has neutralized her.

"What is this, Pip?"

She glances up and seems to gather exactly what I mean by the look on my face, because her gaze immediately falters. I've never seen her falter.

"Siena. What the hell are you doing here?"

She takes a breath. "On a normal day? I'm here doing my job running the family business. Today?" To my surprise, she breaks into a smile. "I'm only here setting things up before I get to sail a charter on my family friends' sailboat."

I imagine her behind an oversized wheel, big sails ahead of her and the wind blowing in her hair. That's a lot more like it.

I whistle. "As in, Captain Pippen?"

"As in Captain Pippen, at least for today. I got certified a couple of years ago, thinking that maybe I could . . ." She loses steam, smile slipping. "Anyway."

She claps her laptop closed and rounds the counter, peeking down a couple of aisles before calling, "Aidan, I'm heading out. You sure you have this under control?"

"All good, Cee."

The little shithead comes out of a door near the counter. I know there's nothing going on between them—I believe Siena when she says she ended their arrangement.

But as far as I'm concerned, anyone who's seen Siena Pippen naked is at the top of my shit list until approximately the end of time.

"Just remember to—"

"Remember to call Brian about the glitch in the POS system. I'm on it as soon as I finish restocking the reels. Don't you have to get down to the docks?"

"Yes, but the shipment of bait arrives at—"

Aidan actually has the balls to look me in the eye, which . . . good for him. "Get your girl on that ship before I jump off the pier and forget how to swim."

I don't know whether I respect him more for rightfully calling her my girl, or for offering to rid me of himself.

Either way, I take the rare opportunity to put my hands on Siena and toss her over my shoulder, sweeping her bag off the counter along with our phones, which I tuck into my back pocket.

She gasps. "Attwood, I swear to God. If you don't put me down right fucking now—"

I march out of the shop, nodding at a customer who pauses just outside the door to watch us in alarm. "Morning."

"*Attwood.*"

"This is probably a bad time to tell you what a turn-on it is when you're stern with me. And I'm already half hard from watching you decimate limp-dicked frat boys, so you're really playing with fire."

She smacks my ass as we move down the boardwalk. "Stern is the least of your concerns."

There she is. My playful girl right back at it, the moment that vitamin D hits her skin.

I whistle. "Do that again and I might drop 'em and bend over for you right here. I've never been spanked, but I think I might like it." I wink at a passing couple, who startle at my words. "We've been dating nine months. Good to shake things up, you know?"

Siena huffs a laugh up on my shoulder. "You're scaring people."

"Nah, did you see that guy's face? Pretty sure he was ready to bend over, too. We're sexual trendsetters. He'll be jacking it in a coat closet in no time."

I find the entrance to the marina along the boardwalk and carry her down the wide dock lined with boats of all sizes. "Which one's your ride?"

Siena grips my hips to steady herself as she cranes her neck around me. "The sixty-five-footer with the black trim down at the end."

"This is the boat you supposedly fished on?"

She sighs dreamily. "Isn't she beautiful?"

Seeing as I know next to nothing about boats, I'll have to take her word for it. I set her down at the mouth of a narrower dock leading to the sailboat and reach to smooth the hair off her face.

She mixes her hands with mine, trying to get me to relent. "I've got it."

My arms drop to my sides. *Can't even fix her hair for her.*

I take her phone out of my pocket and tuck it into hers. "What time do you dock tonight?"

"Six thirty, but I need to get a couple things done at the shop before heading home. If it's too late for you to pick me up, then don't worry about—"

I sigh, probably louder than I have in my whole life. What is this fucking nonsense?

Who the hell made this woman feel like she was anything remotely close to a bother? She's the most self-sufficient person I know.

"You will call me when you're back on land, and I will come get you. Don't argue with me on that." I take her by the shoulders and turn her toward the boat. "I'll see you tonight, Captain."

Chapter 23

Brooks

"Brooks, have you seen this?"

Summer's French braids sway as she hurries across the rehab center with a copy of *Around the League*, a national sports publication, tucked under an arm and her phone in her hand. I don't know which of the two the *this* in question is coming from, but the panic is plain on her face and plentiful enough to raise my blood pressure. The rehab center, adjacent to the UOB gym facility, is empty but for us this early in the morning, dotted with various training equipment and plush tables like the ones I'm perched on.

Parker's hands pause on my knee, which he's been obsessively tweaking since the injury. "No. Nope." He shakes his head. "Take whatever bullshit you've uncovered away from here, Prescott. We're dealing with enough."

I tend to agree with him. Summer grimaces in apology as she reaches us, handing me her phone. "I can't believe Josh hasn't been calling you. There's . . . a video."

The screen is open to the *All-Stars* website, the same gossip site that anointed me Siena's boyfriend just a month ago. "*Are Cece Pippen and Brooks Attwood bringing a new meaning to the words* play fake?

This video suggests they might be," I read out, dread prickling at me as I hit play on the video in question. Parker rises to have a look.

It's me and Siena, back at the alumni game. Rather, us on the jumbotron, half of which shows me jogging down the field after a touchdown, grinning at her. While she sits in the stands in my number eleven jersey, arms and legs crossed. Looking annoyed as all hell as the crowd around her celebrates. Conveniently, the video cuts off before I hauled her onto the field. Before she kissed me.

I know she had trouble faking it in those early days, but that's a look that plainly says *I can't fucking stand you.*

"Josh is going to kill me." I scroll through the article speculating about the validity of our relationship. The comments section seems divided between those accusing us of faking it, and those wondering what I must've done to end up in the doghouse that night. "Why is this coming out *now*? It's been a month since."

I scroll back up. The video is being credited to an anonymous source. Between this, the knee, and the resurfaced back-alley photos that started all this, I seem to be suffering from a bad case of karmic retribution. Something—or some*one*—out there doesn't want me playing again. Seems to be doing whatever they can to prevent it.

"It's not too bad, is it?" Parker tosses me the black fabric knee brace I've started wearing during our sessions. "You've been seen since, looking a lot more . . . together."

"It's 'not too bad' that the only reason the Rebels think I've got my act together is being called into question?" I consider calling Josh myself, but leave my phone buried in my bag. It's only a matter of time before he starts losing it, and I'll take the breather while I can.

Parker winces. "Right. It's bad."

I pull on the brace and test my knee by bouncing on the balls of my feet. Parker's really worked his magic on it. It'll be good as new by the time I hit the Rebels training camp. Assuming I get an invite.

Which, with this fresh hell I've just been dealt . . .

"At the risk of giving Josh a run for his money as the bearer of bad news," Summer says slowly, flipping open her copy of *Around the League*.

I groan. "You're kidding, right?"

"They've ranked all the NFL's unrestricted free agents by position and likelihood of starting the season on a roster." Parker joins her up on the treatment table where she's sitting and flicks the end of her French braid out of the way to get a better look at the magazine in her hands.

"And?"

"You're number three among receivers."

I shut my eyes. "Doug McDaniels is number one?"

"I'm sorry. They're predicting he'll go to the Rebels."

Fucker. *Fucker.*

"Don't sweat it, man. These lists are bullshit." Parker plucks the magazine from Summer's hands and tosses it away.

"It's not bullshit. Josh is in touch with their general manager every day, trying to suss them out. It sounds like they're fifty-fifty between us, and that was without people wondering whether I'm injured, or faking a relationship just to get signed. Josh thinks there's a chance that we'll both be invited to training camp, which would be . . ."

Spending time with my ex's affair partner, while the woman in question sits in the stands watching?

Hell. It would be hell.

A phone chimes from somewhere in this room, loud over the sounds of weights hitting the black rubber floor and grunts from beefy dudes out in the gym. It grates on me, but I suck a breath into my lungs, trying to unwind the tension in my shoulders. "I hate that any part of this comes down to anything I do off the field."

I'll bet all Doug McDaniels has to do is play well, flash the Rebels a dumb smile, read them his mediocre stats.

"You need to forget all this chatter. Stay focused on what you can control," Parker says. "Let them hear how you're entertaining the Tigers. Play the part with your loving girlfriend. I can shuffle around some of my clients to put in more time training you, if you want."

My stomach pangs. "You think I need to put in more time?"

"Not what I meant. I'd rather we take a week off, give that knee time to fully heal." Parker lifts an eyebrow. "But I'm not stupid enough to think you won't take this as a sign to spend more time in your gym at home. If you're going to keep running yourself ragged, I'd rather you do it under our supervision."

"You've been going easy on me since the Tigers scrimmage—"

"Yes. Kind of the point."

That ringtone picks up again, and I scan the empty facility. "For fuck's sake, whose phone is that? Answer the damn thing."

"That would be yours, jackass." Parker toes my bag, sitting on the floor between us. "Cute new ringtone, though."

I dig through the bag. When I tap the phone to life, I find Siena's picture of the bay underneath several notifications. "It's Siena's. I must have switched our phones by mistake." Guess I know why I haven't heard from Josh. The phone goes off again. Her mom calling.

"Answer it," Summer suggests.

"I can't. That would be in clear violation of the *no meeting friends and family* rule." I stare at her picture of the water. I hope she's having a great time out there. I've never seen her come to life so fast as when she mentioned the charter.

"Uh-oh," Summer says. I look up in time to see her and Parker exchange a smug look. "It appears we've hit a snag in the fake relationship. Namely, it isn't fake anymore."

"Not according to the internet."

They both stare at me like they're ready to argue to the death the moment I start denying it. But I've spent the past couple of weeks hitting a wall with Siena, and it's draining enough. I pluck a pack of gummy worms from my gym bag, needing the pick-me-up as I lie back on my treatment table. "You really wanna hear all this? You always complain your clients treat you like their therapist."

"You're already moping on my treatment table. Besides, you know how Parker likes to meddle in relationships. He's salivating for it, look."

Parker bumps her with his shoulder. "*Thanks*, Sum."

I laugh because it's true. He'd done his fair share of meddling in his sister's life a few months ago, puppeteering a reunion with our friend Zac.

"Maybe I learned my lesson. I'm minding my own business." Parker watches Summer kick off her sneakers and wince as she stretches out her leg. "Tight?"

"I added weight to my deadlifts yesterday."

"Attagirl." He catches her leg and coaxes it up between them, digging his thumb into her hamstrings. "So, what's the issue with Siena? If anyone asks, you can say it's real now."

"It's not real. Not for her, anyway. She says she won't date athletes since her ex."

Parker glances up from Summer's thigh. "Why?"

"She hasn't felt the need to explain." I rub my face roughly. "Lately I've been thinking . . . Maybe it's bullshit. Maybe it's her way of letting me down easy."

After our breakup, it became abundantly clear that Naomi hadn't liked much about me other than the lifestyle I gave her. The fancy parties, attention from fans, and celebrity connections to the team. It hadn't bothered me in the thick of it, but the moment I caught her with McDaniels, it clicked. I could have been plucked clean from the picture, replaced by anyone else with some kind of status, and she'd have been happy.

Not that I've gone out of my way to date in the time since I emerged from a literal and metaphorical back alley, but it's not as though I've had a line of women come knocking. That couldn't be a coincidence, could it? I lose football, and suddenly I'm undesirable.

What, exactly, have I offered Siena, anyway? Grief over being in the wrong place at the wrong time that first day? An orgasm? Hell, I hadn't even achieved that on my own.

I sigh, loud and unrestrained in this empty treatment facility.

Midnight skinny-dips. Somehow, even the memory of Siena's voice from that first day helps clear the fog of insecurity. *What's your thing? When you're sighing that hard?*

How sad is it that I think *she's* my thing?

Us in a bed, lights off. Just listening to her soft voice in the dark, telling me stories.

"You're spiraling." Parker is watching me carefully.

"Yeah. I'm spiraling."

"If this is about Naomi—"

"No. It's nothing to do with that." I lie as firmly as I can. Because how humiliating is it that she was able to mess with my head like this? "Siena doesn't see it with me. If it's up to her, we end the second I get signed."

Summer tears her gaze off the trajectory of Parker's fingers over her leggings to turn a sharp look on me. "Brooks, you know I love you to pieces."

Parker smirks. "So why does it sound like you're gonna rip him a new one?"

Summer shrugs. "I'm only going to point out that, this time last year, he thought he'd never step onto a football field in full gear again. And now, the top industry publication is predicting he lands on a roster before the first kickoff of the season."

"Technically, they say I'm third in line."

"The point remains," Summer insists. "So what if Siena doesn't see it with you right this second? It doesn't mean she never will." She

jabs a finger in my direction. "You're not the type to sit around feeling
sorry for yourself. You're a fighter. So act like one, goddamn it."

Siena's phone rings, **MOM** flashing across the screen again.

Parker shrugs. "Pick it up. What's the worst that can happen?"

Chapter 24

Siena

I'm still buzzing as I make my way out of the marina and onto the boardwalk, which is quiet except for the predictable line coming out of Molly's Chowder Cove down at the very end.

Unless I count midnight swims in the bay, I haven't been out on the water in the years since Dad passed. I'd expected it to feel at least a little painful, being back on the ship where he and I spent so much time. But that was the place we shared so many laughs. Where he'd let me swim around as he fished, effectively scaring away any potential catch and not caring one bit. Indulging in those memories, and the heat of the sun on my skin, eclipsed any kind of pain I might have felt.

I've got a mountain of administrative work for the shop after playing hooky all day. But today has got me wondering if I can somehow juggle both. Maybe talk Evan and Carla into letting me run a couple of charters a week. Finally put that certification to good use the way I'd planned to, before I had to take over Ship Happens.

I blink down at the phone I pull out of my bag. I hadn't had a second to check it on the ship today, but the moment I tap it to life I realize it isn't my phone at all. The home screen is littered with unopened notifications, over a picture of a gigantic German shepherd. Brooks must have handed me the wrong phone this morning.

I chuckle, admiring both the picture of his dog and the fact that Brooks is so head over heels for him that he'd give Peter this kind of prime real estate. It's downright adorable.

And then I take a proper look at the text previews within his notifications. There are a handful from his agent Josh, demanding Brooks returns his calls, interspersed with some from an unknown number.

207-826-5848: Pip, if you see this, we mixed up our . . .

207-826-5848: I answered your phone when your . . .

207-826-5848: She broke her leg falling down the stairs . . .

My heart sinks into my stomach at the words, and then right into my gut when I recognize the phone number. Brooks has been texting from my mom's phone.

~~~~~

I follow the sound of the tap running in my parents' tiny kitchen. Stupidly, I expect to find Mom at the sink, blond hair pulled off her face with a tortoiseshell claw clip the way it normally is.

Or maybe I hoped to see her there, that Brooks's texts had been wrong. That my sweet mom, who already lives in severe pain given her arthritis, hadn't fallen, hadn't broken her leg, hadn't tried to call me while I was unable to get to her.

It's not Mom at the sink, though. It's Brooks standing with his back to me, so intent on the dishes he's washing that he doesn't even look around.

My heart sinks and lifts at the same time.

"Brooks."

He starts so hard soapy water splashes back on him. Brooks wipes the suds off his forehead with the back of an arm, staring at me carefully like I'm a skittish animal about to take off.

"She's in her room. She's okay. We just had some dinner."

Dinner? He fed my mom. I gulp down the sob building in my throat. It gets stuck halfway down, a thick and painful lump. I'm seconds away from losing it in front of him.

"I'm going to check on her." I escape before he finishes a single nod, throwing my hair into a messy bun on top of my head, sweaty from my lung-searing run home to get to Mom.

I crack open Mom's bedroom door and peek inside to find her in bed with a cast on her leg, propped up on a stack of pillows. She does look okay. Cheerful, even, as she crochets the atrociously yellow and teal blanket she's been working on, her latest endeavor to help maintain the joints in her hands. The weight sitting on my chest since the moment I checked Brooks's phone lifts. I take my first full breath in nearly twenty minutes.

"Siena?" Mom says without looking up from her crochet hook. I swing the door open wider. "You're staring like you expect me to burst into flames."

She tucks her work aside when I sit at the edge of the bed. "I'm sorry I missed your calls. My phone—"

"Was with Brooks. He filled me in." She says *Brooks* with so much familiarity, it's like she's known him for years. "He's lovely, angel, and I sure put him through some drama. He took me to the hospital to get fixed up after I fell down the stairs, then let me beat him in several rounds of cribbage all day."

A chuckle bursts out of my mouth. "He knows how to play cribbage?"

"I taught him. He's *terrible*." Mom reaches to stroke the hair off my face. "I'm sorry I worried you. But I'm glad I finally got to meet your boyfriend."

My guilt is a living, breathing thing inside me, rearing its head at the sight of Mom practically glowing on the word *boyfriend*. It's exactly why I never wanted them to cross paths. She'd been so disappointed when my last relationship ended, waved a tearful goodbye to any chance of a wedding and grandbabies in the near future. And seeing as Tom never had an ounce of Brooks's charm, I'm guessing this impending breakup will hit her even worse.

"I know you said it isn't serious, but if you ask me, there's nothing more legitimate than showing up to look after your girlfriend's old goat of a mother."

A new kind of guilt twists inside me, sharp like the razor tip of a knife. Brooks and I agreed to surface level. I'm his fake girlfriend, a means to an end, and he certainly never signed up to save my poor mother on a random Thursday, when he likely had a whole host of better things to do.

You'd better hope you're worth all that trouble.

I get to my feet and make it to the door before turning back to plant a kiss on top of Mom's head. "I'm glad you're okay."

Mom must see the acute guilt in my face because she hisses, "Siena, do not go out there and sabotage this relationship. Do you hear—"

I snap the door shut behind me, drowning out her hushed warning. I'm not going to sabotage it. If anything, the situation requires quick and thorough damage control.

Back in the kitchen, I find Brooks wrestling with a layer of plastic wrap, trying to get it to cling to a plate of chocolate chip cookies on the counter.

He shoots me a sheepish smile when he finds me staring. "These are fine sitting out for a couple of days, but I'd probably put them in the fridge if they're not gone by Saturday."

My gaze falls to the plate. "You made those?"

"It's my mom's recipe. I learned to bake before I could ride a bike." He peers down at the plate, moving as though he means to offer me one but thinks better of it for whatever reason. "They don't look like much, but your mom said she liked them."

He's tentative in a way I've never seen from him, usually so collected and confident.

When I don't do anything but stare, Brooks adds, "I know we said we wouldn't cross this line. But she kept calling while I was at the gym, and you weren't on land. I couldn't leave her hanging."

My stomach plummets. "You skipped training to come look after my mom?"

"Of course I did, Pip."

I picture Mom, crumpled up at the foot of the stairs. While I was out on the ship, having the time of my life. Unable to do anything to help even if I'd known. And Brooks, the guy who wouldn't let the pain in his own body keep him off the field, who wants this comeback more than anything, had to take the day off to step up when I didn't. Pressure builds in my chest, so heavy and goddamn painful.

After another too-long silence, he tucks his hand in his pockets and asks, "Have I upset you?"

Dagger straight to the heart. The soft tone of his voice, the question on his gorgeous face.

I find that I . . . very much hate Brooks uncertain.

I hate Brooks questioning whether he's done the right thing. I hate him losing his swagger, that confident edge. Especially when he's done a very, very right thing. Saved my ass in a way I could never repay him for.

I'm unraveling. That pressure surges up my throat, and I'm on the verge of damn tears again. I'm filled with the overwhelming urge to hold him or touch him in some way, to thank him and beg him to tell me everything will be fine, and how I can make this up to him. The titanium crate inside me where I keep every miserable thought and agonizing memory is bloating fast, threatening to burst and take me down with it.

You'd better hope you're worth all that trouble.

Brooks must be able to tell how close to the edge I am, because he begins moving around the small island.

"Stop." I throw up my hands before he can get any closer. I know there'll be no holding it together if he lays a finger on me. Brooks stops so quickly he kind of sways on the spot. "I really don't want to cry."

I take breath after breath until I can think about my stupidly sweet, pretend, temporary boyfriend bridal-carrying my injured mom out of this house, without my body screaming for tearful release.

Brooks stares back with a soft smile. He holds out his arms. "Please come here."

"I'm really okay."

"I said please, Pip. My next move is pouting, and you *really* don't want to see me pout. It's extremely convincing. Like, lethal levels of convincing. And I'd rather you come to me of your own free will."

"Brooks . . ."

His deep brown eyes go earnest and round.

"Oh my God." I huff a laugh. This man has a screw loose, I swear.

Brooks's lips curve down at the corners, exaggerated to the fullest. And then he sniffs.

Sniffs.

My fit of giggles threatens a different type of tears. The good kind, often and presently accompanied by a warm tingle up my arms and a flutter low in my stomach. And now we're just standing here, grinning at each other like a pair of fools.

"I told you it was good." Brooks's arms come out again. "Can I hold you now?"

I let him. The fingers of one hand dig into the hair at the back of my head while the others spread on the small of my back. I lean into his body, surprisingly at ease considering it's the first time we've touched like this without an audience.

"Brooks, thank you. I know how much this comeback means to you. I don't take it lightly that you missed training to do this for me."

"I was happy to, Pip. Well—not happy about Rachel breaking her leg. You know what I mean."

I pull back to look at him. "Rachel? You're on a first-name basis with my mom now?"

"I let that woman hand me my ass at cribbage for an entire afternoon. You bet your ass we're on a first-name basis." Through the tangle of hair caught between his fingers, Brooks strokes his fingertips along the back of my neck. "And by the way, I think she withheld a few key points when she taught me how to play. Because there's no way I'm that bad. I refuse to believe it."

I prop my chin on his chest. "How can I pay you back for this? I swear, I'll do anything. Clean your toilets. Walk Pete every day until you move back to LA."

Brooks gazes down at me for a long, quiet moment. "I'd rather you tell me who made you feel like you owe people for looking after you." He shakes his head when I start to deny it. "Offering to clean my toilets, Pip? You work in your parents' shop even though you very clearly hate it—"

My heart attempts to leap out of my throat. I clap a hand over his mouth before he can say any more, shoot a glance over my shoulder. "She can hear you."

He glances through the kitchen doorway. "She's in her room with the door closed."

"Trust me, you can hear everything from the bedrooms." I grip the front of his shirt and tug him into the small backyard, closing the sliding glass door carefully behind us before facing him. "Brooks, I appreciate everything you've done today, but you don't get to come here and blow up my relationship with my mom because you think you know what's best for me. I don't need saving."

His gaze remains steady on me. "I know you don't. I only want to understand."

"There's nothing to understand. I'm doing right by my parents. They gave me everything when I had nothing."

I plan to leave it at that, because today has already gone well past surface level and I'm really itching to go back inside and be that thirty-one-year-old who curls up in bed with her mom.

My feet stay rooted on the spot, though. I'm stuck on the patience in Brooks's eyes.

"Siena, who made you feel like this?"

I can't tell whether I need *him* to know or *someone* to know.

Because I'm exhausted. Keeping this inside for seventeen years has been *exhausting*.

But I can't do it here. Not where Mom can hear.

"Okay," I tell Brooks. "I'll give you this, if you give me something I've been missing."

Chapter 25

Siena

"Fuck, fuck, fuck, fuck."

I do my best not to giggle.

Not at Brooks's stream of words in the speaker in my ear, nor at the way his fingertips dig into my waist as we rip down the final stretch of deserted dirt road cutting through pine trees. I bring my bike to a smooth stop at the opening of a clearing I've visited more than once in my lifetime.

Instantly, I miss the wind flapping through the ends of my hair. It's as close to the feeling of sailing a boat as I can get on land. The freedom, the weightlessness.

Brooks hadn't been wrong to gripe about my lack of leathers that first morning he picked me up for work, so I wore a leather jacket tonight to appease him. After making sure Mom was set up for a little while, we'd picked him up his own jacket and a brand-new helmet before we took off.

Despite his sheer terror during the ride, Brooks looks so good coming off my bike—swinging his long leg off the side so gracefully, shedding his helmet, tunneling his fingers through the unruly waves on his head. Tugging off his black leather jacket and tossing it on the seat of the bike, over mine.

He's so damn stunning, it's sick.

He stares around at the surrounding pines. "Josh would kick my ass into the ground if he found out I did that."

I comb my fingers through my hair. It's a lost cause, though. Back up it goes into a chaotic bun. "Why's that?"

"Our livelihoods rely on my body remaining intact." He follows me through a small break in the trees on one side of the road. "And both NFL contracts I've signed included several clauses against anything like the death trap you just made me ride."

"I don't know, Attwood. You can't convince me you didn't love that." There's a fresh hop in my step, not unlike the one I had coming off the sailboat a couple of hours ago.

The trees fall away, and we're left with the most gorgeous view in the county. The edge of the cliff overlooks the sprawling bay. Boats dot the water, with the boardwalk in the distance. Dirt and dried-up pine needles under our feet. I'd stare up at this cliff from the boat whenever Dad and I used to take it out, until I finally found a way up here years ago.

I like to pretend I'm the only one who knows about it, even though the tire tracks in the dirt road leading up the small mountain tell a different story.

Brooks sits at my side on the bed of pine needles, feet dangling off the cliff face. There's not a foot of space between us. He blinks around with something of a smile.

He feels it—the same exhilaration, persistent adrenaline flowing through me. From the ride and the endless water below us.

I knew he'd like it.

Brooks Attwood has a little reckless in him, too. I'd felt it on that gala dance floor. Heard it in the way he said nothing had matched the adrenaline rush of playing football in the years since he retired.

I doubt this measures up to his dream of winning a championship with the Rebels, but maybe it helps to know there's more than one way to fill whatever void he's felt. Football isn't the be-all and end-all.

He's so much more than that.

"This feels sacred," he says without looking at me. "You bringing me to your secret spot."

"The house we were just in is just as sacred to me. My mom is sacred to me. May as well go all in."

He nods. "Are you upset I did that today?"

"More . . . uncomfortable. I prefer to handle my own business." I reach over the edge of the cliff to roll up the pant legs of my jeans. With a soft grunt and a *goddamn it* under his breath, Brooks grips the back of my T-shirt, as though to stop me from falling into the bay.

He's sweet. Too sweet.

Making me feel things I shouldn't.

I can feel his heavy stare. Acute awareness presses against every inch of me—my cheek, my arms, down to my toes. I should tell him to stop, to add a bit of distance between where we sit now, but nothing comes out of my mouth.

"Do you trust me?"

His question catches me off guard, but it's his soft delivery that really squeezes my heart. He's so stripped back today. Careful, more than a touch vulnerable, and I don't know what to do with it.

"Do you want me to?"

"I do. Very much." Brooks pauses. "I trust you."

What are you trying to do to me?

My throat closes up, nose prickles. I don't know where this is coming from, but I take a moment to fight the responding sob building in my throat.

This—*we* are moving in such a stupid, irresponsible direction. Feelings were not meant to be part of the equation.

"I lied to you," I say. Hoping he flies off the handle. Gets his guard up.

Brooks doesn't even flinch. "Okay."

"You asked a while ago whether I went looking for my birth parents. I told you no, but I did see them again. A year after they left. They were passing through town and tracked me down at school. Said they wanted me back."

My heart pounded so hard it hurt, when that familiar voice called my name from across my high school parking lot. I'd been heading home at the end of the day, turned and found the woman I'd last seen in our old kitchen the night before she left me.

I didn't go looking for them, but it was certainly a lie by omission. Still, all Brooks says is "Okay."

It was easier when I couldn't stand him. I fiddle nervously with the anchor charm around my neck, trying to figure out where to start. I've never told this to anyone. Not my parents. Not Shy.

"By the looks of their back seat, they'd been living in their car. And the years I was with them . . . well, you know about that." I shake my head because it's my history, things I've actually lived, and it still feels unbelievable. "I don't know what possessed me to do it, but I told them about the Robertses. And that I wasn't going to leave with them."

"You don't have to justify not wanting to go back to that."

"Well, they didn't like it. Whatever reason they had for coming for me . . . it was gone the second I told them. Their parting words were *you'd better hope you're worth all that trouble.* And I didn't understand the full extent of what they meant until later."

Brooks stares off into the distance, the rapidly setting sun streaking blues and oranges across the sky. His body looks tense, locked up. Like he's anticipating a kick to the gut.

"The way my parents took me in wasn't exactly legal. I had a maternal aunt I should have gone to after my birth parents left, but she wasn't much better than my birth mother."

My parents had gone about their research discreetly, and they'd figured out quick that seeking legal guardianship would likely have me taken away. But they hadn't been the only ones to realize it.

"You want to know how I know you can hear everything from the bedrooms at the house? A year after I last saw my birth parents, I woke up in the middle of the night to my mom crying in the kitchen. She and Dad were talking about my birth parents, how they'd come around earlier that day. To *collect their payment*, Brooks."

A bird lands on the edge of the cliff, just a few feet away. It ruffles its feathers, pulling my attention from Brooks's growing frown. I'm grateful for the distraction and take a moment to soothe the squeeze in my stomach, the nausea that always comes when I let myself dwell on this part.

"Apparently, they'd come by the house after I refused to leave with them the year before. Threatened to go to the police because I wasn't staying there legally, and began extorting my parents for more money than they could afford in exchange for keeping their mouths shut about it. My parents had to remortgage their house to afford it." I grind my teeth together, denying the tears. "Can you believe that? They'd been *paying* to keep me. Who does that for a strange kid they picked up off the street? After they caught me stealing from them. I wasn't the easiest kid, either. Had gone years without parental supervision, and it showed."

I never had the guts to ask my parents about the conversation I'd overheard. Can only assume Patricia and Tyler Pippen showed up every year until I turned eighteen, when it no longer mattered where I lived.

"It's a level of kindness I can't even . . . It still makes no sense to me, to this day. My own birth parents didn't care to look after me. I grew up hearing how much of a fucking burden I was to them, every single day. And they turned me into one for my new family. They neglected me, abandoned me, and still couldn't let me just be fucking happy, for *once*—"

My throat closes and the tears I've been fighting come, full force. A sob cuts through the summer sounds around us.

Fuck.

The last thing I see is the shock in Brooks's face before I press my palms into my eyes, fighting for control so hard I'm actually shuddering.

"Hey." Brooks's hand lands on my shoulder.

"Don't. Don't say anything. I don't like to cry."

"I know. Take a breath for me."

I do what he says, force one into my lungs.

"Now hold it."

I cut myself off, keep the air in my lungs, and after a moment it starts to center me. The sob falls back down my throat, the burning in my eyes dims. My shoulders fall from where they'd crawled up to my ears.

"Good." His warm thumbs stroke the sides of my neck. He smiles gently when I resurface from my hands. "You're okay."

Which dimension of the universe did we stumble into? That Brooks Attwood—*Brooks Attwood*, the player Dad and I marveled at for years, the man who'd accused me of fangirl stalking only a month ago—would become the only other keeper of this secret.

Would show me so much grace and compassion, without once treating me like the wounded bird I'm not.

"You asked how I can stand to keep going with the shop when I hate being there. Letting my parents keep paying those people off . . . it's the most selfish thing I've ever done. So, tell me it isn't the least I can do to honor my parents for doing so much for me. To help repay the debt they took on to keep me."

"I have to confess something, Pip. Rachel showed me old photo albums of you today—" He pauses, visibly course-correcting. "Okay, the truth is that I begged her to show me old photos of you. I swear, she has ten for every year she's had you, filled with pictures of everyday things. You at the shop. Swimming in the bay. Eating hot dogs."

My laugh comes out as a puff of air, and he chuckles with me. "She was always obsessive with a camera."

"Oh, I got that." He shakes his head. "There was a whole section dedicated to pictures of your dad painting your nails."

I close my eyes, caught in the same nostalgia as earlier today, on the ship. The hurt and joy that comes with remembering Dad. "I came home from school that day and mentioned I'd never painted my nails before. Mom handed Dad the brush so she could capture my first manicure."

"Somewhere around the fifth photo album, your mom started crying. She said it really breaks her heart that she missed your first thirteen years. All those other firsts."

My heart squeezes, both at the knowledge of my mom's tears, and that she'd felt comfortable enough to shed them for Brooks.

"Your parents love you," Brooks says simply. "The unconditional, never-fades kind of love. Took me half a day with your mom to know that. I think they'd hate knowing you ever felt like you had to repay them for the things they chose to do for you. That you felt like you were any trouble at all and were making yourself unhappy every day for their benefit."

"I know. I know that, deep down. But this kind of thing just . . . *sticks*, you know?"

Brooks nods. "It would stick for me, too."

My brows go up. "That's it? You're not going to try to talk me out of it?"

"How could I, with everything you've just told me?" Brooks's unfocused gaze drifts over my head. "But, broken bones and cheating at cribbage aside, I had so much fun with your mom today. She reminds me a lot of mine. Rachel's leg is broken, and I could tell her knuckles were bothering her, but she still insisted on making sure I was fed and comfortable in her house. I had to order her out of her own kitchen."

Typical Mom. "How'd you manage to convince her?"

"I pouted, Pip. I told you, that thing's fucking lethal." He tips his head, watching me ride out my laugh. "But it's more than just about liking your mom. I liked that I was doing it for you. You're not a chore or a responsibility to me, and the only type of trouble you've ever been is the kind that has me riding a goddamn death trap against my better judgment. Doing all that today made me happy. It made me feel wanted and needed, and that's important to me in a relationship. Pretend or not."

I'm not sure how he managed to make me choke up and choke with laughter with a single speech, but I'm quickly realizing that that's Brooks in a nutshell. The type to get you off on a gala dance floor, shamelessly flirt and play with you, only to turn around and let your mom embarrass him with a deck of cards for an afternoon and then bake cookies in her kitchen.

Something truly worrisome *thunks* in my chest. Drop-kicks the beehive lodged in my stomach, setting free its occupants. They buzz around in a way that excites me, tickles my insides. Terrifies me.

Because there's nothing pretend about putting his day on hold to care for my mom, nor the care with which he handled me just now. Nothing fake about this buzzing in my stomach, nor the way I want to touch him, just to feel the warmth of his skin.

All of this for a man actively working on moving across the country in a matter of weeks.

A strong breeze, warm and providing no relief from the summer heat, slices the air around us. It ruffles the wisps of hair fallen from my bun. We move for them at the same time, Brooks's fingers tangling in the air with mine, hovering at the edge of my face.

He'd been visibly disappointed this morning on the dock, after I'd swatted him away from my ruffled hair. He looks it again now, hand falling limply at his side as he simply watches the strands tickle my cheeks.

I'm not sure which of us is more surprised when I clasp my hands together. Lift my chin in invitation. But Brooks picks up his cue. He smooths back my hair, tucking strands behind my ears. Dragging his thumbs over my cheeks as he does. An indulgent move more than anything, leaving behind a scintillating feeling. Like Pop Rocks hopping along my skin.

This is going to blow up in your face so spectacularly once he leaves.

Brooks tucks me against him, rests his chin on top of my head.

I let him, because that's just me. Reckless to the bitter end.

Chapter 26

Siena

It's under the coverage of the running tap in Mom's kitchen and Carla's vivacious laugh in the living room that I let myself whisper, "Don't tell your mom this. But I think I like my pretend boyfriend. And I don't think we're pretending anymore."

From the floor, Rosie blows a raspberry.

"Ouch. Tough crowd." I straighten in time to catch Shy sneaking a bite of cheddar off the cheese board we've been putting together for our parents.

"In today's most predictable news," she says, deepening her voice like she's reading off the six-o'clock news. "But I'm impressed you admitted it out loud."

I throw my hair up into a mess of a bun. Not because I rode my bike here—Brooks still insists on keeping my helmet in his possession, though we've taken the bike out together a couple more times since the evening on the cliffside. But my body temperature has skyrocketed with the confession.

"I've never been one for inner thoughts. Not around you, anyway." I cinch the hair tie before picking up a knife and slicing through some more cheese. I sneak Rosie a bite as she uses my skirt to clumsily stand up. "And was it really that predictable? He called me a stalker the day we met."

"After staring at you like his favorite slice of cake on that field. Like, lick-the-plate-when-he's-finished-and-leave-no-crumbs-behind kind of staring."

"I'd rather be the plate in this scenario."

Shy lifts Rosie to sit up on the counter. "Except you're still not sleeping together."

I point at her with the tip of my knife. "Correct. I can't stop my heart from acting a fool, but I can definitely keep this pussy on lock." I look down at my crotch. "Sorry. I'll let you off the leash soon, I promise."

"With your not-pretend boyfriend."

I tip my head from side to side. The gesture is noncommittal, but damn if things shifting with Brooks doesn't feel . . . inevitable.

There's only so many times I can cycle through the contents of my bedside drawer before needing something better than silicone. Needing to bring to life those fantasies of his inked-up body moving above me. The way we might curl up together after, his strong arms around me as we drift off to sleep . . .

Not that I'd allow that. Post-coitus cuddling would be a hard limit in the event of a hookup. Fortunately, I have a proven ability to manage casual sex. Because this could go no further. Not with the man working on shipping himself to the other end of the country.

My knife goes down on the counter. "This is all a little . . . familiar, isn't it? Dating a guy on the verge of leaving? I don't know how I ended up here twice."

Shy pulls a sympathetic face. She'd been my rock in the months following Tom's trade to the Ravens. I'd clung to her extra tight as my relationship fizzled, my abandonment issues on humiliating display.

By the time he'd left, Dad had died, and I wasn't exactly free to fly across the country at all times while running a business. Tom liked

LA so much, he stayed there in his off-season. We were stuck in a never-ending game of phone tag as he built a whole life out there without me. Even when I could visit, I felt so out of place.

I was practically begging for Tom's attention by the time I finally ended the relationship. The same way I'd spent my childhood begging for my birth parents' attention, before they moved on without me.

And here's Brooks, with a built-in life on the West Coast. A home, teammates, and friends. His parents. His sister and nephew. It'll be so easy for him to fall back into his life there.

I can't. I just can't put myself through that again, no matter what I feel for him.

"Maybe this is a nonissue." Shy stares off thoughtfully. "How likely is it he gets signed out there?"

"Likely, if his agent has anything to do with it. He's brought on a publicist to help with all the fake-relationship rumors." All that aside, the Rebels would be crazy not to sign him. I know Brooks is worried about it, constantly running himself ragged with training, but he looks better than ever. I'd know, having watched him play with Dad until his retirement.

I rinse off my hands but leave the tap on when I finish to cover our conversation. I watch Shy adjust Rosie's blond pigtails. She's got to be the cutest little girl I've ever seen. Perfectly cherubic, always smiling. Dressed to the nines in glittery sandals I wish my feet could fit in.

Her mom, though? She looks tired. *Exhausted*. Shy's wrapped herself in a baggy cardigan over her leggings, blond hair loose but a little frazzled. There are dark circles under her eyes, and now I feel guilty for complaining. Maybe I'm headed for heartbreak, but Shy's stress levels have been through the roof with Max away.

"How're you doing, Shy? Getting enough sleep?"

"Sleep?" Shy laughs and hands Rosie a piece of cheddar. "She's started sobbing every night at two in the morning, like clockwork. Refuses to go back to sleep unless she's in my bed. Don't you, Ro?"

"Yah!" Rosie gives us both a proud, toothy smile.

I wrap my arms around Shy. "Why don't you ever call me when you need a break? You know I love hanging out with my girl."

"We've been okay. Really. My parents have stepped up." Shy stares down at the counter for a quiet moment. "You want to know the truth? She wakes me up at two in the morning, but the kicker is that I'm pretty much guaranteed to have stayed up until then anyway, just worrying. This thing she does now . . . She calls every guy we come across *Daddy*. It kills me, Cee. We get on the phone with him as much as we can, but it's not the same. She misses Max so much. I'm terrified it'll mess her up long-term."

"Daddy!" Rosie chirps, flailing her head from side to side and making her pigtails flutter.

My heart squeezes, and I fold my friend into my body just as tightly. "Speaking as someone with experience in matters of abandonment, you know what I bet helps? Seeing her mom bust her ass to make sure she's happy, healthy, and safe. Rosie is so lucky to have you worrying so hard about her. And to have a dad who can't wait to come home to you both." I stroke Rosie's little cheek. "And in the meantime, I'll be mommy number two, if you want me to be."

"I've never heard you say you wanted kids."

I've always been neutral about it. Figured I'd have kids if my future husband wanted them. "I'd have them with the right person."

"With your not-pretend boyfriend?"

I think of Brooks shamelessly dancing with the junior cheerleaders all those weeks ago. The patient way he'd corrected kids about my name at the Huskies camp. How playful he'd been coaching them through drills and a game of flag football. He's got *dad* written all over him.

And yet, we've just spent the past couple of minutes discussing the pitfalls of raising a kid whose dad isn't always around.

"With my best friend Shyla. Especially if that kid's name is Rosalie." I *boop* the tip of Rosie's nose. She giggles, so I do it again.

"Okay, that's enough moaning from me." Shy disentangles us and reaches into the fridge for the near-empty bottle of pinot grigio our parents have been working on all night. "What's next for you and your not-pretend boyfriend?"

In the living room, Mom *whoops* at what I can only assume to be a victorious round of cribbage. Finally, I turn off the tap.

"I've been roped into a photo shoot this week," I tell Shy as she lifts Rosie off the counter while I pick up the cheese board. It's Josh and this new publicist's grand plan to counter the online chatter. Us at Brooks's house, looking like a happy little family with Pete. "They want me and Brooks half naked in a spread in *Around the League*."

"What did I just hear? You're spreading out half naked with your boy toy in a magazine?" Carla calls from the living room. "What kind of photo shoot is this?"

Evan mutters his signature *for shit's sake, love*. My mom laughs. But all talk of nakedness and spreading is promptly forgotten when Shy, Rosie, and I come into the room, cheese board first.

Chapter 27

Brooks

Truly, there is nothing more sobering than spending the majority of your existence in a gym, only to be told you need your abs shaded in with makeup anyway.

The *Around the League* crew has taken over my house since the crack of dawn, shortly after Siena arrived to get a tour of the place before someone realized she'd never set foot here in her life.

All day, she's watched them put my half-naked body through various shoots. In my home gym, wearing just a pair of shorts. Pretend-fetching a football with Pete, for some reason dressed in the lower half of a football uniform. Apparently, this is meant to be a behind-the-scenes look at my home life. To convince people that Siena and I are the real deal, making me more attractive to the Rebels.

Not sure why I need to be shirtless for it, but what do I know?

Now, I stand in the middle of the living room dressed only in a pair of jeans as hair and makeup people fuss over me. I stare longingly into the kitchen as Siena, Shy, and Summer laugh together.

Siena's wearing a fluffy white robe given to her when they sat her down for hair and makeup. Her hair is loose and waved around her shoulders, feet in slippers. Like it might be a Sunday morning here with me, drinking coffees and watching Pete run around the lawn.

I know how long and boring these shoots can be, so I enlisted Summer to come keep her company, and told Siena to bring Shy along, too. Predictably, they all took to each other immediately. I knew they would. Summer is awesome, Shy already has proven good taste in friends, and it would take a pretty severe head injury to keep someone from falling for Siena.

Maybe not even then, considering I've had one of those and can't keep my mind off her.

My motives weren't completely pure. I like the idea of carving a place for Siena in my life, with my group of friends. I want to tangle us up together so much that she forgets all about *pretend*.

I want her to like me. Fall for me.

The way I'm falling for her.

"Don't take it personally. They're really good abs," April, the makeup artist, jokes. "Who knows, you might even like how this turns out. I did it for my husband once, and it boosted his ego so good we had the best sex of our lives that night."

My laugh mixes with the one coming from Maggie, the hair stylist hovering above me with the help of a kitchen stool.

Across the room, Siena freezes mid-conversation with Summer and Shy. She stares at me, or at the way April crouches in front of me. She looks . . . irritated?

And hell if it doesn't send a thrill down my spine. Cool and collected Siena Pippen, jealous of a makeup artist who's innocently shading in my stomach.

Come on. Get over here, all hot and territorial.

But Summer draws back her focus and Siena seems to forget all about me.

"Your dog is terrifying, by the way." April blows on the bristles of her brush before dipping into the brown powder. Pete is curled up just feet away, bored with the mayhem after living it all day.

"He's a massive softie. Nothing to be scared of."

April finally rises to her feet. Her gaze snags on my tattoos and she pokes at one near my wrist. "What does this one mean?"

Across the room, Siena catapults off the counter.

There you are.

"You should see the one on his ass," she says loudly, giving April a look that would make me crawl under a chair for safety. "He had me bite it once and got the imprint of my teeth tatted on."

April and Maggie exchange startled looks. Siena hops onto her toes, kisses my cheek before brushing my ear with her lips. "You kidding me with the touching, Attwood?"

I palm her hip and tug her closer. "You jealous, Pippen?"

She pulls back to look at me. Siena is always stunning, knocks me flat on my ass with her bright eyes, silky hair, and the adorable sun freckles over her nose. This close up, though? She's a revelation.

Our only kisses have been for show, and it kills me.

I want to taste her for real, alone in this home with the afternoon sun streaming in, warming the air. With no one watching this time, so that I can feel more of her. Touch her everywhere. Feel her touch everywhere.

Siena's fingers toy with the hair at the back of my head. I hear a sigh somewhere around us. Probably the hair stylist, who'd been meticulously arranging me for the past ten minutes.

Siena's gaze flickers to my mouth. "New rule: no one gets to touch you."

"Except you?"

She pulls her hand from my hair. "That would be against the other rule. Which means the only person touching you until further notice is you."

"And who gets to touch you?"

My fingers curl into the terry cloth over her luscious ass. Just that one, tiny feel of her is enough to make my dick twitch.

She wets her lips, staring at mine, body tense. That beautiful head of hers is an impenetrable fortress most of the time, making it near impossible to figure out where she and I stand. Whether things have veered away from *fake* for her. Whether she'd opened up on that cliffside because she's interested in more, or if she'd been confessing her heartache to a friend.

Whether I'm worth her time. Long-term, far past the end date we agreed on.

But she wears her desire for me plainly on her face, her body, in the jealous bite of her words.

"I hate to interrupt a moment, but are we ready to go?"

Annie, the fuchsia-haired creative director, steers me into place at the end of the couch against the dark leather armrest. April helps Siena shed her robe, all animosity apparently forgotten.

Oh, fuck.

As if the situation wasn't delicate enough, Siena is wearing a royal-purple jersey, oversized so that it hits the midpoint of her bare thighs.

Not just any jersey, either. It's my old Rebels jersey.

Goddamn. I could jerk myself raw, over and over, and my cock would still strain against these jeans at the sight of her like this.

Annie positions Siena so that she leans into my side, legs curled underneath her, and goes to check in with our photographer.

"I'm gonna need you to come a little closer, Pip." I shift her so that she's leaning farther into me, giving me some coverage. "My dick is hard as a fucking rock for you right now. And I don't think Josh pictured that kind of photo shoot when they booked this spread."

I haven't been touched in a year and a half, and I'm suffering. My cock, already aching from her proximity, is begging for the woman beside me. Her hand, her mouth. What'll surely be the prettiest pussy I'll ever lay eyes on.

Siena tosses her hair over her shoulder. "Full disclosure: they actually brought generic jerseys for me to wear, but I was snooping around your room and found this in the closet." She takes me in. "Why didn't I get this reaction the last time I wore your jersey?"

The image of her in Huskies maroon floods my mind. "Because I no longer give a fuck about pretending, that's why."

Siena draws back to look at me. A quiet look, like I've just confirmed something she's long suspected.

That I'd spend every day playing cribbage with her mom if she asked me to. That picking her up in the mornings is the best part of my day, and dropping her off at night is the worst, because it means another twelve hours without her.

Good. I hope she knows.

I'd tell her if she ever gave me a sign that she wanted me back.

Annie claps her hands together, drawing our attention. "Let's get started. We're going for a cozy night in, so just get comfortable, focus on each other, and let us do the rest."

We face each other, grinning almost awkwardly. Like we haven't done this before, smiled for the cameras.

"What trouble did you three get up to today?" I speak just loud enough for her to hear.

Siena tucks her hair behind her ear. "Oh, you know. We talked about books. The sad dating pool in Oakwood. You."

"Covered a lot of ground." I run lines along her hip with my thumb. "You know I'd tell you anything you wanted to know, right? You only have to ask."

A camera flashes nearby, but it's all I register of the crew now that I'm sitting so close to Siena. I'm drenched in her sunny scent, the smile coming from those almond-shaped eyes.

"Really? You'd have voluntarily told me about the time on spring break when you got so drunk on piña coladas you disappeared for hours, then showed up wearing one of those puffy sumo suits with no idea how you got it?"

Fuck, Summer went deep into the vault with that one.

"I'll do you one better, Pip. I'll admit to you, and only you, that I know exactly how I ended up in that sumo suit."

Her eyes go wide, so sweetly excited. "You remember?"

"'Course I do. I just didn't want those jackasses to hold it over my head for the rest of my life. I'll tell you as long as it stays between us."

"Only between us." She smiles. "I like having secrets with you."

"I like it, too."

We exchange a look loaded with conspiracy. Pretend-dating, in-game injuries, and cliffside confessions will do that to you. I couldn't have hoped for a better partner in crime.

"All right, I was nineteen and out of my mind off piña coladas." I adjust her anchor charm where it sits over my old Rebels jersey. "And let's take a minute to appreciate how much rum must have been in those things. Because I've always been a big guy. So, it takes quite a bit just to get me buzzed."

She nods briskly. "Noted. Appreciated. Do go on."

"Somehow, I ended up at a neighboring resort during one of those performances they put on for their guests—well, *backstage* at one of those performances. Which that night happened to be . . . let's just call it a Magic Mike retelling. Really charming stuff."

"Oh my God." Siena nearly doubles over in a laugh. "Please tell me this is going where I think it is."

"Of course it is. One second I'm backstage, wondering where the hell I am. The next second someone shoves me *on* stage, to wondering where the hell I am and also why about two hundred people are look-ing at me expectantly. *Cheering* expectantly."

"Brooks." Siena's face falls into her palms, shoulders shuddering in a laugh. Someone behind the camera *tuts* their disapproval. Gently, I pry away her hands and lace our fingers together.

"Yeah, so, obviously I start stripping."

"The logical thing to do."

I flick a strand of hair off her cheek with our intertwined hands. "You're trying to tell me you wouldn't have played into it?"

She licks her lips, and I can tell she's delighted that I have her so pegged. "I definitely would have stripped."

"Exactly. So, I get down to my underwear, tossing my clothes into the crowd, really *feeling* it, you know. All that cheering as you get naked does wonders for your self-esteem."

"Note to self: cheer the next time Brooks gets naked."

I clutch my chest, widen my eyes. "Oh, would you please?"

Note to *my*self: spill all my embarrassing secrets if it means keeping that look on her face. Pure enjoyment and . . . affection?

I think that's affection.

For the cameras, or for me?

"Where does the sumo suit come in?" Her smile doesn't drop an inch.

I fill my lungs dramatically, as though recalling a fond memory. "Well, Siena. The thing about throwing your clothes into a crowd is, you're pretty much guaranteed never to see them again. So, there I am, in my underwear. A whole two or three resorts to walk through to get back to mine. And apparently, modesty came crashing down on me at the end of my performance. I found a sumo suit left over from the previous show. And the legend was born."

The morning after had been unbearable, between the hangover and Naomi's irritation when I'd skipped our workout to sleep it off. But it had been nice to have a moment. Just doing something stupid for the sake of it, when my focus had been on football for nearly my whole life.

Siena smiles. "You're a pleasant surprise, Brooks Attwood. I think we could've gotten into the best kind of trouble together, back then."

I pull her in, needing her closer. "What's stopping us now?"

Chapter 28

Brooks

I sink into the sofa with a grunt, preemptively lifting an arm for Pete to snuggle under. Predictably, my boy hops up beside me and moves right in. Lays his massive head on my knee, demanding a snuggle-head-scratch combination I really wouldn't mind for myself.

The *Around the League* crew left hours ago, and after dropping Siena off in Baycrest I headed to the gym for an evening workout to make up for training I missed today.

I'm sore and fucking beat, and all I want is to be huddled on this sofa with Siena. I rub a hand over my face, trying to force the image of her in that Rebels jersey out of my head. It's promptly replaced by the image of her coming on that dance floor, which is even better material to get my dick going.

Jesus Christ.

"Petey, I need some space, man. You don't want to see this."

I pat his head and get to my feet, reaching for my phone on the kitchen counter. There's a new picture at the top of Siena's social media account, one Summer snapped earlier today. Siena's eyes shine with laughter as she looks at me, looking hot as sin in my jersey. And even though this picture was part of the plan—one that seems to have worked, given the number of gushing comments—I can't help but smile, seeing us together all over her profile. Looking every bit the real couple I want to be.

I already miss her. I want her here, shamelessly teasing me. I want to listen to her complain about her day, watch her fiddle with that sparkly anchor around her neck. I want *her*. So fucking badly. After spending that time pressed together on the couch, I can barely stand to be in this room without the visceral need to jack off.

I scroll through her page until I find the selfie I'm looking for. It's an old one, on that boat she used to sail all the time. She's not even fully in the shot—it's just half her smiling face with the water in the background. But what I can see of her looks so damn happy and free, I can never go long without finding it again. Just staring at it.

This is where I'm at.

I'm so far fucking gone I'm about to jerk off to this picture of half her face and the goddamn bay. *Someone, please. Save me from me.*

I'm turning back toward the living room, fixated on the picture. But I almost wipe out tripping over Pete, who's apparently come to investigate what my hard-as-nails dick and I are up to in the kitchen. The phone goes flying out of my hand as I catch myself on the kitchen island and skitters across the hardwood.

"Shit. Sorry, buddy."

I pat my pup on the head and scoop up my phone just as a direct message comes through on the app.

Siena Pippen: Why are you sending me a blurry picture of your ceiling?

Sure enough, there's a blurry picture of the living room light fixture right above her message. The impact with Peter must have set off the camera.

WhatIsAFootballDaddy01: Accidental blurry picture. What are you up to?

Three dots appear. Disappear. Appear again.

Siena Pippen: In bed reading a book.

Siena Pippen: Go away. You're interrupting.

WhatIsAFootballDaddy01: Must be one hell of a book. What is it?

Siena Pippen: Just something Summer recommended today. Stop messaging me.

Hold the fucking phone.

I drop onto the sofa, staring at my screen.

WhatIsAFootballDaddy01: I know the kind of books Summer reads. What's got you so absorbed, Pip?

Siena Pippen: I'm putting my phone away now.

WhatIsAFootballDaddy01: Come over. Bring the book. Take the bike if you have to.

Three dots flicker, over and over. She's considering it.

She's fucking considering it.

Siena Pippen: Can't. You have my helmet.

I'm about to tell her I'm on my way there when another message comes through.

Siena Pippen: My panties are around my ankles and this is killing the mood, Attwood.

WhatIsAFootballDaddy01: I've never been more sorry in my life. How do I make it better?

This time, the dots flicker for so long I'm pretty sure I'd find a skeleton staring back at me in the mirror. They disappear. And a video call appears onscreen instead.

Fuuuuck.

I answer the call faster than I've done anything in my life.

Siena fills the screen. And it's so much better than the half-face-half-body-of-water photo I was just staring at. She's pink in the cheeks, bright-eyed, sucking that plump lip into her mouth. Dark hair scattered over a white pillowcase, lights dim around her. Pale pink bra straps hanging off her shoulders.

She looks like every wet dream I've had since the moment I met her.

"Hi," she says breathlessly.

"Hi." I'm just as out of breath, drinking her in. "I missed you."

"You know what, Attwood? I missed you, too." She sucks on her lip harder, fighting a smile as my stomach straight-up summersaults. "What are you doing over there?"

I sit back against the slouchy leather. "I'm sitting here thinking about you. And me. Me fucking you, to be specific."

She makes the sexiest little sound from deep in her throat.

"Tell me what naughty things you're reading about."

Her smile turns part smirk. Not an ounce embarrassed. "It's not all naughty. I was choking up a couple chapters ago."

"Tell me about the part that got your panties around your ankles."

Siena licks her lips, wrenching a groan from my chest. "She's blowing him in the back seat of his car."

Fuck, I am so hard. Pre-cum stains the front of my sweats.

"Yeah? That got you all wet, Pip?"

"Mm-hmm."

"Show me." I can't help grinding the heel of my palm over my cock. "Show me how wet you are."

There's no hesitation on the other end of the call. The screen jostles as she shifts around and tilts the phone down her body. I am on fucking fire.

She's in nothing but that pink bra, laid out on a fluffy comforter. "Your body is insane."

She huffs a laugh. "I jiggle when I walk."

My eyes fall shut. "That's my favorite part."

There's a bright pink vibrator vaguely shaped like a dick sitting by her hip. But I can't pay it more than a second of attention because her hand drifts down her bare stomach. She angles the phone to let me watch her swipe her fingers over her pussy once, twice, before dipping her fingers inside.

"Spread your legs, baby," I damn near beg. She does, rewarding me with a tease of a view. Pink and perfect wetness. "Wider." Her thighs spread wider like the sweet, perfect girl she is. I groan into the living room, nose practically touching my phone like I'm trying to dive into the screen. Dive into *her*. "Fucking *soaked*, Siena. I wanna fuck you so bad."

I watch Siena finger-fuck herself, slicking her fingers over her clit a few seconds before dipping back inside. She's moaning softly, and there's no helping it—I move a hand over my own sweats.

She pulls out of her pussy, moves the phone back up to her face, flashing me her soaked fingers. "Do I pass the test?"

I swallow, but my throat is parched. "Lick them off for me."

Again, zero hesitation from my girl. She sucks on her fingers, staring at me through the phone.

"So fucking jealous, Siena. Your pussy tastes so good."

She pulls her fingers from her mouth with a pop. "Are you hard?"

"Fuck yeah."

"Show me."

I pull my cock out from my sweats, hold the phone out so she can see me stroke it. The tip is wet. My entire body is aching. Dying for her.

"I love your cock. Loved watching you fuck your fist in that closet. I know I'm not supposed to admit that, but I really did. I always think about it. Always think about you."

My head falls onto the back of the sofa. Pretty sure this'll be the last day of my life. Death by Siena's dirty talk. What a glorious way to go.

"What are you thinking about?" she asks.

"I'm thinking about you blowing me in the back seat of my car."

"I'm thinking about that, too."

"Yeah? You want my cock in your mouth?"

She actually fucking sighs. "Really bad."

"Prove it. Show me what you'd do with it if I let you have it." I swipe my thumb over the head of my cock, using the moisture as I keep fucking my hand. "Use your little pink friend and show me."

Siena feeds me the filthiest smile I've ever seen. She sits up, tits so fucking perky and mouthwatering in that bra. I lose sight of her for a moment as she moves around the bed, but then she's back with the phone propped up on something, gifting me the view of a lifetime.

She's lying on her stomach, propped on her elbows, tits damn near spilling out of her bra. She lifts the vibrator, moving slowly enough that I know she's doing it on purpose. Torturing me with her pace as she brings it to her mouth and licks the tip.

She hums, smirking at her phone. "Tastes like me."

"Fucking fuck."

I whip off my shirt. Lean forward onto my elbows like the new angle will bring me closer to her. When it doesn't work, I prop the phone on a stack of books on the coffee table, freeing both hands. One to keep stroking my cock. The other to dig through my hair, because I'm going fucking crazy right now.

"Suck my cock, Siena. Show me how bad you want it."

She doesn't keep me waiting. My dirty fucking girl sucks on the toy's tip for a moment before drawing back, licking her lips and pushing it into her mouth. She swallows a couple inches then pulls back, leaving it wet with spit before taking a few more. It's not especially thick, doesn't stretch her lips the way I would, but it's long enough for her to struggle to take it all.

I stroke my cock, move down my shaft only as many inches as she's got in her mouth. "All the way, baby. I know you can do better than that."

Siena moans around the vibrator and lifts onto her knees. She stares right at the phone as she works the toy into her mouth, deeper, deeper, until she gives a little choking sound.

"Fuck, Siena. You look so fucking good."

She moans again, bobbing her mouth over her toy, sucking it down, making me lose my fucking mind as I stroke myself.

"Choke on it again. Put my cock at the back of your throat and gag on it."

She does what she's told. Feeds the toy into her mouth, all the fucking way until she gags. She looks utterly perfect. Brows twisting with effort, mouth slick with spit, tits heaving from exertion. Working so damn hard. Putting on a show for me.

I duck my chin, let my own spit fall over my cock. She must see it clearly, must love it, because Siena moans around her toy, and I use the slickness to stroke myself, trying to keep with her pace, pretending it's her mouth on me.

Siena shifts again, reaches down, and cries out around her mouthful as she plays with her clit.

I'm an inch away from death, I swear.

"That feel good, sweetheart? Does sucking cock make your pussy hurt?"

She whimpers, nods frantically.

"You want my cock down there, too?"

She nods again, still sucking on her toy.

"Then stop. Take it out of your mouth and show me how you'd ride me."

She yanks it out of her mouth, falls forward on her hands with a grateful sob. "Brooks, this is so fucking hot."

I'm panting, trying to keep myself in check. "It's all you, sweetheart. You're so perfectly fucking beautiful. Let me watch you fuck yourself."

She scrambles around, angling the vibrator between her thighs.

"Siena." She looks up. "Lose the fucking bra."

I groan when she unclasps it, throws it away like the burden it was. Then she looks right into the phone, right into my soul, and lowers herself onto her toy, taking it into her pussy inch by agonizing inch, whimpering softly as she goes, until she's sitting her ass right down on her ankles.

And then she lifts up and starts fucking the damn thing. Hard and fast, hips working, bouncing on the mattress, moaning so loud. My hands flies over my cock, stroking just as fast.

I am nearing delirium, eyes stuck to her.

"Fuck, baby. I can't wait to feel you like this. You're gonna make me come so hard right now, I swear. I fucking love watching you like this."

"I like it," she pants. I think she tries to say more but moans instead. I don't need her to, anyway. I know exactly what she means.

"You do, don't you? My dirty little attention whore. Coming for hundreds of people in your pretty dress. Fucking yourself on camera for me now."

Siena moans, tits bouncing as she keeps fucking her toy. The second she gets a finger on her clit she starts to shudder. "Brooks, I'm going to come."

"Then fucking do it. Give that greedy little pussy exactly what it wants."

Siena sobs in her room, like my words were the permission she'd been waiting on. She moves her hips back and forth, drawing herself over her toy until her head falls back, hair slides off her shoulders, and she cries out so loud the sweet sound of it fills my living room from miles away. I watch her shudder on her bed, captivated, until she falls forward and flings the toy out of her pussy like she can't take anymore.

The second she's still, my hand moves over my cock with a fucking vengeance. I groan, feeling everything tighten. My eyes stay open long enough to see Siena lift her head off the bed to watch me come, empty myself out on my stomach.

"Oh my God." She falls flat on her face again, panting into the comforter. My head hits the back of the sofa. "Brooks, you're so hot."

Who am I, in this world of eight billion people?

What did I ever do to deserve this, become the chosen one? Someone Siena Pippen would deign to show her flawless body to, let alone fuck it for my viewing pleasure.

Where am I?

When am I?

I throw an arm over my face, laughing into the room even though nothing about this is funny. Or maybe it is.

Watching Siena come has given me a full-on existential crisis.

Her husky laugh comes through my phone and I lift my head to watch her shoulders shake against her comforter. She's writhing in uncontrollable laughter. "Remind me to call you whenever I touch myself. Never doing this without you again."

Siena picks up her phone, bringing me closer to her smiling face; I do the same, looking just as stupid satisfied. This might be the best sex I've ever had, and we're not even in the same town.

"Deal. You've got yourself a deal, Pip."

Chapter 29

Brooks

Siena throws me another look over her shoulder as I follow her into Ship Happens, humming cheerfully since the moment I picked her up this morning.

Oddly enough, it has nothing to do with the image of a naked Siena that's been playing on loop in my mind for the past couple of days.

A naked Siena fucking a sex toy on camera for me, calling my name, making those breathy little gasps, staring at me with wide, desperate eyes through the phone. Telling me how bad she wants me . . .

Cool the fuck down. We've got things to do today.

Siena pauses behind the counter to gaze at me suspiciously. "You're acting really weird, Attwood."

I hike the gym bag over my shoulder and she zeroes in on it dangling at my side. Guess she hadn't noticed me taking it out of the trunk earlier. "I'm ready to go whenever you are."

Her eyes narrow on the pale yellow swim trunks I'm wearing and I can't stop smiling.

"And where are we going?"

I tip my head at the door. "The *Lilly Grace* is due to set sail in ten minutes, Captain. I chartered it for the day, and you're coming with me."

After a moment of surprise, Siena's gaze falls to her laptop. "No, you didn't. The *Lilly Grace* has been booked out for months, and Carla spent all of cribbage night complaining about today's charter. It's a bachelorette party for . . ." She trails off as I slide a slip of paper across the counter: the invoice for today's charter, with my name in point-forty font across the top. "Brooks Attwood."

"Present and accounted for."

She blinks slowly. "Brooks. What did you do to the bachelorette party?"

"I offered them alternate arrangements." I check the time on my phone. "Emma Horton and her twenty best friends are currently in limos on their way to wine country. Their first tasting starts at one. But they're having a boozy brunch at the Ivy Hotel first, which is where they're staying tonight."

"At the *Ivy*? No one can afford the Ivy."

I shrug. "I can."

Siena makes a startled sound, a rapid rotation of emotions crossing her face. I can't tell whether she wants to kill a smile, kill me, or both. It's adorable. "You organized them a different bachelorette party so you could have the ship to yourself?"

"It's not the ship I want to myself."

She stares like she doesn't have a clue what I'm on about. Personally, I think I'm being pretty damn clear with my words, so I leave them there for her to do what she will.

Siena tugs the tie out of her hair, letting it fall free around her shoulders as she massages her temples. "You need to train. And I need to be here at the shop."

Aidan strolls out from aisle three with impeccable timing. "Hey, man. You ready for today?"

"Born ready."

He turns to Siena. "The live bait delivery comes at five thirty. You've got Ben coming at one for maintenance on the security system. I'm going out back to wait on the shipment of waders right now. Have a good day on the water."

Siena watches, wide-eyed, as Aidan claps me on the back on the way to the back of the shop.

Look at me, so generously mature. Making nice with her ex-fuck-buddy instead of snapping his fingers for having previously touched her, like I've fantasized about doing since I learned of his miserable existence.

Nice guy, though.

"Brooks, this kind of sounds like a date. You see that, right?"

"Of course it's a date. There's no *kind of* about it." I've rendered her entirely speechless and I've achieved no bigger thing in life. I hold out my hand. "You with me, Pippen?"

~~~~~

They say even the best laid plans are flawed.

Apparently, that's absolutely true.

When I came up with this idea, I'd been laser focused on my goal: getting Siena to let go of the self-imposed responsibility of running that business, and getting a day on—specifically *in*—the water.

The flaw in this particular plan happens to be the dark, bottom-less pit of doom that is Oakwood Bay.

I fucking *hate* open bodies of water. I don't know who I thought I was, going out there with my chest puffed up. Trying to save my girl from her own dissatisfaction, when I've actively avoided any type of water that doesn't come out of a tap since I was about ten.

It's hot and humid even for July. Though I wouldn't be surprised if meteorologists declared a strange heat phenomenon originating on this very sailboat, in the form of the dark-haired stunner sitting on this wooden swim platform with me.

Siena swishes her feet in the water. She's the picture of relaxation compared to me, with the breeze in her loose hair and the way she lifts her chin to the sun, soaking in its heat. She's wearing this insane blue bikini we picked up at a shop down the boardwalk, on our way to the marina. She's already been in the water twice since she sailed us out here, while I've been content to watch her float.

She really is at home on the water, on this boat.

"I have to say, paying off an entire bachelorette party to charter their ship is unhinged behavior. But it's also the sweetest thing anyone's ever done for me."

"You're worth every penny, Pip."

It's not lost on me that, other than the moment she'd stuttered at the shop, Siena hasn't once told me how unnecessary it was to have done this for her. Hasn't asked how to repay me. I hope it means her thinking is shifting, that she understands she's perfectly entitled to take from me.

I can't come up with a single thing I wouldn't give her. I'd spoil her rotten if she'd let me.

Even if she didn't.

I trust her not to take advantage of it, the way my ex did.

I pick at the assortment of food I packed us for the day. Brownies I baked from my mom's recipe. Pretty much the entire menu from the diner back in Oakwood. I covered all my bases, in case she was craving something specific.

"You look so good out here, Captain. The water suits you."

"There's no place I love more."

"I can tell. You belong here."

Siena's chin touches her shoulder when she looks at me. "Whenever I was able to visit LA and needed to kill time alone"—she doesn't specify, but I assume she means visiting her *ex*—"I'd sit on the beach in Marina Del Rey watching charter sailboats go past and wishing I was behind the wheel. There was this one I used to drool over with a teal hull. Just so pretty. And I became obsessed with this idea that I *could* take the helm one day. Got certified and everything."

"And then what?"

"You know what."

"Right." Her father passed away and she inherited a family business that seems to be slowly draining the soul from her body.

"Would you ever consider shutting it down?"

"The shop?" Siena widen her eyes, as though sickened by the idea. "I could never, not with something so important to my dad. Besides, Mom needs the income. Second mortgage and all that."

"And what if you didn't run it yourself? What if someone ran it for you?"

"I'm the one Dad left it to, trusted with it. And I don't trust anyone to put that same kind of care into it. To anyone else it would be just another job. And to me, it's . . ."

"An obligation?" I say, before I can stop myself.

"Brooks."

Shit. "I'm sorry. I know it means a lot to you."

"It means a lot to me not to let my dad down." Siena helps herself to a brownie square from the container behind us. "These are amazing, by the way. Another one of your mom's recipes?"

"Everything but the pretzel bits. I was feeling adventurous."

Siena hikes up one knee as she turns to face me. "Speaking of adventurous, what are we doing on a boat when you're terrified of open water?"

"Who says I'm terrified of open water?"

"I've worked along the bay for a long time, Brooks. I know thalassophobia when I see it, and I'm staring it right in the face."

I force my eyes wide. "Please tell me there's a cream for that."

Siena bursts out laughing, shoulders shaking so hard the anchor charm bounces off her chest. She's already sprouted a handful of new freckles from our time in the sun. There's a really sweet one under her right eye I can't stop staring at.

This is what it's come to.

There's an absolute bombshell sitting next to me, perfect body from head to toe, and all I want to do is smile like a fucking fool at that freckle.

"We've been on this boat for hours, and you haven't dipped your feet in once. You're not even *looking* at the water."

"Okay, the looking part is your fault, because, I mean . . ." I run my gaze over her again. The wet hair tickling her arms, the little bows holding up her swimsuit bottoms digging into her curvy hips. That damn freckle. "There's only so much you can ask of me as a man, and keeping my eyes off you isn't one of them."

"What a line." Siena attempts a whistle, laughs when the sound comes out sad and wet.

She's so fucking cute. I want to devour her. Lick and nip every single damn part of her.

"As for the dipping-my-feet thing, you can go ahead and blame the water itself." I peek over the edge of the platform. "Why is it so *dark*? How do you know what's down there?"

"You freaked out when a weed brushed against your foot once, didn't you?"

I release a very real gag. "That's just it, isn't it? It's so dark down there it could have been anything. A weed. A shark."

She laughs quietly. "You're so . . ." She stares as though searching for the end of that sentence on my body. "You're really nothing like I expected."

In a good way, or . . . ?

But she doesn't elaborate. Siena reaches for another brownie in the container behind us. I hook a finger in the chain of her necklace, making her come to me instead. She doesn't even fight it. Lets me bring her close, until I'm lying back on the platform and she's hovering with her arms on either side of me, her body across mine.

The anchor charm swings back and forth between us with every wave crashing against the side of the boat. Her tits are damn near bursting out of that blue top and grazing my chest. And that freckle is close enough to lick now.

It's such an immaculate view. I'm fairly certain I just shot out of a cannon aimed straight at heaven.

"I'm suddenly understanding the boat's appeal."

My fingertips skim her spine, along the trail of star tattoos I've thought about since I found them at the gala. Her eyelids drop a fraction, lips part, and she's close enough that I can hear the soft breath come out of her. If she ever opened the door to it, to us, our bodies writhing together, I'd take her up on it without hesitation.

"I never had a death wish until I met you."

She coughs out a startled laugh. "What?"

"I have had this recurring dream since we met, where I have my face buried between your tits and just . . . pass away. So happy, straight to heaven. And then I wake up, actually sorry to be alive because it means it never happened."

Her whole body shudders with laughter, completely missing that I am *very much* serious about wanting to die this way. "I think they call that a nightmare."

"Nightmare, wet dream, who cares."

She taps my forehead right between my eyebrows. "Sounds empty in there today."

"It's not. It's full to the brim. Pictures of the other night on repeat. How perfect and beautiful you looked fucking that toy for me."

Not even a hint of a flush in her cheeks, my shamelessly horny girl. "I liked doing it for you."

"I like you."

Her mouth stretches playfully. "Makes sense."

"Yeah?"

"I'd like me, too."

"You'd be crazy not to." With the bright sky above her like this, there's a pale halo of light framing her head. "Tell me something you like about me."

Her eyes are all amusement. "Fishing for compliments, Attwood?"

I am, blatantly.

I'm falling for her so fucking fast, and I'm desperate for a real sign that she's falling with me.

Damn my oversensitive heart; I need her to tell me that my ex had been wrong. That there's something inside me worth liking, sticking around for besides my career. Maybe even worth loving, one day.

"Come on. There must be something you like about me. I like plenty about you."

She rubs her lips together. "Like what?"

We really are the same, me and her. Hiding behind confidence, with the same innate need to feel wanted. To know that she's worth loving, being cared for, after the way she grew up and got left behind.

I lift my chin, run my mouth along her jaw just once. So fucking smooth.

"What are you doing?" She's holding her breath, and her mouth is a sliver of space from mine.

"I'm telling you how bad I want to lick down the cute slope of your nose. How that sweet line you get between your eyebrows when you think makes me want to stack the densest books in front of you, just to watch you focus for hours."

That line between her eyebrows appears, and I can't help a smile.

"You're the most beautiful woman I've ever laid eyes on, and what's truly frightening is that your looks aren't the even the most extraordinary part about you. Your strength is. The way you've gone through more than most people do in a lifetime, and came out of it resilient. Caring. Loving life." I pause. "Or maybe it's the way you're so fiercely loyal. The second I figured you out, I never once doubted that you were in my corner. Even when I hadn't done anything to deserve it."

Her lips form a perfect little *O* shape of surprise.

"Now you go," I nudge.

She averts her eyes, traces the tattoos over my chest. "I like these. How long did they take you to do?"

I work to swallow my disappointment. Still, it twists inside me, coiling around my heart. Making my throat ache. "About twenty hours over a few sessions."

"And this?" She hesitates, then runs her finger along a bit of bare skin by the inside my elbow. "It's a heart. Was it for your ex?"

"No. It's not even a heart. The shapes just happen to come together that way, like this." I use her finger to trace it out. Then press her palm to my chest, just for the sake of feeling it there.

"Oh. I see it now." Her throat works through a swallow. "All this ink and you never got one for her? Eight years is a long time."

"Back-alley hookups, Pip. Which were soon followed by several *come to Jesus* therapy sessions that ended in very stern advice from my therapist not to sleep around without serious feelings involved. She screwed me up so badly, I couldn't recognize myself for months. I'm grateful nothing ever possessed me to get one for her."

"I still can't believe she did that to you."

"The worst part is that I decided to quit football for *her*. Or the eventuality of her, and our family. That concussion scared the hell out of me. I was convinced I'd done lasting damage. That I'd have all these kids one day and could never . . . I don't know. Play catch in the yard with them without seeing double. That I'd forget things about them that I shouldn't. I thought I was doing the right thing for us by retiring, but she . . . she called me a coward for it. And then had an affair."

Siena shakes her head in disbelief. "You thought you'd marry her one day?"

"I thought there was a chance. I'd never been close to proposing or anything."

"After eight years together?"

"I think my heart knew something I didn't." Siena hums a thoughtful sound. "She was never right for me. Made me feel like my identity was football, and nothing else—it's all we ever talked about when we were together, and the minute I couldn't play anymore, she made it clear exactly how little I mattered beyond my roster status. I lost my value the second I chose to give it up." I really didn't want today to be about this but there's so much relief in letting out these words. In the soft way Siena looks at me while I do. "I've spent the past couple of years unpacking that mess of a relationship. Trying to convince myself that there's more to me than football, that I could have the things I wanted outside of the game—the things I quit for. But I've come up short on all fronts. I like to think I'm better than this, but it really makes me wonder."

Siena swallows. "Wonder what?"

"Was she right about me?"

I feel stupid the moment the question flies out. Because as much as I'd like to pretend it's rhetorical, that I know better than to believe something like that, I haven't exactly been thriving since that relationship ended. And the only woman I've wanted since keeps finding ways to put me at arm's length.

Siena hangs her head, buries her face in her hands. "God fucking damn it, Brooks. I'm going to kill her."

Chapter 30

Siena

Brooks tells me all this matter-of-factly, but there's pain in his eyes that tangles a heavy knot in my chest, aching even after he stop speaking.

Now you go.

There has to be something you like about me.

I thought he was kidding around, fishing for compliments, being a flirt. But it all thunks into place for me now. The reason he's been so fixated on this comeback, running himself down and pushing his body past its limits. The reason he'd been so desperate for me to agree to our scheme. This woman—what she did to him—has put it in his head that he needs this career in order to thrive. In order to be wanted, and worthy of the love and the family he's dreamed of.

Turns out, after years of struggling in lonely silence, I've stumbled upon my twin soul. Collided with him on a football field where I'd felt like my dad was leading me on the anniversary of his death. Underneath all the charming smiles and casual bravado, Brooks is just a man who needs the validation of knowing he's worth liking. Loving.

Just like me.

It's tragic, really. That Brooks would feel anything like I do, when he doesn't deserve to. When he's so *good.*

Tragic that I'd find what could very well be my other half in someone who's set on following his joy across the country, where I can't follow. Not with my mom here, the family business, my best friend raising her kid on her own.

I think it's plenty fair for me to guard my heart against the inevitability of our goodbye, the way our lives are literally moving in different directions. But it's not fair to guard it at his expense. He's an amazing guy—everything I'd want under different circumstances—and he deserves to know it. Deserves everything he wants out of life, and then some.

"Listen closely, Brooks." I sit up, then take him by the shoulders and heave him upright. His eyebrows draw together. "That woman is a sociopath. I'm sorry, but someone needs to say it."

He barks out a shocked laugh. "What?"

"Your ex is a sociopath," I enunciate. He begins to laugh again but I shake my head. I've never been more serious. There are times that call for eloquence and poetry, and this isn't one of them. This is a man in need of cold, hard facts. "She's deficient in a way that's truly worrisome for the general population. Public menace levels of idiocy. That's what it must be, if your career is all she saw in you."

Brooks's gaze swings to either side of me, like he expects someone to appear and explain what the hell's gotten into me.

He's gotten into me. Every sweet gesture. Every time we've lapsed into shared, uncontrollable laughter. I crave his company when I'm alone.

Ache for it.

"You want to know what I see in you? What I like about you?" My eyes devour his gorgeous face—the dark features, the scar. His casual smile and the way his eyes are tight, trying to play it off but silently telling me *yes, I need to know.* "You make me laugh more than anyone I know, and you don't take yourself seriously—but you're serious when it matters. You're open with your feelings in such a brave, enviable way. In a way that's so hard for me to do, but feels easier with you. The fact that you've been calling me out on my baggage for weeks, without once making me feel weak or stupid, or like I'm wrong for feeling the things I do—the fact that you even *noticed* it, and took the time to ask? You're attentive, and so damn . . . *kind*."

I blow out a breath, trying to organize my thoughts. To slow down, so that this really penetrates that absurdly beautiful, sensitive head of his. Brooks's gaze is fixed on my face, his attention rapt, and that almost does me in on its own.

Fuck that woman for making him doubt himself. *Fuck* her for making him need to hear this in the first place.

"Brooks, what you did for my mom that day, when you owed her nothing, didn't even know her? She means so much to me. And it meant a lot that you put that much care into looking after her when I couldn't. You're dependable, and . . . the most charming person I've ever met. In a really up-front, cocky kind of way. But somehow, it bundles together in this perfect package of . . ." I gesture at him helplessly. Trying to find a word less juvenile than *amazingness*, but I'm on a breathless roll, words tumbling out. "And those cookies you baked her are seriously, without question, the best I've ever had. These brownies, too."

Brooks chuckles at that. "It was my mom's—"

"Your mom's recipe. I know, and it doesn't matter. They'd be burned to a crisp if I'd tried making them. Salty instead of sweet. You *bake*, Brooks. Do you know how ridiculous that is? As if you weren't perfect enough. And—and you dancing with those kid cheerleaders? The way you made their day like that? Equally as ridiculous. But it's something I could totally picture my dad doing when he was alive. I know you'll never get to meet him, but God . . . I really wish he could have known you."

My eyes burn as I picture it. Dad and Brooks in the tiny yard at home, beers in hand. The way Dad might have talked his ear off about the massive striped bass he'd have caught while we were on the ship earlier in the day. The way Brooks would have indulged his enthusiasm, maybe even suggested they go fishing together next time, even though he can't stand the open water. Because that's just who he is.

I'd give anything to see them together even once.

"I'm convinced he'd have loved you as much as my mom does. She won't shut up about you—keeps asking when I'll bring you around again. Seriously, if I don't marry you, she might." Brooks's brows shoot up, and I curse myself for the slipup. "Not that I'm going to . . . It was a . . . You know what I mean."

He's visibly holding back laughter at my stuttering, but nods briskly. "I'm marrying your mom, then. Got it."

See? This is what I'm talking about. I want to grab him and shake him. He's so good at defusing tension. Knows exactly when to push, and when to back off.

I take his face in my hands. "And just in case you need to hear this, too . . . You're incredible on the field. You're focused, and dedicated, and talented. Any team would be lucky to have you. I wish you'd be more kind to yourself in the process, but I really do admire your drive and how hard you work at something important to you." Brooks's gaze flits across my face while mine does the same over his. "Brooks, you're a catch from all angles. And you know what? I'm so glad we were cornered into a pretend relationship. Imagine if I never got to know you? What a loss that would have been."

His brows are furrowed, like he's in silent conversation with the freckles on my nose. "You like me."

A laugh bursts out of me. "Yes. In summary, I like you. For about a million reasons besides your job." My gaze falls to his mouth. His stunning grin goes as big as I've ever seen it. Fire ignites under my skin, every inch of it. It hurts. It feels fantastic. "Like that smile. That smile could melt a glacier in the dead of winter, Attwood."

And I'm falling for you.

And it's scary, knowing you're probably moving in just a few weeks.

And we should probably slow this down so I have a shot at recovering when you leave.

Brooks moves closer, and the thunder of my heart drowns out my brain's insistent attempts at common sense. He sighs dramatically. "Be still my fucking heart, Siena. I knew I'd get you to fall for me. It was only a matter of time."

I smack his chest, but he catches my hand and keeps it there. His heart is racing.

He can't feel it, but mine is, too.

"I really needed to hear that," he whispers. "It's like you said on that cliff. When you know it's bullshit deep down, but the bad thoughts just stick."

I nod, feeling so deeply sad for him, but comforted that I'm not the only one. "Then I'll do whatever I can to make them unstick."

"Thank you, baby."

Baby. It sounds so right rolling off his tongue. Feels so right sinking recklessly into my heart.

He lifts my hand, kisses the inside of my wrist, and how outrageous is it that I've never kissed this man? *Really* kissed him, without frustration or an audience?

"Hey, Brooks?" I lean in. He looks serious now, but there's that usual playful spark in his eyes. "You go left."

The second my lips touch his, Brooks is moaning into my mouth. The sweetest moan, so *Brooks* in its vulnerability, because that's exactly who he is. Open and vulnerable. Confident but soft. It's the same way he kisses me now, guiding my chin with gentle fingers to tilt my head, kiss me deeper.

Brooks's fingers tangle in the lengths of hair at the back of my neck, and he's both pulling me closer and pushing me back. Like he can't settle on how he wants this to go. Whether he wants to stay patient, wait for me to come to him, press my body to his. Or to cut to the chase and take what he wants. What we both want.

God, I want to fuck you.

He seems to have the same thought because he decides for us both, pushes so that my back hits the ship. His hands are everywhere, hips pushed up against mine. His cock digs into my stomach, making demands of its own. My fingers feel the firm muscles at his sides, up to his shoulders, before sliding down to his hips.

I toy with his waistband, even though I know I can't go further, not here. I may not mind playing a little in the open, but I've shared Brooks enough since I've known him. This—having him—it'll be just for me.

"Siena," he says against my mouth. It's all he gets out before getting distracted, sucking on my lower lip, licking into my mouth.

"Brooks." I rock my hips, find an angle, grind against his cock.

"Fuck yeah. More." He grunts when I give it to him. Hooks an arm under my hips to lift my weight as I all but fuck him from below. His mouth is on my neck, kissing, licking. "I've been so good, Siena. So fucking good, for so long. Let me be bad for you." His cock hits my clit over and over, and I'm gasping. "Take us to land. Come home with me."

I tug on his neck, looking for more of his mouth. He relents, letting me kiss him another moment before breaking it off.

Brooks's hands sweep along my body, toying with the blue triangles keeping me covered. He pulls one aside, freeing my nipple, grazing it with a rough thumb. The sound I make is somewhere between a mournful whimper and a needy moan.

"Come," he presses a kiss on my neck, "home," another on my jaw, "with," Brooks takes my mouth again, "me."

And it's a fucking lost cause.

Chapter 31

Brooks

"You want a drink?"

Siena glances over her shoulder, leaning her elbows on the porch railing at the back of the house. She stayed out here watching Pete buzz around out back while I showered upstairs. The sun had set by the time we made it back to my place, after stopping by hers so she could have a shower after our day on the water. The lights spilling from inside illuminate just enough to see her bare feet, the frayed denim shorts she'd changed into.

"It's okay. I'm not thirsty."

I go back inside for a beer, because what the hell. I've held off for months, and it's been a great day.

Most of them have been since Siena came into my life, but today especially.

I confessed what I'd felt was a shameful insecurity, embarrassed that my ex's idea of me still hung over me the way it did. Only to come away feeling seen. Wanted.

I'm not sure there's an overnight cure for it, just like that evening on the cliff couldn't possibly have erased decades of pain my girl has held on to. But she helped today—this no-bullshit woman, who never minces her words or fakes her feelings.

It all clicked into place. Damn near caused me to float off that swim platform.

The way she smiles at me, eyes twinkling from under those mile-long lashes. The way she'd softened against me on that cliff, let me hold her in her mom's kitchen. Every time she laughs with me, those little touches.

It's definitely affection. And it's definitely real.

Because Siena Pippen can't fake romantic emotion worth shit. I've known it since our very first appearance as a couple, when she'd sat tongue-tied meeting fans.

If she calls you a dick, it's because you're being one.

If she tells you you're worthy . . . it's because you are.

When I return, Siena is focused on the dark grounds and the glow-in-the-dark marker on Pete's collar as he zooms around.

She's so fucking pretty it's almost comical. Unnatural. There's got to be a mad scientist out there who cooked her up in a lab, my dream girl, and sent her here to turn my life upside down. I'm tumbling down a hill, falling for her so fast there's no stopping it.

Anticipation thickens the air around us, already dense and hot with summer humidity. The only light is what's spilling out from the house and the warm glow of the hot tub running down on the patio.

"What are you thinking about so hard?"

She glances at me. "Us fucking. I'm trying to decide if it's a bad idea."

Maybe her words should put me on my heels, but they have the opposite effect. My fearless, dive-in-head-first girl never hesitates. Never overthinks.

The fact that she is now? It tells me that this matters.

Means something to her.

We're not something easily brushed off in the morning.

"How could it be?" I tuck her hair behind her ears and kiss her, like it's all the answer she needs. But just in case it isn't, I add, "We both know what bad looks like, and this isn't it. There's not a single bad thing about us."

She doesn't say anything as Pete bounces up the porch steps, collar clinking and breaking the thick silence. He goes straight through the open glass doors into the house, and it's just us again.

Me and Siena, in the warm summer air.

I reach for the back of my shirt and tug it off. Do the same with my shorts, leaving only my boxer briefs. With my beer in my hand and her eyes on my back, I make my way down the porch steps and into the hot tub.

From up on the porch, Siena watches me take a long sip of my drink. I'm not going to say anything to get her in here. She either wants this or she doesn't.

Siena actually glances from the hot tub to the open back door.

"Heading out?" I ask when she stays quiet.

She gathers her hair in a messy pile on top of her head. "Heading in."

Hell yeah.

I sit up straight, grip tightening on the neck of my bottle with every step that brings her closer. She sweeps her shirt over her head. Unzips her shorts, letting them fall down her body.

Somehow, the glass bottle doesn't shatter under the strain from my fingers.

She's perfection in sheer mesh, the red fabric barely covering the nipples straining against them. The matching red thong is see-through as anything, digging into the soft skin at her hips.

When she climbs over the edge of the tub, I rub a soaked hand over my mouth to stifle a groan at the sight of her ass as she moves for the spot directly across from mine. Whoever created her, sculpted those full, soft curves, should be elevated to sainthood.

Siena settles in, face smooth except for the wild fucking glint in her eyes. I take a long sip of beer without looking away. I couldn't look away. It's the mess of hair on top of her head, with loose tendrils framing her face. The way the water has pulled one of her bra straps off her shoulder so that it sits bare above the swell of her tits.

She sucks her bottom lip into her mouth. Ruthless, senseless jealousy rages inside me. I want that lip to myself.

Want her whole fucking body for myself.

Siena raises a hand out of the water to rub at her collarbone, like she's feeling all the same things. Nods at the edge of the tub. "Aren't you going to offer me a sip?"

I lift the beer to my mouth instead and take a long pull before placing it carefully back on the edge of the tub. "Come here and get it."

The words hang in the hot air between us.

Siena stands, giving me the view of a fucking lifetime—her body soaking wet, water streaking from the mesh cupping her tits, down her stomach. That bra strap still hangs loosely off her shoulder as she moves through the water. Her knees brush mine as she reaches for the bottle.

She downs a sip of beer as she backs away from me.

I tip my head. "I didn't mean come here and steal it."

"It's not stolen. It's confiscated. I know what you're trying to do, looking at me like that."

"And what am I trying to do?"

"You want me to make the first move."

"The first move for what?" When she only throws me a sexy-as-hell smirk, I continue, "See, I don't like that. This is my house. My hot tub. My beer. I'm the one who confiscates."

"And what is it you want to confiscate?"

She's still standing, beer in hand. I jerk my chin at her. "Lose the top."

Her lips part. "You're confiscating my bra?"

"My house, my rules. No bras in the hot tub."

I think for a split second she might decline, but this is Siena. She sets the beer down on the edge of the tub, unclasps her bra, and lets it fall away from her body.

Fuck. Full breasts, perky nipples begging for attention. I'm aching everywhere, desperate to get at her.

I've never wanted someone more in my life.

"I'm obsessed with your body." She bites her lip, just soaking in my attention. "New rule: No bras, ever. For as long as I live. I'm going to burn that fucking thing."

Siena dangles the bra out between us, offering it to me. I crook my finger at her. She shakes her head, takes a step back.

"Come here and get it."

I don't know if she means for me to come get her or the bra, but the second the words leave her mouth I'm moving, lurching through the water. I rip the bra from her fingers and toss it out of the tub. Dip, grip the backs of her thighs, and pull her up into me. She gasps the sweetest fucking sound as our bodies collide.

I fall back into my seat and take her with me, locking my arms under her ass to hold her in place above the water where I can see her. Get my fill of her.

She stares down at me, lips parted, panting, hair messy around her face. Her hands grip my shoulders, nails dig in, and that's it. I'm done. Control lost in the fucking wind.

I palm her breast, groan as my mouth finds her other nipple, teeth scraping against the sensitive skin, my soul bursting at the sound of her moan.

Her hands fly to my hair, the back of my head, bring me closer.

"Fuck, please don't stop. Brooks, don't stop."

As if I could.

Siena doesn't take her eyes off me, dipping her chin to watch me suck her, lick her, grab every part of her I can reach—her tits, her waist, that goddamn ass. Every inch of her is soft perfection, fills my palms so satisfyingly. I'm not sure how I'll ever get enough of her.

I might fuck us into an early grave tonight.

She writhes as I kiss down her stomach. "Fuck, I missed this."

"No, you didn't." I nip her waist. "Can't miss what you've never had. How ever you think it feels to be thoroughly fucked, have this pussy filled up? Forget it. None of it will compare to this. I'll give you what you need."

She gazes down through her lashes, chest heaving when my hand slips between her thighs, and she gasps my name the second my fingers feel her through her panties. There's nothing patient or exploratory about the way I touch her. It's pure hunger, driven by my aching cock and the sounds she's making for me. My fingers move over her pussy before pushing her panties aside and finding her clit.

She pants in short, tight bursts, not taking her eyes off me. "And what is it you think I need?"

"Me." I wipe my thumb over her clit. "Touching you here." I move down, press a finger into her pussy as far as the angle allows and her soft cry fills the silence around us. "Fucking you here."

She whimpers. Squirms into my hand. "Oh, fuck. Please, can you give me more? Please, Brooks—"

I cover her mouth with mine, swallowing the rest of her pointless words. Her hands go to the back of my neck and move right into my hair. Pulling it, scraping my scalp.

Yes.

"You don't beg." I kiss along her jaw, move down her neck. "Say the word and I'll fill this hot pussy with everything I have. My fingers, tongue, cock. I'll fill you up with my cum if you want. You never have to beg with me."

The fingers in my hair turn merciless. "Shouldn't my begging get you off?"

"You know what gets me off?" I withdraw my finger, sink it right back in her pussy. "Giving you whatever the fuck you want."

"Then I want everything. All of it. Tonight. Now." I give her another finger and her eyes squeeze shut. She's up on her knees, above the surface of the water, and everything inside her pussy is pure, wet need—her body responding to mine.

I'm being rough enough that her tits bounce in my face as I fuck her with my fingers, but every one of the pretty sounds leaving her mouth tells me I'm doing it right. We look down, watching my fingers disappear in and out of her. She mumbles something inaudible. Cries out when my other fingers find her clit, both hands working hard for her. I flick her nipple with my tongue, scrape it with my teeth before sucking it into my mouth.

"Yes," she gasps. "Yes, yes, yes. Brooks, I'm so close."

"I know, baby." I lick at her nipple, move to the other. "I know those little gasps. Know exactly what they mean."

"So put your dick in me. Fuck me already."

"You'll get it as soon as you come for me."

Her pussy clenches around my fingers, and it's a tight fucking fit but I add a third inside her, fucking her fast and hard. Playing with her clit, biting her nipple as her fingers twist in my hair.

"Brooks—*Brooks*—"

That final gasp cuts off. Her brows furrow, lips part, eyes go wild. First, a tiny cry, and then the next one, loud and drawn out as her head falls back. She shudders over me, around my fingers, and I fuck her through it, drawing out as many more of those cries as she can give me until she slips, sinks into the water, and slumps against me.

"So fucking pretty when you come, Siena." I nip her lip, soaking in her dazed look. "Are you going to take more tonight or does my sweet girl need a good night's sleep?"

Dazed eyes turn to pure fire and she reaches into the water, wrenching my fingers from her pussy.

"Shut up," she mumbles against my mouth. She nips at my smirk, then wipes it clean off my face when she cups my dick, strokes it once before pulling it out of my shorts. I grunt when her weight comes down on me. It's everything I fantasized about since the day I met her. Siena sits her pussy right along my straining cock and grinds. I tip back my head, clamp my teeth. My entire body throbs as something hot and sharp shoots down my spine.

This is the moment I figure it out.

When I know with absolute certainty that there's no way—*absolutely no fucking way* I'll last a second fucking her. It's been nothing but me and my fist for a year and a half, and I am so *fucked*.

She glides easily, stroking her clit along my cock as she holds her panties to the side. The notes coming out of both our mouths sound so good together, filling the outdoor silence. It's a good thing the houses on this road are set far apart, because there'd be no hiding this from the neighbors.

My hands find her hips. "Slow down for me. You're making me so fucking crazy."

Her eyes shut as she keeps grinding on me. Every movement brings me dangerously close to the edge as it is. But then she starts to lengthen her strokes, all the way along my cock. Water splashes around us.

We gasp together when my tip unintentionally slips inside her. She freezes. Our gazes clash, and then she's gone again, sitting up on her knees.

My heart dunks straight into my gut at a devastating realization: I don't have any condoms.

I don't have any fucking condoms.

"I'm clear. I got checked—I'm okay," she pants, backtracking fast to the conversation that got lost in a needy shuffle.

"Me too." I swallow hard, trying to calm my breath. "Baby, please tell me you're on something. Otherwise, this is a terrible time to confess that I don't keep condoms in the house."

"No condoms, no temptation?"

"Yeah. I'm not tempted at all." I lift an eyebrow, looking down between us. "So, tell me, Siena. Am I fucking you tonight or not?"

Chapter 32

Siena

I don't even finish nodding before he's moving.

Brooks winds an arm around my waist and stands, taking me with him and sending water splashing out of the hot tub when we crash into its other side. He sets me down on the edge and we're frantically stripping off my soaked panties and his shorts. I toss mine overboard, but Brooks gives up on his as soon as he kicks them off. They float in the water behind him.

There's a voice in my head begging me to be careful, protect my heart. It shouts that I've tried the long-distance thing, and it failed so spectacularly.

But so what?

Later. A problem for later.

"I've wanted this since the second I met you," I confess as he licks up my neck. I tip my head to give him more room to play. "Since you knocked me down on that field."

"I know, I could see it in your eyes. You were fucking me in your head before I ever said a word to you." Brooks's fingers reach for my pussy again, drawing soft circles over my clit as he kneels on the seat between my thighs. "Is this how you pictured it, Siena? Sitting on the edge of this tub, pussy full of my fingers?"

He watches me pant through it, every stroke sending a rush down my legs before he slips inside me again. His fingers are heaven, long and thick, perfect for catching a ball. Even better for dulling the ache inside me.

Dulling but not quenching.

I grip the edge of the tub, trying not to fall over the side. "I pictured a lot more than this."

"I didn't." Brooks's fingers slow, fuck me at a gentle pace. There's a fresh rawness to his voice and I find him staring like he's only now realized I'm here. Like he's in awe of what he sees, can't believe his luck. "I wanted you, but I never expected it to be like this."

My heart stutters. I don't think he's talking about my body.

I shove the thought out of my head. Refuse to linger on the emotion behind it because, quite frankly, I don't have the capacity to address it right now. He's still softly thrusting his fingers into me and we need to refocus, here.

I grip his hair and pull him to me. He comes without hesitation, groaning into a kiss. He tilts his head, deepening it with slow and gentle strokes of his tongue. Maybe it's not the filthy kiss I was after, but the second I reach for his cock it turns frantic enough to bring more pressing matters to the forefront.

Brooks scoops my ass off the edge of the tub, lining up our hips. I keep my hands planted behind me for leverage. We look down between us, at the way his cock slides along my pussy, wet with more than just water. God, we already look so good together.

"Slip me in." Brooks grazes my jaw with his teeth. "Let me wreck my perfect girl."

I press him down so that he slides inside me. He watches my face as he slowly moves us together, pulling me to him and pushing his hips at the same time, bringing with him a steady burn as he stretches me. My breath catches, nails scrape on the plastic tub.

Brooks stops moving. "Does it hurt?"

"It's . . ." I look down between us, at the way I'm working to take him. At the inches left to go. "It's a lot."

He runs a thumb along my jaw. "Take a breath for me."

I gasp air into my lungs and laugh it back out, feeling silly and inexperienced in a way I'm definitely not. "I can't tell you how sobering this is. Never thought I'd get taken down by Brooks Attwood's massive dick."

He laughs into a kiss. He's being sweet and careful again, but this time it's exactly what I need. I can feel my body relax with every stroke of his tongue, every nip he gives my lower lip.

"Almost." It's a statement and not a question as he dots kisses over my jaw. His fingers circle my clit and the tension in my body is gone. "There it is."

The burn turns delicious. I shift my hips and he takes the hint, laying his forehead against mine as we watch him slowly disappear inside me.

"Perfect fucking fit," he murmurs when he's all the way in. "In every single way."

My stomach bursts with warmth, heart glows in agreement.

But I squeeze my eyes shut, trying to block everything out but the feel of him inside me. Brooks draws all the way out at a pace so slow I feel every single inch as he moves. He punches his hips and he's back, filling me all the way and shoving the breath from my lungs.

His thumb strokes my cheekbone. "Open your eyes. Open them and watch me fuck you. It's such a pretty thing."

His voice is so thick with pleasure that my eyes pop open. It feels so good, what he's doing, dragging every inch out of me in a way I feel down in my bones. He leaves me completely empty and damn near whining for him before shoving his cock back in with a single, hard stroke. Does it over and over, taking away the pleasure before slamming me into a wall of bliss.

But it's the sight of him that really does it for me. His biceps strain with my weight as he holds me above the water, fingers gripping my ass. His abs flex with every hard stroke into my pussy. He watches his cock work me with all the concentration in the world, his brows furrowed, hair falling onto his forehead. His body is incredible but his careful focus might be the hottest part about this.

"Such a tight little cunt. Perfect like the rest of you. It's so fucking good, Siena."

I nod, because it is. Then Brooks unclenches his jaw and releases the deepest, most beautiful grunt as he slams into me next, and *that's* the hottest part about this. Every single sound he makes.

"Gotta be kidding me. I'm supposed to go another second of my life without fucking you?" He scrapes my jaw with his teeth. "Gonna lock you up in this house and fuck you whenever I want. Whenever you need."

My body is overheating, the air steaming from the hot water beneath us. Brooks fucks me so torturously rhythmically and I love it, love every bit about it, but it's no longer enough.

I use my leverage on the edge of the hot tub to push into him, not letting his cock slip out all the way this time, and building a quicker momentum.

"You want it harder?"

"Please. Faster."

He grunts, forehead hitting my shoulder. "I'm already close. I'm telling you right now, I fuck you like that and I won't last. You'll be dripping with me a lot sooner than I want you to be."

Oh.

Forget the concentration.

Forget his sounds.

This is the best part. The way he looks to be hanging on the edge of his control, with nothing but a single, final finger holding him there. I take in the pure struggle in his face, the curls sticking on his forehead, damp from the steam rising from the water.

I'd forgotten how long it's been since he's done this. But the reminder that he hasn't been with anyone else in almost two years, that I was the one to tempt him like this, is a high I might never come down from.

"Do it." I practically shove myself off the edge of the tub. Fucking him harder. Faster. He lifts his head, searching my face. "Come on, Attwood. Show me how crazy I make you, or I'll have to call you a liar."

With a frustrated growl Brooks pushes me onto the edge of the hot tub, hikes a knee up beside me, and starts driving into me at such a ruthless pace my breath cuts off completely. I don't even miss the air. The way he fills me, bounces me up and down his cock, and grunts with the force of it, fill my lungs with something so much sweeter.

"Is this what you wanted? Me losing my fucking mind over you?"

"Almost, baby." My words come out choppy from the force of the way he fucks me. I scrape my nails through the hair at the back of his head. "Come on, fill me up, Brooks. You're really hot when you come. I've fucked myself so many times picturing you. Thinking about this, you fucking my pussy so hard and deep I—"

"*Siena*. Fuck."

With a deep groan, so loud every single person down the street must hear it, Brooks goes off. His firm body slumps against mine. I hold him to me as he shudders, feeling his cock throb inside me. Just listening to the sweet sound of his ragged breath as he comes down.

It's a new one for me. I've never been so satisfied, so completely, blissfully sated, just from feeling a guy come. That says something about him and what he means to me. But before I can examine the thought too closely, Brooks pulls out of me. He takes me with him as he climbs out of the hot tub like a man on fire and loving every second of it.

I gasp, clutching his shoulders for balance. "What are you doing?"

He doesn't answer. Brooks kicks a patio chair away from the massive wooden table, sends it flying across the lawn. This has to be some kind of athlete recovery shit, because the man was near comatose in my arms a second ago.

Brooks drops my ass on the table, throws my thighs open, and falls to his knees on the concrete.

There's no way.

His cum is dripping out of me, and *there's no damn way* he's about to do what I think he is—

Brooks smooths his palms over my thighs, holding me wide open for him. "You're not getting off that easy."

Oh my God.

He runs a finger through the wetness along the inside of my thigh, collecting his cum before sinking that finger inside me. Adding another. And dropping his mouth to my pussy with a groan.

I bow off the table, moaning his name. I'm hallucinating. That's it, isn't it? Because there's no way I'm really living this, what has to be the filthiest moment of my life: spread open on a table outside, with the most gorgeous man I've ever seen on his knees, licking my pussy and whatever bit of himself he has smeared over me.

I only realize my jaw has dropped when he looks up and returns a smirk.

He licks and kisses along my pussy, finger-fucking his cum back into me as he goes, before settling on my clit. Licking at it, sucking it into his mouth so perfectly I'm a writhing mess above him. His cock had already primed the hell out of me minutes before, so my orgasm comes quick. One scorching hot pull down my spine, up my thighs, and I'm crying out into the night, thrashing on the table, grinding my pussy into Brooks's mouth, needy for every little bit he gives me.

With a sigh, I go still, but Brooks's mouth stays put. He mumbles something over my skin, seems to realize I can't hear him with a mouth full of pussy, and pulls away.

"Open your mouth." He pulls out his fingers and presses them at my lips in an offering I eagerly accept. "We taste so fucking good together. Don't we?"

I suck his fingers clean, tasting us both. I can't say I have a point of comparison for this, but it's hard to imagine anything ever coming close.

Brooks watches me greedily. "Say we taste good together."

"We taste good together."

It comes out muffled around his fingers, which amuses him greatly . . . until I start sucking on them harder, twirling my tongue, hollowing my cheeks. His jaw slacks.

Brooks plucks his fingers from my mouth and shifts around between my thighs.

"You ready?"

I blink down. "For what?"

"Did too good a job cleaning you up, sweetheart." He stares at my pussy, head tilted like it's the view of his lifetime. "Think I like you better dripping."

Brooks rises to his feet, yanks me so that I hang off the edge of the table, and oh my *fucking* God he's hard again—

I think I might die tonight.

His cock sinks inside me with one merciless stroke, and all I manage is a needy cry that echoes around us. He fucks me so hard and fast, the heavy table scrapes over the patio concrete. My hips sting with his death grip biting into my skin.

This time, when I feel the tight pull inside me, the burst of heat, it catches me off guard. All I can do is clutch at the edges of the table, surrender control, and ride out every ruthless punch of his hips as another orgasm sinks its claws in me.

"Brooks," I gasp. "*Brooks*. Oh my God, I can't . . . How—"

He groans, brows pulling together, and watches me come apart below him, shuddering so hard I rattle the table. This might be the longest orgasm of my life. Wave after wave, winding me up, releasing me. Winding me up.

"Fuck, I'm already—" I lift my head to find a wild look on his face. There's a sheen of sweat over his forehead. "This pussy is—swear to God, Siena—you ruined me." Brooks comes with his head thrown forward, without taking his eyes off us, mesmerized by the sight of his cock moving inside me.

If he's ruined, then I'm destroyed.

"Oh my God," I mumble, falling flat on the table with my heart pounding and nothing left to give. I stare up at the dark sky. No moon, but there are a handful of stars scattered around. "That was . . ."

"Worth the wait."

I chuckle, because how long did I make him wait, really? We met barely a couple months ago.

Brooks plants a hand on either side of my head. His face blocks the sky but I'm more than okay with it. He's a much better view, with his mussed-up hair, blown out pupils . . . glistening mouth. He's gazing down almost dreamily, like he's looking at something treasured.

Something worth the wait.

My heart soars with hope, want. Sinks with dread.

Don't, I plead with him. *Don't make this something it can't be.*

Brooks kisses me hard, then tosses me over his shoulder. "Let's get you inside."

Chapter 33

Brooks

I don't make it far.

I set her down on the sofa and grab the throw blanket hanging over the back, a gift from my mom when she last visited and claimed that the house was sorely missing homey touches.

Siena is shivering, skin still damp from the hot tub, so I bundle her up underneath it. Her cheeks are such a pretty rosy color, eyelids heavy, lips puffy from kissing. She looks so blissful and satisfied, my perfect girl. If I could quit my life again, this time exist with the sole purpose of putting that look on her face, I'd do it without question.

She winces as she fiddles with the elastic band in the mess of damp hair on her head.

"Here, let me." Once it's free, I sink my fingers into her hair, rubbing the crown of her head.

She groans, eyes closing. "That feels like heaven."

So, it's not just me, then. Because I'm fairly sure this *is* heaven.

I scratch at her head until she's sunk deep into the sofa, then get to my feet.

"Where are you going?"

"Getting you a towel." She starts to stand but I gently push her back down. "No, you'll stay put. You know I respect the hell out of your need to look after yourself. But when I fuck you, I take over. That's nonnegotiable."

"So bossy," she murmurs. Still, she wraps the blanket tight around herself.

"Yes." I kiss her and go to leave the room. Then double back to kiss her again because it's official: I am addicted to Siena Pippen. "Okay, I'm going."

But she's looking at me like I've lost my mind now, so I bend to kiss that look off her face.

She giggles against my mouth. "Brooks."

"I'm going." I cannot. Stop. Kissing Her. "Now." I just can't fucking stop. "Right now. I swear."

She's full-on laughing, so out of control I can't kiss her through it. I go for the second-best thing and dot kisses over whichever parts of her face I can reach.

"I'm going to clean you up and cuddle you so hard, Siena Pippen. Prepare yourself." I plant a final kiss on her forehead and force my feet to move.

"Prepare myself how?"

"Mentally," I call over my shoulder. "Physically. Philosophically."

Her laugh follows me into the bathroom. I'd been so fixated on the idea of fucking her that I'd forgotten about the best part—the part you get when you do it this way, with someone you're falling for, and not in a dingy back alley outside of a nightclub with a woman whose name you've already forgotten.

I'm really fucking crazy about her.

Like, move her in, have her babies, love her until the day I die kind of crazy.

And I'm gonna cuddle that woman so good. Cuddle us straight into a real relationship.

When I'm back in the living room, towel and cold glass of water in hand and Pete at my heel, Siena is sitting on the sofa, looking deep in thought.

Pete jumps up by her feet and she snaps out of her trance, grinning up at me as I follow my dog's lead. I climb on top of her with a growl and unwrap her from the blanket with my teeth.

Siena's face is pure amusement. "You are so weird after sex."

It has nothing to do with the sex, mind blowing as it was. This is all her, bringing it out of me. I love the person I am with her. Trusting and playful. Optimistic.

Anyway, her amusement is gone when I run a towel over her thighs, wipe myself off her pussy, and press a kiss over her clit just to see her squirm again.

"What are you trying to do to me?"

I offer her the glass of water and she props herself on her elbow to drink. "Make you delirious enough to tell me everything you like about me again."

Her face turns soft. "I'd do that for free, Brooks."

She sets down the glass and lets me shuffle her around so that she lies on top of me. We're naked, cocooned in this blanket, with Pete's giant body curled up at our feet. I couldn't have pictured anything better if I tried.

I'm already starting to doze off, but even with my eyes closed, I can feel her thinking hard. "What's going on in that beautiful, slightly unhinged head of yours?"

She hesitates. "I'm thinking about how terrible your therapist must have been. So much for no fucking without serious feelings, huh?"

"I don't fuck without serious feelings. Haven't in a long time." I settle into the leather underneath me, tucking her closer. Feeling around to make sure the blanket is still covering her. "M'falling asleep. You got everything you need?"

She must be on the brink of sleep, too, because it takes her a moment to answer.

"Yes, I'm fine." She slides off my chest to tuck herself into my side. "Brooks?"

"Mm?"

"How many cars do you have?"

It strikes me as an odd question, but I'm barely conscious anymore. "Here or in general?"

"Here."

"Just the one. Left the fun cars in LA."

She nods, and the feel of her soft skin brushing against mine lulls me to sleep.

~~~~~~

Minutes or hours later, I jolt awake to a thump in the front hall.

The living room is dark, only slightly illuminated by the lights underneath the kitchen cabinets. Peter still sleeps soundly by my feet, but my arms are tragically empty. No Siena to speak of.

I frown at the dark ceiling. Why was she asking me about cars? Right after I said . . .

There's another thump, a whispered *shit*, and I jerk upright.

Right after I essentially admitted I'd been fucking her with feelings. Serious ones.

No.

"Siena." I leap off the sofa and scramble out into the hall with the throw blanket wrapped around my hips.

She's already halfway down the front porch by the time I catch up. She hasn't even bothered putting her own clothes on—she's swiped my T-shirt, and her outfit from earlier is gathered in a fist.

"Hey—*hey*." I catch her hand as she reaches the driveway and turn her around to face me. "Where are you going?"

A teasing smile stretches across her face, but I catch the panic there before it. "I'm leaving you wanting more, baby."

"Siena. Where are you going?"

That sad excuse for a smile dies right off her face. "I'm going home. Tonight was great. But if we're doing this hookup thing, we need to reset some boundaries. That includes no sleepovers."

"Don't give me that." Every time I think I find my footing with this woman she blindfolds me, spins me around, and sends me on my merry way off a cliff.

"That's the point, Attwood. I plan to give you a lot more of *that*." She punctuates the word with a wink before turning on her heel and moving down the driveway.

My fingers tunnel roughly through my hair. "Are you planning to walk all the way to Baycrest?"

"Don't be ridiculous." She lifts what I recognize as my car fob in her hand. Unlocks the doors and hops into the driver's seat. My stomach plummets.

There's just no way she's about to steal my only car, knowing I couldn't follow her.

No way in hell.

But I stare, struck fucking dumb, as she fires up the engine and peels out of the driveway.

Chapter 34

Siena

"Young lady, you could use another five hours of sleep."

It's a startled Mrs. Robbins who meets me in my building's lobby this morning. My sweet, elderly neighbor gives me a gaping-mouthed up-and-down. Her little white furball of a dog Spike sniffs at my sandals, patiently waiting for his moment outside.

I stare down at my rumpled skirt, hair falling messily into my eyes from the untidy bun on top of my head. "Maybe another eight. I didn't get much at all last night."

With a hearty chuckle, Mrs. Robbins offers me Spike's leash—the ultimate vote of confidence considering my haggard appearance. "I'd only blame you if you did. I've seen that man of yours on TV. He has a fabulous backside."

I force a laugh. "It's really something, isn't it?"

I hurry down the steps outside our building, to let Spike relieve himself but also to escape any more talk of Brooks. My head is enough of a mess without Mrs. Robbins singing his praises so early in the morning.

I stared at the ceiling for hours last night before my brain powered down.

Away from the steaming hot tub and Brooks's ruthless fingers, ruthless mouth, ruthless *everything* to distract me, it was impossible not to focus on the other stuff. The way he looked at me like I was something precious. The way he held me on that sofa. The sweet words weaved in with the dirty ones. He outright admitted he had serious feelings for me last night.

And I panicked so damn hard.

But I owe the man an apology, and that's exactly why my first order of business today is to pick up breakfast from the diner in Oakwood that's been fueling my daily caffeine intake, and then return Brooks his car.

Hope that he's not too furious to give me a ride back to Baycrest.

"Have a good day, Mrs. Robbins!" I call over my shoulder once I return Spike. I dash back down the steps, trying to remember where I parked Brooks's car.

"Why, hello there."

Please no.

I inhale a long breath before turning to find Marty strolling out of the building toward me. My landlord approaches with a toothy smile, raking his gaze over my body before blatantly fixating on my tits.

"Siena." My skin crawls at the sound of my own name. I hate the way he says it. Like it's some dirty secret he's trying to rope me into. "What a coincidence, finding you out here."

I live here, you creep.

"Hi, Marty." I try my best not to sigh the words.

"You've been avoiding me."

I most certainly have—*always* have, though I'm not sure what's inspired him to call me out on it today. I usually leave early enough in the mornings to miss him completely. Then, I perform the extent of my daily physical exercise when I dash past his apartment on the way to mine in the evenings, because he cooks dinner with an open front door wearing nothing but a pair of briefs. He always makes a point of shouting invitations inside as I rush past with my head down.

"Do you still need the lock on your door fixed?"

He's not looking me in the eye—why would he, when there are breasts in the vicinity?—but something in the way he asks makes the hairs on the back of my neck stand up.

The question almost sounds rhetorical.

Like he knows the lock is back in perfect working order, even though I never mentioned it had been fixed. I'd been asking him to do something about it for months before Brooks handled it.

"Marty, I better get to work—"

"Did your boyfriend fix it for you?" he asks my tits.

My blood chills.

How do you know the lock is fixed, you fucking trespasser?

I've never once noticed anything out of place in my apartment, but I feel this down in my gut. This is why he'd dragged his feet on getting the lock fixed.

When had he been in there? Had *I* been in there while he'd been?

"Yes, my boyfriend did fix it."

I fist my hands, willing myself calm. If there's one thing I learned from growing up with strangers coming in and out of my birth parents' house, it's never to confront the creeps capable of *mistakenly* entering into your space while you're in it. No matter how badly I'd love to throw up, then punch them in the throat.

They're too unpredictable. You never really know what they're capable of.

"I'm going to work." I turn before he can get another word in, sprinting to the back of the parking lot.

"I'll see you for dinner tonight?" he calls after me.

Fuck. How the hell do I fix this? I can't keep living here now, not knowing this.

My footsteps stop abruptly when I catch sight of Brooks's car. Specifically, what's waiting for me beside it. "Oh, shit."

In the spot right next to the black SUV sits an identical car in white. With an incredibly sexy man leaning against its driver's side door, inked arms crossed tight over his chest. Brooks watches me come toward him with hard, hungry eyes.

Like he's about ready to devour me. Or murder me.

Devour me *then* murder me.

"Okay, hear me out before you kill me. I have a whole list of reasons why you shouldn't." I throw up my hands in surrender as he simply glowers. "Number one: My blow jobs are top-notch. I know you got a preview over video, but they really are something else. I'm telling you, you're gonna want one." I pause, pretend to think. "Actually, that's it—that's the whole list."

"I came to get my car, you little thief." Brooks straightens off the white car, shaking his head at me. "Who was that talking to you just now?"

"My landlord." I check over my shoulder, but Marty's gone. "I thought you only had the one car. Who's going to drive this one back with you?"

"No one." Brooks's gaze lingers behind me, as though he can still see Marty there. But he moves to the front of the white car, dropping his keys onto the hood next to a stack of papers that he flips through. He slides its final page toward me. "Sign this."

"You've just given me the last page of a contract and expect me to sign it without reading it? Not suspicious in the slightest."

"Sign it, Siena."

He thrusts the pen in my hand and flicks his gaze pointedly at the sheet of paper. Not an ounce of patience. So, I do one of the stupidest things I could do. I sign it.

"Good." Brooks dangles a key fob from his index finger. "Now take it."

"I don't follow. Are you lending me one of your cars?"

"This car was mine for the sum total of four hours, from the time I bought it this morning to transferring ownership to you ten seconds ago." He glances at the vehicle. "I hope you like white. It's all they had in the showroom."

I gape at him. "You're *giving* me this car?"

Brooks collects the document, folds it in three, and hands it to me. "Gave."

What the actual . . .

"Wow. I knew I was good at sex, but this is a whole new level of appreciation. I would have given it up again for free." I pat over my panty line. "Nice work, down there."

"To be clear, I do want it again." He leans into the open window of the white SUV and hands me a to-go cup of coffee smelling of vanilla. Before I can take a sip, he grips the back of my neck and brings his mouth to my ear. "But the next time you want to run off scared in the middle of the night? I'd like to be able to chase after you."

My heart stutters.

Brooks draws away, looking me right in the eye. Daring me to disagree that that's exactly what it was last night. I ran away scared.

"Would it kill you to be more emotionally stunted? Seriously, there's so much beauty in repressing your feelings."

Brooks shoots me a look. Not so much into the jokes this morning. "I'm going to need you to find a way to articulate exactly *why* you ran away scared, because I don't plan on leaving on uncertain terms. I told you feelings were involved last night. You freaked and stole my car. Why?" He nudges my chin when I hesitate. "*Talk*, Siena."

"All right. *All right*." I clasp the ownership papers in a fist. "You're gunning for a contract with the Rebels. And seeing as you're pretty much one of the best wide receivers I've ever witnessed, I have to assume you're going to get signed. Which means you'll be moving back to LA before the start of the season, which I can't do seeing as my business is here."

Brooks contemplates me. "You hate running that business."

"Doesn't mean I don't have a responsibility to it."

"Then we'll do long-distance."

"I've tried that," I say delicately. "My ex demanded a trade to LA halfway into the relationship, and it was . . . hard."

"We'd still see each other all time."

"We wouldn't. It isn't a couple of hours in the car, Brooks. That's a whole country between us. Add to that your training and travel schedule . . ." I shake my head, because it's crazy how history has a way of repeating itself. "And then there's the Rosie of it all."

Brooks's brows pull together. "Shy's Rosie? How does she fit into this?"

I shove a loose strand of hair off my face. "Never mind. Look, I lived this. Thinking I was in a solid relationship when he was here. Seeing each other every free minute he had when he played nearby, traveling together during the off-season. Then barely anything once he moved. He created this whole life out there without me. And I've been an afterthought too many times to go through it again."

I don't have it in me to pour my heart into another relationship that, at best, has me lonely and missing him. And at worst, ends up being yet another time I wasn't worth holding on to.

"I'm not your birth parents. And I'm nothing like Tom."

"I know you're not." He already means more to me than Tom ever did. There'd be no bouncing back if things went the same way.

Brooks rubs his face in both hands, muttering "Thomas fucking Ivers" under his breath. "So, what now? You think this can't go anywhere, so you cut it off today?"

"I wasn't going to cut it off. You still haven't been signed, and it matters to me that you are. I'm with you until you leave. In the meantime . . . we enjoy this for what it is."

"Siena," Brooks's stare could cut through concrete, "if you call us fake, I swear to God I will lose it."

Ellie K. Wilde

"It's not fake. It's . . . an expirationship. We keep this light and
fun until you move, and then it ends. Exactly how we planned from
the start. No harm, no foul."

For some reason, that only seems to amuse Brooks. He closes the
gap between us. My breath catches when he cups the nape of my neck
and brings me closer. Brushes our lips together.

"Yeah? You think you can keep this going, and then see me off across
the country in a few weeks with nothing but a smile on that pretty face?"

I swallow. "Yes."

He crushes his mouth on mine and damn it, I'm instantly moaning. I almost lose my grip on my coffee. Because whether I like it or
not, there's a whole lot of *rightness* in the way Brooks kisses me—the
way our lips move in perfect sync.

Brooks pulls away abruptly, and stares down at what must be a
dazed look on my face with a smirk on his own.

"Liar." He slips something into the pocket of my skirt. The fob to
the white car. "Now, get in your shiny new car and get to work."

I finger the fob. "You know you don't have to buy me stuff, right?
I meant what I said yesterday. I like you without all that."

"I know. You're nothing like her." He assesses me. "You stole my
car because you're afraid. And you're afraid because you have real feelings for me. Do I have that wrong?"

My heart melts for him all over again. "No. You're not wrong."

He presses a kiss to my temple. "Good. And just so you're aware?
You aren't an afterthought to me. You are *the* thought. From the moment I wake up to the second I fall asleep. It's you."

Brooks doesn't wait for me to say anything. He heads for the
driver's seat of the black car as a voice in my head cackles, in absolute
hysterics. *You are so screwed. You really think you can let him go?*

He's reliable and trustworthy. Emotionally available and he cares
about me. That's what makes me gather the nerve to stop him before
he gets into his car.

"Brooks, can I ask you for something?" I wait until he turns. "If I needed you to handle things with my landlord—nonviolently—would you be able to help me?"

I can't remember the last time I had the heart to say the words *help me*. Not even the night Dad caught me pilfering their kitchen. But I trust Brooks to have my back, and this is one problem I'm not stupid enough to try to handle on my own.

Brooks stands perfectly still, maybe recognizing how monumental a moment this is. "Siena, I would help you with anything, no questions asked. What do you need?"

"I think he was sneaking into my place before you fixed that lock—*fuck*, please don't kill him." I wince when Brooks swears, shoves agitated hands through his hair, and laces his fingers on top of his head. "Maybe just a stern talking-to, to tide me over until I move in with my mom."

"You're moving in with me." He holds up a hand when I start to interrupt. "Call it the expirationship special. You want light and fun? You let me move you in until you find another place to live. Otherwise, I give you everything you don't want. Romantic dates. Talking about our feelings. Beating this landlord to a bloody pulp."

Terrible idea. The worst yet.

"Okay," I say anyway. "Just until I find somewhere else. And I'm giving you the car back."

"That car doesn't legally belong to me, so best of luck with that." Brooks holds out an open palm, crooks his fingers. "Now, give your temporary boyfriend the keys to your place and let him deal with this."

Chapter 35

Brooks

"I'm half joking when I say this, but are you sure about this girl?"

I watch Parker scan the wall behind Siena's soft green sofa just a few feet from the kitchen, where I'm wrapping up her dinner plates destined for a storage locker. He's staring with a mixture of mirth and alarm at Siena's crudely reworked vacation pictures, where Shy's face now sits over her ex's.

Slightly unhinged, she'd called it, and herself, the day I first saw them.

Ironically, it's the gist of how I've felt since the moment I crashed into her on that field. Slightly unhinged rubs off on you, apparently. And all I want is more of it.

I woke up at the crack of dawn today to bribe the guy who'd sold me my SUV into driving Siena's new car three hours to Oakwood from the city and hand me the keys.

Then there's the lucky-to-be-alive motherfucker two doors down, probably cowering in his shower right now. Siena's ex-landlord started shaking like a leaf the moment he found me on his doorstep. Telling me without telling me that Siena's instinct had been right on the money. If he wants to remain in possession of all his limbs—which

I suspect he does, by the way his entire pathetic body blanched as I spoke to him—she'll never hear from him again.

I don't think I've ever been as persuasive as I am when I'm working for Siena. Which is why Summer and Parker are here now, dutifully helping me pack up her apartment.

The dinner plate in my hand is badly chipped and rimmed with a faded blue pattern. Still, I bundle it carefully in a thick, protective layer of packing paper. I chuckle at Parker, who seems entranced by the batshit crazy pictures on her wall.

"I can't look away. Why can't I look away?" he mutters. "Who is this blonde?"

The chuckle is a real laugh now. "That's her friend Shy. She's married. Has a real cute daughter."

"I wasn't asking if she's single. I was asking if she's going to crawl out of these pictures at midnight and haunt me to insanity. This is some kind of horror-movie shit. You lay eyes on it, you get haunted." Parker finally tears himself away from the photo wall, shakes it off, and resumes stacking the contents of Siena's bookshelf into a box.

A flash of blond hair in my peripheral vision has me jumping out of my skin, almost dropping the plate in my hand. As though Parker summoned her, Shy stands silently giggling at the kitchen opening, eyes fixed on Parker's back. She's holding her adorable little girl on her hip, shushing her with a finger over her mouth, and does the same at me when I start to say something.

Shy tiptoes over to Parker, who's elbows deep in a cardboard box.

"*Seven days*—" she rasps into his ear.

"*Fuck!*" Parker jolts so hard his head crashes into the bookshelf.

Shy staggers back, nearly doubled over in laugher and clutching her daughter to her. The little girl shrieks her own delight. She glimpses me laughing over her mom's shoulder, and her smile doubles in size.

She's so damn cute. I want one.

Parker rubs at a red mark on his forehead. He's laughing by the time he sizes up Shy, who retreats into the kitchen to sit Rosie on the island. "Hey, freaky picture girl. Nice to know you're as nuts as your friend."

"Oh, no. I'm the sane one." Shy grins as I come over to wave at Rosie. "The sweet to her spice. The Lois Lane to her Harley Quinn."

"Do I hear Shy in here?" Summer strolls into the open kitchen-living room and hugs Shy. "This must be Rosie-Wosie! Nice to meet you, little one."

"Say *hi* to Auntie Cee's friends." Shy moves Rosie's arm in a waving motion. "Siena texted that there was a packing party going on, and we wanted to get out of the house. Didn't we, Ro?"

"Daddy," Rosie says, reaching for Parker.

Shy grimaces. "That's not Daddy, Rosie."

"Daddy." Rosie reaches for me this time, and fuck if that doesn't break my heart. I remember the little girl had done the same thing the day I met Siena.

"Also not Daddy." Shy's cheeks flush, and Siena's unfinished point from this morning falls into place.

The Rosie of it all.

Shy's husband is deployed for another few months. The little girl misses her father so fiercely, she searches for him in every man she comes across. And Siena is holding it up as yet another hazard of long-distance.

How the hell do I counter *that*?

"How's the packing coming along?" Shy looks around the living room. We've been at this all day, and, between the three of us, have managed to pack up the entire place.

"I think we're almost done," Summer says. "Brooks, the bedroom's all packed up except her underwear drawer and nightstands, because I chickened out of opening them. You can't unsee that kind of stuff."

Shy points at Summer. "Smart girl."

"Thanks, Sum," I say. "I'll take care of that."

Parker finishes slotting the picture frames into a box and plops down on the sofa, propping his feet on the coffee table. "Still can't believe you're moving her into your place. You're going to pretty great lengths to trick her into a relationship." Parker's gaze cuts to Shy. "For the record, she'd be lucky to have him."

"He'd be lucky to have her," Shy counters.

I tape up the box of plates and move into the living room to sit next to Parker. "I'm not trying to trick her into anything. I just want her to wake up one day and feel like she can't live without me."

"I think it's sweet that you're moving her in." Summer joins us on the couch. "That's the dream. A hot, rich, knight in shining armor who becomes obsessed with you, threatens your creepy landlord within an inch of his life, and moves you into his ranch-style mansion."

"Hot and rich? Is that your criteria?" Parker asks.

"At this point, my criteria is *man*. I haven't been on a date in months."

For better or worse, our group has been consistently single for years. It's been impossible to feel lonely when we're in it together, able to keep each other company. But these moments seem to happen more often now. Zac followed Melody to the city. I've, quite frankly, become obsessed with Siena. Parker's out doing . . . whoever Parker is doing that day.

And then there's Summer. The unrelenting romantic, looking for her person despite the ex who decided marriage wasn't in the cards for him, only to turn around and get engaged months after their breakup. Despite the weird blind dates and terrible luck on apps.

"Maybe Siena knows someone," Parker tells Summer.

"Oh!" Shy snaps her fingers, securing her squirming daughter to the counter with her other arm. "How do you feel about guys named Aidan? We grew up with him, and he's big on surfing, too—you could go together!"

Summer wrinkles her nose. "Isn't that the guy Siena was hooking up with before Brooks?"

Fucking Aidan. "He's all right," I concede.

Summer gives a mournful shake of her head. "Don't worry about me. You all go on being loved up. Or whatever it is you do in that apartment, Park."

"What's that supposed to mean?"

My laugh quickly turns into a cough when he shoots me a look across Summer. In a small town like Oakwood, I'm devastated to say I've heard stories about the kind of stuff Parker apparently gets up to.

Summer doesn't seem to be afflicted by awkward. With an unrepentant smirk, she brings her wrists together and extends her arms toward him, as though waiting to get handcuffed.

Parker's gaze bounces from her face to her wrists and back again. And then . . . his jaw tenses. Just for a split second, before he blinks it away with a disturbed shake of his head.

Uh. What the fuck was that?

Summer is laughing to herself, completely oblivious to the look he just gave her. Shy seems to have caught it, though, staring between them with calculating interest.

When she catches my eye, she mouths, "Are they . . . ?" She pinches together the tips of her forefinger and thumb and pokes her other forefinger through the hole. The universal hand signal for fucking.

I shake my head. The two of them have always been close—damn near inseparable since I met them in college. It makes sense, given they work together, live across the street from each other, and have been friends since their preschool days. But I've never noticed anything remotely close to . . . whatever that look was.

"I'm going to get a few waves in while the sun's out." Summer heaves herself off the couch with a grunt that's completely unnecessary, seeing as she's in even better shape than I am. Parker digs into his pocket and tosses her the key to his Jeep, which she drives whenever she's towing around her surfboard. Summer pulls her own car keys out of her purse and hands them to him. "Thanks. Brooks, I can be over later to help unpack Siena's stuff."

"I owe you one, Sum."

"No, you don't. Just do me a favor and get the girl. You deserve it." She waves me and Shy a goodbye. Then playfully clips Parker in the shin, bobbing and weaving to dodge his responding nudge.

"Sit the fuck still and take it." Parker catches the back of her shirt to hold her in place and delivers the tap back. Summer laughs.

"Bye-bye, kids," she singsongs on her way to Siena's front door, blowing Rosie a kiss on the way.

Shy turns to Parker the second the door shuts. "So, I get we just met. But I'm nosy enough to ask anyway. How long have you been into Summer?"

Parker scrolls idly through his phone. "Brooks is moving Siena into his house. What makes you think he's into Summer?" He does a double take when he sees us both staring. "What?"

Shy laughs. "I wasn't talking about Brooks."

His brows shoot up his forehead. "I'm not into Summer."

Rosie blows a raspberry from her spot on the kitchen island. Shy nods. "What she said."

"I don't know about being into her," I say truthfully. They've both hooked up with other people for as long as I've known them. "But you just gave her a look. A *look*, Park."

We watch Parker debate whether or not to deny it, but finally he deflates, groaning at the ceiling. "I really need to get laid. I'm giving Summer a look. *Summer*. We were in diapers together, for fuck's sake."

"What do diapers have to do with anything?" Shy asks.

I get to my feet and pick an empty moving box off the living room floor. "And why do you talk like you haven't been seeing a new girl every week?"

Parker scratches at something on the couch. "I'm not fucking them. I'm dating them. Or trying to date them. I don't know, I haven't done this in a while."

I pause, box in hand. "What do you mean, you're dating them?"

Can't remember the last time Parker seriously dated anyone. A flush creeps up from the neck of his shirt, and he grimaces at the coffee table.

"I mean, I'm trying to meet someone. Not that it's going well, but can you blame me? My twin sister and childhood best friend got engaged a couple months ago. Summer's bound to meet someone eventually, and you're tricking Siena into being with you—"

"*Hey*—"

Parker waves me off. "She'll go for it, don't worry."

"Yeah? You think so?" I look at Shy, who's still staring at Parker with all the amusement in the world. "Will she go for it?"

Shy gives me a small smile. "I've known Siena most of my life, and I still can't predict her next move. But I hope she does go for it—if anyone deserves to have a man bend over backward for her, it's Siena. I think you're perfect for each other."

"I think so, too." Empty box in hand, I head down the hall to pack up the last of Siena's bedroom—the panties and bedside toys we're going to have so much fun with the second she gets home tonight.

Before I can get there, though, my phone goes off in my back pocket.

"Pack your bags, Brooksy." I haven't heard Josh this pumped up in years. Not since the day he handed me a pen to sign my insane second contract with the Rebels. "You've got a Rebels training camp to crush."

Chapter 36

Siena

"Jesus, Sum. What the hell did you put in these?"

Melody—the tiny blond woman known as Brooks's first fake girlfriend—coughs into her fist after a gulp of her pink, sugar-rimmed drink. She turns watering eyes on her best friend as her fiancé, Zac, thumps her back.

Summer looks up from a glass she's filling with more of the pink liquid. "What? We're celebrating Brooks!"

"And we'll all be passed out on his living room floor by eight o'clock at this point. Just what a guy who isn't drinking right now wants to see."

I shrug, arranging an assortment of lollipops into a glass. "Apparently, it's my house now, too. And I say it's totally fine."

Lollipops arranged, I take in our handiwork: The candy covering the kitchen counters, jugs of the drink Summer dubbed the Summer-ita. A celebratory banner hanging above the dark cabinets.

The banner reads *You Did It!* and has small graduation caps printed over it, but it was the best I could find on short notice. I'd barely turned off the *open* sign at Ship Happens when Brooks texted about his invite to the Rebels training camp in two weeks' time. I ran out to the shops in my shiny new car, and had Summer rally his friends for a surprise party at my new home. Their friends Zac and Melody made the drive down from the city, and I'd snuck them all in to set up while Brooks went out for his evening run.

Timing for the news couldn't be more fitting after our talk this morning. I'm ecstatic that Brooks has the opportunity to show off for the Rebels. He's earned it.

But it means we're one step closer to our goodbye, and that stings, regardless of how hard I tried to pretend this morning. Moving in with him will only make it worse. But if I have him for just a few more weeks, I've decided to go all in.

Soak him up while I can.

Shy materializes at my side just as Summer passes me a Summerita. She tries to pluck it from my hand. "Mom's night out. Don't make me fight you for that cocktail."

"How old is your daughter?" Zac asks.

"She turned two a couple months ago." Shy takes a long sip of her drink. "My parents are watching her overnight."

Summer throws an arm over Melody's shoulders and tugs her into her side. "Don't go giving Zac any ideas, Shy. We locked down Mel's wedding dress the other day, and let's just say there's no room for both mommy and baby in that kind of number."

Parker uncaps a couple of beers and passes one to Zac. "While we're on the subject, Mels, Mom wants to know if they can park the RV at your place in a couple months. Sounds like they're headed back to town."

Mel frowns at her brother. They look hardly alike for twins, with her light features and Parker's darker ones. "Why is she asking *you* about parking at my house?"

"Why does Mom do a lot of things?" Parker shrugs. To me and Shy, he adds, "Our parents are . . ."

"Eccentric?" Zac supplies, visibly suppressing a laugh.

"So polite. Gold star for the son-in-law." Melody pats his arm. "They're straight-up weird, okay? They sold their home and all their belongings a few years ago to travel the country in an RV."

"Is it bad that I love the sound of that?" I ask.

"Is it bad that you couldn't pay me to do that?" Shy counters.

"Uh . . . hi?"

I spin to find Brooks hovering uncertainly in the kitchen opening. He's mouthwatering in a sweat-soaked T-shirt that clings to him in all the right places. His waves are in tighter curls now that they're damp with exertion, and he has a sweetly confused look on his face as he takes in the banner covered in graduation caps.

"Oh—surprise!" I throw out my arms.

The rest of the kitchen has noticed Brooks, and they all shout their *surprises* in a highly disorganized fashion. Which is right on the money for me, honestly. I was so fixated on the assortment of candy I didn't think to properly rally the troops for a coordinated grand entry.

Brooks doesn't react. He just stares into the now-silent kitchen. And . . .

Oh, it's awkward.

My stomach inches down my body. I think maybe I miscalculated.

I genuinely thought he'd enjoy this, but they're very polarizing things, surprises.

Maybe he hates them.

I'm on the verge of turning to the group, saying *thanks but no thanks, please get out of my new home and take that ridiculous banner with you* when Brooks clears his throat. He becomes deeply fascinated by the wooden beams soaring across his vaulted ceiling, as though it's the first time he's noticed them.

Oh God. He's visibly touched, and my heart melts into a gooey puddle in my chest.

"Thank you," he says softly.

My heart tugs. Literally *tugs* me over to him.

Summer clinks a glass behind me, pulling everyone's attention off us. "Okay, kids, who needs a drink?"

Brooks tucks me against him. "You did this for me?"

"I'm proud of you. You deserve to be celebrated."

"Thank you, baby. This is so . . . But you know it's only a tryout, right? It might not go anywhere."

The fact that he's trying to brush off the accomplishment, that he looks so floored that someone might have done this for him, makes me murderous. I'm not sure I've ever hated someone as viscerally as I do his ex.

"It's a tryout you've worked your ass off to get invited to. I can't think of a cause more worth celebrating."

He beams at that, the warm smile that touches every inch of his flawless face, and I absolutely preen.

~~~~~~

Slipping away from the party, I follow the sound of running water behind Brooks's bedroom door. It's a gorgeous room, neat and understated with its dark blue colors. There's a well-worn Pete-shaped spot on his massive bed. The three of us would easily fit, if he hadn't given me my own space across the hall.

After devouring a handful of candy, Brooks had gone to freshen up. I find him in the steaming shower. Naked, perfect, shoving his soaked hair off his face. He catches sight of me just as my shirt hits the slate floor, and stands there watching me like his prey as the rest of my clothes come off. He's stunning, this man of mine. Just *stunning*, in a way I can barely stomach.

I pull open the foggy shower door. "You packed my blow-dryer, right?"

With a nod, Brooks pulls me under the spray and runs his fingers through my hair. "You live here all of two hours and you're already throwing ragers while I'm out?"

I smooth my palms over his shoulders. "Tell me the truth: How many teeth is Marty missing?"

His eyes close when I wrap my fingers around his cock, stroking gently. "You asked for nonviolent, you got nonviolent. You won't hear from him again, though."

"What did you do?"

A soft breath hisses from his mouth. "Paid off the rest of your rent so he has no reason to bother you. Threatened him, his livelihood, his cat. Five generations' worth of people on his family tree, if he breathes the same air as you again."

"The cat, too? Vicious." I run my thumb through a bead of pre-cum and drag it down his length. "I was thinking about Mrs. Robbins and her dog . . ."

"Your ex-landlord will be taking on your Spike duties, while he contracts people to build a ramp into the building so that your neighbor can make it outside on her own. I mentioned I'd be coming by periodically to check on his progress." Brooks's gaze rakes down my body, lingering everywhere. "And when that's done . . . A guy I used to coach with is brothers with the county sheriff. He'll be paying your old landlord a visit. We can't leave him there to do this to another tenant."

I've done it, haven't I?

Found that perfect guy you only dream about, don't really believe exists. Except that he's actually in front of me, so caring and thoughtful. Gloriously naked and wanting me.

I'm not sure how I got this lucky.

"Thank you for doing that. For the rent and for moving me in. I couldn't have handled it on my own. I really don't deserve you."

Brooks licks a stream of water running down the side of my neck, nips my shoulder. His hands start roaming over my body. Down my arms, across my stomach, palming my breasts.

"You deserve everything. Even better than me." He pauses his movements. "Scratch that. You deserve exactly me. No more, no less, just some guy named Brooks Attwood whose house you already live in."

"Convenient."

"Isn't it?"

"Almost sounds premeditated."

"Almost."

Brooks's hands wander lower, fingertips skimming my stomach. He toys with the folds of my pussy before slipping a finger between them. I sigh and he gently strokes me, dips inside me, returns back to where he started. He repeats the trajectory over and over, staring calmly at my face as the shower amplifies my quiet moans.

"You're so good with your fingers. I could come so hard, just like this." His chest rises with a breath. It wasn't hard to notice the effect of my words last night.

My beautiful athlete loves his praise. Loves the validation, being told he's the best at what he does.

Needs to feel wanted, just like me.

I step out of his reach and kiss down his neck, chest, the crease where his perfect leg meets his perfect body, until my knees hit the shower tiles.

He looks unbelievable from this angle. Towering, imposing. Sculpted to perfection.

I can't believe he's mine. Even if it's not forever, I can't believe it.

"What are you doing?" His voice is soft, overpowered by the shower water hitting our skin, the tiled floor.

"Tying your shoelaces."

"Not if this is a thank-you. No paying me back, least of all with this mouth." Brooks takes my chin between his fingers.

"It's not a thank-you. It's an I need you." I suck one of his balls into my mouth and he grunts. "Bet you'll like this even better than my pussy."

Brooks shuffles us out of the direct spray from the showerhead. "You have the sweetest little cunt, Siena. Squeezes so good around my cock. I highly fucking doubt anything'll be better than that, but you're welcome to try."

"Oh." I give him a doe-eyed, innocent look as I pretend to think on that. Then flick my tongue over the tip of his cock. "What about that?"

His fingers slide past my cheek and comb through my hair, smoothing the soaked strands off my face. "Not sure."

I shuffle closer on my knees, run my tongue down his length. Double back to suck just the tip into my mouth and keep it there, playing with it with my tongue. I stroke the rest of him with a fist. Brooks anchors a hand on the shower wall behind me, groaning over every little slide of my tongue.

I pull back. "And that?"

He grips the back of my neck, tugs me back in. "Think I'm gonna need a bit more to decide."

I wrap my lips around him. Suck on him, take more, draw back, take more. He's rubbing his thumb over my cheek, staring right back at me and looking like he's suffering some terrible pain.

Brooks's fingers gently scrape the back of my head. I think he means for it to soothe me but I take it as a challenge. I remove my hand, grip his hips, and swallow even more of him. He groans as he hits the back of my throat, over and over.

"Such a sweet fucking girl. So good to me."

He looks like a god like this, shamelessly taking pleasure from my mouth. So sexy and confident standing there with a hand on the shower wall, another on the back of my neck, never letting me stray too far off his cock. He has his head tilted and an amused little smirk on his gorgeous face as I work him.

"Look at you, working so fucking hard for me."

The huskiness in his voice takes me over the edge. I reach between my thighs, and moan around the cock in my mouth. *Fuck,* the relief is instant.

Until Brooks takes my elbow and pulls away my hand. He laces our fingers instead. I whimper in protest, maybe in pain.

"I know, sweetheart. I know it hurts. I'll make it feel good once I'm done, I promise." His grip on the back of my neck turns firm. "I need to fuck your mouth now. Okay?"

I stop moving, letting him take over. He never slams into my throat but fills me just past my limit. It feels good because I trust him. Know I'm safe with him.

"Fuck, Siena." His groans echo around us and my clit aches in response. "Sweet pussy. Sweet mouth. Bet you're sweet in other places, too."

I gag once, then again, and his hand closes softly around my throat to pull me off him. Brooks lifts me and turns me around. My palms meet the glass shower wall, back meets his front, and his fingers run along my pussy again. They dip inside, and there's nothing gentle about the way they fuck me this time. There's hungry purpose behind every thrust, every brush of his thumb over my clit. It's burst after burst of intense heat rushing down my legs as I moan his name.

"Look up, sweetheart." Brooks nips my earlobe and grinds his cock into my back. He takes my chin and angles me toward the mirror across the shower. "I want you to see how sweet you look when you take cock. So trusting and needy, that talented mouth parted and begging to be fucked some more."

My hands slip, smearing over the foggy glass. It's me in the oversized mirror, writhing into Brooks's hand. Hair soaked and sticking to my shoulders. I look so small with Brooks towering behind me.

"*Ohmygod.*" The words are a single slur out of my mouth.

"Perfect. Fucking. Girl," Brooks whispers in my ear, every word punctuated with a hard drive of his fingers. My moans bounce around us as my tits slide up and down the shower wall. "Getting fucked with all her new friends downstairs."

My breath catches and pussy clenches, and his grip on my face turns rough as we both feel my orgasm coming. In the mirror, I watch as my mouth rounds, fingers curl, nails scrape ineffectually over the wet glass. I come so fucking hard it rips through me in one powerful, knee-buckling burst, accompanied by a cry I do my best to contain what with the party downstairs.

The sound is barely out of my mouth before Brooks tugs me back by the hips and bends me over. He grabs my elbows from behind for leverage and sinks into my pussy.

"Fuck."

The word bounces off the walls twice, in his deep growl and my breathless pitch.

He's angled us so that I can watch his cock move inside me in the mirror. I rock back into him, a silent plea to fuck me harder, to knock the breath out of me.

Brooks stares, chin tucked to his chest, as my ass bounces over his cock. "Could watch you fuck me like this forever."

My next sound is half laugh, half whimper. "Another time. Please."

Brooks picks up his pace, absolutely *fucks* me just as hard and fast as I demanded last night. He pinches my clit and I'm done. My moans catch in my throat and I'm coming, shuddering into him. He clutches me in a death grip, grunting with effort as he uses me to come. I'm stuck on the mirror, captivated by the way he looks. I swear, I'll never get enough of watching him come. I'm addicted to him.

He turns me around and tucks me into his chest under the spray of hot water. "Regret throwing this party yet? Could've made a mess of this house instead."

"Kick them out. All of them. Right now."

Downstairs, we hear the sound of a glass being clinked and Summer's voice floating up the stairs. "Let's dial this up several notches, shall we? Who needs another Summerita?"

Chapter 37

Siena

"What the hell is in the water in Oakwood?"

Shy presses her nose into the wall-to-wall windows looking out onto the lush green lawn and thick line of mature pine trees behind Brooks's house. Beside me, Melody does the same, as does Summer at her other side.

I don't need to ask what she's referring to. That would be the three gloriously sculpted men throwing around a football outside, oblivious to their audience of salivating women.

"I think Brooks might have been engineered in a lab somewhere." I track his movements—the way he effortlessly catches that ball, keeps his footing when Parker tries to tackle him.

"Zac is definitely part Greek god. You should see him naked." Mel's eyes are glued on her fiancé. "Actually, don't ever see him naked. I'd kill you. Brutally."

"Did you know Parker has a bondage kink?"

Our gazes swing to find Summer staring out of the window with a deep tilt to her head. She isn't drooling the way Mel and I are, though. She looks more curious than anything.

Melody widens her eyes. "Are you and Parker—"

"*No.* I heard it through the grapevine. It might not even be true."

"The *grapevine*? Is that code for your vagina now?"

Summer nudges Mel. "I am *not* fucking your brother. It's code for Sammie Waters, who heard it from Georgia Irving, who heard it from Ava Anderberg, who apparently once spent a whole afternoon happily tied to his headboard."

"*Really?*" I appraise Parker. "Consider me impressed."

"Word on the street is twelve orgasms. *Twelve.*"

Mel makes a choking sound.

"I volunteer to find out for sure," Shy chimes in.

I swat her arm. "Shyla! You're married!"

"I know." Shy groans, burying her face in her hands. "God, I miss Max."

I make a sympathetic sound. I've been where she is, and the over-active libido without a satisfactory outlet was nothing short of torture. "May I suggest phone sex? Highly recommend."

Mel nods with enthusiasm. "Zac and I spent a couple months apart before he was able to move to the city with me, and . . ." She blows out a long breath. "It was so good I've been tempted to role-play long-distance. He's all cool and calm and the voice of reason, but the man has a mouth on him."

Shy gives me a funny look. "I can't picture your ex ever being into phone sex."

"I didn't mean my ex." I push my forehead onto the glass, staring at Brooks. "Tom and I were two ships passing in the night when he moved. Phone sex is a newer discovery."

"And it all makes sense now." Summer loops an arm around my waist and drags me to the kitchen island. "Come on, people, let's let the Summeritas guide us through a manifestation session."

I stumble up on a stool, feeling the major effects of the copious cocktails. The Summeritas are strong.

The Summeritas are *very* strong.

Mel hops onto the island with Summer, both sitting cross-legged and facing me on the counter. She takes a long pull of her pink drink and sags into Summer's side. "Why am I still drinking this? I'm manifesting a hangover cure for tomorrow."

Shy props herself up beside me. "Can we manifest better snacks? Brooks ate all the gummy worms, Parker demolished every donut but the plain ones, and Zac left us . . . two Cheetos." She stares into the picked-over bowl. "Scratch that. I'm manifesting myself their metabolisms. Can't believe they all look like that and eat the way they do."

"That's not a good metabolism, that's living in a gym." I top off my own glass from a pitcher of Summerita. "I prefer my endorphin kick with a side of dirty talk. Which is what I'm manifesting more of."

Summer drops a maraschino cherry into my glass. "And I'm manifesting a time when Siena realizes how lucky she is to bag a guy like Brooks, and doesn't throw it all away. Also, a hot boyfriend for myself."

I groan at the ceiling. "This isn't a manifestation session at all. You're trying to friend shrink me!"

"Friend shrink?"

I jab a finger in her direction. "Friend shrink! Where we all sit around and talk about my baggage until I have an *ah-ha* epiphany in the span of five minutes, then ride off into the sunset like all my problems vanished on the spot." I take a swig of my drink, working hard to swallow when it almost refuses to go down. "Well, let me disappoint you right here. My problems aren't made up. They're not hypothetical scenarios where I assume shit will hit the fan. I've *lived* this before. Tom was amazing until he wasn't. All over me when he was here, and forgot I existed when he was there. I'm in exactly the same place I'd been then, running a business that can't have me flying across the country whenever the hell I want. And I'll never be okay living three thousand miles away from my future husband. Not now, not ever."

I lift my glass, the liquid inside sloshing around as I silently toast Summer, who doesn't look at all deterred by my diatribe. In fact, she looks plenty pleased with herself.

"Why do you look so smug? I just dashed all your dreams."

"No, you didn't. Your drunk ass just called Brooks your future husband." She grins over at Mel, who's been making faces at Pete over the side of the island. "I'm so excited there are three of us now! Oh, *four* of us, including Shy. And Rosie! Look at us, upsetting the group's testosterone supremacy in a single sitting. Well done, everyone."

"I totally just called Brooks my future husband." I fold forward, laying my cheek on the cool countertop. It feels divine against my drunk-flushed skin. "Somebody friend shrink my baggage away. Please."

"We're trying." Mel jabs my elbow with her toe. "Stop resisting."

Summer cracks her knuckles and rolls her shoulders back. She moves her head from side to side like she's hyping herself up. "Okay, here I go: I get not wanting to live across the country from each other. But what's stopping you from going with him?"

"Oh, you know. Just a job she hates," Shy pipes in.

I lift my head off the counter. "I love that shop!"

"Cee, I don't know who you're trying to fool with that. You can't act worth shit."

"Excuse me. I acted in plays all through high school."

"*Acted*," laughs Shy. "You were Munchkin Number Three in *Wicked* and Servant Number Five in *Macbeth*."

She has a point, but I do my best to sound outraged anyway. "Fucking rude, Shy! You said I made an excellent Munchkin Number Three."

Mel snorts. "Try to sound mad again without giggling through the words."

Summer claps her hands. "Let's stay focused, people. Are you completely opposed to LA, then?"

"I have nothing against the city, if that's what you're asking. The few times I was able to visit my ex . . ." The sun, the beaches, the sprawling city and assorted cultures. I *loved* it, and every return home became harder than the last. Knowing there was a whole world out there, but that my place was in a town roughly the size of a postage stamp. In the cramped square footage of the shop.

And then the shame would come, for dreaming of a way out of the better life I was given by people who owed me nothing. Still, it's hard not to feel as though I've gone from one small world to another. Stuck either way.

I press my palms onto the counter. "LA is a bigger, sunnier Baycrest. At least, the parts along the ocean were. I love this area, but it's . . . there's not much to it."

"I get that—I always preferred the city. It's why I left." Mel contemplates me with her cheek on Summer's shoulder. "It all comes down to the family business, then. It's the only thing keeping you here?"

"There's also my mom."

"Who's basically in a platonic throuple with my parents. Rachel would be fine, Cee," Shy says.

"And you and Rosie?"

"Nope, you're not adding us to the list of things keeping you in Baycrest. You know my parents are already over-involved grandparents." Shy stares thoughtfully out the window. "If you're dead set on staying here for the shop, then isn't the solution obvious? Why aren't you asking Brooks to sign with the Tigers and play nearby?"

I don't need to answer the question, because the awkward silence from two of Brooks's best friends does it for me. Summer and Melody both wince, knowing just as well as I do what playing for the Rebels means to Brooks.

And I'd never ask him to give that up.

Chapter 38

Brooks

"Bye, lovers! I wish you a night of hot, dirty sex I wish I was having."

Summer waves enthusiastically from her position hanging over Parker's shoulder as they head for his Jeep, passing by Zac, who's tucking a snoring Mel into his own car. Shy already snuck up to bed in one of the spare rooms.

"Are they going home together?"

I chuckle. Pretty sure Siena means to whisper it to me, but my girl got hit hard by the Summeritas and she ends up shouting the question through the open front door.

"Their apartments are directly across the street from each other. Parker lives over a bar, Summer lives over a yoga studio." I shut the door once everyone has driven off. "How much of that stuff did you all drink?"

The guys and I had come inside to complete mayhem in the kitchen: Mel and Summer lying on the kitchen island, curled up in laughter. Siena wrestling with Pete on the floor. And Shy scrambling for the bathroom, struggling to hold her bladder with the force of her laugh.

"You'll have to ask them." Siena melts into my side, fully rubbing up against me. "I barely had any."

I snort. "Babe, you're wearing Pete's collar around your neck. How did that even happen? *Why* did that even happen?"

She digs her fingers into my hair, gives it a little tug. Flutters her dark lashes at me. "So many questions. How about I give you an answer for every item of clothing you lose?"

"Siena . . ."

"Fine. I'll give you an answer for every item of clothing *I* lose." She sweeps the straps of her dress off her shoulders, letting the fabric drift down her body. Stands there in a tiny pink thong and the bra I recognize from the night she fucked that toy for me. My entire body goes rigid with want.

But she's drunk, wearing my dog's collar, and needs to get her sexy ass to sleep.

She squeaks when I toss her over my shoulder and start up the stairs. I whistle into the house. "Pete, come. Let's escort our girl to bed."

Peter rushes out of the living room and climbs upstairs in pace with us. Such a good boy.

"Have I ever told you how good of an ass you have? Because you do. It's phenomenal. Top tier. A-plus-plus, absolutely no notes." Siena slips her hands into the back pockets of my jeans and gives a healthy squeeze. "Give this man's ass the Lombardi."

I chuckle. "My ass just won the Super Bowl?"

"And the Stanley Cup. The Commissioner's Trophy. What do they win in basketball?"

"The Larry O'Brien."

"Well, your ass gets that one, too."

She gives me a satisfied smile when I lay her down on the bed in her new room. I'd been so tempted to move her into my own bedroom, but getting her to agree to live with me had been a miracle in itself. I figured we should probably ease into anything further.

I'm in it to turn this *expirationship* to a *permanentship*. I'll play the long game if I have to.

Siena pats the mattress beside her, does that little shimmy I love—curves bouncing, tits damn near spilling out of that nothing bra.

I rub my face. "You gotta stop doing that. Or do it more. I don't fucking know."

"Does this do it for you, Brooks Attwood?" She shifts onto her side, propping her head on her hand. "Me in Pete's collar?"

"*You* do it for me. Anything and everything you do does it for me."

"So get in this bed and prove it."

"Please believe me when I say there's very little I want more in life than to fuck us both into a coma right now. But you're drunk and wearing my dog's collar. Are you ever going to take that off, by the way?"

"Never."

Siena bounces off the bed and beelines for her dresser. The piece of furniture had been there before, but those insane pictures she'd had in her living room now hang above it.

"Can I take another shower? I'm going to take another shower."

She roots around, making a mess of the perfectly organized drawers Summer helped me with. I stand there just smiling stupidly at her in that tiny thong and bra, wreaking havoc on this bedroom, clothes flying everywhere. So sweetly chaotic.

Siena throws back her head and growls at the ceiling before flopping back onto the bed. "I can't find your shirts."

"My what?"

She throws out her arms. "Your shirts! The ones you put in my bag when we were out with the Tigers. I wear them to sleep."

Fucking hell.

I'd put those in there in a blind, jealous rage that morning, never once imagining that she'd actually wear them.

I tug my T-shirt over my head. "Here. Plenty more where they came from."

"Thank you," she sighs. Then she melts my heart by bringing the shirt up to her face and inhaling deeply. That simple action pummels the voice in my head forever trying to plant seeds of doubt and insecurity.

My girl. My light at the end of a dark, hard tunnel. Just as in this as I am, whether she wants to admit it or not.

In her adjoining bathroom, I run the shower, holding my hand under the water until it's hot. I lay out a fluffy towel on the counter for her. When I turn, she's leaning in the doorway just watching me with a smile in her eyes.

"Checking out my ass again?"

"Checking it all out. You're the total package, Brooks." She reaches behind her. Her bra falls to the ground, followed quickly by that minuscule thong. "Will you shower with me again?"

"Just a shower. No fucking tonight."

"Just a shower." She nods meekly. "I don't want to say goodnight yet."

I tip my head toward the steaming shower, then drop my jeans and follow her in. I pull her into the overhead stream and run my fingers through her hair until it's soaked, then reach for the shampoo I'd packed from her old apartment and massage it into her scalp. She makes soft, satisfied sounds as I work it into her hair. By the time I move to conditioner and rinse it all out, her body has melted completely into mine.

I'm hard; her hips are squirming. But when she turns to look at me, her eyes have a dreamy quality to them.

"Brooks, can you tell me something honestly?"

"Anything."

"If you close your eyes and picture your dream future, what does it look like?"

"I don't need to close my eyes. It's standing right in front of me." Surprise widens her eyes. "I want you, Siena. I want you and your chaos. I want all your laughter and the tears you refuse to cry. I want you and all those walls you live behind."

"You *want* my walls?"

"I want you to make me part of them. Your walls are there for a reason, and God knows you can handle yourself. But I want to protect you whenever you can't. I want to have your back whenever you need me to. I loved doing that for you today."

"Why?"

That single word just eviscerates me. It feels like I'm meeting thirteen-year-old Siena. Scared, starved, stealing food to survive. Unwanted by the people who should have stood by her, and questioning whether she's worthy of the strangers who saw something in her worth keeping.

"Do you know how I knew I was wrong about you?"

She stares up at me, water running down her face. "I told you my mom introduced me to my ex. That I didn't go looking for him."

I shake my head. "Before that. I knew the day I met Aidan and realized you'd actually gone through with breaking things off with him, even though you couldn't stand me. I knew the day I realized you'd been turning down thousands of dollars so it wouldn't derail my career. When you looked at me with your heart in your throat on that Tigers sideline after I injured my knee. You showed me your character without even trying, without even knowing those were things I needed, and you never even noticed the trail of fairy dust you left behind."

"Fairy dust?"

"It's how I feel when I'm around you. Like I'm hovering a few inches off the ground." I lean forward, just for the sake of being closer to her. "You've drenched me in your fairy dust, Siena. I find it everywhere. On my pillow. In my clothes. Embedded in my skin."

Siena tunnels her fingers through my hair in that way I love. "You make me feel so good, you know that? Are you allowed to kiss me in Pete's collar?"

I do, slow and full, pouring every bit of want into it. Leaving none of it close to the vest as the water runs over us. Making sure that she knows, without a doubt, that I'm hers. And she's it for me.

My tough-as-nails girl. My beautiful captain. My chaotic mess.

My little thief, stealing the heart right out of my chest.

Chapter 39

Brooks

One day, far into the future, someone will ask me to pinpoint the best moment of my life.

I'll tell them I was lucky enough to have thousands of my best moment.

Just me, Pete, and our Siena.

Every single day, at seven fifty-five on the dot, Siena skips down the stairs at home, freshly showered and dressed down after work. She trails that sweet scent of hers into the open living room–kitchen. Pete comes for her at a run. She ducks at the last minute, letting him assault her with puppy kisses before grinning over at me in my spot on the couch.

I'm looking cool and relaxed with my feet up on the coffee table, and not at all like a man who just spent the last couple of hours pacing the house because I couldn't wait for her to get home.

Siena gives Pete a final kiss on top of his head, which he accepts with the posture and wagging tail of a very good boy. He's come a long way since the day I picked him up from the rescue, all skittish and distrustful of humans.

He's just like us, isn't he? Passed over and waiting for his people to claim him.

"Brooks?" Siena gets to her feet.

"Hm?"

"You're staring."

"And you're pretty."

She shakes her head, smiling to herself. "How was training today?"

I arch my back in a stretch. "Not bad. We're ramping things up to get me ready for training camp."

"Should we ease off, then? Are those extra hip thrusts tiring you out?"

"No. They're vital to my training. Absolutely critical. Quitting now would set me back months."

She sucks in her cheeks. "Yeah?"

"It would ruin my career. You wouldn't want to be the one who kept a four-time all-star off a roster, would you? Think of the fans."

My skin sizzles in the nicest way, watching her move around the kitchen. She fills up the kettle we adopted from her apartment and lays out two colorful mugs, also from her place. She loops the tea bag strings around the handles to stop them from splashing into the water.

She's at home here just a week and a half in, and I feel like I'm living someone else's life.

I'm a tea drinker now. This herbal kind, with turmeric and chamomile, that she always has after work.

I hate it.

Hate it. It's equivalent to pouring hot tar on my tongue. But I'll choke down a gallon of it a day if it means I get to keep watching her twist those little strings on a mug handle.

I bought this house at the tail end of a depressive bender, shortly before moving back here to coach at UOB after what felt like one long, dark night. I was at my absolute lowest, but doing my best to come out of it.

It was just somewhere to live. A roof over my head with a ton of land out back, for the dog I figured I'd adopt and pour my energy into.

Now, though? I think this house might be heaven.

Siena puts our steaming mugs on the coffee table and drops next to me on the sofa.

"Hand me the goods, Attwood." She holds out both hands, curling her fingers greedily.

She's so fucking cute.

I pull my sweater over my head and pass it to her.

"Thank you," she singsongs, slipping it on. She swims in it, has to shove the sleeves up to expose her hands, but she looks so content as she tucks her legs neatly underneath her and settles in.

Hot tea and a hoodie imbued with my body heat. It's the compromise she negotiated so that I can keep the AC running as high as I want. I'd run it all winter if it means I can keep seeing her in my clothes. Watch her inhale the fabric around her neck when she doesn't think I'm looking.

"How was work?"

Siena heaves a sigh, and her head hits the sofa back. "Draining. Which makes no sense seeing as it was a standard day. Zero drama, just me standing by the door like a brain-dead scarecrow, pointing in the direction of the stupid live bait at the stupid back of the stupid store."

She demonstrates, tongue lolling out of the side of her mouth and pointing to the kitchen with a stiff arm, before burying her face in her hands.

"I'm sorry. That came out a lot more bitter than I wanted it to. I love that place. It's nice seeing the water right outside the window."

She says it into her hands, in a soft, quiet voice that tells me she isn't talking to me. Maybe apologizing to her dad. Maybe talking herself into loving it. It hurts my heart either way.

"Should we go skinny-dipping?" She'd mentioned the day we met that it was her favorite thing to do whenever she feels down.

Siena surfaces from behind her hands. "It's still light out."

"Fair point." I get to my feet and pull her up with me. "Then we'll go for the next best thing."

~~~~~

Siena strips off her bike helmet and shakes out her hair from underneath it. I swear to God, this woman is a walking wet dream.

In my old, oversized hoodie. In a skintight dress. In the tiny pajama shorts she wears around the house that can't contain the full underside of her perfect ass. In those white overalls. There's just no view of Siena Pippen that doesn't have me immediately salivating.

We walk the short path to the cliffside clearing we've ridden to more than once since the first time she brought me here. We hang our feet over the edge, and spend a few minutes in peaceful silence, just watching boats motor across the bay, either to or away from the marina.

I get why she likes it up here. You feel omniscient, seeing the activity on the boardwalk; the cars moving around the small patch of town known as Baycrest beyond it; the scarce traffic through the pines on the opposite shore of our cliff, lining the road leading to Oakwood; the boats dotting the endless water and people floating in the bay. All while no one knows you're here.

But I suspect I could be sitting at the very bottom of the bay, quickly running out of air, and still love it if Siena were there beside me.

Siena's feet swing side to side over the edge of the cliff. She folds her hands in her lap as she stares right down at the water. Heaves another sigh before looking over, smiling when she finds me staring.

"I blame you. I always felt stuck here. But now I feel *stuck*, you know? It's going to hurt so bad when you go."

"We don't know I'll get signed. I might blow this camp, and then this poor town will never get rid of me."

Siena stares down at her sneakers a moment before asking, "What about the Tigers? Are they still open to you?"

The question puts me immediately on edge. If she ever asked me to sign with the Tigers . . . I'm not sure what I'd do. Playing with the Rebels has been the dream my whole life.

But Siena is the dream I never saw coming.

"Josh is a dick, but he's a great agent. He's got the Tigers waiting on me for an answer."

She seems to think on that for a moment, then nudges me with her shoulder. "You won't blow it at camp, Brooks. The Rebels would be so stupid not to have you. You're amazing."

"Thank you," I say, even as disappointment pangs inside me. Turns out, I want her to ask me to stay. Reaching for the back of her neck, I stroke my thumb along her hairline. The tension in her shoulders deflates.

"I love it when you do that."

"I know. You do this purring sound whenever I do."

Her eyes widen. "Do I?"

"Yeah. It's my second-favorite thing that you do."

Her shoulders shudder in a laugh. "You're just going to dangle that in front of me, huh? Dare I even ask?"

"I dare you."

"What's your first-favorite thing that I do?"

"I love that you trust me enough to complain about your day. I know how uncomfortable it is, especially complaining about something that meant a lot to your dad. But it makes me feel as important to you as you are to me. And that feels really, really good."

The breeze pushes strands of hair over her cheek. She sits patiently as I brush them away. Then she damn near gives me a heart attack as she shuffles onto her knees along the cliffside.

I fist her T-shirt. "What the hell are you doing?"

"Coming over." She shifts around so that she straddles me, with her back to the bay.

I clutch her against me and inch away from the edge of the cliff. "So fucking unsafe, Siena."

"No, it's not. It's the safest spot there is."

Her arms circle my neck. She sits in my lap without a fear in the world. I think I'm doing that floating, fairy dust thing again. If I look down, we might be inches off the ground.

"Brooks, you *are* important to me. I need you to know that, without question. You and Pete are the best part of my day. I sit in that shop just dying to come home to you. Wondering how the hell I survived it before, not having you to look forward to after such a lifeless day."

I love you.

The thought pops into my head, loud and clear. Oddly unexpected, seeing as I'm attuned enough with my own feelings to know I've been falling for her for weeks. I guess all that was missing was the final shove over the edge. To hear her vocalize that I mean something to her, despite her guard and the limits she's set on our relationship.

She doesn't show her love with those three words, but she tells me in plenty of other ways. Maybe it won't be an easy, straight line to our forever. But we'll get that forever. I've never seen it as clearly as I do now.

I'll wait as long as it takes for her to realize it, too.

I am so damn in love with her, and the day I catch a single sign that she'd be ready to hear me say so, I'll shout it from this cliffside. Get it written in the sky. For now, I lift my chin and kiss her—telling her with every lick of my tongue, nip to her lip. Pretending that each one of her soft moans is her saying it back.

Siena trails kisses along my jaw and down my neck before setting her forehead on my shoulder. "Can I admit something? I've been expecting you to try to talk me into quitting the shop."

"I've been tempted. But I can't tell you what to do with your life. Least of all with something as important as this."

"Then give me a small nugget of wisdom. I could really use it today."

I stare at the sky beyond her. The sun is beginning to set, and orange swirls above the far treeline. "You talk about the shop the way I talked about coaching. I was so close to where I wanted to be. Just a few feet on the wrong side of the sideline."

"Yeah." She nods earnestly, cheek brushing my neck. "That's it exactly. I'm a few feet on the wrong side of the boardwalk. How'd you get over feeling that way?"

"I quit. In fairness to you, I didn't have family obligations anchoring me to land."

"Pun intended?"

"Yeah. Pretty proud of that one." I squeeze her. "Siena, if this is about the second mortgage . . . I would love to help you, if you let me."

She pulls back to look me in the eye. "Thank you—truly. But money isn't all it's about, and I need to deal with this one on my own."

"Will you tag me in when you need it?"

"You'll be my first call." She presses a long kiss on my neck. "Can I sleep in your bed tonight?"

I gasp. "Siena actually wants to be cuddled to sleep?" A week and a half into living together, and we've never woken up in the same bed. We'll fuck in my room and then she'll tiptoe away after just a couple minutes of spooning. But, for whatever reason, she never closes my door on the way out. Never closes her door, either. "Next, she'll finally admit that she swerved the wrong way on purpose to kiss me on our first date."

She throws back her head in a laugh. "You are *never* going to let that go, are you?"

"Not until you admit it."

"Except there's nothing to admit. Either *you* kissed *me*, or you have an alarming inability to distinguish between left and right."

"Respectfully, you're completely delusional." I kiss the tip of her nose. "But I'm so glad you did it."

Chapter 40

Siena

A handful of giant men tear down the otherwise deserted Huskies field. With the start of the Rebels training camp just days away, Brooks's agent recruited a few recently retired NFL players to come put Brooks through his paces for one last practice.

After half a day of directing customers to the live-bait section at the back of Ship Happens and staring at the sunny boardwalk outside the window, I threw in the towel and joined his friends at the stadium. I couldn't stomach spending yet another day under the fluorescent lights at the shop, instead of soaking in *his* light while I still have it.

Brooks's gorgeous smile, the butterflies he sets off in my stomach.

Hell, Brooks doesn't give me butterflies. He gives me fire-breathing dragons, wreaking havoc on my insides. Burning me up, disrupting my sense of gravity.

He has his back to me on the field, but Brooks stands out easily as the tallest of the bunch, wearing a number eleven practice jersey. Also, I'd recognize that bubble-butt anywhere.

"So, what do you think?" I ask Summer and Parker. The question draws Zac's and Mel's eyes to me from their places on Parker's other side. "You happy with the way he's playing?"

"I think he looks like a fucking NFL star." There's unmistakable pride in Parker's voice.

Summer nods her agreement. "And I think we're awesome at our jobs."

"Damn awesome."

Without looking away from the field, they sync up for a fist bump between their seats.

Ass aside, Brooks is so captivating when he plays. He was even before his retirement, but he's even more so now that I know just how much each of those runs costs him. How hard he works to condition his body into being able to block a defender the way he just did.

"What the fuck?" Zac's voice is quiet, but his words carry enough trouble for us all to look over. He and Mel are peering at his phone, both a little ashen.

"What?" Parker asks sharply.

Zac hesitates, then lifts his phone to show us. It's open to the homepage of the *Around the League* website, with the lead story in big block letters across the top.

BATTLE OF THE RECEIVERS: REBELS HOSTING ATTWOOD AND MCDANIELS AT UPCOMING TRAINING CAMP

Doug McDaniels. The guy Brooks's ex left him for. My stomach hasn't just dropped—it's left my body entirely.

Parker's thumbs fly over his own phone as he flicks from website to website, like he's hoping one of them will contradict the news. They don't.

I swallow. "Is this normal? Inviting two receivers to compete for a spot?"

Zac stares grimly out at Brooks. "It is. But that's not the problem."

I know what he means. It's bad enough that the Rebels are pitting Brooks against his ex's affair partner, but there's a very real chance it'll mean Brooks comes face-to-face with the woman who broke his heart for the first time since she left him. During a week that'll be high stress and high stakes enough as it is.

He's worked so hard for this. Wants it more than anything. Deserves it more than anyone. And if seeing that woman throws him off his game, after everything she's already done to him . . .

"I know the whole reason I'm going there is to show these people that he's settled down. But how bad would it be if I lose my cool when I meet her?"

"Who, Naomi?" Summer seems to be giving my question real thought. "What would you do to her?"

"I can't decide between scratching her eyes out or some kind of public humiliation."

"If you're looking for someone to talk you out of either, you're with the wrong people," Zac says.

Summer nods. "Public humiliation. It's what she deserves."

Parker smirks proudly. "And make sure you tell her I say *hi*. She fucking hated me."

I lean around Summer to get a look at him. "Why?"

"He was the only one out of all of us to see her for what she was, right off the bat," Summer tells me. "And he wasn't shy about warning Brooks."

Parker shrugs. "Not that it worked."

I glance between Parker, Zac, and Mel. Brooks had mentioned that Parker had conned them into a weekend trip together a while ago, to force them to deal with their baggage after a decade apart.

"You're kind of a meddler, aren't you?"

Zac chokes on his laugh. Mel shoots her brother an amused look. Parker sinks into his seat.

"He's protective," Summer chimes in. "Don't get me wrong, sometimes it's wildly misplaced. But when he's right, he's really right. Case in point: Naomi." Summer nudges him playfully, and Parker shoots her a grateful look. "*Not* case in point: every bad date he's ever failed to save me from."

"I just got called a meddler. What do you people want from me?"

"Yeah, well. Maybe you should meddle. You're all going to get married with babies and have to designate a room in your family homes for sad, single Aunt Summer."

"I'm still single. Do I get a designated room?"

Summer makes a face. "Not at the rate you're going. The Oakwood tourism bureau may as well designate your apartment a landmark, the way you've been hosting tourist girls the past few years."

"Nice one." Parker nods appreciatively.

"Yeah, you liked that?" Summer grins at him. "See? I'm cute and witty and I still can't find a man. Hold on to yours tight, you two. It's dire out here in the trenches."

She says it to Mel, too, but gives me the pointed look.

Parker follows her gaze. "Please don't make me meddle. Because I will. Give me a reason and I'll have you moving out to LA in no time."

I snort. "Are you threatening me with a happily ever after?"

"Absolutely, I am."

Summer pats his thigh. "Easy, big guy. We'll keep that in our back pocket."

We fall silent as Brooks lines up at the line of scrimmage with the rest of his practice squad. The quarterback calls the play and we all watch Brooks power down the field, getting himself open for the pass. He makes the catch easily and runs out of bounds as a defender approaches quickly.

Another whistle on the field. The play clock starts, players get into position, the ball snaps.

Brooks leaps into the air to make another unbelievable catch. This time, though, his feet don't touch back down. One of the defenders catches him around the waist. Brooks crashes to the ground with the man's heavy weight on top of him. I hear their combined grunts of pain as their lower bodies hit the turf.

And then absolutely nothing but ringing in my own ears as Brooks's neck snaps back with the force of the tackle, and his head bounces sickeningly off the ground.

The offending defender scrambles upright, and the other players hurry over. Brooks lies there, perfectly still on the ground.

No. No no no no—

Through the ringing in my ears, I hear Melody whisper something that I think might be *oh God.* I can't be sure, though. My entire body—arms, legs, my fucking heart—is frozen in place.

Summer hops the barrier and heads for Brooks at a run. Parker looks like he's got the same idea, but for some reason he crouches at my side instead, bringing himself at eye level with me.

He's mouthing something at me, looking deeply concerned. I blink at him a few times before I register that he's asking me to take a breath, over and over, as though I'm the one lying completely prone on the football field—

"He's all right. Siena, look—he's fine." Zac's calm voice yanks me out of my panicked haze.

Out on the field, Brooks sits up. He gets to his feet on his own strength, tosses the ball he'd caught at the defender who took him down. They exchange words that better include one hell of an apology for such an irresponsible tackle, before Brooks follows Summer back toward our sideline.

My heart hammers against my chest—trying, I think, to launch itself out of my body so that it can latch onto his.

That's when it truly sinks in. The little jerk actually pulled it off.

That competitive, too-sweet-for-his-own-good absolute little jerk made me fall completely in love with him, despite my best efforts not to. And I'd be livid about it if I wasn't so relieved to see him walk off the field, chuckling with Summer.

His grin falters when he spots me.

Damn you, Brooks. I love him. I really, really love him.

Parker squeezes my knee and gets to his feet. "Thanks for the heart attack, jackass. Shaved about ten years off our lives."

Brooks doesn't spare him a glance. "Siena, come here."

I practically stumble into his open arms. Brooks lifts me over the railing and onto the field, and I wrap my legs around him as he walks us to a quiet corner of the sideline. It's a relief like no other, feeling him under my hands. His sturdy, healthy body, and warm skin against my cheek as I tuck my face into the crook of his neck. He sets me down on a bit of railing a few yards away, but I refuse to disentangle.

"I'm sorry I scared you. Just got the wind knocked out of me." Brooks rubs my back in soothing circles. "I'm okay, I swear."

"Okay enough to play catch in the yard?"

He pulls back just enough to look me in the eye. "What, now?"

"You said that after your injury, you worried you'd never be able to play catch in the yard with your daughter without seeing double."

His mouth stretches in an amused smile. "My daughter?"

"I picture you as a proud girl dad. Little Brooke."

Brooks laughs quietly, looking at me like I'm insane. "Here's hoping we come up with something more creative than Brooke."

We. Me and Brooks. With our Pete and Brooke.

Or something more creative than Brooke.

"Well." I give a casual half shrug. "She'd be your daughter. Name her whatever you want."

"*Our* daughter, and I've been thinking about Sophia."

"You've already picked out your daughter's name?"

"Our daughter. The name's pretty. Matches yours." There's a dangerous, ecstatic rush through my entire body at his words.

"Well . . . either way, will you promise me something?" I wait until he nods. "Swear that whenever you get hurt on that field, you think of Sophia. And if it's bad enough that you can't play catch with her one day, you sit your ass on the bench until you're medically cleared. This dream of winning a championship with the Rebels is important, and you should keep chasing that with everything you have. But not at the expense of the other things you want out of life."

Brooks tucks a strand of hair behind my ear. "I'll pause the scrimmage now. Get the doctor in the athletics center to clear me before going back out."

"Thank you." I slide my fingers through his hair and pull him in. Kiss him like he's mine for good. Moan at the uninhibited way he kisses me back, the decadent slide of his tongue against mine.

"You make the prettiest sounds when I kiss you," he murmurs against my lips.

"Pretty sure I'm the one who kissed you."

With a gasp, Brooks tips his head back, looking up to the sky. "You hear that, world? Siena Pippen finally admitted that *she* kissed *me*."

I huff a laugh. "Please shut up."

"Hey, Brooks?" Summer hurries down the row of seats to reach us, holding out a phone. "Josh is calling."

"Do I even want to know what for?" His eyes narrow as Summer and I exchange a look. "What? What do you know?"

I nod at his phone as another call from Josh lights up the screen. "You better answer it."

Chapter 41

Brooks

The nerves hit the moment our plane touches down on the tarmac.

After months of training, running my body into the ground, sucking up two of my best friends' free time, faking a relationship with the woman who'd go on to steal my heart in a very real way . . .

It all comes down to this. Tomorrow is my first scrimmage with the Rebels since I retired.

It would have been pressure enough without knowing it also means laying eyes on Naomi for the first time since the front door of my house shut behind her. And competing against her affair partner for a contract with the only team I've ever wanted to sign with.

The sky outside the terminal is pitch-black. We took the last flight out to LAX, but the airport is still an obstacle course of people and suitcases that Siena and I weave through on the way to the car service the Rebels set up for us.

My girl is just about the only reason I'm not having to tackle unsuspecting travelers standing between me and safely throwing up in passing garbage bins.

Her soft hand in mine tethers my sanity. She's so damn cute, marching us through this crowd with authority, ponytail bouncing, suitcase trailing behind her. Siena glances over, checking on me like she has multiple times over the course of our six-and-a-half-hour flight. She gives me a smile that feels a lot like the conspiratorial ones we'd exchange during appearances, when this thing between us was pure pretend.

You with me?

And fuck, am I glad she's with me.

I know, unequivocally, that I couldn't handle the next few days without her.

She's my person, my sounding board. Always in my corner, looking out for me. Wanting the best for me. Making me feel worthy of every single thing I want in life.

The contract, the championship. The wife, the kids. The growing old together.

We round a corner on the way to the escalators when Siena hits the brakes with a gasp.

"It's you." She drags me through the crowd to a newsstand, stopping at a magazine rack to pluck a copy of *Around the League* off the stand. "Is this our issue? I didn't know it was coming out this week!"

I grimace at the sight of my own face on the cover. That stupid shirtless, football pants and padding ensemble they put me in.

I look like an absolute tool.

"I mean, come on. The audacity of this cover." She flips it around against her chest, exposing it to anyone walking past. She's beaming, the picture of pride. "You're so hot it's just rude to other men."

A woman pauses at Siena's proclamation. I shuffle a couple of steps to block her view of the magazine, hoping she moves on.

"A little subtlety, babe." I take Siena's wrist, trying to get her to hold the damn thing less prominently. I wonder how I can go about buying every copy of the magazine in this airport without looking self-absorbed.

"Subtle for what? You look unbelievable. Do you think our shots together made the cut?"

Siena flips through the magazine until she finds my spread: four back-to-back pages of whatever words vomited out of me when they interviewed me that day, along with various photos. Including a full-page shot of me and Siena.

We're in the living room, huddled on the couch. Me in just a pair of jeans, her in the Rebels jersey she'd dug out of my closet. It's so reminiscent of the picture that started all of this. The one up in the coaches' booth at UOB.

She's tucked under my arm, hand splayed over my chest, and I'm looking down at her exactly the same way I had that first day. A perfect storm of awed and stunned. Like a guy who isn't quite sure how he ended up there, but it would take an act of God to tear him away.

Except, this time, Siena's looking right back at me.

Her mouth is tilted in a way that's a little perplexed, as though she's trying to figure me out. But her eyes tell the rest of the story. They're crinkled in a bright smile, sparkling with pure . . . adoration. If we don't look the picture of head over heels in love, I don't know who would.

Siena stares down at the magazine for several seconds. I can tell she senses exactly what I do through this picture. That even though neither of us have said the words, this picture shouts *I love you* through the page.

"We look really good together," she says at last.

"We are really good together." *And I love you.*

"I'm going to buy it." She hesitates, then lifts every copy off the rack, giving me a sheepish look. "Just in case your mom wants a couple when we see her."

~~~~~

"You're fidgeting."

Siena leans in the bathroom doorway of our hotel suite with a towel wrapped around her, watching me fiddle with my watch.

I got her naked the moment the door swung shut behind us, which offered as good a distraction as they come, seeing as just the prospect of Siena's body could lift me out of a ten-year coma. But then she went to have a shower, and I really should have just followed her in because all I've done in her absence is pace around the suite.

I'd have much preferred staying in the house I kept here, which only ever gets used by my sister, Josie, and her family when they visit LA. But the Rebels put us up in a hotel closer to their practice facility, and we're making the drive out to my parents' place right after camp, anyway.

Siena moves into the room, gaze lingering on the neat row in which I nervously organized all her shoes. She reaches for me, straightening out the hem of my T-shirt just to slide her hands underneath.

"Talk, Brooks. You're worried about tomorrow. Seeing your ex?" What a role reversal. Siena getting me to talk about my feelings.

"Yeah," I admit. "It's one thing to be on a field playing against McDaniels, or in the same stadium as her with thousands of other people. I'm a professional and I could have handled that. But having to make nice? Trying to convince this team to sign me over him? Siena, you'll be sitting in the stands with her."

"Don't worry about me. I can hold my own."

"I know you can. But they don't deserve to breathe the same air as you."

She combs her fingers through my hair and I inhale the sweet scent of her. "You're the one she screwed over. I think you meant that the other way around."

"No, I didn't. You're a queen. Too good to trifle with someone like her." I sigh into her bare shoulder. "I'm worried I'll do something stupid."

"Like what?"

"Break his face, for starters."

"He'd deserve it. But you won't do that. Because if I'm a queen, you know what that makes you?"

I bite the crook of her neck, soothe it with a lick. "Your peasant. Your court jester. I'm at my best when I make you laugh."

She does then, this soft laugh against my cheek. "If I'm a queen, that means you're a king. And you're better than either of them. There are much more important things than the temporary satisfaction of giving him a bloody nose. You deserve to play for whichever team you want. To win the championship you worked your whole career to have."

"And if I choke?"

The question hangs in the air, revealing the other, more pressing reason for my nerves. I don't want to disappoint her. Humiliate myself. Prove once and for all that I'd been stupid to think I could nail this comeback, after two years retired.

With a hand on my cheek, Siena forces me to surface from the coverage of her shoulder. Her face is soft, dripping love and compassion.

"Choke or don't choke. I'm with you regardless."

Just like that, the weight lifts off my chest. But then that voice in my head does its best to drag me back down.

She's only with you if you do choke.

Because succeeding, leaving here with a contract, could mean saying goodbye.

Siena tucks her fingers into the waistband of my sweats and tugs. "Let's get some sleep. You have an early morning."

"Not sure I'm gonna get much sleep tonight."

She scrunches up her nose in sympathy. "Then let's do something fun. Get your mind off it." She smirks when I open my mouth, and adds, "Something that doesn't involve your dick rearranging my insides, Brooks."

I drop into an armchair, swiveling it from side to side. "Then I don't want it."

She laughs like I was kidding. Siena moves toward her suitcase and throws me a coy look over her shoulder as she pulls out a pair of overalls.

"I have an idea."

Chapter 42

Brooks

I grunt, stumbling on the sand as I attempt to hop out of my boxers while hurrying down the deserted beach.

"Do you not understand the concept of sneaking around, Attwood?" Siena hisses in the dark. "You're supposed to be quiet."

She's long stripped out of her overalls, leaving them somewhere behind as we run for the moonlit ocean.

There's no reason to hurry, really.

It's the middle of the night. Siena has dragged us to a deserted, dark patch of beach which she'd apparently frequently visited whenever she'd been out here for her ex, though he'd never joined her. There's no sound around us but the ocean crashing on shore.

"You're the one dragging me naked into the goddamn ocean, Siena. You know how I feel about open bodies of water." Our feet splash into the Pacific. "You're sure no one will find us?"

"The only living things you need to be concerned about right now are sharks."

I hit the brakes with the water lapping at our calves. "That's supposed to help?"

"Yes, actually." Siena takes my hand, threading our fingers, but she doesn't make a move to pull me in. It's dark enough that I can't completely make her out—just the perfect outline of her naked body, the shape of her eyes when she moves closer. "Come on, Brooks. Swim with sharks with me."

My grip on her hand tightens, and with a breath we forge ahead until we reach waist-deep water. There, Siena grips my shoulders, bobbing as she wraps her legs around my hips. If the idea was that I'd forget about tomorrow's scrimmage, she's succeeded. "Look at you. Brooks Attwood, with his phobia of open bodies of water, swimming butt naked in the ocean, in the dark, with possible sharks around. You're fearless, baby."

"Trust me, the fear is there. I feel the fear."

"And yet, you're doing it. Fuck the fear." Her arms circle my neck. "Fuck the fear right now, in this water. Fuck the fear tomorrow, on that field. Can I tell you something?"

My hands settle under her ass, helping to support her. "Tell me."

"I'm so proud of you. You've worked so hard for this, chasing this dream, and you've stayed the best version of yourself the whole way. So kind and loving. Playful. Dependable. Anything I could ask for. Brooks, they'll be falling over themselves to have you back on the team. And even if they don't, I'll be there in the stands. Falling over you myself."

She presses a kiss to my forehead, and something so damn sweet blooms inside me. I don't think I've ever felt loved like this.

"Thank you for caring this much."

"I don't need a thank-you for caring about you, Brooks. It might have been the easiest thing I've ever done." Her lips dust my temple, across my cheekbone, the scar I got in the very last game I played from the helmet that clipped me in the face after mine flew off, a moment before my head hit the turf.

"Can you tell me something else?" With a soaked hand, I tuck her hair behind her ear. "If you close your eyes and picture your dream future, what does it look like?"

Siena's breath is soft, barely audible over the sounds of the ocean. "It's with you."

My heart soars into the pitch-black sky at the words. Sinks to the bottom of the Pacific at the unsaid caveat.

And I know what I have to do. How we get to keep this. How I get to be there when she needs me. Be there even when she doesn't. When she loves me and when she can't stand me. She's where I want to be. There's just no way I can let her go.

But I push it all aside for now.

I kiss her instead, focusing on the slide of her tongue, the moan she releases in my mouth. Her nails dig into my back, scratching as she shifts her hips, pussy searching for my cock that's already hard and waiting.

"Thought you said no more rearranging."

"I changed my mind. Are you complaining?"

"Fuck no." A breath hisses through my teeth as she rocks her hips, grinding along my cock. She whimpers softly in my ear. "I'm addicted to your body. Since the second I met you, it's all I think about. You're all there is." My grip on her ass tightens and I help her move over me. "You want me to fuck you right here, Siena? Out in the open, where anyone could find us?"

She nods into a kiss.

"You're trouble, you know that? The very best kind." I lift her, line up my cock. "My little troublemaker. Little thief. Stealing my common fucking sense. Stealing my heart."

I release her. Let her slide down my length, luxuriously slow, taking her time with every inch.

"Oh my God," she mumbles. And then her eyes fly open. "We should get out of the water."

"No." With nothing but her to hold on to, I can't do much more than to punch my hips a little, meeting her rhythm. "We're busy."

She gasps a laugh against my mouth, sliding up a few inches only to drop again. *Fucking bliss.* "The water isn't . . . This beach is a lot prettier in the dark."

Fuck. "Don't you fucking stop, Siena." I'm moving for the pier to the right, knees damn near buckling as she presses her arms into my shoulders and uses the leverage to fuck herself on my cock. I press her back against the elevated edge of the pier, wet sand at my feet, and bless this angle. I can fuck her so much harder this way.

"I love your cock." She's panting, letting me take over. "You're so fucking good at this. My very favorite fuck. Best I've ever had."

I groan. Pin it on decades working my ass off to be the best at what I do, but it turns out I have a praise kink I never figured out until sex with Siena. Her words send blood rushing straight to my head, to my dick, and I fuck her harder, wanting to be the best at this for her, too.

"I'd do anything to make you feel good. You know that? Whatever you want. Anywhere."

"I want you everywhere all the time."

She's absolutely perfect with her sighs, the way her body arches into me, her pussy clenches my cock. But it's the way she moans my name that gets me most. My fingers knead the fullness of her ass, inch between her cheeks to brush the sensitive skin there. She breathes out the sweetest little *oh*. Rocks her body into my hand, demanding more.

"You want me here, too?"

"Yes," she whispers. "Please."

"Open your mouth." I press two fingers past her lips, slide them over her tongue. "Suck. Make them wet. Get them ready."

She does, twirling her tongue over my fingers. She sucks them deeper into her mouth, teasing me with that talented tongue, letting her spit coat them, soak them. When she releases me, I position my fingers between her ass cheeks and the next time she sinks down on my cock, she takes a finger inside her, too. She clenches everywhere and gasps such a grateful sound. I'm fucking glowing. My skin feels so alive at the sound of her satisfaction.

I lick up her neck and she tucks her chin down, kissing me. She's taking my cock deep, and after a while I press another finger into her ass. She sucks my tongue into her mouth and I've never felt more complete.

"I can't believe it's this good." Her words are breathy gasps. "Brooks, it doesn't feel real."

"It is, Siena. It's real, and we'd be stupid to let this go."

She's moaning, writhing against me, water ebbing and flowing around us. I'm not sure how I find the mental capacity to notice it, but in my peripheral vision I see two streams of light bounce over the sand in the distance. The dark outline of a car no bigger than a golf cart coming our way.

Fuck.

"Baby, there are people coming." She mumbles something I can't make out. I palm her hip, grinding her harder over my cock. "I need you to come for me, okay? Now."

"Don't stop," she moans. "Please. *Please.*"

"Not stopping." I dip to take her nipple in my mouth—bite, suck on it. Her head falls back with a cry. "Touch your pussy. Play with your clit, Siena. Help me make you come."

She does, slipping a hand between us, and she's already shuddering. The headlights move closer. "*Hey*—who's out there?"

Siena whimpers, bouncing, grinding over my cock, taking my fingers inside her, tugging at my hair as we fuck fast and hard. I can't make out the voices anymore but the headlights are coming closer. What I can make out is the eager smirk on Siena's face. She loves the danger in this, my rebellious little tease. I can't help but gasp a laugh.

I can picture the headlines if we get caught, the angry calls from Josh. But I can't seem to make myself care. She's done that to me, like she has all summer—reoriented my priorities to put her, us, first. More important than my career. Exactly how it should be.

Her face falls into my hair, nails dig hard into my back. She gives me my favorite sound—those breathy gasps. One, two, three of them before she whispers my name and breaks, pussy clenching around me. Her wet skin slips against mine as she shudders, and with an unrestrained groan I come inside her, edges of my vision going darker than the sky.

The headlights swing several feet in the wrong direction.

"Oh my God," Siena mumbles in my hair. She's limp in my arms, surrendering her weight to me.

I don't give us the time to recover. The second I'm strong enough I tear down the beach, clutching her to me, ignoring the shouts from security guards and scooping our clothes off the sand as I go.

I run faster than I ever have in my life, Siena's blissful laugh mixing with mine.

Chapter 43

Siena

I arrive at the Rebels practice facility the next afternoon, feeling so jittery you'd think I was the one in a helmet and padding, warming up on the field for a make-or-break scrimmage. Half the players are wearing black practice jerseys, the other half royal purple, all kneeling on the turf in a synchronized stretch routine.

Spread out over four rows in the stands behind me are women I take for the other partners. I scan them blatantly, trying to figure out which one of them could be Naomi. She's a brunette, according to the internet digging I did early on. But so are half of them up there, and I can't remember her face.

I've mentally composed about a dozen things I'd love to say to her, knowing I won't say a single one of them.

I will be the bigger person. Because today is about Brooks.

He'd been gone by the time I woke up this morning, still so cozily bundled up in the comforter that I know he must have tucked me back in before he left.

I find number eleven on the field, but even with his back to me and a helmet on, I know it isn't Brooks. It's not even about the man's height and build. It's the way he carries himself. He's got none of the casual grace Brooks has on a football field, the easy confidence in every movement.

I will never, ever get sick of watching Brooks run after a ball.

It'll shatter me, slowly rip the soul out of my body, but I know I'll be watching him long after our relationship ends. That I'll be glued to my TV for every one of his kickoffs, still as proud of him as I am today.

If caring about Brooks is the easiest thing I've ever done, trying to fall out of love with him will be the hardest. But I can't dwell on that.

If I do, I might do something stupid.

Something I've considered more than once over the past couple of weeks, but have refused to indulge. Because asking him to sign with the Tigers would be so utterly selfish.

I spot Brooks with his helmet off, on the turf stretching out his hamstrings. He thrusts his hips in a way I've seen several times before, though never with more than eight—maybe closer to nine—inches between our bodies.

I find myself turning to the rows of WAGs in the stands, just to make sure none of them are staring at him in a way they shouldn't.

Especially not *her*. Whichever one of them she is.

"Hey." Brooks approaches the railing at the bottom of the stands and, after I tear my gaze off the other women, I hop down the remaining steps. "You look beautiful."

I shimmy when I reach him, even though my dress is second-skin tight, not loose enough to flutter cutely around my thighs. Hate to admit it, but I dressed up today with his ex in mind, hoping I hold a candle to her in the looks department.

"And you look like an absolute snack, Attwood." I reach for him, pushing the hair off his face and taking in the dark circles around his eyes. "You didn't sleep."

"Not one bit. I'm about to get smoked out there."

"No, you're not. You're Brooks Attwood. Tough as nails. You go on naked midnight swims with sharks, and you're better than any of these other chumps even on your worst day."

Brooks's gaze drifts over my shoulder. "Are you going to be okay sitting with them?"

"Is she here?"

He nods, eyes on me, knowing exactly who I mean. "You'll be proud of me—I managed to greet McDaniels with a nod instead of my fist."

"Setting the bar high in the maturity department. Guess I can't do what I'd been planning." I wiggle my fingers, showing off my bright red nails. "Your friends gave me permission to scratch her eyes out. Got a pointy, bad-bitch manicure and everything."

Brooks barks out a laugh just as a whistle on the field goes off. Behind him, the other players start moving into position either by the benches or at the fifty-yard line.

"Here goes nothing," Brooks says.

I grab his jersey before he gets too far. "Give it everything you have, but don't forget about Sophia. She needs her future daddy in one piece. I need you in one piece."

His shoulders soften beneath his pads. "For you and Sophia, huh?"

"And Peter. Can't forget about Pete."

Brooks's eyes close a moment. All traces of nerves and fatigue are gone. "Siena, I . . ." He pauses. Bites his tongue, I think even literally. "The things I'd do for the three of you, if you'd let me have you. You have no idea."

My heart thumps in my chest. Fingertips tingle. Because I think that's as close to an *I love you* as you can get without saying the words.

I pull my anchor necklace over my head, slip it over his, and tuck it under his jersey.

My silent *I love you, too.*

And he knows it, from the way Brooks fingers his jersey around the shape of the anchor, eyes soft but standing several inches taller.

"I'll take good care of it" is all he says.

"I know you will."

Another whistle sounds. Brooks leans in for a quick, hard kiss. "Good luck up there."

"Good luck down there."

Turning on my heel, I climb the steps to the first row of WAGs all chatting among themselves. Scan them again as though I expect a sign to appear above one of their heads that says, *I'm the kind of woman who cheats on a guy like Brooks Attwood.*

"You must be Cece!" The woman sitting at the end of the first row clears the seat next to hers to make room for me, flinging her designer purse to the ground like yesterday's trash.

Are you her?

"I'm Monica—Cam Guerdy's wife."

My guard drops at the introduction, and I manage a smile. "It's Siena, actually. Nice to meet you."

"Siena." Monica crosses her legs, bouncing a foot dressed in the most gorgeous strappy pink heel. "We were all just saying how excited we are to have Brooks around again! Most of us have been here since before he retired."

"He was always so fun at team events," the woman next to her pipes up.

"The *best* with our kids," a redhead behind me says. "Seriously, we'd all just put them in a room with Brooks and let him entertain them for the night. It was awesome."

My smile is wide and genuine now, because I can picture it exactly. I watched him at the Huskies Tots and Touchdowns camp all those weeks ago. He loved them. They loved him.

He's going to make the best dad.

"Ask any one of us, and we'll tell you we hope he gets signed."

Monica pauses abruptly, smile slipping a fraction as though she's just been caught saying something she shouldn't.

"Really, Monica? You're admitting that out loud?"

Monica widens her eyes at me before turning in her seat. I follow her gaze to the brunette woman three seats over, and I don't need to ask.

I know it's her.

She's absolutely beautiful, with her luscious chestnut hair and deep brown eyes. Thick, perfect lashes. Immaculate makeup, so flawless I'd beg her for a tutorial if I didn't automatically despise her.

Below us, the scrimmage has kicked off. I spot Brooks in his number nineteen jersey successfully luring a couple defenders, leaving his teammate open for a pass. Up here, though, it appears another type of battle is being waged.

Naomi turns a blank look my way before focusing on Monica. "You do realize Dougy's trying out for the same spot on the team, right? You all know him, too. They left the same season."

I take a deep breath.

I will be the bigger person.

"Of course." I've only just met her, but I can tell Monica's smile is less than genuine. "We all wish him the best of luck today."

Damn.

Is that the WAG equivalent of a salty *bless your heart*? It wasn't pointed at me, but I feel the gut punch as though it was. And I certainly see a couple of others fighting their smirks.

Safe to say that if there are teams in the Brooks versus Naomi battle, most of the women around me are decidedly Team Brooks. As they should be.

Me, though? Now that I'm here, now that I see her with my own eyes, feel the tension in the air . . . I want nothing to do with it.

Brooks greeted McDaniels with a nod, and I'm prepared to do even less. I'm here to support Brooks. He's out there chasing his dreams today. Nothing else matters.

My body relaxes into its seat, and I follow number nineteen as he weaves through opposing Rebels players. He sprints downfield with his eyes on the ball spiraling in the air high above him, and makes the catch.

He's phenomenal. *Phenomenal.* And he has this in the bag.

"I'm sure he's told you everything."

I find Naomi's gaze is fixed on me. Somehow, I manage to stop my sigh before it escapes. "Yes, I do know what happened."

There. Nice and mature. I am zen.

Gandhi levels of tranquility.

"I'm sure he's told you terrible things about me."

Zen. Gandhi.

Peace and tranquility.

"All the ways I ruined our relationship."

Oh, fuck this. I've never been zen in my life.

"Has that ever worked for you?"

The sad puppy dog eyes she'd been feeding me spark with something like triumph. "I'm not sure what you mean."

"That bad, sad sack act. It's an interesting choice, considering everyone here seems to know your claim to shame."

Her lips part.

"Oh, I'm sorry. Is that not what you wanted to talk about? All your lying, cheating, letting go of the best dick I've ever had?" She scoffs and tucks her hair behind her ear. I shoot Monica a smile. "I haven't walked straight since I met him, but I guess we all want different things out of life."

Monica presses her lips together, fighting a laugh.

"That's not—"

I flick a hand in Naomi's direction, stopping her before she can get going. "Changed my mind. Let's not talk at all. I'd rather watch my man make a fool out of yours."

I settle back in my seat to see Brooks looking up from the benches.

I'm sure he's just witnessed me interact with his ex, and the sly looks being exchanged by the women sitting between me and Naomi.

"Not bad," Monica mutters in my ear. "And I was dead serious about us wanting Brooks to get the contract. We adore him."

"So do I."

Brooks raises his brows at me. It's his big day, he's the one competing against his ex's affair partner. But as always, he's checking in with me. Putting me first, making sure I'm okay.

To say that I adore him doesn't even scratch the surface.

"Nice ass," I mouth silently.

Brooks shakes his head, trying and failing to kill a smile.

Chapter 44

Brooks

Siena's dress swishes around her thighs as she says something to Cam Guerdy, the Rebels quarterback and one of my closest friends back when I played here.

I hadn't kept in contact with any of these guys after I moved to Oakwood, though they'd tried to keep in touch. It was too painful a reminder that, while I was out there coaching college ball and hating every minute of it, they were back here. Still living my dream.

Even though I'm here on uncertain terms and not for the entirety of training camp, the past couple of days have been incredible. So good that even seeing McDaniels's and Naomi's faces every day hasn't made a dent in me.

I don't give a fuck about them.

It's been everything I ever wanted for myself when I was younger. I'm on the Rebels field, playing better than ever. With my teammates and friends. In my home state. With the girl of my dreams watching in the stands, a smile on her face whenever I look for her.

After the initial scrimmage on day one, we'd been slotted into daily training sessions based on positions. Running drills, conditioning work. Meetings with the owners and coaching team.

Josh's genius really showed itself here. I caught Leonard Dupont, the majority owner in the Rebels franchise, chatting up Siena in the stands earlier today. No doubt trying to suss out whether I'm still the loose cannon who left the state almost two years ago. He'd worn a satisfied smile when they parted ways.

Siena threw me her signature *nice ass* when she saw me looking, which has somehow become our code for *all good*.

It's shocking how different things feel this time around. I haven't been this excited by the prospect of playing since my earliest years in the league. Never felt such certainty that if everything went to hell for me on the field tomorrow, I'd be just fine. Because I'd have Siena.

After tonight's team dinner, my portion of training camp wraps up and we'll be heading to my parents' place in San Diego tomorrow. Now, Siena is right in the middle of the small crowd of players and partners gathered at the bar in the restaurant the Rebels booked out. She's chatting with them like they've known each other for years, laughing, smiling wide. Checking in with me once in a while with a look over her shoulder.

"You good?" she mouths at me where I sit at the table, content just to watch her charm the guys in that magic way of hers.

"Nice ass," I mouth back. She laughs into her wineglass.

The words *I love you* are eating away at me. Tormenting me, poisoning me slowly. I've had to catch them from the very tip of my tongue so many times in the past few days. I'm not sure why I'm still holding on to them. Maybe I'm waiting for a perfect moment I haven't yet found.

"I'm sorry," a soft but familiar voice says at my side. "That must be hard to watch."

A glance to my right shows Naomi in Siena's chair. We've managed to go four days without exchanging words. I'm not sure what's inspired her to break the fortunate streak now.

From what Siena's told me, she's been putting on some sad puppy act with the other partners, probably designed to get a rise out of Siena. Maybe to set me off, throw me off my game.

Thing is, I feel nothing toward her anymore. Nothing seeing her all week. Nothing hearing her voice now.

I finger the outline of Siena's anchor charm under my shirt. "Why would that be hard to watch?"

I fix my attention back where it belongs: on Siena, who lines up to take a shot at the bar with a handful of other wives. I love that she's letting go, enjoying herself, not shying away from getting to know these people. The easily deluded man in me hopes that means she's warming up to the idea of moving here. Being part of this with me.

"I met Dougy at one of these team dinners."

Somehow, I resist the urge to roll my eyes.

Siena takes the shot like a fucking champ, with barely an after-shudder. She high-fives Cam Guerdy, meets his wife, Monica's, hip bump. Throws me a saucy wink over her shoulder, even as her gaze lingers to my right, where I assume my ex still sits.

I love you so goddamn hard.

"You know, you looked good out there today, Brooks."

I lace my fingers behind my head, sinking comfortably in my chair as Kiara Lowndes, a tight end's wife, throws an arm around Siena, who drops her head onto Kiara shoulder like they're already best friends. I used to babysit for the Lowndeses back when I lived here. Their daughter, Nicolette, was the cutest little thing. Made me wear a paper crown to match hers whenever I came over. She must be huge now, two years later.

"You've looked good all week, actually. I've been so impressed."

Monica calls for another round of shots and I laugh when Siena actually buries her face in her hands at the prospect.

"Are you listening to me?"

I jump when I feel a hand on my arm. For reasons unknown,

Naomi is still sitting next to me. She's looking at me expectantly, and it occurs to me that she must have been speaking the whole time.

I clear my throat. "Sorry, what?"

Red splotches blossom on Naomi's cheeks. "I was saying you looked good during practice. You know, even with the damage to your knee?" She leans in before whispering, "I was sorry to hear about that, by the way. It must be so hard on you, realizing you're not where you used to be."

Naomi's eyebrows furrow in a move I think is supposed to look sympathetic. Regretfully, I know her better than that. And I know right then, without a shadow of a doubt, who's been stirring the online rumor mill these past couple of months. It's exactly her style: kicking me while I'm down to punish me for no longer giving her the life she wanted from me. And then securing her own status and position here in LA at my expense.

She doesn't say anything more, maybe waiting on me to blow up, lay into her. Maybe I would've, in a different timeline. As a different man. But I did everything I could to make sure I get signed. I trained hard. Fought for my reputation. Gave this camp my all. Whatever she's done no longer matters. It's out of both our hands now.

And if I don't get the spot, I'll still have the laughter, play, and levity Siena brings to my life. A reason to exist off the field, away from the sport. I'll be just fine. I doubt Naomi could say the same.

All I can do now is chuckle, shake my head at her. "It must be so hard on you, realizing you're about to lose all this because of me. All over again."

Naomi's flush deepens.

"Oh my God, save me." Siena rushes over to where I'm sitting, head ducked but laughing quietly. "The girls are trying to enlist us to take over for their sitters so they can go out and keep the party going."

I push my chair back from the table, thrilled by the interruption. "Tell them we have plans."

"I did! They refuse to take our naked party for an answer."

Siena hesitates behind her chair, which Naomi is still occupying, then rounds me to grab a different seat.

"No. You sit here." I tug her into my lap.

She settles in comfortably, smoothing her hands over my chest. "Are you bored?"

"Having the time of my life."

"Just sitting here?"

"Just staring at you."

Siena makes a happy sound in her throat and buries her face in my neck, planting kiss after kiss above my shirt collar. "You smell amazing. Have I ever told you that? When does the naked party start?"

"Whenever you're ready to say goodbye to your new friends." Siena shivers when I run my fingertips down her back and bring my lips to her ear. "All I could think through dinner was how much better your pussy tastes. I want you bent over the second we get back to the hotel. Need to lick you from behind."

She squirms in my lap. "Now. We're saying goodbye right now."

I give her thigh a couple taps. "Then get going. I'm starving."

Siena's up and making her rounds with the people at the bar by the time my dick calms down enough to get to my feet.

It's not until I collect Siena's purse slung over the back of her chair that I register Naomi is long gone.

Chapter 45

Brooks

"Naughty boy, Attwood. You taking me skinny-dipping in broad daylight?"

I laugh into the top of Siena's head, planting a kiss over her hair as I guide her from behind with hands on her hips. She's blindfolded with one of my ties, but evidently knows the bustle of Marina del Rey well enough to figure out where I brought her, sight unseen.

Still, she lets me walk her down the marina's long dock lined with boats until we reach our destination.

She blinks once I whip off the blindfold, eyes acclimating to the bright, morning sunshine. The weather couldn't be more perfect for us.

"Brooks. You did *not*." Siena's hand flies up to her mouth. "I thought we were going down to meet your family."

With the remaining weeks of Rebels training camp only geared toward players on their roster, we'll be spending the weekend at my parents' place in San Diego before flying back to Oakwood. We couldn't be leaving LA on a better note, either. Josh called me over the moon late last night, praising our performance with the Rebels. He'd already spoken to the some of the coaches and, based on what he's told me, I'd put money on me joining that roster sooner rather than later.

"We'll make it to San Diego in time for a late dinner. Hence getting you out of bed at dawn."

Siena stares at the sailboat docked in front of us. Massive, pristinely white sails and a teal hull—I'd taken a shot in the dark that this was the one she'd spoken about so longingly that day we spent on Shy's family boat.

"Is it the right one? You said you'd stare at a ship with a teal hull whenever you came here. This was the only one I could find."

She hurries to brush away her tears before they fall. "Who'd you pay off to get this to ourselves this time? There's no way it wasn't booked for the season."

"You don't need to worry about that." I nudge her chin, loving the dreamy look on her face and the fact that I was the one to put it there. "Is it the right one?"

Siena reaches past the dock, runs her fingers over the sailboat's spotless surface as though confirming it's really there. "It's her."

"Good." I reach into the back pocket of my shorts and pull out a sheet of paper that I press against the swaying side of the boat. I hand her a pen. "Sign this."

Siena stares at the sheet uncomprehendingly. Then, with an audible intake of air, she turns her wide eyes on me.

"Brooks."

"Sign it."

"We're not doing this again."

"Sign."

"Brooks, you are *not* buying this boat."

"Already did." I take her hand and guide it to the line at the bottom of the ownership papers. "And I'd rather it belong to you."

She stares in disbelief. "*How?*"

"I'm very persuasive when it comes to getting you what you want." I hold her arm out, pen poised over the final page of the contract. After another shocked moment, Siena signs it. Her signature comes out choppy from the waves and maybe her shaking hand, but it still counts. I fold the page and tuck it back into my pocket. "Good. We get to sail it today, then I've arranged for it to get sent to Baycrest. Carla has a spot waiting at the marina."

Unless you agree to stay here with me, boat included.

Siena splutters a half laugh, half gasp. Her cheeks are pink. Eyes wide. "Brooks, you're insane. You've lost your damn mind."

"Yes." I shrug. "You're only realizing this now?"

~~~~~

"How big is Pete now?"

Leo, my six-year-old nephew, lies flat on his back on the checkered rug spanning my parents' living room. He stares thoughtfully at the ceiling as though contemplating the meaning of his short life.

Or maybe how it is Mom manages to get these brownies to taste so goddamn good.

I stare at the half-gone piece in my hand. Seriously, they look like just any other brownie. Though cut into squares rivaling the size of my hand, which is oversized to start with.

But how does she get them so *light*? Gooey. Fucking perfection. I've followed her recipe to a tee multiple times, and could never replicate it.

"You saw Pete only six months ago, Lee." My sister, Josie, spreads out on the couch I'm leaning against, her foot hanging off the edge and landing on my shoulder. She throws an arm over her eyes, the physical manifestation of my stuffed insides after the feast Mom and Dad served.

The food is still spread around us in the living room, covering the coffee table and multiple folding side tables. The Attwoods don't do dinner tables. Never have.

We're the *pile into the living room with plates on our laps* kind. On the sofas, on the floor. Music pounding in the background and even louder voices as we talk over each other, until we eat ourselves into comas like we have today. With Josie and her husband, Colton, on the couch behind me. Me propped up on the floor next to Leo. Mom curled up on Dad's lap in an armchair.

"Oh, Pete is huge now. Ginormous."

Leo pops his head off the ground to stare wide-eyed at Siena, who sits on the ground across from me, legs tangling with mine.

She's grinning at my nephew, nodding in earnest. "*Huge*. Like, T. rex big. The floor shakes when he moves around the house."

"Woah," Leo whispers. "T. rex?"

"T. rex." Siena shifts onto her knees, crawls ominously toward Leo. Making this growling sound from inside her throat.

She's bright-eyed, rosy-cheeked. There's a golden glow to her skin after today's boat ride, and a whole new set of freckles dot her face. She's sun-kissed perfection as she wiggles her fingers threateningly over Leo, who's already laughing hysterically even though she hasn't laid a single tickle on him yet.

Josie props herself up behind me to watch, and Mom and Dad grin wide. I can't help a satisfied sigh as Siena descends on Leo with merciless tickles, growling and roaring in an apparent T. rex imitation as the kid shrieks with delight.

Tonight's been an excruciating glimpse at what our life together could be like if this works out the way I want it to.

In that easy way of hers, Siena swept my parents off their feet within the first half hour. Josie kept shooting me excited looks throughout dinner. And Leo . . . well, the kid looks like I delivered him his new best friend.

I can't believe I found her the way I did. Who the hell meets the love of their life, their future wife, the mother of their children, catching an errant pass on a football field?

Who the hell manages to convince someone like Siena Pippen to fake-date them, only to fall wildly in love with her in the realest way?

What kind of wonderland did I stumble into?

Siena and Leo are now in a roaring contest, each working to outdo the other in length and pitch as the rest of us watch and laugh. Mom is in hysterics on Dad's lap, who turns a knowing gaze on me before tipping his head toward the French doors leading out back.

Colton takes over Siena's position in the roaring competition and she sits beside Josie, laughing. I squeeze her knee. "Gonna step outside a minute. You okay in here?"

"More than okay. Go brag to your dad about me."

I touch my lips to her ear. "I want some of that growling later tonight."

She laughs. "Yeah? Does that do it for you, Attwood?"

"I already told you—*you* do it for me."

I kiss the top of her head, catching Josie's delighted look as I follow my dad through the doors. By the time my eyes adjust to the darkening sky, he's sitting at the large wood-top table overlooking the lawn. Dad sinks low in his seat, relaxed with the glass of white wine he's been nursing since dinner.

Most people who meet Sara and Rory Attwood tend to say Josie and I take after my mom in the looks department. Our bone structure is all her. But my dark features are all Dad, with his thick dark eyebrows, near-black but graying hair.

"You're looking good, old man. Still hitting the gym five days a week?" I drop into the chair at the head of the table so that I can look at him while keeping an eye on Siena through the glass doors.

"Not so much these days. But I could still kick your ass at a hundred-meter dash." He swirls his wineglass and sets it down without taking a sip. "Tell me about training camp."

"It went as well as I could have hoped for. Coaches seemed happy with my performance."

"And you? Were you happy being back there?"

A pad of paper and pen sit on the table from earlier, when Mom scribbled down our take-out order. I reach for the pen and twirl it along my fingers. "I really was. I gave it all up too quickly the first time around. I love that coaching team. I've never played with the kind of chemistry I have with Cam, and I think we'd have a real, honest-to-God shot at the championship this year. It was the best I've ever felt on a field."

Through the doors, I watch Mom push a fresh, hand-sized brownie on Siena, who wisely relents without much of a fight. She's grinning at Josie, who's speaking. When they both lapse into laughter, and Mom looks on with a quiet giggle to herself, I know I've struck gold.

I've always known, but now I *know*.

Siena fits seamlessly in every single part of my life. With my friends, my family, in my home. Even early on, when I didn't want her there, she carved herself a spot in my heart. Widened it until there wasn't a single part of me where she didn't belong.

And the idea that she'd let her guilt win, wouldn't let us keep this? It's eating me alive.

"We were all nervous to meet her," Dad says suddenly.

"Yeah? Why's that?"

Inside, Leo is showing off a plastic T. rex toy to Siena, who *oohs* and *ahhs* with perfect enthusiasm. I don't know how she put her finger on his T. rex obsession earlier, but I wasn't surprised.

"They don't really teach you how to interact with your son's pretend girlfriend."

"Yeah . . ."

Wait—what?

Dad looks amused as hell. "Come on, you talk to your mom more than I do, and we live in the same house. You really thought we'd believe you went almost an entire year without mentioning a girl you were seeing?"

I chuckle. "Yeah, fine. I probably should have told you. It was Josh's idea."

"And yet, you're now here looking at her like I look at Mom. Like Colton looks at Josie. Like Leo looks at T. rexes."

"She's not my pretend girlfriend. She's the one." I swallow past a fast-forming lump in my throat. "But she wouldn't move with me if I got signed. And the distance is an issue for her. Living on opposite sides of the country and all that."

Dad hums thoughtfully but doesn't offer anything else.

"Is that it? No wise, cryptic monologue telling me how to change her mind? No smack to the back of my head for the moping?"

"It's a valid concern. Opposite sides of the country is no joke, let alone with your travel schedule once you get signed."

"Whose side are you on?" I fiddle with the pen in my hand, clicking it rapidly. "What am I supposed to do if she ends it?"

"You keep being the man we raised you to be. You keep doing the right thing, and know that if it's meant to be, the right things will come to you."

I squint at the sky. "What does that even mean?"

Dad gives a low laugh. "You asked for a cryptic monologue. Who am I to deny you?"

He rises when Siena comes out onto the terrace. Dad pauses behind my chair and smacks the back of my head.

"*Ow*—what the hell, Dad?"

He laughs to himself, giving Siena a soft pat on the shoulder as he heads inside. "That's for all the moping, son."

Siena turns a bewildered look on me once the French doors are shut, leaving us alone outside. The quiet evening breeze catches in the slit in her pale yellow, flowy dress.

"You need me to go in there and defend your honor?"

"Nah, I'll get him back, don't worry." I tuck the pen behind my ear and help her settle in my lap.

"Your family is so sweet. Exactly how I thought they'd be." She's got her head on my shoulder so I can't quite see her face, but there's a smile in her voice.

"They love you. I half expect Leo to come out here and fight me for you."

"It wouldn't be a fair fight."

"Leo would win?"

"You'd win. You'd always win, Brooks. There's no competition." She fingers the heart-shaped gap in my tattoo near my elbow. "I still can't believe this is there by accident. What are the odds it would all come together like that?"

I release a long breath, surrendering to the words that have begged for release for what's felt like ages. "What are the odds I'd smash into the love of my life on a field she was never supposed to be on in the first place?"

Siena's gaze travels every inch of my face, as though searching for a hint of a prank. Which is insane, considering I know she already knows.

In the same way I don't need her to tell me to know that she loves me back.

"Brooks . . ."

"I know. I agreed to keep things simple. But there's nothing simple about the way I love you, Siena. It's risky and complicated, and I have no idea how it'll turn out. But you've given me the ride of my life since the minute I knocked you over. And I want to stay on."

Siena nods in a way I can't quite decipher, then she reaches for the pen tucked behind my ear. She stares at it between her fingers for one silent moment before clicking it open. That sweet line carves between her eyebrows as she smooths her thumb over the skin right below the crook of my elbow and draws over my skin.

The smallest **S+B** right there, in the middle of the accidental
heart.

My phone rings on the patio table the moment Siena opens her
mouth to say something.

It's Josh.

Chapter 46

Siena

Sara places a stack of soft throw blankets at the foot of the bed in the room where Brooks and I are staying.

Unnecessary, considering it's the middle of summer, there's already a thick comforter there, and her son turns into a furnace at night. But as she fusses around the room, I sense this isn't about hostess duties. It's the same fussing my mom does while building the nerve to say something.

So I wait her out, seated in suspense on the edge of the bed. There's already a fifty-pound weight sitting on my chest. What's another ten?

Brooks is in the kitchen taking a call from Josh, and my hands haven't stopped shaking since he showed me the caller ID nearly half an hour ago.

I know it in my gut. He's received an offer from the Rebels, and this is it. The moment I've been dreading since I realized he was a man I could truly fall for.

"What plans do you have around Thanksgiving?"

I blink at Sara, who's stopped fussing and now looks at me with a cautious smile, hugging herself into the soft cardigan she's wearing over her pajamas.

"Oh. Well, it's just me and my mom at home. We typically spend it with some family friends."

"The ones who play cribbage? We'd love to meet them all. Would they consider joining us for the holiday?"

The holiday that's not for four months. Brooks and I might not survive the weekend.

But he loves me.

A sob bubbles up my chest, settling at the base of my throat. "Maybe. I could ask them."

I glance at the door, hoping for Brooks. Not because I need saving from this conversation, but because I can't fucking stand this.

I can't stand not knowing for sure.

"I never thought we'd see him happy in a relationship again after the way things ended with that—" Sara halts, forcing a slow breath through her nose, clearly resisting the urge to say something unforgiving about Naomi. "That *person*. But it's been so lovely to see him like this today. There's all this business with football, and I know that's part of it. But he's been there before, at the top of his career, and still, he never . . . *glowed* like he has today. That part is all you, Siena."

Are the walls closing in? They feel like they're closing in.

"He does it to me, too. He makes me glow," I admit. Might as well douse my own heart in kerosene. It's about to blow up regardless.

Sara beams and moves across the room to scoop me off the bed into a warm hug. "It's such a pleasure to meet you, Siena. Truly."

Just light the fucking match, already. Put me out of my misery.

If today was part of Brooks's plan to show me how well we fit, how meant for each other we are, he's done it.

He's won.

Finally—*finally*—Brooks appears in the doorway just as Sara releases me. He gives me a half smile and that's all the answer I need.

"Our bedroom is upstairs," Sara tells me, oblivious to the tension. "You knock on our door if you need anything."

She kisses Brooks on the cheek before leaving, shutting the door behind her.

Brooks hovers across the bedroom. "I have an offer from the Rebels."

This is what it must feel like to be a helium-filled balloon, trying its hardest to float euphorically into the sky while firmly chained to the ground. His words bring me such simultaneous joy and dread that my body doesn't know which way to go.

Do I want to jump up on this bed or crawl underneath it?

I force myself to go to him, sink into his arms. "I'm so happy for you. Is it a good offer?"

"A lot more than we expected, given my age. Including a no-trade clause and a generous relocation budget for you and me."

You and me.

The hopeful question in his voice threatens my precarious façade. I'm just a woman put together with glue sticks and silly putty. Any more of that hope and I'll crumble.

"You deserve every bit. I'm so proud of you."

His body tenses and the silly putty goes first. Melting away, leaving jagged cracks and open sores all over.

"They want us to come to terms tonight. And for me to report back to camp tomorrow." I can hear him swallow. It takes a few tries, and then he whispers, "Please don't break up with me."

The glue holding the last pieces of me together goes, and I just shatter.

It starts as a wave of dry sobs, these pathetic little sounds like my body doesn't quite remember how this goes. Tears fill my eyes so fast they don't even teeter on the edge of my eyelids. They spill free and fast down my cheeks. After a heartbeat in which Brooks goes still, he crushes my shuddering body against him.

"B-Brooks." I'm fighting the sobs as hard as I can, gulping down air so that I can get these next words out. So that I can do this selfish thing I've fought for weeks, and just hope he'll forgive me for it one day. "Please don't sign it."

Brooks pulls back to look at me. I fist his shirt for courage, tears still pouring. "I need you to sign with the Tigers. Okay? If they make you an offer—*when* they make you an offer—I need you to take it. Because—"

Brooks opens his mouth, but I interrupt him with a shake of my head. I wipe my cheeks with a trembling hand, but it's no use. My face is soaked again.

"Let me get this out. Because it's long overdue, and I need you to know that I love you. And that I don't want to be without you. And that I want everything you want in life with the family, and the kids and the dogs, and I want it all with you. So, I need you to sign with the Tigers and not be an entire country away from me, because Brooks? I'm a survivor. I've been a survivor since I was a kid but I'm pretty sure that being without you would slowly kill me, and there'd be nothing I could do about it. So, please say you will."

It takes me a second to decipher the look on Brooks's face, because it looks like none of the expressions I'd imagined. He doesn't look angry I've asked this of him. He doesn't look happy that I just confessed my feelings.

Brooks looks devastated.

And that there should be my sign that this isn't going to go my way. But the stupid, reckless hope in my chest refuses to die until the moment he opens his mouth and says, "I can't."

My entire body sags. My brain goes empty. I back out of his arms to sit on the edge of the bed. "Oh. Okay."

"Siena, I'm so sorry." He crouches at my feet and goes for my hands, but they're bundled so tightly together he grips my ankles instead. "I can't because . . . the Tigers aren't going to sign me. I called Josh the night we landed in LA, after we got back from our swim. I asked him to go to the Tigers for a contract. But they want nothing to do with me anymore."

I think of the dark circles around his eyes the first morning of camp. This is what kept him up?

"What happened? Why don't they want you?"

Brooks's shoulders lift and drop. "They're not happy with the spread."

"The spread . . . in *Around the League*?" I frown at a copy of the magazine on the dresser off to the side of the room. Brooks's stunning face stares up at the ceiling, the picture of understated confidence. And then it clicks. "Because I wore the Rebels jersey."

Brooks nods. "Josh tried everything, but the way they see it, I've publicly humiliated them. It was widely known that they were courting me, and then . . ."

"And then your girlfriend wears a rival team's jersey in a national publication."

"I had Josh reach out to every other team on the East Coast, and they all feel the same way. It's the Rebels, or it's nothing."

An odd laugh gurgles out of my throat.

Because my nosy ass went digging through Brooks's closet that day. Found his old Rebels jersey and thought, *Wouldn't it be funny to watch him sweat if I wore this and nothing else?*

And now . . .

Why the fuck can't I stop laughing? The dry, pathetic sound echoes around us. Brooks gives me a sad smile.

I snort into a fresh peal of laughter, because I've done some truly stupid things in my life and they all pale in comparison. Anyone with half a brain cell could have seen this one coming. Meanwhile, that stupid magazine holds photographic evidence of my own obliviousness.

I chuckle into my hands, truly blown away by my own ability to self-destruct. "I really fucked us good, didn't I?"

"Siena . . ."

"So I guess that's it, then. You stay and I go, and that's it." I jump to my feet, jostling Brooks in the process. I throw open the closet and start tossing things into my open suitcase with shaking fingers.

There's no folding, no care, no fucking common sense.

"Siena, stop."

He's blurry when he turns me around. The tears must be back. "I need to pack. I'm leaving tomorrow."

"You just told me you love me and in the same breath you're telling me it's over?"

I wipe my tears to get a better look at him, but now he looks . . . pissed off. I'm not even sure he's breathing.

He taps at his phone. Lifts it to his ear.

"What are you doing?"

Brooks doesn't answer, but doesn't take his eyes off me, either. I hear the ringtone on the other end, over and over until it cuts out.

"Josh? We're telling them no."

Chapter 47

Siena

I leap for the phone, but Brooks dodges my hand.

"Brooks, stop."

He stares right back, and if it weren't for the sound of an angry voice on the other end of the line, I'd think he was bluffing. "I really don't give a fuck, Josh. That's my decision—"

I snatch away the phone. "Josh, ignore all that. He'll call you back later." I end the call before Brooks can do more damage. All he does is glare. "There's no way you'll quit for me."

"How can you even say that? As though there's a reality that exists where I wouldn't quit *everything* to be with you. You need me to live in Baycrest? I'll do it. You want me to fly home to you every free second I have between games just to glimpse you from the tarmac before having to fly right back? I'll do it. You want me to move you across the country with me? *I will do it*."

"That came out wrong—I mean that you *can't* quit. I could never forgive myself, and you've worked too hard to give up playing now. We always . . ." My chin quivers again, damn these tears. "We knew this was how it would be. We talked about it. I was honest that I can't move, and that I'm not happy with any scenario that has us on opposite ends of the country. You're telling me you'd be okay only being with me in your off-season?"

Brooks paces across the room, more agitated than I've ever seen him. I sit on the bed again, because I'm exhausted.

The emotional burden of waiting for this day has been exhausting, and now that it's here, I'm depleted. I want to lie in bed with blankets over my head and Brooks at my side and pretend we're somewhere and sometime else.

When Brooks comes to a stop in front of me, it's with a final calming breath. Still, I can see he's struggling—fighting for his innate optimism, now that he's faced with the reality of the very thing he's refused to accept despite the conversations we've had.

"I'm absolutely not okay with only being with you in my off-season. I want you out here with me. I want to buy us a house on the water for all our midnight skinny-dips. I want to spoil you rotten, buy you two of every kind of boat there is. I want the privilege of seeing your hair turn silver, lines form around your eyes, and I want our kids making fun of us for being a dirty old couple who still can't keep their hands off each other sixty years later. *That's* what I'm okay with."

Deal. I want it. Give it to me.

Anything less and I'd be an empty, bitter old woman on my deathbed.

"I want that, too. But that doesn't make it possible. It doesn't erase responsibility and duty, or the love and respect I have for the people who gave me my first real home." I watch him tip back his head to stare up at the ceiling. He takes a deep breath and holds it. It's the same way he'd coached me to hold back tears on that cliffside weeks before. "Brooks, I'm so sorry. Hurting you was the last thing I wanted. It's why I fought this so hard. Ending this was never going to be easy."

With pink eyes, Brooks scoops me off the bed and onto his lap on the floor. He runs his thumbs over my cheeks, tucks my hair behind my ears. "Don't apologize. You're right—you were completely clear from the start, and I live with a bad case of delusion. Should probably get that looked at." He's making light of it to spare my feelings and that only hurts worse. "I'm the one who's sorry, Pip."

Something clicks in my head. "You haven't called me *Pip* in a long time."

One single corner of his mouth tugs in a half-hearted smile. "Delusion. In my head, you weren't going to be a Pippen much longer."

My chest caves in on itself.

Brooks dots kisses over my face, my temple, cheeks, the tip of my nose, searching for permission until I take a handful of his hair and pull him in for the real thing.

I kiss him hard. Every lick of my tongue is an *I'm sorry*. Every nip to his lip an *I wish things were different*. Brooks combs his fingers through my hair, all the way through like he's trying to savor the feel of it before doubling back to anchor my head and deepen the kiss.

"Brooks," I whisper against his mouth. He reaches for the hem of my shirt in response, tugging it up and over my head once I lift my arms.

It's the mistake of all mistakes, doing this again. Having him now just to let him go in the morning.

But I've done an excellent job of breaking my own heart already—and worse, breaking Brooks's heart. What's one more shove of the ice pick? I'm already broken.

Brooks's hands are everywhere—down my spine, along my waist, through my hair again. He sweeps my shoulder, my elbow, feeling every bit of me. I scrape my fingers under his shirt, up his stomach, trying to touch him everywhere the same way.

I need to be able to recreate him in my mind, even years from now. Every rise and dip of his body, every callus on his hands. I want to close my eyes and find the precise length and shape of the scar on his cheek among memories of his body swaying with the waves on a sailboat, and the way he bites into a lollipop because he's too impatient to let it melt.

Brooks lifts his arms and lets me tug off his shirt, snaps off my bra and flattens me to him like he's trying to absorb me. Give me no option but to stay. He grunts when I shift on his lap.

I'm straddling him on the floor, our bodies grinding together, searching, demanding the right kind of friction. My shorts ride to the side and my bare pussy meets his sweats. My clit barely makes contact with his straining cock before he lurches forward so that I'm flat on the ground.

Brooks groans softly, looking down between us. "Look at what you've done." His thumb moves through the slick, wet patch on the front of his sweatpants I left behind. "Made a pretty little mess on me."

He smooths his thumb over my nipple, spreading my own wetness. Licks it off, swirling his tongue and grazing with his teeth.

I pant into the room, tucking my chin down so that I never lose sight of him as he moves along my body, kissing every part he'd explored with his hands, like he needs to remember me both ways. How I feel, the way I taste.

He yanks my shorts to the side, freeing my pussy, and kisses the skin all around it, too.

"I want that mess on my face, Pip." Brooks shoves my legs apart, holding me wide open. "I need you to soak me. Okay? I need to wake up with you on my lips. I want the sweet taste of your pussy to linger for days, to keep me warm when you can't. I want it imprinted in my fucking brain, Siena."

I writhe into the ground but his hands force me still as he licks one long path along my pussy. His teeth scrape over my clit and I almost shoot off the ground.

"Oh my God."

"That's what I'm saying."

He nips my clit before sucking it into his mouth. He does that over and over until the heart that had evaporated from my chest appears right there, in my clit, beating hard and heavy as Brooks winds me up.

I feel hot and swollen, needy in a way I've never been. If I'd ever let myself picture goodbye sex with Brooks, the love of my life, it wouldn't have been this.

There's no soft and sweet; no timid, parting touches. It's all greed and desperation.

"That feels so good." My fingers grip my own hair.

"Yeah? Are you gonna come hard for me, Pip?"

"Yeah." Vaguely, I process his persistent, renewed use of the nickname and the new wave of bitterness inside me that comes with it.

I don't want to be a Pip or a Pippen or anything that brands me as anything but his.

Brooks nips my clit, soothes it with a wet lick. "Good. I want you coming so hard it haunts you for the rest of your life. I want to ruin you for anyone else, want you to remember how *mine* you are every time another man looks at you."

There'll never be anyone else, I mean to say, but Brooks licks me back into his mouth and this time stays put, flicking his tongue, sucking, pushing his face into me like he's begging to suffocate in me. I hold the back of his head, rock into his mouth, and he groans his appreciation.

I'm doing my best to stay quiet, seeing as we're in a house of sleeping people, but all that means is that the room fills with the wet sounds of his mouth sucking on me. Brooks lifts off me just long enough to mutter *louder*, before continuing to lick me.

My fingers twist in his hair. "It's—" I bite down on a moan. "Your parents—"

"I said *louder*. You aren't going to let me fuck you one last time just to withhold your sounds." He bites my clit again. "Everyone is upstairs, on the other side of the house. Make my ears ring, Pippen."

My stomach twists. "Don't call me that."

"Why not, Pippen?" His fingers bite into my thighs before he

releases one and works a finger into my pussy. "Does it hurt, Pippen?"
He adds another finger, pumps inside me. "You want the kid gloves,
Pippen? You want me to pretend you didn't just piledrive my heart,
Pippen?"

"Don't say that."

"It doesn't even matter." His voice goes soft. "Break my heart.
Love it back. Rip it right out of my chest. It's yours, anyway. Do
whatever you want with it."

Brooks's fingers fuck me hard, shoving me up and down the rug,
hitting all the right spots. It cuts off my air supply, makes it impossible to string together a coherent thought.

"I need you to moan for me, Siena."

I do. A drawn-out moan, drenched in relief, like the command
was that final permission it needed to release. He relents at the sound
of it, brings his mouth back to my clit. Lets me set the pace as my
hips move into him. I hook a leg over his shoulder, dig my heel into
his back for leverage.

Brooks's entire body shifts with mine, and I realize he's rubbing
his cock on the rug beneath us, hands too preoccupied with me to
bother with himself.

I am ruined. I am wrecked. My own fingers couldn't bring me
relief after this.

"*I'm gonna come, I'm gonna come, I'm gonna come,*" I chant. Brooks
grunts, grinding into the ground and sucking on my clit with renewed enthusiasm. My entire body clenches to the point of pain. To
the point of lifting off the rug only to collapse right back down as I
come, shuddering into Brooks's mouth.

I'm not sure how it happens, but one second I'm flat on the
ground and the next my back hits the soft bed. Brooks blinks down
at me. Mouth, chin, everything soaked with me. Eyes unfocused, hair
thrown around from my handling. He's a mess.

My mess.

"Come here," I urge him. "Put your cock in my mouth. I need to taste you, too."

Brooks crawls over me, shoving down his sweats as he goes. He angles his cock into my open mouth, scraping it over my tongue. He grips the headboard, staring down at me as I take my turn tasting him. He fucks my mouth, kneeling over my head. His face still glistens from me, and I feel my own chin and cheeks soak the same way as I swallow him, over and over.

He mumbles a barely coherent stream of *fuck*s and *Siena*s as he strokes into my mouth. He's flawless—a fucking masterpiece with his abs flexing over me. I reach around him to feel the way his muscular ass tenses with effort as he fucks my mouth.

My pussy clenches on nothing, begging for more like the greedy thing it is.

I need to feel him inside me.

"I need to be inside you," he grunts, proving how thoroughly he's weaved himself into my brain.

Yes.

Please.

Take anything you want.

Brooks wrenches out of my mouth, scoops me up, and sits me on top of him. He calls out my name when I inch down his cock.

"I'm close." He nips my lip when he's all the way in, hitting me so beautifully deep. "Really fucking close, Pip."

I nod frantically because so am I. I'm grinding my clit on his body and rocking above him. Brooks strokes down my back, grips my ass in both hands, and moves me faster, harder. He breaks our kiss to push his fingers into my mouth. I moan around them, skin coming alive with anticipation.

"Nice and wet," he murmurs, watching me eagerly suck his fingers, coat them, make them slick. "So greedy to be fucked everywhere, aren't you?"

Only if it's you.

He withdraws his fingers and I'm trembling, holding my breath, waiting for the push. His fingers trail between my cheeks, work their way inside.

"Brooks," I whimper.

"Breathe," he demands. I do, and his fingers inch into my ass. "Good. Now, back up into it, baby. Take them as deep as you need and come for me."

It's hard but satisfying work. I sway back and forth, taking his fingers, taking his cock, kissing him hard. I cry into his mouth as the pressure builds. Sink my nails into his shoulders as it peaks and hurls me off the edge without mercy. Brooks takes over when my body stills, fucking me from below. At the last second, he twists his head, releasing my mouth. My cries fill the room, loud and broken from the force with which he fucks me.

"I love you." My words are breathless, slip out without a thought. His eyes widen. "Brooks, you're mine and I love you and—"

"Oh, *fuck*." Brooks digs his palms into my thighs to stop my movement. He keeps his cock deep inside me as he comes with an unrestrained groan.

It's still echoing around us as he cups my face and kisses me hard. When he breaks away, it's with the same fire I find in his eyes whenever he hits a football field. Determined. Competitive.

Refusing to back down.

"This isn't over for me. Tell me you don't want this to end."

"I don't want it to end. Brooks, if there was a way, I'd be here with you."

"Then find a way." He rakes the hair off my face, kisses my cheek, my forehead, my mouth. "Find a way, because I'm yours, Siena. I'm yours now, yours tomorrow. I'll be yours even if you decide you're no longer mine. But, please, don't let today be that day."

His words embolden my heart as it fights, gasping for life. Because none of that felt like a breakup. None of it.

It felt like me and Brooks, and the kind of love that makes you do crazy things just to keep it. Like trying to quit your dream career a second after you get it back, or paying people off to keep raising their daughter yourself.

Turns out, Brooks was right. When it comes down to it, I don't have it in me to let him go. "We're not breaking up."

Relief floods his perfect face. He kisses me hard. "Thank fuck."

"I need to go home. To talk to my mom. "Figure out a way to be here."

"And if you do?"

"Then I'll come back." I stroke a wave off his forehead. "I promise."

Chapter 48

Siena

Hey, it's Brooks. Leave me a message . . . and I'll call you back.

Mismatched schedules, missed calls, and spotty text conversations all confirm what I already know: long-distance fucking sucks.

I've heard that voicemail recording so many times over the past week, I could recite it in the same cadence as his deep voice. Could cue the exact moment two barks sound in the background, and Brooks trails off on the word *message* as his focus shifts to Pete before finishing his thought.

I rest my head on the metal shelf behind me, hiding out deep in aisle four to spare customers from my sulking. Brooks looks up at me from the phone in my lap, in a mirror selfie showing off the brand-new Rebels jersey they handed him this morning with his name on the back. Whoever had taken his number eleven in the years since he retired appears to have given it back. The silver chain from my anchor necklace peeks out from the collar. I left it, and my heart, back across the country.

I am so happy for him. Unbelievably proud of him.

And so fucking miserable without him. I've dated an in-season athlete before and know just how hard it is to get their attention, during camp especially. But this is the first time I've lived it while loving a man so deeply, and every unanswered call or delayed text reply feels harder than the last. If I'm not at work and unable to get to my phone, then Brooks is. If I'm not falling asleep waiting for him to call me after being released from late team meetings for the night, then he's passing out exhausted by the time I answer that I'm still awake. And any time I do hear his voice feels like taking a single bite of my favorite dessert, without knowing when the next spoonful will come.

Brooks has been so patient with me all week, hasn't needled me in the slightest about dragging my feet on talking to Mom, but I know the uncertainty can't be easy on him. Pete misses Brooks just as much, if his limp tail is any indication. It's made me feel doubly guilty for avoiding Mom all week so that she won't notice my misery and force me to talk before I'm ready. But it's cribbage night tonight, and I've run out of time. A no-show would be the ultimate tell.

How do you go to one of the most important people in your life and tell her you're leaving her? That you're jumping ship on her husband's legacy, who sacrificed so much for you, a child he picked up off the street?

Between the guilt over leaving Brooks across the country and avoiding Mom, and the guilt over my desire to abandon the shop, I haven't had a proper meal in days.

I blow out a long breath, listening to the light chatter around the shop and the bell above the door as people come and go. Probably with a hefty pile of stolen lures and live bait because I've left the checkout counter unmanned for the past twenty minutes, and Aidan is off competing in one of his surf events in Hawaii.

"Excuse me, do you know where they keep the live bait here?" someone asks toward the front of the shop.

I allow myself one last deep sigh before slapping on a smile that likely looks more psychotic than friendly and dragging my feet toward the register.

"Uh . . . You know what? I don't even know what that is. Like, worms?"

My steps stutter at the familiar voice. I emerge from aisle four to find Parker looking around the shop with mild interest, hands tucked into the pockets of his athletic shorts. He's wearing a UOB T-shirt, light brown hair pushed back and curling around his ears under a backward baseball cap.

"Parker? What's going on?"

"Cee!" Summer emerges from aisle one. She's closely followed by Shy who, in a rare occurrence, doesn't have Rosie trailing her. Which is a shame, because I could have used that little girl's smile today. "There you are. We had gaps between clients down at the rehab center."

I let Shy tuck me into her side. "And you decided to shop for lures to fill your time?"

"Rumor has it you need some company." Parker tips his head to one side, assessing me. "Do you know your shirt's inside out?"

Sure enough, it is. I've been too much of a nervous wreck to notice. "Does this rumor happen to originate from a six-foot-four football god with an ass to kill for?"

"If you mean Brooks, I'll have to take your word for it." Parker wrinkles his nose. "Can't say I've ever sat staring at my friend's ass."

Shy's shoulders pop with a chuckle. "Keep telling yourself that. Maybe one day you'll actually believe it."

It might be the cribbage-induced nerves, but I think I'm missing a joke. Parker seems to get it just fine, though, given the warning look he gives Shy. And hey, if he's been secretly checking out Brooks's backside, I wouldn't blame him in the slightest.

But then Parker's gaze cuts to Summer, whose head is tipped all the way back to stare at the bejeweled lures dangling from the ceiling, not paying this exchange any mind. His eyes linger on her signature sun-bleached French braids, then fall down her back, all the way down the pale gray leggings hugging her killer legs before he blinks away.

Fascinating.

"This is cute," Summer says of the décor, so sweetly oblivious to the way she's just been the subject of what had to have been a filthy-as-hell fantasy. She gives me a small smile. "Mr. Ass to Kill For is worried about you, Cee. And he'll be expecting a full report from me and Parker when we fly out for Fans and Family Day tomorrow, so we recruited Shy and decided to do what Parker does best: meddle."

Brooks had mentioned the Fans and Family Day that the Rebels host during training camp, gently hinting he'd love for me to come. But I don't have the heart to leave again without having spoken to Mom. Without bringing Brooks some kind of clarity as to our living arrangement. I know the distance has been hard on him, too.

Parker leans his elbows on the checkout counter, taking up his best friend's study of the ceiling. "Am I ever going to live down that meddling, d'you think?"

"Not if I have anything to do with it." Summer gives him a snarky smile before returning her attention to me. "Look, we're not going to pretend to know your life better than you do. But I also like to think we're all friends now, and that means we're allowed to dish out some tough love."

"Avoiding your mom, Cee?" The look Shy gives me has my stomach pinching with guilt. "Since when do you hide from your problems?"

I fiddle with the inside-out hem of my shirt, and the tag on the side that's been hanging out all day. "I'm not hiding, I'm . . . thinking. You really expect me to show up at her place all, 'Hi, Mom! I've decided to move across the country, and I have no idea what to do about the shop, but it's your problem now!'" My gaze moves around us, as though I expect the answer I've been searching for to materialize in the fluorescent lights or the scuffed floor. A good, solid plan I can lay out for Mom, that will mean leaving the shop in hands that'll treat it with the love and respect it deserves. I'd never be careless enough to hand it to just anyone. And shutting it down isn't an option, seeing as Mom's still chipping away at that second mortgage. She needs the income. "I *don't* hide from my problems. I solve them. Always have. And this one is . . ."

My gaze falls on the display of football-shaped bobbers on the counter, spinning as Parker messes with it. I look at that thing every day. Stand next to it for hours on end, this silly thing that Dad had been so proud of when it arrived years ago. It's him in a nutshell, the two things he loved more than anything. How am I simply supposed to say goodbye to it?

Leave this place without a care for what happens to it, or to my mom?

But given the way I've got Brooks's voicemail memorized only a week in, the distance isn't sustainable. It's already draining me of life, resurfacing the abandonment issues I've worked hard to forget over the years.

"Oh, Cee." Shy wraps both arms around me this time as the tears that've lived so close to the surface all week threaten to pour. I love her to pieces, but I so badly wish she were Brooks. I miss the feel of his arms around me. The way I fit so perfectly in the crook of his neck. The stockpile of T-shirts I stole from him is starting to lose his piney scent, and I feel every single one of the three thousand miles between us in the hollowness of my chest.

"This place *is* my dad, you know? It matters to me what happens to it."

"Even if it means not going back to LA?" Summer's expression is soft, devoid of judgment even with the note of apprehension in her voice.

I split from Shy, shrugging helplessly. "What choice would I have if I can't figure this out?"

Shy purses her lips in obvious disapproval. "Is that really something you're considering?"

"He thinks you're going back." Parker exchanges a loaded look with Summer. "Please tell me you didn't say that just so he'd let you go."

"I didn't—I meant it." Their silence rings around us, broken only by the sounds around the shop—footsteps from customers milling the aisles, the ventilation system working overtime against the blistering August weather, causing the dangling lures to gently sway overhead.

Hearing it said out loud, this possibility that's lurked in the back of my mind, makes me more than a bit nauseous. It won't come to that if I can help it. I meant every word I said to Brooks—I want to be there with him. Just as soon as I find a way out from this place that I can live with.

"Well, I guess that's that." Parker heaves a sigh and moves for the door. He loops an arm around a startled Summer on the way, dragging her with him. "Should we go to lunch? I assume you're stuck here, Cee. But you're welcome to join us, Shy."

I . . . *what*? "That's it? You came all this way just for that?"

"Nice as this was, rule number one of meddling is recognizing a lost cause when you see one." He doesn't even look at me. "Obviously, you've asked your mom at least once if you could give up the shop. And the answer was no."

"That's . . . Were you tuning me out, just now? I've never asked her that."

Parker ignores me. "And I'm sure you've told her you overheard them talk about all that remortgaging and bribery. And she made it clear that they were happy to do it so long as you made it up to them with your blood, sweat, and inside-out shirts. Worked here forever and a day, no matter how unhappy it made you."

My lips pop open. "She would never say something like that."

Parker turns a confused frown over his shoulder. "Really? Could've fooled me."

Summer mutters something that has Parker chuckling, before he wheels them both back around to face me and an amused Shy. "All right, Cee. I have an idea for you."

I grimace. "What, another subtle attempt at reverse psychology?"

"No, I'm serious as can be now. I swear." Parker lays his right hand over his heart, and though there's a tilt to his mouth, his dark blue eyes are kind. "What if, just this once, you hit pause on this idea that you need to handle everything on your own? You go to your mom—the woman you just said would never want to see you unhappy. Put your faith in her and believe that she loves you enough to find a solution for you. Maybe you'll even find one together."

I'd been preparing to clap back at more of his nonsense. Had a whole slew of jabs just simmering on my tongue, waiting to be unleashed. But they fizzle to nothing at Parker's words. Because he's read me so clearly, has laid out just how unfair I'm being to Mom by keeping all this to myself. By not letting her be the mother she's been to me since the moment we met.

"That was . . . annoyingly wise."

A dimpled grin breaks over Parker's face. "Not bad, huh?"

"You were right," Shy tells Summer, who beams at her best friend with overt pride. "He is good at this meddling thing."

Chapter 49

Siena

"Well, well. If it isn't the prodigal daughter, home at last."

Mom looks up from her crocheting, the colorful blanket she's been slowly working on for weeks sitting on the kitchen table of my tiny childhood home. Her leg is propped up on a chair, with the cast she got what already feels like a lifetime ago. But as I creep into the kitchen, practically tiptoeing as though I'm doing something I shouldn't, she straightens in her seat and nudges another chair out for me. I've shown up here early, hoping to catch her before the cribbage crew arrives.

"Hi, Mom. Missed you." I give her a hug before sitting.

Her brown eyes narrow playfully. "Really? Could've fooled me the way you've been avoiding me all week. How was your trip?"

There's a half-finished plate of pasta on the table. Though my stomach rumbles enough to entice me to help myself to some, I lose my appetite the moment the spaghetti touches my lips. I drop the fork, barely meeting Mom's bemused gaze. "The trip was good. Great, actually. You saw he got signed?"

"I did—I sent him a text message as soon as I heard." I manage a smile. Of course they'd have saved each other's numbers after their day together. "*He's* replied to me, at least."

My stomach pangs with guilt. I pick up her fork again, pushing around the sauce-covered noodles. "Yeah, I've . . ." *Come on, you can do this. For Brooks, Pete, and Sophia.* All the thought does is make my nose burn, though. Cause tears to well. "It's been really hard, leaving him there. Feels wrong."

"Oh, angel." Mom leans over, catching my tears. "Long-distance isn't easy. Especially with your history. But it'll get better, I know it."

Now. Do it now. Say the words: I'm not doing long-distance. I'm moving there with him. Please don't hate me for it.

But then Mom reaches for her crutches and gets to her feet. She pulls me to mine and wraps me as best as she can in that hug of hers. The one where she squeezes me tight and gently strokes my hair, silently promises that she'll keep me safe. It's the same way she hugged me when I showed up here for dinner the day after she and Dad caught me in this very kitchen.

It feels so damn wrong, telling her here. The ultimate betrayal, confessing my desire to leave her and offload Dad's pride and joy, in the very home they opened up to me as a child.

God, I wish Brooks were here. That I could've done this with him. Holding his hand, soaking in his soothing presence, his calming voice. I've never ached for someone's help more than I do now, wishing for his. I'd texted him this morning, telling him tonight was the night. That I'd let him know how things went with Mom. But aside from the few messages we exchanged before he headed into camp for the day, he's been unreachable.

Mom releases me several silent seconds later, balancing on her crutches. "Are you hungry? Should I fix you a plate of pasta?"

The doorbell goes off before I can answer. I check the clock on the microwave—I'm running out of time. "Bit early for cribbage, isn't it?"

Mom shakes her head. "Can't be them. They've never rung this doorbell in their lives."

She goes to open the door, patting Pete's giant head as they cross paths in the kitchen doorway. He'd wandered into the house when we got here, but he comes to sit next to me now, regarding me with baleful eyes.

"I know, I'm being a wimp." I rub his head. He groans his disapproval. I narrow my eyes at him. "You don't have to be so judgy about it. I'd like to see you do what I'm about to."

"Siena?" Mom calls from the hallway. "Could I get your help out here?"

Pete follows me down the hall. He pauses with me when I stop to gape at the floral arrangement Mom gingerly tucks against her body. It's massive, flowers ranging every shade of blue I can imagine.

"Who are they from?" I hurry over to help her, eyeing the white van backing out of the short driveway.

"I couldn't say. There's another one with a card addressed to you on the porch."

I place the arrangement on the small table by the door and shuffle around her to get to the porch. *What the hell?* It's another blue arrangement, about twice the size of Mom's. I grunt with the effort of lifting the beast, staggering into the hall under its weight, my back hitting the wall. Useful, frankly, because I need the help supporting our combined weight.

"Rachel, thank you for . . ." Mom's voice trails away. I pivot to get a better look at her from around my flowers. She stares at the card she must've produced from her flowers. "Well, isn't that sweet? They're from Brooks."

"What does it say?"

Mom hands me the small white card. *Rachel, thank you for raising the love of my life, for taking her in, putting her on a path where we'd meet one day. I'm so grateful to you and Logan, I'll happily let you keep kicking my ass at cribbage. Looking forward to a rematch very soon.*

God, I love that man.

The writing isn't his—obviously, seeing as he's currently across the country. But it's so him, that perfect blend of sweet and playful. I feel each of his words dust over my skin like a warm caress, a hint of pine bridging the too-many miles between us. Like he knew I'd need him tonight. Like he's right here with me, holding my hand through one of the most painful things I've ever done.

Mom leads me back to the kitchen, where I set the second arrangement on the small island. I have to stand on the tips of my toes to reach the card tucked between the petals. *Come on, Siena. Swim with sharks with me.*

The knot in my stomach fully unravels, reading the same words I gave him the night we arrived in LA. If Mom's note was Brooks taking my hand, this one is his arms wrapping around me on the back of my bike. The first nervous dip of his toes in the ocean at midnight. His legs dangling off a cliffside, warily eyeing the long way down.

It's that little push I've been giving him all summer, the one he repeatedly answered with blind trust in me and courage he didn't think he had in him. I feel it nudging the words up my throat, the ones I've been trying to perfect all week, making my jaw unclench to let them out at last.

"I want to move to LA." *Good grief, woman. So much for easing her in.* I'm so loud my voice actually bounces off the walls and cabinets around us, momentarily distracting me from the sounds of a chair scraping against the worn kitchen tiles.

Mom slowly sinks into her seat, eyes glued to me. "What?"

I clutch Brooks's words for courage. "I'm sorry, Mom. That's not how I meant to tell you—to *ask* you."

"I don't understand. Why are you asking me to move to LA?"

I sit with her, shoving away the leftover spaghetti as Pete trots back to my side, curling his massive body around my feet. Either knowing I need the mental support or determined to bully me through this conversation with a well-placed snap of his teeth, if I chicken out again. "Well, the thing is, Mom . . . I know I let you think earlier that Brooks and I were going to do the long-distance thing, but that's never quite worked for me, and—"

"No, I understand *why* you'd move to LA. Frankly I was shocked you'd stay here, what with the way things with that other one turned out." Her mouth flattens into the hard line it adopts whenever Tom comes up in conversation. She never really got over the way he treated me. "I'm asking why you, my grown woman of a daughter, are *asking* me to move to LA as though I have a say in the matter."

"You do have a say in the matter." *Brooks, Pete, and Sophia. Brooks, Pete, and Sophia.* "Because of the shop."

"The shop." Mom's voice is even, face is blank.

"I wanted to . . . to see whether there was something you and I could work out. Some way that we could keep it in the family, make sure you're still able to pay off the second loan on the house, and that I could—"

"The second loan on the house?" Mom's eyes grow in alarm. "Siena, how do you know about the second loan on the house?"

I hesitate. "I overheard you and Dad talk about it, the day before you went to the bank."

"You weren't—" She pauses, perhaps remembering the extent of that conversation. The one where she'd cried over the way my birth parents had been bleeding them for money. Mom's face drains of color. "How much of that did you happen to hear?"

"All of it," I whisper.

"Fuck." Mom drops her face into her palms, and I'm momentarily stunned. The woman never swears. "You weren't meant to hear *any* of that, Siena. I am so sorry."

"*You're* sorry? Mom you were being extorted." My throat starts to close up, tears start to well. "You and Dad had already gone above and beyond when you took me in, and your reward was to slowly become bankrupt just to keep me. If anyone here should be sorry—"

"Don't you dare." Mom blinks rapidly. "Don't you dare apologize for something you had nothing to do with. Don't you dare apologize for the choices Dad and I made. That was the least we would have done to keep you."

She grabs her crutches and starts pacing the kitchen.

"Mom, you should be sitting."

"I can't sit. How can I sit? I'm fucking *furious*. You're telling me you've been carrying this with you since you were *fourteen*? How could you not—" She turns to face me. "Don't tell me this is why you're still here. Don't tell me this is why you're so worried about the shop. Please tell me it's because you love working there, and you don't want to let it go."

I rub my lips together, the guilt so heavy on my chest. Peter huffs, his breath hitting my toes. "I don't really love it all that much, Mom. You and Dad loved that place more than I ever did."

"Do you mean to tell me you've been working there as . . . what, Siena? An act of guilt? Obligation?" She closes her eyes when I don't respond, breathing deep like she's searching for patience. "I need a drink. Do you need a drink?"

I chuckle. "I could use a drink."

Mom takes out the pinot grigio she's been cooling for the cribbage game and shocks me to my core by taking a swig right from the bottle before handing it to me. She watches me take my own sip.

"You know, this is the second time you've broken my heart in this kitchen."

Slowly, I lower the bottle from my mouth.

"The first time you were about this tall." Mom holds out a hand at shoulder height. "Skin and bones. I could see the holes in your sneakers even though the lights weren't on. Dad asked what you were doing with a backpack full of food from our fridge. And all you said was *I'm hungry*. I swear, you could have heard my heart shatter across the country."

I'd been so fucking scared that night. In all my forays into foreign kitchens, I'd never been caught before.

"And then you made some silly joke about the police and juvenile detention, and I swear, Dad fell in love with you on the spot. That hadn't even happened with *me*—it took him ages to ask me out when we met." She laughs fondly before her expression clouds over. "Siena, you owe us nothing. Do you understand me? We'd have done anything for you, whether you asked us to or not. We love you in a way that isn't earned or repaid. I'm sick to my stomach knowing you've spent even a moment thinking that you owed us for doing what any parent in their right mind would do for their child."

"I'd do anything for you, too. I don't even want to think of where I'd have ended up without you and Dad taking a chance on me."

"Oh, you silly girl. You still don't get it, do you?" Mom shakes her head. Her smile is sad, her eyes damp. "The day we caught you breaking into this house was the very best day of my life. Every day since, I've thanked the universe that you chose to steal from us that night. That Dad got up for a glass of water when he did. That you let us love you when you'd been disappointed so badly before and had every reason not to trust us. You're the best thing that ever happened to us. Even now, when I'd love nothing more than to shake some sense into you for thinking such ridiculous things."

Air gusts out of me, tears pouring from my eyes. Body deflating like a mammoth balloon just burst inside me—one I've ignored nearly all my life, where I kept shoving every difficult thought I didn't want to have, every unhappy feeling I didn't want to linger on. It feels like relinquishing decades' worth of insecurities, and so much pressure to be deserving of the new life given to me.

It's like I told Brooks the first time I brought him to our cliffside: I never doubted my parents' love. Always knew my fears were likely unfounded. But that didn't make them any less hard to ignore.

Doesn't make it any less meaningful to hear from Mom how wrong I've been, with all our secrets out in the open.

Mom tips her head toward the hallway. "Come with me, angel. I want to show you something."

I follow her slow pace out of the kitchen and to her bedroom. Mom heads straight for the closet to the right, the one that's sat untouched for two years, and throws it open.

That ever-present ache at the base of my throat—the one that ebbs and surges depending on my mood and on the ways in which I remember Dad on a given day—swells with a vengeance as I take in the contents of his closet. The familiar sweaters and jeans, the pairs of worn shoes lining the ground. It's possible it's just in my head, but I inhale deeply because I swear, it still smells like Dad.

I want to dive into that closet face-first. Live in it, wrap myself in all his belongings and pretend it's him holding me. Simultaneously, I want to shut its doors, block it from my sight for good.

Mom indicates a battered box on a shelf at the very top. I pull it out and sit at the end of the bed with her, where she sorts through the box's contents before handing me a stack of yellowing papers.

It takes me a moment to realize I'm staring down at my dad's handwriting. Pages and pages of his rough scrawl indenting the paper, the funny way he writes his *E*'s. I used to tease the hell out of him over those *E*'s, but I finger them now as though I might feel him through the ink. I read his words as Mom looks on quietly, every new line deepening my frown. Blurring my vision.

"What is this?" I ask, even though I really don't need to. It's all there, laid out by Dad. Every word detailing what appears to be his original retirement plan from Ship Happens. Figures and data points, pages of research on the merger with the local marina he'd wanted to propose to Carla and Evan so they'd eventually take it off his hands.

"He and I spoke about this for years." Mom smiles wryly. "Most marinas similar to theirs tend to have partnerships with local shops like Ship Happens. The marina already funnels us most of its business. Carla and Evan would essentially be doubling down on their own clientele, gain both streams of revenue."

I swallow, barely daring to believe it. Selling them the shop would mean repaying Mom's mortgage. Keeping Dad's legacy intact, and in good hands. "This was your plan all along?"

"We only set aside the idea because you seemed to love working there. You spent every waking minute there. You got a business degree specifically to take it over one day. So we kept it for you."

"You're kidding me." I puff out a laugh—a rueful one that's part relief, part grief. And so much shame that I let guilt and assumptions needlessly dictate my past and almost ruin my future. Mom tucks me into her shoulder. She squeezes me tight and strokes my hair, relieving the tension lingering in my body. My lungs expand in a way they rarely do on land, welcoming the air like they've been badly depleted for years. It's the same kind of freedom I only ever feel on the water, or with Brooks's heartbeat against my back as he holds me to sleep.

We sit like this a while—my head on Mom's shoulder, hers resting on mine. Both our tears soak her shirt. Dad's handwriting is in my lap and his warm scent seeps from the closet, surrounding us like he's with us, too.

Eventually, Pete wanders in, sitting in front of us with perfect attention. *Don't worry, Petey. We'll see him soon.* I wipe my tears with the back of my hand as Mom does the same. "You think they'll go for this? Carla and Evan?"

Outside the bedroom, we hear the timely creak of the front door, shortly followed by Carla's distinct laugh as she and Evan make themselves at home.

Mom pats at her leftover tears. "I guess we'll find out. But even if they don't, we'll find another way, my California girl. I need you to go out there and do what you love and be with that man of yours and give me a brood of grandchildren with exceptional athletic talent.

And I promise to teach them to be much better cribbage players than their father, because . . ." She chuckles and shakes her head. "I say this with all the love in the world, but the man truly has *no* idea what he's doing with a cribbage board in front of him."

I muster a genuine laugh. Pete whines and nudges my knee with his nose, as though taking the jab to Brooks personally and demanding I defend his honor. I ruffle his fur. "It's true, Petey. Nobody's perfect. We were bound to uncover a flaw eventually."

Chapter 50

Brooks

"Brooks! There you are."

Summer and Parker edge through the crowd, past an elderly couple watching their pint-sized grandson chatter at me excitedly.

We caught up quickly before this morning's training camp scrimmage, part of the annual Rebels Fans and Family Day held at our practice facility, but I haven't had a chance to see much of them otherwise. Given the sheen of sweat along Summer's hairline and my old Rebels jersey clinging to Parker like a second skin, they've been braving the sweltering heat in this busy parking lot since, loitering during the autograph session and indulging in the food trucks around the perimeter of the busy parking lot, according to the sweating cup of lemonade in Summer's hand. They pause when they reach me, noticing the little guy dressed head to toe in Rebels swag.

"My friend Jake Wallace says his dad is having a party to watch your first game of the season and everyone is invited!" The kid, Weston, is talking a mile a minute, eyes stuck to me. "He's going to be so jealous when he finds out I got to meet you. He couldn't be here—he's on family vacation!"

"Well, you tell Jake hopefully he can make it here next summer.

I'd love to meet him, too." I beam wide as I can until I notice what he's wearing. "Hold up. I know you're not out here wearing someone else's jersey. You should be wearing mine. Turn around—let me see whose butt I need to kick."

Weston wheels around to show off Cam Guerdy's jersey. "I had yours from before. But it doesn't fit anymore, and the people at the store said they don't have yours in stock yet." He jabs a glum finger over his tiny shoulder, presumably indicating the pop-up pro shop at the opposite end of the parking lot, which I can't see through the sea of fans enjoying the event.

"Well, we can't have that. Here." I straighten and tug the game-day jersey over my head before handing it to Weston. I'm instantly relieved to lose the extra layer over my T-shirt. The sun is merciless this morning. "Should take you a few years to grow out of this one."

Weston's eyes damn near bug out of his eyes. He shouts his *thank you* at me, practically shuddering as he rushes over to his grandparents to show off his new gear. He's real cute, his excitement contagious, and I swear, this has got to be the first real smile I've worn all week.

Summer throws an arm around me when she and Parker reach me. "I don't think I'll ever get used to seeing people fawn over you like that."

Parker laughs. "If only they knew what a pain in my side Golden Boy Brooks was in the gym."

"If only they knew my trainer was a raging sadist."

"Hey, it got you here, didn't it?"

"Yeah, I guess it did." I actually manage a real laugh, feeling a surge of affection for my friends. I'm glad they were able to beg off work to fly over for the event. They deserve it, given how hard they worked to get me here. "Couldn't have done it without you guys."

Not for the first time, I scan the crowd for a head of familiar shiny hair, knowing I won't find it. Chances were always slim that Siena would have everything settled enough at home to make the trip back so soon after leaving. Especially when she'd only spoken to her mom last night. Still, part of me held out hope.

A few yards away, my parents chat with Josh, all three wearing my pre-retirement jerseys. They're far from the only ones wearing them—my name is all over the sea of purple in this parking lot. The cheers were loudest when they announced me before the scrimmage, my line the longest at the autograph session. The fans have welcomed me back with open arms, and so have my teammates. My family lives just a drive away. I'm so grateful for it all; it's everything I wanted when I decided on this comeback. Everything I thought I needed to be happy again, after years of torment.

And yet, my chest sits empty. Heart beating in the hands of a woman across the country. I haven't seen Siena make a cup of tea in too long. Have no idea if the sun freckles on her face are where I left them, or how many she's gained since I last saw her.

I don't know how other people do it. She was right. The distance is torture.

It's like she took half of me with her when her plane took off in San Diego, and the only time I don't feel the crushing weight of loneliness is when I'm focused on avoiding a tackle at work. Like all the fairy dust has been scrubbed from my life, and the only doses I get are the few times our schedules and time zones line up for a phone call.

"You look miserable as hell, man." Parker eyes me like he expects me to melt down here and now and is ready to step in at a moment's notice. "Still haven't heard anything?"

I pull my phone from my back pocket for the thousandth time today, staring at my text thread with Siena. There's the message I sent her before passing out after a long-as-hell day yesterday, and then the unanswered ones from before this morning's event.

BROOKS: Been thinking about you. Did you talk to your mom?

SIENA: Sure did. Fill you in soon. ♥

BROOKS: Shit, I fell asleep. How soon is soon?

BROOKS: How'd it go?

BROOKS: How are you feeling?

"Still nothing. I'm losing my mind, guys. She was stressed enough about the distance, and then she talked to her mom, and . . ." The disappointment that I haven't heard from her is bad, but worse is the anvil of dread weighing down my body. It makes me check my phone every other second, wishing I could be across the country with her, making sure she's okay.

She put a heart emoji in her last text, which might be a good sign.

But she also hasn't answered since last night—*late* last night, considering the time difference and the hour at which I managed to escape my meetings. Had she been tossing and turning in bed after talking to her mom? Had it gone that badly?

Maybe she's avoiding me. Trying to figure out how to break the news that she's staying in Baycrest, and that heart emoji is meant to soften the blow. Maybe she's . . . Fuck. Maybe she's about to dump me, and she's working up the nerve to do it.

"How bad was it when you talked to her?" She'd been putting on a brave face, talking upbeat whenever we managed to speak, but I know she's been unhappy. And I've been helpless on the other side of the country, unable to do much about it but sneak texts to her between breaks in practice and meetings. I sent flowers to her mom's house last night, just hoping they'd give her a boost.

Summer and Parker exchange a look, which Summer quickly tries to cover with a smile. "I'd rate it about a five out of ten on the meltdown meter."

"A *five?*" Parker barks a laugh. "Her shirt was inside out, Sum."

Fuck.

"Seriously, Park?" Summer gives him a wide-eyed look of warning. "Are you really in a position to judge her fashion choices when you've got about six hundred Hawaiian shirts sitting in your closet back home? You might want to try turning *them* inside out. Might help you look a little less ridiculous when you wear them."

Parker staggers back, exaggerating as though she just punched him in the gut, but he's clearly enjoying the teasing. "Take that back, Prescott. The Hawaiian shirts are great."

"They're pretty fucking bad, man," I chime in, checking my phone again. Still nothing.

Summer gives Parker a triumphant smile before refocusing on me. "Look, Brooks. Siena loves you. Misses you more than anything. Enough to think about giving up something that's been part of her life for years. I know you're nervous but hang on to that."

"Besides, she's still got Pete," Parker adds. "No way he'd let her forget about you. He's even more infatuated with you than the kid you just handed your jersey to."

"And then there's this." Summer plucks at the chain around my neck until Siena's anchor pops free from inside my T-shirt. "She wasn't wearing it yesterday. Had an inkling I might see it here."

I finger the charm, the stones glinting under the glaring sunlight. Every swipe of my thumb over them steadies the jitters inside me. Because they're right.

We've come a long way since I first knocked her over on the Huskies field. This woman, who hated me mere months ago, handed me this necklace—handed me her *heart*. This week apart has been nothing short of torture. But a few days is nothing to what I'd spend waiting for me and Siena to figure us out. That's my true best friend, my love, my future wife. The second this event is over, I'm going to call her and make sure she knows it.

I focus on Remy the Rebel, the eye-patched mascot posing for pictures nearby, hoping to absorb some of his enthusiasm for this event. "How much longer do you think I have to stick around here without getting fined for leaving? I need to call her. Make sure she's okay."

Parker glances over my shoulder, suddenly wearing a look of deep satisfaction. "You know what? I'd say she's just fine."

"Didn't you *just* say she wasn't? Inside-out shirt, remember?"

Summer's gaze meets mine after a quick look over my shoulder. She's grinning wide. "Seems she's remembered how to dress herself."

"What the hell are you guys . . ."

And that's when I hear the sound of a familiar, happy bark behind me.

Chapter 51

Brooks

I know it's her even before I hear the smattering of bird whistles from the crowd. Before I'm shoved forward from the force of Peter launching himself at me from behind, then accosting me with a series of excited barks and nuzzles at my legs.

I know it's Siena because my own heart left me to live with hers a long time ago, and I feel it there, humming. Like a homing beacon making its way back. She kept it strong and loved and healthy, and that's how I know, regardless of what happened last night with her mom . . . we're going to be fine.

"Petey-Pete!" I crouch to let our boy cover my T-shirt in dusty paw prints and my face in excited puppy kisses. His tail is going wild like a fur-covered chopper. Beyond him, Siena strides through the crowd of fans, laughing at us both. She's as stunning as ever with free, wavy hair, sun-kissed skin, wearing a purple dress that flutters in the breeze. I don't know if she's here for good, or if I only have her here for the weekend, but this is good enough for now.

She's here, she loves me, and is smiling at me, and I don't care about the rest.

"I'm so happy you made it!" Summer intercepts Siena before she can reach me, enveloping her in a one-armed hug, but it's worth it just to see them together like they've been friends for years.

"This one's been miserable all day." Parker tips his head in my direction.

Siena catches my eye over my Summer's shoulder. "Maybe keeping this a surprise wasn't my brightest idea. I've been flying all morning."

"It was a great idea," I tell her.

"A heads-up might've been nice." Parker dodges the elbow I try to dig into his side.

"Come on, Park. I hear TJ Hunt is single. Wingman me an introduction?" Summer links arms with a now-frowning Parker and drags him toward my teammate.

Finally—fucking *finally*—Siena closes the gap between us. She's beaming, my personal ball of sunshine, brighter than anything above us as she winds her arms around me.

"I missed you so much," I tell her.

"I love you so much."

I'm aware that people are watching and snapping pictures, but I don't have it in me to care. Let them get their fill. See this for the real love it is.

"You have no idea how . . ." I inhale the scent of her hair, attempting to drown in it. "You were right. The distance is brutal, and I think we need a new rule where you come to me every weekend."

"Just a quick round-trip across the country, huh?" She sits her chin on my chest. "Can you come inside with me? I need your help with something."

"Lead the way."

Siena takes my hand and we weave through the crowd, Pete bringing up the rear. We pause to say hi to my delighted parents on our way inside the practice facility. It's quiet in here, away from the excited voices and blaring music, with only a couple of security guards manning the entrance.

"Thank you for the flowers last night." Siena squeezes my hand and leads us down a quiet hall, toward the team parking lot. "I can't tell you how much I needed it."

"I wish I could've been there with you."

She stops me, then lifts onto her toes to kiss me. "It was like you were."

"How long do I have you here?" Pete circles around us, looking for an opening to join the embrace. I pat him on the head. "I'll get my ass handed to me if we leave this event now, but I'm willing to risk it."

Instead of answering, Siena tugs me a few steps down the deserted hallway . . . to where three person-sized suitcases sit along the wall, so stuffed they're practically bursting at the seams.

"Siena." I stop dead. My heart picks up its pace. "You should know my hopes just flew through the roof. Please tell me this means what I think it does."

Because that looks like more than a weekend's worth of stuff. And I'm suddenly ready to run ten laps around this building, this city, this fucking country. It's gameday levels of adrenaline. Jump-through-a-brick-fucking-wall levels of adrenaline.

"It means what you think it does." Siena stares down at her own bags like it's still surreal. Like she hadn't packed them, flown them over here herself.

"How?" is the only word I muster. I'm pretty sure that if I activated my vocal cords any longer than that, I'd end up roaring victoriously.

"I spoke to my mom. I told her everything, and she was . . ." Her eyes go wet, and I hate it, not seeing the usual light in them. But I sense there's a new comfort with the tears—this woman, who normally fights crying with everything she has. "She was pretty fucking angry I took so long to tell her how I was feeling. But it was nice to finally let myself ask for that validation. To let myself ask for help. And to have so many people happy to come through for me."

I thumb the tears running down her cheeks. "I'm so proud of you, baby. I know how hard that must have been. How unnatural it must have felt."

"I couldn't stop shaking all night. And we don't have it all straightened out, but . . . Carla and Evan are looking into whether they can take it on as an additional business. Dad had apparently planned to propose the idea in the first place. They're going to oversee the shop now, while we figure out if we can make it work." With a deep breath, she dries her cheeks with the back of her hand and smiles. "It felt wrong not to figure it out for myself, but all night I kept thinking . . . if someone as good as you thinks I'm worthy of that kind of love and support, there's no way I can't be."

I nod sagely. "Because I know everything."

Siena gives me my favorite sound in the world: that husky laugh I'll never get enough of. "You know what? I think you might. Remember the night of the Tigers' gala while we were talking in bed?"

"Vividly. It was like a switch flipped that weekend, and there was only you."

Those eyes smile up at me. "That's the night you started falling for me?"

"Sweetheart, I started falling for you the moment I quite literally fell for you on that field. Stupid me, trying to break your fall like a hero. Only to realize that I wanted you to fall for me more than anything."

Siena reaches for the chain around my neck, fingers the blue-gray stones. "That weekend, I said I thought Dad put me on that field so I'd have some way of fixing everything that was going wrong in my life. And you said . . . you said maybe things went wrong to bring us together."

"You laughed when I said that."

"And you said you didn't believe in things being meant to be."

"Which proves I know absolutely nothing." I didn't believe it, then. The things I'd gone through two years prior, the injury, the cheating, the dark hole I'd dug for myself in the months after . . . They were too harsh to accept that I was put through them for a reason.

But I think I was.

I think it was one long, rough road to bring me right where I needed to be that day. On that field, down on my luck, trying to save the future love of my life from an errant ball.

I went through what I did to understand what I deserve from a partner. What I deserve out of life. And in came Siena, blowing my expectations right out of the water. She's raised my standards to a level I never aspired to.

And Pete. I got Pete out of the deal, too.

I hold her face between my hands, admiring the way my palms mold to the apples of her cheeks as she smiles. "You're really moving here?"

She nods, practically shuddering with excitement. "I'm sad to leave home, and Mom, and Shy. And leaving the shop does feel like losing an arm in a way, because I've been there half my life. But I think Dad would have loved this for me. You, me, Pete, and Sophia. With our house on the water and midnight skinny-dips with sharks. You winning a hundred Super Bowls and me sailing a hundred ships."

Perfect. She's laid out the perfect life, and fuck, I can't wait to start living it.

I squint past her, down the hall. "Is that, like, a hundred ships at the same time, or . . ."

Siena gives a split second of a laugh before I pull her in, bring our lips together. I part her mouth in a slow, indulgent kiss, all sliding tongues and soft moans from us both. Her fingers are all over me. My hair, my cheeks, down my neck. Like she's confirming I'm really here. They slide over my shoulders and glide down my biceps, finding that spot below the crook of my right elbow. The accidental heart she loves to trace. Siena pulls away, tracing the raised and still-sensitive skin inside that heart. A permanent version of the tiny "S+B" she'd drawn on me before she left. I only made it two feet out of the airport once I dropped her off before knowing she and I belonged there for good.

"Brooks." Her shoulders tremble in a soft laugh. "I'm really fucking happy."

"Me too. There's really only one thing that could make this even better." With a dramatic sigh, I slide down the wall next to her suitcases, pulling Siena to the ground with me. She shimmies around in her dress, fighting with the long skirt until she can straddle me.

God, my body missed her.

"It would be the perfect cherry on top." I rake my fingers through all that gorgeous, shiny hair. "You finally admitting that you kissed me first on purpose."

Her jaw drops. "You cannot be serious. How are we still on this?"

I nudge her mouth shut with a finger. "Admit it."

"You're truly deluded."

My mouth hovers just half an inch from hers. I jerk back when she leans in. "Admit it."

"Oh my God." She's in fits of laughter, her forehead meeting mine, and she's actually blushing. Her fingers hold the back of my head, gently scraping through the hair.

Heaven. All of this.

"Brooks." Siena brings me closer, leaves only a sliver of air between our lips. Smiling from her eyes. "I totally kissed you on purpose."

Epilogue

Seven months later

Brooks

There are times in life when you don't recognize a moment for what it is.

Like that euphoric split second about three years ago to the day, right before the tackle that rocked my world. Like scrambling after a ball at just another practice, only to smash into a woman I never even knew existed.

Both life-altering events that yanked my unsuspecting ass onto paths I never saw coming. Paths I'd never have taken if fate hadn't rightfully decided I was ill-equipped to choose for myself. Took matters into its own hands, and delivered me everything I needed, though I didn't see it at the time.

This isn't one of those times.

This time, when I launch myself in the air and that brown leather bounces into my waiting palms, when my feet hit the turf and I weave past the last of the defense as the stands fall in silent anticipation, I know it's the biggest day of my life.

For multiple reasons.

Everything around me erupts the second that ball passes the goal line. I barely have the space to let it sink in before I'm accosted by royal-purple jerseys. Men scream in prepubescent pitches, driving me back into the tall barrier behind the end zone with the force of their collective embrace.

Because there are six seconds left in this Super Bowl game, and we're up by four. We're about to kick for the extra point, and I don't want to get ahead of myself, but . . .

I make it to the sideline with my heart pounding louder than the frenzied Rebels fans in the stands. Cam winds an arm tight around my neck in an affectionate choke hold as players line up for the kick on the field.

"You scrappy motherfucker." The quarterback pulls me into his side and rubs a rough hand into my hair when I strip off my helmet. "You stupidly pretty, scrappy motherfucker. I fucking love you, you know that?"

I manage an exhilarated laugh inaudible to my own ears. There's nothing more capable of turning grown-ass men into foul-mouthed saps like being seconds away from winning their first championship.

It's the slowest six seconds of my life. I scan the boxes framing the midsection of the stands looking for mine, where my family watches. I spot them up there. Josh, looking more dishevelled than I've ever seen him. My parents, my sister and Colt, Leo, Parker, Summer, Zac, and Mel. Shy and her husband, Max, who's holding tightly on to Rosie. Rachel, Carla, and Evan.

It's about as perfect a picture as it can get. Every one of them on their feet, practically hanging over the edge of the railing in anticipation of our win.

But that picture is missing the most important person.

The crowd roars and in a blink, I'm dragged back onto the field, surrounded by a screaming sea of purple as confetti rains down on us. It's a bizarre fucking feeling. Surreal, despite the full sensory experience of it. The sounds, the crushing assault of my massive teammates. The pure ecstasy overtaking every inch of my body.

Because I'm a fucking Super Bowl champ.

Holy fuck.

Holy fucking—

Someone shoves a victory baseball cap on my head. Matt, one of our PR people, fists my jersey and starts tugging me toward a half circle of cameras already surrounding Cam.

But then there's a break in the sea of players, coaches, and media, and I find her. Siena, with a wild bun on top of her head, scrambling over the barrier at the foot of the stands.

A neon-vested security guard rushes her the second her sneakers meet the turf, but it's too late for him. My little trespasser has locked eyes on me, smiling so fucking big, and the poor man doesn't stand a chance. She bodychecks him out of her way like he's made of nothing, and charges toward me.

"Brooks, we need you for interviews."

I pry Matt's hand off me. "Find me later."

My girl is flushed, wild-eyed, mouthing "oh my God, oh my God, oh my God," but the second she jumps into my arms and winds her legs around my waist it turns into *I love you, I love you, I love you* in my ear.

"I'm so fucking proud of you—"

My mouth crushes hers, cutting off the rest of her praise, because I know she is. She tells me she's proud of me about fifty times a day, gushes freely about every little thing I do. Makes me feel like I'm Bob the fucking Builder when I so much as replace a burnt-out light bulb at the new house. Like Evel Knievel whenever I dip a toe into the ocean out back, like I'm performing some kind of wild, death-defying stunt.

I've been on top of the world since the morning I loaded her suitcases into my car, and she hasn't let me stray off that peak once.

I'm stupid happy even just watching her at the kitchen table, ironing out the final logistics for the business she'll launch this spring. Because she'll be living her dream. Running charters on the *Ship Happens*, the teal-hulled sailboat bringing her dad's legacy to the Pacific Ocean, while the shop lives on back home under her family friends' ownership.

When she pulls away, Siena's got tears streaking down her face. "Brooks, I'm so happy for you. I can't stop shaking, I'm so happy. I've peaked. This is it. Nothing gets better than this."

Wanna bet?

With a surge of adrenaline rivaling the one that carried me into the end zone, I start to lower her to the ground. But she winds her legs tighter in protest.

"Baby, I need to put you down for a second."

"No, you don't. Just go about your celebrating like this. You won't even notice I'm here." She mimes locking her mouth and throwing away a key.

I shake my head at her, chuckling at the innocent look she's giving me. The crowd around us swells as the other families finally make it onto the field, in a more sanctioned manner than hers.

"Nothing's ever just a straight line with you, is it?"

She mimes unlocking her mouth. "Straight lines are boring."

"They really are." I hike her up in my arms. "Take out the necklace." Her eyebrows pull together and I tuck my chin down, indicating my chest. "The anchor necklace. Fish it out."

The shimmering anchor surfaces from under my jersey, alongside a different kind of sparkle. I'm all laughter as Siena's eyes go as wide as I've ever seen them, staring down at the ring.

"Brooks Attwood."

"Siena hopefully soon-to-be Attwood. I love you so damn—"

"Oh my *God*, yes. Is that even a question?"

"I haven't even asked—"

Siena shoves the ring on her finger, chain and all, and cuts off any hope of getting a single other word out when she crashes our mouths together. Kissing me stupid, right here, in the middle of this chaotic football field. Covered in confetti, in a mosh pit of people, cameras clicking around us.

The whole thing is so her. Nothing like how I rehearsed it.

And everything I've ever needed.

Acknowledgments

This story and its special characters have been a long time coming, and I am so beyond thrilled to finally be sharing them with the world. While book one in the series, *Only in Your Dreams*, is the one that started my journey within traditional publishing, it's Brooks and Siena who gave me the push I needed to try for this new chapter in the first place. They were a complete joy to write, came alive so easily and vividly. And the love they got from their earliest readers had me truly believing, perhaps for the first time, that my stories were worth taking this leap for.

Besides Brooks and Siena (Briena?), I'm so lucky to have a long list of people to thank for helping to bring their story into the world.

First and foremost, to every reader who has supported me by reading, reviewing, and sharing about *Only in Your Dreams*: you've made this new chapter possible for me and for that, I'll be endlessly grateful. Thank you for your love of my stories and characters, and for so patiently waiting on this one.

To my husband and family, who all pitch in to let me continue writing while also keeping a semblance of a home life. Doing this would be impossible without you. Thank you for your encouragement and your belief that this dream career of mine is worth making some sacrifices of your own. To my son, the happiest, sweetest boy that ever was, I hope that one day, this drives you to chase your own dreams.

Shelby and Maria, thank you for being the first to read this story and assure me that I wasn't crazy for having fallen so deeply in love with these characters. I'm so grateful for all your help in making it even better, for hyping me whenever I needed it, and for listening as I spiraled on more than one occasion.

To Aarti, Ada, Athena, Aubrey, Chris, Kathleen, Lauren, Sam, Samantha, Serena, Shannah, and Vanessa: I couldn't have asked for a better group to share this story with. Your love for this novel was the push I needed to take this series in a new publishing direction, and your lovely and truly hilarious commentary throughout its draft has lifted me out of funks more times than you can imagine.

Jenn, your insight and encouragement truly brought this story to the next level. Thank you as always for your invaluable feedback. And to Claire, thank you for your keen eye and attention to detail!

Lauren and Hannah, I can't thank you enough for putting me on this new path, for loving these stories, answering 1,001 questions, and talking me back from the ledge every time I needed it. I'm so lucky to be able to lean on such deep expertise.

Melanie, thank you for your thoughtful feedback and for brainstorming with me to make this story endlessly better than the way it came to you. I'm so sorry for what I put you through with chapter eighteen, but your reaction to it will forever be my favorite! Thank you also to the team at Atria, including Elizabeth, Jessica, Zakiya, and Camila, and the one at Simon & Schuster Canada including Chloe, Natasha, and Mackenzie. Thank you for championing me and for everything you've done to bring this story into the world.

Finally, to the me of three years ago, who dared herself out of her comfort zone on a late November night. Who self-published her first book hoping that maybe one person might read it but expecting absolutely nothing to come of it. Thank you for taking that leap.

About the Author

Ellie K. Wilde is a Canadian writer of contemporary romances and romantic comedies that make you laugh, swoon . . . and maybe require a cold shower or two to recover. She enjoys writing stories with dirty-mouthed, cinnamon-roll heroes and the fiery women who bring them to their knees.

When she's not daydreaming about her next book, you'll find her devouring other romance novels, bingeing reality TV, and snuggling with fur babies. You can keep up with Ellie through her website at EllieKWilde.com and on Instagram @EllieKWildeAuthor.